D0845702

The Waimea Gathering

Mahealani Shellabarger

authorHOUSE®

AuthorHouse™
1663 Liberty Drive
Bloomington, IN 47403
www.authorhouse.com
Phone: 1-800-839-8640

This is a work of fiction. Except for historical facts and references, names, characters and incidents are products of the author's imagination or used fictitiously. Any reference to persons,(living or dead) or events recounted are purely coincidental.

© 2010 Mahealani Shellabarger. All rights reserved.

No part of this book may be reproduced, stored in a retrieval system, or transmitted by any means without the written permission of the author.

First published by AuthorHouse   3/30/2010

ISBN: 978-1-4490-9483-6 (e)
ISBN: 978-1-4490-9484-3 (sc)

Printed in the United States of America
Bloomington, Indiana

This book is printed on acid-free paper.

Other Books by Mahealani Shellabarger

Lanikai
Lanikai Flowers
Kahala Sun
Children of Kahala Sun

booksbymahealani.com

mahe@booksbymahealani.com

Dedicated to

My dear childhood friend
Bina Mossman Chun
Whose "own works praise her in the gates"
and quiet giving never ends

and

The Maui Gang
Who fill my thoughts with memories
and my heart with love

The Waimea Gathering

They met in a beautiful Waimea Home
After forty five years from where they'd roam:
Six girls who attended a special school
At Kamehameha where they learned the golden rule:
To do unto others and serve them well;
Some would excel and others fell,
But they each carried Pauahi's creed;
Eventually they'd all succeed
To become the women they aspired to be
And live their lives in harmony.
Six lovely valleys were their homes in Hawai'i
From O'ahu, Maui, the Big Island to Kaua'i:
Puakea, from Palolo who used her fists,
Kanoe, the serene from Kahana's mists,
Kalihiwai's Nani, vivacious and fun,
Lihau, homely in Ha'iku's sun,
Kia, a thorn from Makaha Valley,
Keala with warmth from Waipi'o, she'd rally.
And so, to a gathering in Waimea, they came
To relate their stories of failure and fame.

Prologue

June 2007

Four women arrived at Keala's sprawling Waimea home on the Big Island of Hawai'i, bordering the immense Parker Ranch and overlooking the slopes of Maunakea. There would be six in attendance. This would be the first time in forty five years that they'd convene in the same place. Keala was the only one who had kept in touch with them, either by phone or through letters. She had arranged the gathering. The women embraced with long hugs and happy faces, all of them relieved to be there after their plane flights, and some with mixed anticipation over reliving the past. They were waiting for one more to arrive. Kia was late.

After depositing their luggage in their assigned rooms, they were seated at a long koa table on the lanai spread with *pupus* which included platters of sushi, edamame beans with garlic seasoning, salted *poke,* lychee fruit stuffed with cream cheese and macadamia nuts and iced soft drinks.

"Where's Kia?" asked Puakea

"Oh, she's late. She'll be here in an hour," replied Keala.

The group expressed their admiration for Keala's seven bedroom home as they sat overlooking the majesty of Maunakea. It was a clear afternoon. The mist had cleared past the mountain, so they were able to view it in its splendor. A wide open pasture spread out in front of them. Four cows grazed on the tall grass. Fruit trees and tropical plants surrounded the house including an umbrella shaped tree hung heavily with avocados. They were all impressed with the lovely setting.

Keala gazed at the four women seated. They seemed to have aged gracefully in one way or another. Puakea was the one with whom she'd communicated on a frequent basis and Keala's favorite. They'd been close friends, but she hadn't seen her in years. Puakea was the animated conversationalist of the group—so much to say and no trouble keeping an audience. Her short hair was streaked with gray. She sat comfortably in white shorts and a blue tee shirt, her standard attire that hadn't changed. One foot was propped on her chair as she hugged her knee. Puakea was all about comfort. Keala appreciated that.

Keala sat at the head of the table. Next to Puakea, Nani was seated. She'd always been the most effervescent of the women. Lovely still, with her olive skin and exotic look, she sat concentrating in rapt attention to Puakea's words. She had been the vivacious song leader in high school and continued to animate that same quality.

Across from Nani sat Kanoe, the quiet spirit, calm and tranquil—her hair still worn long to her waist with streaks of white running through chestnut tresses. She smiled as she sat there. Keala remembered how she'd always brought a serene quality to a room. Lihau rested her arm around Kanoe's chair, clearly elated to see her after such a long time. Keala noted that Lihau's former shyness had been replaced with a more confident air. She wore designer glasses now, her face starting to reveal her age, but her smile showed how happy she was to be there.

The state of Hawai'i consists of hundreds of valleys created by the volcanic action that occurred to make these crevices. The six women who had planned to gather for five days were each raised in a valley— Nani from Kalihiwai on the island of Kaua'i and Keala from Waipi'o Valley, not too far from her present Waimea home on the Big Island of Hawai'i; three came from valleys on O'ahu: Puakea from Palolo, Kanoe from Kahana and Kia who had not arrived yet, from Makaha. Lihau's island of Maui was referred to as the Valley Isle. She was raised in the quaint community of Ha'iku.

They heard a car in the circular driveway and assumed it was Kia. Keala went to greet her and returned to the patio with her arm around her shoulders. Some had mixed feelings about seeing her again. Their smiles were cranked down a bit, but still plastered on their faces as she entered. Kia was not exactly the favorite. Nevertheless, she had been a vital part of their group.

She stood there wary of their welcome, spectacularly put together in a three piece Chanel suit, looking refreshed and ultra-sophisticated after a limo ride from her home in San Francisco, two airplane flights, and another limo ride from the Kona Airport to Waimea. They all rose to hug her; she stiffened when Kanoe was the last to extend the amenities. They had not left each other as friends when they had parted over four decades ago. Kia had definitely changed in her appearance, not a hair out of place, dyed a medium brown and highlighted in a short glamorous style. Her face was smooth as rose petals, and her trim figure surpassed the one she had in high school.

The association for all six women originated in high school. Some had been merely acquaintances during their time at Kamehameha School, but all were assigned to the same Senior Cottage in the last six weeks of their graduation year. This experience had instilled a lifelong impression on each of them and the reason for the gathering.

Senior Cottage, Kamehameha Girls School
Forty Five years earlier

"I think the baby's sick," said Lihau with a panicked face as she stood at Puakea's bedroom door.

Puakea got out of bed, groggy from a deep sleep. "What time is it?"

"It's about two in the morning. He got up screaming and he won't go back to sleep."

"Alright, I'm coming. Why me, Lihau?"

"I don't want to wake Miss Paul. She's already on my case…and besides, everyone knows how much he likes you."

Puakea went to retrieve him from his crib. His name was Bradley. In eight months, Bradley had been nurtured by almost thirty teenage mothers and one housemother. Puakea cooed to him, and his crying was reduced to a whimper.

"Get me a cold, clean washcloth," she said to Lihau.

Lihau came back with it. "What are you going to do with it?" she asked.

"I think he's teething, I'm going to let him chew on it. It might soothe his gums."

"Oh, I don't think Mrs. Paul would like that."

"Well, what she doesn't know won't hurt her, will it?"

Bradley started to chew on the washcloth and stopped crying. "See I told you," said Puakea.

"Wow, you're a lifesaver, Pua. I couldn't figure out what to do. I changed him, gave him his bottle which he refused, and he's been crying for an hour. Amazing."

"There, there, Bradley. It's no fun being a baby. Aunty Pua will sing you to sleep," said Puakea as she rocked him in the rocking chair.

"I don't think I'm going to make a very good mother," said Lihau.

"You'll be fine. I've just had more practice babysitting kids in Palolo. They're really not all that hard.

The first Senior Cottage was started in 1912. It was later expanded when Kamehameha School was situated on Kapalama Heights. At the time there were three cottages which were dormitory type buildings located at the the highest end of the campus overlooking the city of Honolulu.

A housemother oversaw and monitored their activities. Every week, they were assigned a different task. After six weeks each girl was to have mastered what she needed to go out into the world to become a decent housewife, mother, or at the very least, someone who was familiar with household chores.

They were graded according to their performance. Their residence was considered a requirement before graduating which included cleaning, cooking, taking care of the laundry, polishing silverware and the most challenging: taking care of the baby assigned to each cottage.

The only perk to that job was the fact that the "mother of the week" did not have to attend school. She stayed home with the baby. In this cottage it was a cherub named Bradley, now ten months old. The Javanese, Hawaiian German baby proved to be quite a handful for the inexperienced girls. For some reason Puakea had what it took to make him happy, and he'd light up whenever he saw her.

"Who's cooking tonight?" asked Puakea the next morning.

"I think it's still Nani's turn," replied Kanoe as they walked down the pathway to school. Their cottage was located at the highest end of the school's site on Kapalama Heights overlooking the city of Honolulu.

"Oh, no. I thought she was done for the week."

"No, she's got two more days. It wasn't so bad."

"She burned lunch yesterday. It takes a lot to burn lunch."

"Now, Pua, it isn't where she does her best, but she makes up for it in other things."

"You always have something nice to say about everyone, Kanoe. I need to be more like you."

"Oh, Puakea, we all want to be like you. You're so much fun."

"Yeah, but my mouth gets me into trouble, when I'm not trying to control it."

Each night after their homework and chores were done, the girls were required to be in their rooms with lights out at nine o'clock. There were two to every room. The housemother would make a periodic night check to make sure they were in their appropriate sleeping areas. After her check up, they'd scramble out of their beds and meet in Keala and Kanoe's room which was the largest. The snacks would come out that were stashed in their closets.

It was a week before senior prom and two weeks before graduation. They were almost rounding the bend before they would be out of the cottage and school forever. These nightly slumber parties had brought them together during the month that they had spent in this unusual place.

Puakea and Kanoe were the only day students and new to this full time boarding experience. Kanoe usually made the long trek from Kahana every day in a car pool. Puakea just caught the city transit from Palolo to the Kamehameha terminal and was transported by the school bus to classes on the hill. Kia, due to family problems and the long distance from Makaha, had joined Keala in the Nu'uanu dorm at the beginning of their seventh grade year, and later boarded in the Kapalama dormitories with Lihau and Nani who entered in ninth grade.

The boarders were used to being away from their families and had now overcome their homesickness which had plagued them in their early years. These slumber events were Puakea's idea. She was not used to all the restrictions and had to make up for them by breaking the rules.

Kia was the last one to enter the room that night. Kanoe had been unusually quiet amongst the giggling girls, who were now spreading peanut butter on Hawaiian crackers as they sat on the floor. Kia always tended to be somewhat more guarded than the others. She was the honor student from the country who had proved herself in her ability to achieve high grades and guaranteed a full paid scholarship to University of California at Berkeley.

Kanoe looked up when she saw her. "Is it true, Kia?"

"Is what true?"

"Are you going with Kamalu to the senior prom?"

"Oh, that. Who told you?"

"Everyone's talking about it at school."

"Well, yes. I am. We were talking one day and I asked him if he had a date to the prom. He said no. So I asked him. No big deal."

The girls sat there silently. Lihau had a knife with peanut butter suspended in the air. "Not good," said Keala who finally spoke.

"I don't see why not. He and Kanoe broke up a month ago. Surely she's over him by now."

"Not good," Nani parroted Keala.

The other three just shook their heads from side to side.

"Well, if you're all going to gang up on me, I'll go back to my room," spewed Kia and turned to walk away, not before she heard Kanoe's last words.

"How could you Kia?"

It was long past that day as they gathered together for the first time in over four decades. They were senior citizens now. Some of them were on their first year of collecting social security. Keala knew that Kia's presence would not be appreciated by all, but she had to invite her and was frankly surprised when she accepted. Keala understood her position as hostess was to handle the occasion carefully with hopes of creating new memories and wiping the unpleasant ones away. After all, they were sisters of a sort. They had shared so much together.

Puakea sympathized with Keala's dilemma and did her best to assist her in this delicate task. She took over the conversations from the time she arrived and was exhausted when she went to bed the first night. Keala came to her room before retiring. "Thanks," she said as she winked at her.

"Thanks for what? For shooting off my mouth all night like I was the most important person in the room?"

"No, that's not what you did at all and you know it."

"So, what did I do?"

"You made it comfortable for everyone."

"Well, not everyone."

"But at least you tried. You've always covered for me."

"Well, my dear Keala, four more days to go. I think you better take over tomorrow."

"Yeah, we'll do it in shifts," she said. "I love you, Puakea. Goodnight."

The next day they spent touring the Kohala Coast and drove down to the Waikoloa Resort for lunch. That night, after they had finished steaks and salads for dinner, they sat in the patio by candlelight and watched the moon come up.

Keala spoke, "We have seven meals left over the next three days. I know this sounds unusual, but I thought we could each tell our story—anything we want to share about our lives over the last forty five years. We can devote time after every meal, and each of us will have an uninterrupted time to talk. We can present these stories and leave them wherever we want, and on the last breakfast, we can finish them. That way we can absorb each narrative and share our conclusions at the end."

There was a silence in the room for a moment. "So, what do you think?" surveyed Keala. Most of them nodded their heads. Kia sat there and stared into space. Keala thought Puakea should be the first one to share.

PUAKEA

***

PALOLO VALLEY

Palolo Valley

PALOLO, A RESIDENTIAL AREA OF O'ahu, is situated four miles from downtown Honolulu and less than a mile from Diamond Head. The back of the valley, primarily agricultural, slopes up to the Ko'olau Mountain Range which was formed from one of the two largest volcanoes on the island of O'ahu. Also located in this area is the extinct volcano of Ka'au Crater.

Palolo Stream flows through the valley joining with Manoa stream to form the Manoa-Palolo drainage canal which empties into the Ala Wai Canal in Waikiki. Palolo's lower portion, where most of its residents live, borders Wai'alae Avenue and the community of Kaimuki. The valley lies nestled between Wilhelmina Rise on the east and Wa'ahila Ridge on the west.

Palolo Valley was the site of a golf course, rock quarry, two dairies and, during World War II, an airfield. In isolated reaches of the valley, a few acres were used for farming at the time.

In 1955 the 7.5 acres of the Palolo Golf Course was replaced by Jarrett Middle School for intermediate students, the 33-acre quarry became a 200-home subdivision after it was closed in 1951 and the airfield was developed into the location for Palolo Valley Housing. The area included low and middle income families, many of whom were coming out of the war to own affordable housing in a rural setting with close proximity to downtown Honolulu and Waikiki Beach.

The neighborhood mainstays of schools, churches and the recreation center were scattered, but grocery stores and a few small businesses were aligned along Tenth or Palolo Avenues, the two main streets of the valley.

Like most valleys that backed up to the Ko'olau's, Palolo's tropical abundance was the result of a continuous amount of rainfall enshrouding its areas farther in with an eerie mist that encouraged many legends from its early days.

1

SUMMER 1958

OUT OF THE CORNER OF her eye, thirteen year old Puakea Flynn watched the six boys who gathered in front of a lifeguard stand rehashing the day's canoe paddling events. They had all done well in their division. Her older brother, Lanakila stood in the group, doing most of the talking; he tended to dominate wherever he was. Charismatic and witty, Lanakila, lived up to his name translated as *victory* in Hawaiian. He was usually the center of attention in any room, but, right now, it happened to be a small portion of the beach. He had just said something that made them all burst into laughter; it was at that moment when he turned to her and shouted.

"Puakea, come ovah heyah, I wanna ask you somet'in."

Wearing a dark green tee shirt and white shorts, Puakea leaned against a canoe waiting for her father after a race at Waikiki Beach. Her eyes kept landing on one of the boys in the group. His name was Thaddeus Crown, shortened to Dee by his friends. She knew everything about him, but he had barely noticed her. Puakea brushed the sand off her legs and stood up, reluctantly walking towards them.

"What?" she said as she approached them

"See dose girls ovah deyah. Who's da one in da blue bayding suit?"

3

Puakea shaded her eyes and looked over at the group of three who were sun bathing on the sand a few yards down the beach. "Oh, that's Ginny Carson. Why?" Ginny was not her favorite person and neither were the girls she hung with. Puakea thought they were stuck-up boy crazy *haoles*. On top of that, they were gigglers, something she abhorred.

"Dee was askin' bout her. Maybe you can fix him up," said Lanakila with a leering grin. "What am I talking about? Fix her up wit' me. I'm da best looking one heyah."

"And what's Connie going to say about that?"

"Oh, well, what Connie doesn't know, won't hurt her, will it?"

"No, but if she finds out, you're gonna be hurting real bad. Leave me out of it. Dee's a big boy, he can fix himself up." Puakea glanced at Dee as she spoke.

He stood with arms locked together across a broad chest, his eyes squinting from the glare of the afternoon sun. Dee's eyes were the most unusual blue she had ever seen, shaded by dark lashes, framed by, what she thought, was a perfect face—prominent straight nose, full lips and ebony hair that curled around his ears. His tall, statuesque swimmer's form made her look away to keep from staring.

He punched Lanakila's shoulder playfully and said, "You didn't have to call your sister over for that. She's right. I'll go fix myself up. Watch me." He puffed out his chest as the boys laughed and walked the few yards that separated them from the girls who looked up with smiles on their faces when he plunked down beside them. Puakea's stomach turned as she watched Ginny welcome this Adonis to their group. She walked away from her brother and his friends as they made comments and laughed about Dee's conquest.

A newcomer to the paddling world, Dee had done rather well over the four years since he had arrived. At seventeen, he was already in the senior men's division; his strong upper body strength and determined stamina empowered a canoe to move faster, enabling them to win race after race.

Dee had come straight from the streets of Chicago landing in Honolulu with his prosperous family who now resided in an impressive home in the upper region of Palolo Valley. Lanakila and Dee first met a few days after he had arrived. Dee had been exploring the back trails of Palolo when he came across a group of five boys in a mountain apple fight. They were throwing the fruit like baseballs at each other, and when they saw this *haole* boy stop in their midst, one of the boys from Palolo Housing started pelting him with apples. Lanakila told him to knock it off, and before he knew it, both he and Dee had a fight on their hands. They became fast friends from that day on.

Dee had not even seen the ocean until Lanakila introduced him to the beach at Waikiki. Once Dee felt the warm waters of the Pacific envelop his body, he never wanted to leave it. Attending the private school at Punahou, where he was soon enrolled, was the only time he did. Otherwise, he was in the ocean for some reason or another. Waikiki became his home base and it was here that he spent almost every waking moment.

Waikiki, originally the playground of Hawaiian royalty, was still untouched by the high rise hotels that would later impose their structures along the coast line. The Royal Hawaiian Hotel, The Moana Surfrider, the old Halekulani and a few others were scattered along the beach. Beach boy stands and surf board lockers were in place for the tourists and locals alike. People were starting to come to this paradise setting, flanked by Diamond Head on the left and the expanse of palm trees and the hotels on the right. Farther down on the right, the Hawaiian Village had just been built, a major sprawling hotel developed by the steel magnate Henry Kaiser.

2

APPROACHING HER FOURTEENTH BIRTHDAY IN a month, Puakea—her name a shortened version of Ho'opuakea which means *bright* or to *shine*—held her own in the paddling world. *Athletic* was definitely a word that described her, and she took easily to almost any sport. Streaks of blonde running through her ash brown hair, cropped short with wispy curls, framed her freckle-nosed face which resembled her *haole* father and was enhanced by the lovely chocolate brown eyes of her Hawaiian mother. With golden skin tanned from the sun, Puakea's figure had not found its full form yet, still growing in adolescence.

She was just in time to meet her Dad as he headed towards her. "You ready to go, Babe?" He never called her Puakea—just "Babe" ever since she was born. She didn't mind. Most everything her father said or did was okay with her. She adored him. His face weathered by years of being in the sun, he was still handsome in his forties.

Jacob Flynn, known as Jake to all, had been one of the few big wave riders, undaunted by the gigantic surf that swept the west and north shores of O'ahu, especially during the winter. He had been one of the most daring surfers of his time and still managed to take on the large waves when he was in the mood, though not much lately. It was too risky, and his large family of five children depended on him. So, instead of facing peril, he took on the task of guiding their canoe club to win victories. Puakea had helped him to hull, shape and build the canoe that they used for the men's division. It had taken almost two years to finish and turned out smoothly with sleek form, able to glide easily over the waves.

Father and daughter, who looked more alike than any of his five children, walked from the beach together after storing things in a locker where they kept their boards, a concession area run by one of his friends. They headed toward a side street and approached his Woody, a classic car the size of a station wagon, which had hauled many surfboards over the years. Lanakila would catch a ride home with a friend. He still had some celebrating to do at one of the beach boy's apartments in Waikiki.

They didn't talk much on the way home. Jake was a man of few words. Puakea was usually the verbal one with her friends and her brothers, but when she was with her dad, they had an unspoken connection that did not require words. He was the only person who gave her a sense of peace. She remembered cuddling up to him as a little girl feeling safe and secure in his love for her.

He was strict with his four boys who were all older than the girl who finally came along. The five children were born in two year intervals. The two older ones, Jacob Jr. and James had joined the army together. Her brother Clinton, who just graduated from high school, received a scholarship to go away to Oregon State, and Lanakila, at sixteen, attended Kaimuki High School.

When Puakea came into the world, her father had mellowed with the discipline required for four boys and reveled in being able to shower his daughter with affection. Puakea and Lanakila were the only ones with the Hawaiian names and the last of the children who remained at home. They both had English first names that they never used. She was Katherine Puakea and he was Jonathan Lanakila.

Puakea's resemblance to Jake was strictly in appearance; she did not have the same temperament. The Irish trait had skipped his generation and landed on her. She was feisty, strong willed and fought for her place amongst her brothers, having to put up with their teasing, taunting and sometimes a little bit of jealousy over her father's obvious favoritism.

Jake drove the few minutes from Waikiki on Kapahulu Avenue towards Kaimuki, then up the road to Tenth Avenue, entering the beautiful valley of Palolo. Their house was located about two miles from the community of Kaimuki where the Flynn children spent their time. They ate *saimin* and take-out *sushi* at Tanouye's or attended movies at Kaimuki or Queen Theater when they had the extra coins to spend. There were barber shops where the boys got their hair cut, Kress Store and National Dollar which became Ben Franklin, and a few other shops which sold their goods on Wai'alae Avenue, the main street in the district. Piggly Wiggly and Liberty House were situated further down the hill at Wai'alae Shopping Center which had just become the site for the Kahala Mall.

With the help of his friends, Jacob Flynn had built their home with views of Diamond Head and the ocean on clear days. Part of the house lay on one side of a small stream and the other portion was connected by a covered bridge, serving as a hallway leading to the other side. The two bedrooms that housed the four boys were located on one side of the stream and the main house on the other. It was not an elaborate structure—a single walled functional habitat where rooms were added on over the years. Its uniqueness lay in its location and its unobstructed views, enhanced by a jungle-like setting with an overabundance of tropical plants thriving on the heavy rainfall of the valley.

Her mother, Lilinoe, stood by the kitchen sink, preparing dinner when they arrived. Lili was now a matronly Hawaiian woman with a radiant smile and an endless capacity to spread her love on her unruly brood and anyone else in her vicinity. Much to her husband's objection at first, she assisted with the family's income by cleaning and caring for other people's houses. She had been doing this for years now, even when the children were younger. After sending them to school, she would go to work at her various jobs and be back by the time they were home. Her paycheck was eventually welcomed to help the growing family.

Because his parents strongly disapproved of their alliance, it was not until both passed away that Jacob Flynn finally married Lilinoe Kahale. By then, she had given birth to her second son. Jacob's father, Robert passed first. Five years later the daunting matriarch of the Flynn clan, Marjorie Hannah died unexpectedly from a heart attack two weeks after she was informed of her son's liaison with Lili. Marjorie had been adamant about refusing to let her son marry a Hawaiian commoner. The Flynns were affluent, society driven and autocratic in their rule over their four children. Marjorie had time before she died to cut her son out of her will as a final parting consequence of his disobedience.

Jacob took it all in stride, almost relieved when left to make his own decisions and live his life without his parents' iron rule. They struggled at first, but when he got a job working for the City and County of Honolulu Sanitation Department, with the help of Lilinoe's income, they were able to make ends meet. He was reduced to spending less time in the surfing and canoe world, but managed to break away once in awhile after work.

Lilinoe had been patient before her marriage and, because of her heartfelt love for this *haole* surfer, she waited to finally become his wife. They had a rocky road in their early days. They met through mutual friends at a wedding *lu'au* and she loved him from the moment they met. Jake took awhile before his loyalty was placed in her hands, but he soon grew to become dependent on her nurturing strength. She filled the void he'd always felt from the lack of a loving mother, and she became both mother and wife to him. He loved the way she treated their children—a combination of a firm hand and affection that knew no bounds. Jake almost envied them their mother and realized eventually that she was an angel with whom they were all blessed.

"Hello, my darlings. How was your day?" Lili asked turning towards them from the sink where she had cut up vegetables for their stir-fry dinner.

"Great," replied her husband. He leaned over and kissed her cheek and walked towards the bathroom to shower. "I'm starving," he called out.

"Dinner will be ready in a few minutes. Where's Lanakila?"

"Lanakila's with the boys. He won't be home for dinner," muttered Puakea. "We came in third. Could've done better."

"Oh, next time, then. There's always another day," her mom winked at her.

"You're right, Mom," said Puakea. She kissed her as she said this. "I'm going to shower first and I'll be right out to help you."

The back part of the Flynn property included a trail that led to a fresh water pool Jake had created for his children. He had maneuvered a part of the stream to a side area and filled it with rocks so that the stream poured over smooth stones to create a waterfall which cascaded into a tropical swimming hole. It was not large, but big enough for four boys to jump off rocks and wade in water up to their chests. The pool was surrounded by torch and white *ginger* and several large trees. One of the trees, a *kamani,* had been used as a fort when the kids were younger. Small boards were pounded to create a ladder that led to the top of the tree secured by a platform of two-by-fours.

The next day, Puakea decided to take her "Gone with the Wind" novel up to this part of the *kamani* to read in solitude. She had been warned by her father not to use the tree fort because the boards were now rotting after many years of being pounded by the rain. After a short time, the sound of her brother's voice interrupted her concentration. Her perch was shaded by branches. Lanakila and his friends, Bobby Makua and Dee Crown who trailed behind him, did not see her.

They all wore shorts, but decided to take them off before they jumped in to go swimming in the small rock pool. Puakea peered between the branches as the boys frolicked in the pool, laughing and ducking each other under water, doing cannon balls and yelling as loud as they could. They finally stood chest high in the cold water and talked for awhile; the subject got around to girls as Lanakila asked Dee about Ginny Carson.

Puakea strained her ears to hear them, put her book down, and in order to get into a better position, braced herself so that she was standing with her legs apart on the rotting boards. She stood there for a few seconds and before she realized it, the boards gave way. She toppled almost headfirst to the ground. In order to brace her fall, she put her arms out as she hit the rocks below, feeling a horrible pain in her right wrist and falling to her side on her shoulder. She screamed in pain.

Her brother let out a string of expletives, but before he went to help her, looked for his shorts to put on. They all did. "Stupid tita," is what he yelled at the top of his lungs when he finally stood over her.

"Oweeeee," she screamed. Dee came up behind Lanakila and crouched down beside her.

"You alright?" he asked.

"No," she cried and found all three boys bending over her.

"What were you doing heyah, spying on us?"

"I wasn't. I was here first," she whimpered and then started crying in pain.

"We'll take you to the hospital," said Dee. They were unaware that they probably should not have moved her, but Dee gathered Puakea off the rocks and carried her in pain through the short trail that led to the house. No one was home at the time, so instead of taking her inside, he headed for his car.

Lanakila and Bobby followed while Lanakila kept reminding her how *stupid* she was. The boys put on their tee shirts and slippers, still with their wet shorts and hopped in the back seat of Dee's 1958 Chevy Impala. Puakea was carefully laid on the front seat.

"You could have told us you were there before we took off our clothes. You were spying on us!" yelled Lanakila.

"Leave her alone. Can't you see she's in pain?" Dee yelled back.

Puakea was hurting too much to reply. She was so embarrassed, and Dee's kindness, for some reason, made her more upset. He attentively carried her into the hospital and waited with her during the admitting process. She wished she could have enjoyed the experience, but the pain overrode the thrill of being in the arms of Thaddeus Crown.

After she arrived at the hospital, the admitting staff at Queen's Hospital got in touch with her father at work. He was there in a half hour to take over. X-rays revealed that she had a broken collar bone and her wrist had snapped in three places. She was put into a cast, given medication for pain, and taken home after three hours. Dee and Bobby departed when they realized she would survive, leaving Lanakila to ride home with her and Jacob.

"Puakea, I told you those boards were rotting and to stay away from the tree fort," admonished her father.

"She was spying on us, Daddy," reported Lanakila.

"I was not. I was reading my book, and then I leaned over too far when I heard you splashing around."

"See, Dad, she was leaning ovah to spy on us. We went skinny dipping in da watah and it was boys only. Den we went heyah one crash and out of da tree comes da tita. She deserves what she got."

Jake turned the car off the side of the road. He pulled Lanakila out of the back seat and took him to the rear of the car. They were about three miles from home, just approaching Tenth Avenue.

"Lanakila, would you like to walk the rest of the way home?"

"No, but..." He couldn't speak any further because Jake put a hand over his mouth.

"One more word and you're walking."

"Okay, okay, I'll shut up."

"Good," said Jake. "Now get in the car and don't say another word."

3

PUAKEA HAD ATTENDED KAMEHAMEHA SINCE first grade. The school, at the time, had several campuses. Kindergarten through second grade rooms were located at McNeil Hall below Kalakaua Intermediate. Third through sixth grade classes were held at Bishop Hall near the Bishop Museum, and seventh through twelfth graders attended school on the hills of Kapalama. While she had attended the first two campuses, the new Preparatory School was in the midst of construction on Kapalama Heights. Puakea's sixth grade classroom was the first in the new school that included all grades in the fall of 1955.

Kamehameha School was the main beneficiary of Princess Bernice Pauahi's last will and testament, an estate that covered over 400,000 acres of which 353,000 were inherited from her cousin Princess Ruth Ke'elikolani just one year and five months before Pauahi died. Pauahi, the great granddaughter of Kamehameha I, married an American, Charles Reed Bishop in 1850, defying her parents who had expected her to ally herself with Hawaiian royalty. Theirs was a love relationship, and he carried on her legacy in 1884 after she died at the age of fifty two.

The favorite of the head mistress at a small missionary school for royalty, appropriately named Royal School, Pauahi was considered a serene, unassuming person who spent her life being a blessing to all she encountered. She had even refused the royal crown when asked to carry on the Kamehameha dynasty. Her foster sister, Queen Lili'uokalani recorded in her memoirs that Pauahi was "as good as she was beautiful". After her death, her humble life instilled the goals in the students who attended Kamehameha. She was their role model, and her memory was revered by all at least once a year with marches, songs, speeches, psalms and a reciting of the 31st Proverb.

Steeped in paternalism, the school, when Puakea attended, had noble intentions for the Hawaiian children under their care. Pauahi's will stipulated its objective to create "industrious men and women", and the opportunities were there to encourage this. Sportsmanship, fair play, table manners, deportment, discipline in every area were used to promote this mission.

During this post-war period, most of Hawai'i was swept up in the need to become loyal Americans and the underlying theme of emulating the *haole* would become predominant. The school followed suit. Hawaiian teachers were sparingly scattered amongst its administration and most of the staff enlisted were Protestant Caucasians. As a result, very little of the Hawaiian culture was endorsed. The institution was run on a curriculum that would have probably been found in a private finishing school in the eastern United States. The Hawaiian monarchs had been taught similar standards and ideals at Royal School. Kamehameha continued its principles.

Kamehameha Schools consisted of a majority of day students and a smaller contingent of boarders. The boarders , some who started as early as seventh grade, were mostly from the outer islands—Maui, Moloka'i, Lana'i, Kaua'i, the Big Island of Hawai'i and one or two from the private island of Ni'ihau. Others came from broken homes or the country areas of O'ahu which were considered too far to travel.

The school's ethnic mix consisted of a handful of pure Hawaiians, but the majority were Hawaiian mixtures with every race inhabiting the islands at the time—the Portuguese, Chinese, Japanese, Koreans, Filipinos, Puerto Ricans, and *haole*. Thus, a variety of race, creed and color represented the student body with the one thread they all had in common—the Hawaiian blood of their ancestors.

Cultural distinction was not emphasized. There were country children who had come from one room schoolhouses mixed with those of the privileged from affluent homes. Class lines were not distinguished nor considered an issue. They were all under the same umbrella and collectively taught the goals of academic achievement and servitude.

Many students thrived under the system. Puakea was not one of them. Her short fuse and stubbornness got her into more trouble—as one of her teachers put it—than a "barrel of monkeys". The scrapes at home with her four brothers carried over to her life at school. Boys became the bane of her existence. The more she reacted to them, the more they taunted and teased her. She pummeled them at recess, beat them up after school, and annihilated them in sports activities. Most of these incidents took place away from the authorities' watchful eyes, but she did manage to get caught on a few occasions.

Once, in fifth grade when the teacher was out of the room, she threw a desk clear across the room at a boy. He had just repeated a verse they'd often taunt her with, "Bewayah, bewayah of Puakea cause she no cayah; she no cayah; she no cayah." She had heard it before, and it was just his stupid attempt at rhyming, but she'd had great disdain for the boy who recited this, and her rage exploded beyond reason. Luckily, she missed him by an inch, but the teacher arrived in class to see the toppled desk on the other side of the classroom. It was a good thing that he was a male teacher who had a fondness for her, and the teasing boy was the one who got in trouble.

Puakea toned down her violence over the years, but it was always on the surface ready to erupt. The irritation of the teasing boys changed in seventh and eighth grade, when they finally started to notice girls in a different way. An increased number of new students were admitted to seventh grade. The kids she had known all her life were now exposed to a variety of people and a whole different climate emerged. Now the boys went *girl crazy* and that irritated Puakea even more. The new boys, who were unaware of her tainted past, were even making advances towards her. Somewhat confused, she had no idea how to handle this unwanted attention, so she shined them on, greatly relieved when they were finally separated in ninth grade.

The boys traded their white shirts and khaki pants for a military uniform that year and began their careers at Kamehameha Boys School, located above the Preparatory Department and below the Girls School which was segregated at the top of the Kapalama campus.

Puakea arrived on her first day at Kamehameha Girls School in a cast that wrapped from the top of her shoulder and extended over the thumb of her right hand. She was not happy.

The girls as well as the boys were separated into five sections according to their academic ability, a stigma that was not enjoyed by some of the better students in the lower sections. Their ability was rated by a test that was taken before entering ninth grade and their section assignment—sections A,B,C,D and E—stayed with them until they graduated.

Puakea was assigned to C Section and her mood improved when she found that Keala Kalia and Kanoe Hunter were also allocated there. The three girls had been in the same eighth grade class, and she liked them both for different reasons. Keala's all encompassing friendliness was contagious, and Puakea had been drawn to protect Kanoe in her shyness.

"Puakea, what happened to your arm?" Keala questioned as the three walked together to their second period class.

"Like an idiot, I fell out of a tree."

"Oh, no," said Kanoe. "How did you do that?"

"I was trying to watch my brother and his friends skinny dip in our pool."

"You have a swimming pool?" Kanoe asked, more amazed at that.

"No, silly, it's just a bunch of rocks surrounding water in our back yard."

By this time Keala had burst out laughing. "Leave it to Kanoe to ask about the pool and not the naked boys in the water. That's what I want to hear about."

"Well, I didn't see much, since I was too busy falling out of the tree."

"So then what happened?" asked Kanoe.

"Then one of my brother's cute friends carried me to his car and took me to the hospital."

"Was he still naked at the time?"

"No, Kanoe, they all got dressed the minute I fell out of the tree. In fact they were more worried about getting dressed than they were about me who could have been dead on the ground."

"Knowing you, Puakea, you must have been screaming your head off, so I'm sure they knew you weren't dead," Keala teased, still laughing out of control.

Puakea sighed and rolled her eyes, "You know me so well, don't you Keala?" The three girls walked into their second period classroom.

4

THE NEXT TIME PUAKEA SAW Dee was six months later at the beach at Waikiki. She was on her surfboard at a spot called Queens in front of Kuhio Beach. "Puakea," he shouted. She sat there straddling her long board as he paddled out to her. "How you doing?" he asked when he finally reached her. The sun reflected on his face—illuminating blue eyes as they took on a turquoise shade—simulating the color of the ocean water that surrounded them. Puakea's heartbeat escalated.

"I'm good," she answered, not able to think of anything earth shattering to say.

"Your arm must be better if you can surf now."

"Just had the cast removed a month ago. It's fine now."

He smiled at her. "That'll teach you to hang out in trees."

She knew her face was turning red now—not from the hot sun that was beating down on them. "I gotta go now. I've been in the water too long."

"You wanna get something to eat with me?" he asked.

Now how the heck was she supposed to get out of this one? "Okay," she finally said.

"I'll race you back to shore."

They brought their surfboards in and laid them down on the sand. While Puakea toweled off, Dee walked off in the direction of a deli stand and soon returned with two hamburgers and bottled Nehi sodas. They sat under a coconut tree, sitting cross legged as they devoured the food. Dee started talking and she began to relax as he spoke. He asked her a few questions about herself, fascinated with the concept of Kamehameha; then engaged in telling her more about his life—some of it she knew, but she became privy to more as the day wore on towards twilight.

"My dad's all about me going to Illinois Tech when I graduate. He's an architect and wants me to follow in his footsteps. It's in Chicago where I grew up. I hate it there and it's not exactly my dream."

"What d'ya wanna do?"

"I don't know. Stay here and surf and paddle. That's what I really want to do. But I was thinking that maybe I could compromise and could go to UH."

"Hmm. Sounds like a plan. Just think, by the time you're done at UH, I'll just be finishing high school."

He tilted his head and looked questioningly at her. "I forgot how young you are Puakea." Their eyes connected. "Such a pretty girl with a long ways to go. Bet you have lots of boyfriends."

She stiffened, sat up straight and moved towards her surfboard. "Don't be slinging hash at me, Dee Crown. You know darn good and well, that I'm not pretty. I think it's mean of you to make fun of me like that, and I have to go."

Dee sat there with his mouth open as she picked up her surfboard and started to walk away. He jumped up to go after her. "Nice exit, Puakea, but how're you gonna get home?" You're not going to walk all the way back to Palolo Valley."

"You don't even know that for a fact. Maybe I have a ride."

"And maybe you don't." You'd have to call your father and then that'd take awhile, so you better let me drive you home."

She stood there with a frown on her face trying to figure out how to recover her pride. She couldn't. So, after a long pause, she muttered, "Alright then."

They didn't speak on the ride home; she mostly kept her face towards the window as Dee concentrated on the road. When they pulled up in front of her house, he turned to her and finally spoke.

"I don't know why you got so mad, Puakea." He enunciated his next sentence. "I… was… not… making fun of you."

"Well, it's better not to speak, if you don't mean what you say."

"About you being pretty?"

She nodded her head.

"Puakea, you're in the dark on that subject. That's what comes of too many brothers around," he argued, "But pretty soon you'll figure it out and you'll be knocking em' dead. You'll have broken hearts lying everywhere." She continued to look out the window as he spoke again. "Now let's see a smile on that pretty face of yours before you go in. After all, I *did* buy you a hamburger."

She turned to look at him and feigned a smile, then opened the door, unstrapped her board from the rack on the roof of his Chevy Impala. He came around to assist her, but before she walked towards the house, she said, "Thanks for the ride, Dee…and the hamburger."

Knock 'em dead she thought later. *Yeah right, if he only knew—broken bodies everywhere, but not hearts that's for sure.*

5

PUAKEA AND KEALA SAT ON the sidelines of a court, wearing their blue shorts and white shirts, after playing basketball in P.E. "I don't know why you hang with that Kia Kea. I can't stand her." Keala looked up in surprise. Puakea continued, "Did you see the way she hogged the ball and pushed me aside to make that basket?"

"Aw, Pua, she's alright. She's my friend. You have to get to know her," Keala protested.

"Uh, uh, not me. She's way too aggressive in sports, stuck up, thinks she's better than us cause she's in A section, and I heard she's going out with everybody's boyfriends."

"Well, you can't believe everything you hear. I know for a fact that she does *not* think she's better than us. She just has a hard time trusting others."

"I think I'm going to beat her up after school," returned Puakea, just to be contrary.

"Puakea Flynn, if you do, you'll have me to answer to. I told you she's my friend. Now, if anyone said something awful about you, I'd come to the same defense. Leave her alone."

Puakea stood up and started to walk away. Then she turned towards Keala with second thoughts, "Okay, Keala, I won't beat her up." Then she walked towards the locker room as she muttered to herself, "Not today, anyway."

Puakea stayed away from Kia after that, primarily for Keala's sake, but also because she could not tolerate her haughty demeanor. Kanoe and Keala became her closest friends. Keala had many others, and Puakea understood that she was unique, never covetous or resentful of her popularity.

And so, the years passed—from freshman they became sophomores, and on into their junior year. Puakea bided her time, which was becoming tedious, and still managed to get in minor trouble that, much to her dismay, did not get her kicked out of Kamehameha. She went to one prom; hated her dress, thought the dance was boring, and ended up punching her poor date who tried to kiss her. She never went to another one. Once in awhile she'd think of Dee's words, *broken hearts everywhere.* Not likely, not for her.

Puakea Flynn did manage to get prettier over time—not that she noticed. But others did. Her *ehu* hair remained short. She had not grown more than an inch since ninth grade, but her body took on different proportions, and her face transformed, losing the scattered blemishes of the adolescent and changing into that of a young girl who could definitely be considered *pretty.* She had learned to control her short temper—except for the night of the prom—but still retained an edge that no one challenged.

She had known Nani and Lihau when they arrived as boarders in ninth grade, but not well until they all roomed together at Senior Cottage. Keala became the mother hen when they were together at the cottage and as a result, they all bonded in an unusual way—all, except for Kia who continued to hold herself aloof from the others.

They graduated together, the six girls from Senior Cottage, each dressed in white along with the handsome boys who wore their military blues. Puakea celebrated the day. She was leaving a place where she had spent her last twelve years.

After graduation parties galore and a summer of get-togethers, Puakea got involved with a group of boys from her senior class. They spent most of the summer hanging out at each other's houses drinking beer, telling stories and playing music. They loved going to her house during the day to swim in the waterfall pool as they lazed around the surrounding grassy area or perched on the rocks indulging in their favorite pastime.

One of them had a grandfather who owned a house in Kihei. In August of that year, they each had permission to go to the island of Maui for a week before everyone went their ways to college or work in September.

It was a last minute trip, and most of them had not even left the island or seen Maui's shores, but at different intervals, they all arrived in Kahalui and embarked on their adventure to Kihei, a lazy little beach area with very few residents at the time. The house had been vacated for a future rental and having no furniture, they had to be innovative. So, three of the boys broke into a vacant house next door, *borrowed* all their mattresses and dragged them over. The house was then furnished with wall-to-wall mattresses—all that the teenagers required for their week's stay in Maui.

Lihau drove from Ha'iku. Keala flew in from the Big Island; Kanoe arrived with Puakea from O'ahu, and the girls found themselves with seven boys for the week. They had invited Nani, but she was unable to come. Most of them had never been unaccompanied by a parent on a trip, and they were free to do anything they wanted. So they did. Lewd, crude, rude behavior followed and the mode was set for the week. They were joined by different characters from Maui along the way. A boisterous party every night with more drinking, singing and storytelling took place in the house of mattresses. Two cars were packed with teenagers on their motor tours, and they embarked on trips all over the island.

On one outing to Lahaina which was also sparsely populated at the time, they visited a handsome *haole* diver who was a friend of one of the guys and lived in a dwelling located in the middle of town. He cordially invited the group into the sunken living room of his house which was so full of broken glass—the result of shattered beer bottles and other liquor containers—that the eleven visitors had to leave on their slippers in order to enter. After they visited awhile, he told them he had to clean up and escorted them outside while he turned on a garden hose and blasted the living area with water—no vacuum cleaners for him—but when they thought about it…how else could one clean a house like that?

On another occasion, a lovely man came over to the Kihei house and taught one of the guys to play the spoons orchestrated to go with their guitar and *'ukulele* music. The next day the same man invited them to breakfast at Kihei's beach park, and they were graciously treated to a Hawaiian feast which he and his sister had so hospitably provided.

At one point, the group split up. Five of them, including Lihau and Keala, trekked up to Haleakala to see the blazing sunrise from the rim of its crater. Puakea and Kanoe proceeded with the rest of the boys on the long enchanting drive to Hana where they spent the night and camped on the grass in a paradise setting complete with an idyllic waterfall garden—and of course—followed by more lewd, crude, rude behavior.

The trip was life changing and would create a bond that would last for the rest of their days. It became a *coming of age* for each of them and from then on, they always referred to themselves as "the Maui Gang". They would all go on to other paths, but that one week, in a moment in time, became their fondest memory...ever.

6

"Daddy, please don't make me go to college. I don't want to go."

"Why not?"

"Because...I hate school. I'm sick of it. I've been going for thirteen years and I need a break."

"But you already got accepted to UH."

"I don't care. I don't wanna go."

"What are you going to do then?"

"I'm going to help Mom with her jobs."

"Cleaning houses? No way."

Puakea eventually did have her way after her promise to attend school the following year. She would cross that bridge when she came to it. Right now, she was so relieved. She had been helping her mother off and on for years in her work. She was industrious, one of Pauahi's goals; the good, humble, virtuous part might come later. For now, she was free to work, surf and paddle, and she was over the moon about it.

Lilinoe had been slowing down, and it was a perfect time for Puakea to take up the slack. Lili's jobs included two houses near Diamond Head, one in Kahala, one on Wilhelmina Rise and in the past two years she had been asked to work at the Crown house in Palolo where Dee lived. She worked once a week at each house for five or six hours and

29

came home in the afternoon. Other people requested her, so she had more than enough for Puakea to take on.

Puakea was willing to do whatever Lilinoe wanted, but Dee's house was definitely not going to be on her agenda even though he had been away at college. Instead of Illinois Tech, he had managed to compromise and ended up going to the University of Illinois to appease his father.

Dee had finished his liberal arts studies the same time Puakea graduated and she heard he was returning home to find a job. *No, she was definitely not going to do the Crown house.*

She had taken on the two houses in Diamond Head and the one on Wilhelmina Rise, leaving Lilinoe just the ones in Kahala and more time to spend at home. Her kids were all grown now and on their own without the need for their mother's added income, and she was happy to give her work over to her daughter.

The homes in Diamond Head were side by side, but completely different in their design. One sat on the cliffs overlooking the water with swimming pool and glass galore—not her favorite thing to maintain, and the other sat further back in a garden setting. The one on Wilhelmina Rise, she could walk to. Even though it was a trek up a steep hill, she loved the views of the city and the person who lived there was her favorite. It was occupied by an aging Hawaiian widow who always had the most delicious food waiting for Puakea after her chores were done.

Her brother Lanakila had joined the Honolulu Fire Department and by that time was well entrenched at Kapahulu Fire Station, located near the zoo and within walking distance from Waikiki Beach. He lived at home on his days off and still managed to give his sister a bad time, not intentionally, but out of habit. She was used to it by now and actually missed his harassing when he was away from the house.

"I'm goin' out wit' Dee, tonight," he announced to his mother at the dinner table one night.

"Oh, that's right, I heard he came home two nights ago."

"Yeah, he's t'inking bout joinin' up wit' da Depahtment, so we gotta talk about it."

"Oh my, what do his parents think about that?" asked Lili.

"I don't t'ink dey know. Be shuah and keep it undah yoah hat, Ma. He's just looking into it." His mother noticed that Lanakila's pidgin had gotten even worst since he hung with all the boys at the fire station.

Puakea was all ears, but she didn't say a thing. A few weeks later he informed them that Dee was indeed interested, in spite of major objections from his father and that he would be embarking on all the tests required. A few months later, he told them that Dee had passed the tests and through a lot of maneuvering, they would be working together at the Kapahulu station.

"Puakea, what are you doing here?" he said the first time they encountered each other. She was sitting in the sand under a coconut tree staring out at the horizon as the sun set at Waikiki. It was probably the same coconut tree she had been sitting under the last time she saw him four years ago.

"Nothing," she replied, unable to utter anything else at the moment.

He stood there, with surfboard under his arm, wearing canvas swimming trunks. She shaded her eyes from the glare of the setting sun and stared. He seemed to look the same as she remembered, but maybe not. She couldn't say...perhaps because she was so stunned to see him. His eyes still matched the ocean; his body had filled out with more of a manly stature and an aura of confidence that seemed to emanate from him.

She remembered that he was a fireman now, and thought that the endurance needed for his work had probably honed a more physically fit physique. Anyway, she thought he looked spectacular and it made her even more nervous in his presence than ever before.

"It's been a long time, Puakea," he remarked. "With the risk of getting you upset, I gotta say, that you look great."

"Thanks," she responded, remembering how strongly she had reacted four years ago to a similar statement. Trying to keep the blood from rushing to her face and to think of something half way intelligent to say, she spoke. "How you doing, Dee?" Now that was earth shaking. She couldn't get her tongue unraveled.

"Fine, just fine," he replied. "You heard I'm working with Lanakila now."

"I did. He talks about you all the time. Says you're a pretty good fireman—one of Hawai'i's best."

"Well, I don't know about that, but it beats pounding the books for four years. Don't even have a degree I can do anything with. But who needs it? I like what I'm doing. What about you?"

She did not want to talk about her domestic profession right now—not that she was ashamed of it, but for some reason, it wasn't what she wanted to relate. "Just finished school and I'm taking a break before I go to UH."

He didn't probe further, but cheerfully said, "Good for you. That'll give you lots of time to beach it and surf all you want."

She smiled then, and felt more comfortable warmed by his enthusiasm. He put his board down, sat down beside her, and they talked for awhile. He did most of the talking about his time in Illinois and how homesick he was for Hawai'i's shores. He asked her if she had a ride home. She told him that she had inherited Lanakila's old car, a 1953 Dodge after he bought a new one.

"I guess I'll be seeing you around, Puakea. I'll certainly be down here as much as I can." Dee got up to leave and turned to her with his parting words, "Take care, and don't be breaking too many hearts."

She saw him often after that, mostly from a distance. He said hello to her and waved with that bright smile of his, but they never had another lengthy conversation. She watched him over that year; each time she saw him, he was surrounded by girls or with one in particular. Her heart stopped one day when her brother informed her that Dee was serious about a girl named Luana and seeing her exclusively. Any information on Thaddeus Crown perked up her ears, but she was not included in his social world. Just as well, she thought. He was way out of her league and always had been.

The year passed and Puakea continued to work in the various homes she cleaned, actually enjoying the satisfaction of accomplishing her chores and the freedom that gave her time to spend in Waikiki.

She attracted guys now, and many approached her, but she wasn't interested in any one in particular, never admitting that there was only one who had captured her interest, making others pale beside the image of him.

7

Lanakila called home one day while he was at work. Lilinoe answered the phone. "Oh, no," she cried. "Oh, no."

Puakea had been sitting at the dining table chopping onions to assist Lili with dinner. "What Mom. What is it?" she asked. Lili waved her away, while she tried to listen to Lanakila. Puakea saw her nod, say a few incoherent things and knew she had to wait until she hung up the phone.

When Lilinoe finally hung up, she took a deep breath and sat down on a chair. "It's Dee," she announced with a voice filled with distress.

Puakea finally got the details, some at that moment, and more from Lanakila the next day. The Kapahulu Fire Station had received a routine call, the kind of emergency that they had handled on several occasions. A man was trapped in a car that had been in an accident on the side of the old Pali Road in Nu'uanu.

Dee and Lanakila and two other firemen were in the process of freeing the man whose car had turned over. Dee approached the car and proceeded to angle himself in a prone position so he could talk to and soothe the frantic man. Lanakila was right behind him, crouching down beside the car. He and the other firemen were trying to jack the door free so they could extricate him.

What happened next was unexpected. They did not notice the car's leaking gas tank. Oil and gas ignited, causing an explosion that knocked Lanakila and the two other firemen off their feet backwards on to the road. The entire car went up in flames until the man's screams could no longer be heard. Dee was right there in the middle of it. He was still alive when he was finally rushed to Queen's Hospital by an ambulance that had already been en route to the scene. The driver of the car was pronounced dead upon arrival. Lanakila was frantic as he rode with Dee all the way to the emergency room.

Queen's Medical Center, was founded in 1859 by Queen Emma and King Kamehameha IV. At the time, the diseases brought by foreigners to the islands were serious threats to the survival of the Hawaiian race. The King proposed his desire to have a hospital for this purpose and to serve the population in providing a facility for all their medical needs. He and his wife went personally to homes to solicit necessary funding which was also assisted with a donation from the Legislature. Even in her overwhelming grief, after the death of their beloved child and the King's passing that soon followed, the Queen worked tirelessly to fulfill this dream.

There was limited treatment for burns at the time, but the staff at Queens could not do enough for the fireman who was brought to them in dire need. He had been diagnosed with second degree burns on the left side of his face and neck and third degree burns in the chest and shoulder areas. The shock to the body fortunately left him unconscious for a period of days, so he was not feeling the pain that would come with his waking moments.

It was the beginning of Dee's nightmare and the end of the quality of living that he had so taken for granted. His parents were frantic and beside themselves when they were informed. At the time, the state of Pennsylvania had just built a Burn Center that specialized in trauma victims like Dee. Through their connections, and their abundant resources, the Crowns had him flown within the week to Pittsburg to be treated.

Lanakila Flynn had not been hurt, but the guilt he suffered and anguish over what happened to Dee affected him deeply. During Dee's hospital stay at Queen's, Lanakila spent every moment he could spare beside him. It was not a pretty sight and added to his culpability, but his self imposed penance was to see him through the agonizing hours. When Dee was finally transported to the airport, Lanakila was there to see him off.

It would be a year before they would see each other again. Lanakila never failed to write him once a week, or call on frequent occasions when he could get through to him.

Puakea felt anguish too. But she could never express how profoundly she was affected to anyone. After all, Thaddeus Crown was just supposed to be a fleeting acquaintance of hers—her brother's friend, someone she saw once or twice on the beach—not what he actually meant to her. And that, she would not put into words…not even to herself.

So, she gleaned information from her brother who was in close contact with Dee and from her mother who told her whatever she heard while she worked in the Crown's Palolo house. It would be a year and a half before Puakea saw Dee Crown again.

8

"MOM, I DON'T KNOW HOW you can ask me to do that. Isn't there someone else?"

"No, Puakea, you're the only one who can take on this sensitive task," insisted Lilinoe as her daughter helped her pack for the hospital.

"I can't do it, Mom. Please don't ask me to."

"Puakea, I very seldom ask anything as important as this of you. It means the world to me and I can't take 'no' for an answer."

Lilinoe was going into the hospital for a gall bladder operation. She would be laid up for a couple of weeks. She had been working for the Crown's as their housekeeper for years, and since Dee's return, she was one of the trusted few allowed in their home. He had a part time male nurse who came in, but the house was now closed off to outsiders. She had recommended that Puakea take her place while she was laid up, and the Crowns had agreed to have her come.

Puakea had heard from other sources about how Dee had become the patient from hell. She hadn't heard the details. Lilinoe was very discreet, especially about anything negative. Unlike Puakea, she only discussed the good things about people.

Puakea arrived one summer morning at the Crown residence. In all the years Lilinoe worked for them, Puakea had never been to their house. The home was somewhat out of place in Palolo Valley which, in those early years, primarily consisted of low income housing and people who resided in average affordable homes.

The three story structure had been built on the side of a steep cliff, overlooking the valley with partial views of the city of Honolulu. A special driveway led up to the front entrance located on the middle floor of the house. She rang the doorbell and Julia Crown, a woman who appeared to be in her late forties came to greet her at the door.

"Puakea, how nice to see you, or should I say, meet you," she exclaimed warmly. She was barefoot and wore a pair of Capri slacks with a short Polynesian print blouse when she answered the door. Her blonde hair was simply drawn back in a pony tail. Puakea was surprised at how youthful she appeared.

"Uh, thanks, same here. I guess you were expecting me."

"Yes, your mom made all the arrangements. I hope she's doing alright. I can't tell you what a blessing she's been to me."

"She's going in for her operation today, so I'll let you know how she does afterwards."

Julia Crown gave her a tour of the house and the location of all the cleaning supplies and equipment; then spoke to her in a subdued voice. "Thaddeus' room is upstairs to the far left of the house. He does not know you're here. You don't have to clean his room today or any day for that matter. His nurse takes care of that. Just know that that room is off limits, for now. He should not be disturbed." Puakea was almost glad to hear this. She was not intending to see Dee, although she had an ongoing curiosity about his condition.

She was amazed at the size and beauty of the house. The entrance led to an enormous living room that took full advantage of the views below. It was sparsely furnished with rattan couches and matching chairs—covered with black and yellow Polynesian prints of ginger blossoms. That was the theme of the room—yellow and white ginger stalks everywhere in large ceramic containers. She gathered that they must have come from their yard, surrounded on each side with patches of ginger, cascading down the hill. Probably the most fragrant of all the flowers in Hawai'i, the scent was breathtaking and the air, inside and out, filled with the sweet smelling aroma. On the one wall that was not glassed in, there was a large bamboo framed picture of the same ginger blossoms next to a waterfall that poured into a rock pool.

A kitchen and dining room off to the left faced the back mountain area, and stairs separated the rooms from the living area—one set leading to the third floor and the other to the lower level. She learned later, that Mr. and Mrs. Crown's bedrooms were downstairs and that Dee was separated two floors above them.

Cornelius Crown was away on a business trip for six months in Japan. He worked as a developer and consultant for various hotel resorts and presently involved in negotiating with several Japanese firms that were investing in American interests—one of them was a proposed resort in Hawai'i.

Puakea tended to her work and got into the routine of caring for the large house. She was scheduled to come two days a week on Tuesdays and Thursdays after her job on Wilhelmina Rise. The second day she was there, she had gone to vacuum and clean the third floor spare bedroom, bathroom and den. The den had now been converted to what looked like a physical therapy room with weights, exercise equipment and a short ramp with bars on each side of it.

She heard shouting and something crashing against a wall. As she emerged from the den, she saw Julia Crown scurrying down the hall. Puakea noticed Mrs. Crown's tearful face and quickly stepped back into the den so she wouldn't be seen.

The second time this occurred was the following Tuesday. The third time it occurred was the next Thursday. There was a variation on the incidents, but they all included shouting, and Mrs. Crown departing from the room in tears.

Puakea's favorite book as a child was the "The Secret Garden" made into a movie that she later viewed on a late night television show. The heroine was played by a young Margaret O'Brien, and a younger Dean Stockwell acted as the crippled rich boy who threw tantrums every night. She remembered Margaret O'Brien stomping into the boy's room to tell him what a brat he was, and that is just what Puakea intended to do after the third incident.

Mrs. Crown, on this occasion was so upset that she went storming out the front door, into the driveway where she got into her Lincoln Continental and sped away. This gave Puakea the perfect opening to march towards Dee's room.

It was quiet now. Instead of knocking, she turned the knob slowly and entered the room which was completely enshrouded in darkness. The thick double drapes were drawn, and not a sliver of light seeped through. Puakea stood by the door for a moment to adjust to the darkness.

"Is someone there? Mom is that you again?" said a voice from the direction of the far side of the room. "I told you, I didn't want anyone in here." The voice was shouting again.

"It's not your mom," Puakea almost whispered. "She left."

"Who is it?"

"It's Puakea." A silence followed…and then all hell let loose. "What the…are you doing here? Get out. Get out right now. Is this my mom's idea?" Shouted obscenities were directed at her, and things were thrown at the wall, things she couldn't even decipher in the dark. Nevertheless, she stood there as if her feet were stuck in cement. Then she moved.

"You know what, Thaddeus Crown, you are a spoiled brat," she said putting on her best Margaret O'Brien impression. "How dare you treat your poor mother that way? Every time, I see her, she's in tears… all because of you and your infantile tantrums. You need to get a grip." Puakea was standing next to his bed right now. Her eyes were getting accustomed to the darkness. She could see that he lay sideways on his bed.

"Puakea, if you know what's good for you, you will turn around and leave this room."

"I can't." More silence. And then more silence. "So, now you're going to freeze me out?" she queried.

"Whatever works," he muttered.

"It's too dark in here. These blinds should be drawn," she announced and started walking to the windows. Before she managed two steps, she felt forceful hands bite into her shoulders, and she was spun around facing the bed again. Dee stood next to her gripping her firmly, towering above her with his breath on her face. She was trying not to show how stunned she was. First of all, she had been under the impression that he was an invalid like the boy in "The Secret Garden". But there he was standing over her, trying to mangle her upper arms in a vice—a pretty strong one at that.

"If you open those blinds, you die," he spat out the words in her face.

She shrugged his hands off as if she weren't shaking in her slippers with fright and said, "Well, I guess I won't open them, then."

He slumped back on the bed and lay there for a minute. She sat on the bottom corner of it, aware that it might be improper, but not really worried about it.

"So, don't you get bored in here?"

All she heard was a grunt.

"Company might be good for you."

More grunting.

"I could tell you about my life and all the houses I clean. That might be entertaining." Still no answer. "You do know that's why I'm here. I took my mom's place. She's in the hospital. Plus I clean some other houses. Do you want to know about them?"

No answer again.

"Well, I guess I will tell you about the houses. I go to one on Monday at Diamond Head and the next day I go to the other Diamond Head one, and on Tuesday, I go to Wilhelmina Rise, and then back to Diamond Head on Thursday for the big house with all the glass. So, now, I have to come to your house on Tuesday and Thursday afternoons and that means…that I can't surf until Fridays."

"Course I do have Saturdays and Sundays off, so I can surf those days too, so I'm not really feeling sorry for myself. Anyway, the surf at Queens has been breaking during the summer as you probably guessed, but it's getting so crowded with tourists that I almost lost my board the other day cause some stupid *haole*—excuse the expression—tried to cut me off. So do you want to hear about the people I work for? The lady at Wilhelmina Rise is pretty cool, but Diamond Head's got some really stuck up people…"

Puakea continued her ongoing monologue until she heard a soft snoring sound. Well, maybe putting him to sleep was not so bad. It was better than the temper tantrum she told herself, and then she quietly tiptoed out of his room.

Lilinoe, recovering from her operation after two weeks, needed to take off more time from work. Jake was reluctant about her working at all, and they continued to have discussions on the matter. So, Puakea returned to the Crown house extending her employment there on an indefinite basis.

It had only been two days since her last visit to the Crowns. She did all her work the following Thursday. Mrs. Crown was not at home that day. She had left a note that she wouldn't be back until that evening due to a charity event that she was preparing for.

Puakea always did the third floor last, and had just completed her chores. She was getting ready to leave when she heard a moaning sound from Dee's room. She walked down the hall and, without knocking again, opened his door slowly.

"Are you alright, Dee?"

"Puakea, get my medicine for me."

"Tell me where it is."

"In the bathroom cabinet. They forgot to leave it on my nightstand."

She walked quickly to his bathroom, and saw several plastic medicine containers in the cabinet. She rushed back to the bed and asked him which one she was supposed to bring him. He told her what to retrieve in a muffled voice wrought with agonizing pain, and she brought it back to him.

"Dee, I can't see in the dark. Can't we turn on the light?" Puakea had leaned forward trying to find the switch on the bedside lamp. Dee lay near the edge of the bed with his head away from her. His immediate reflex was to stop her and, in so doing, his elbow hit her cheek right below her eye.

"NO," he groaned.

"Ow," she yelled. She held her hand near the eye that was throbbing now. "You didn't have to hit me."

"I didn't hit you. Your face was in the way when I tried to stop you."

"Well, you still packed a wallop on me," she moaned.

"You'll be fine." He just couldn't spit out an apology. "Wanna trade places?"

"No. S'okay. You're right, my fault," she grudging replied.

Puakea sat beside him on the bed and handed him the medicine container. She could hear him fumbling around as he reached for the glass of water on his nightstand.

"Okay, did you take it?" she asked.

"Yes."

"Good, then I'll let you sleep now," she whispered and slowly got up to head for the door.

"Puakea?"

"Yes."

"Don't go yet."

Well, that threw her for a loop. She thought she was his number one nemesis. This was certainly the last thing she expected from him.

"Okay, I'll stay."

She fumbled back to the bed in the darkness and sat at the foot of it, cross legged while she waited for him to speak again. It was a few minutes before he did. She knew the medicine had to take effect. She could hear the difference in his tone.

"Tell me some more stories," he petitioned. So she did.

9

EVERYONE WHO SAW HER THAT week commented on the bruise that was now prominent on her face. "Puakea, what happened to your eye?" her dad questioned when he saw her at dinner that night.

"Ah, surf board mishap," she responded.

"I didn't know you were at the beach today."

"Oh yeah, I went right after work."

"You better see to that eye, and put some ice on it."

"Okay, Dad, I'll be fine."

She returned the following week to the Crown's and when she once again finished the last of her chores on the third floor, she noticed that Dee's bedroom door had been left open and wondered if it was an invitation. Only one way to find out and what did she have to lose?

So, she stood by the door this time. The room had more light now that the door was open. She noticed him propped up on his pillows in the shadows; the drapes were still drawn.

"Come in, Puakea, and shut the door," a gravelly voice commanded.

She shut the door and walked over to the bed, then seated herself in her usual position at the foot of it. A light immediately shone in her face, and she shaded her eyes reflexively. "What are you doing?" she cried.

"Trying to see the damage, I did."

"That's not fair, you get to see me, but I don't..."

"Leave it alone, Puakea," he muttered as the light illumined her face and then down her body.

"You hit me in my face. Why is that flashlight going elsewhere?"

"Just wanted to see the whole package." The light went back to her face.

"Hmm. I guess I owe you an apology," he slumped.

"Well, don't pull your teeth out to do it." she sighed, rolling her eyes. For the first time, she heard a snicker out of him which was pretty close to something like a laugh. "It's just a bruise."

"Okay, next subject," he said brusquely as the flashlight went off and he slouched down more in bed. "How's your mom doing?"

"She's coming along. Not up to work yet, so here I am." He didn't ask too many questions after that. She sensed it took some effort. Most of his words were muffled and she could tell he was talking out of the side of his mouth.

"Do you want to hear about the time in first grade when they made me stay after school to eat the liver we had for lunch. I hated it so much that I sat there for hours in front of my plate. Everyone else had figured out how to stuff it into the table legs or sneak it into their napkins. Not me...there I sat forever until the bell rang. You know. I don't care what you do to liver. You can smother it with onions, mushrooms, ketchup, soy sauce, or whatever...and it still tastes like mud."

Thus, once again, Puakea commenced with her montage of anecdotes, some from the present, others mostly from her illustrious past including all the boys she beat up in school, her Maui adventures, living with her brothers and anything she could think of to entertain him. This time she did manage to get a few laughs out of him.

She missed coming the following Thursday and he noticed. His mother almost fell down when she turned around in the kitchen and saw him standing there that late afternoon.

"Oh, my gosh, Thaddeus, you scared the daylights out of me."

"Sorry," he said. He had limped down the stairway and was still wearing a robe and his pajamas.

"Now what do I owe the honor of this visit to?"

"Well, you're always nagging me to get out of my room, so here I am."

"Well, in that case, have a seat and have dinner with me."

He wasn't ready to be *that* social, but he didn't want to ruin the excitement in her demeanor. They talked a minute and then he got to the real reason for his trek down the stairs.

"Um, what happened to Puakea?"

"Oh, she couldn't come today. Had to take her Mom to the doctor's."

When Puakea arrived the following week, he was ready for her. She finished her chores and noticed the door open again as she walked down the hallway. She peered in and stared in astonishment; his back was facing her as he sat on a stuffed chair next to his bed looking out the... window. The dark double drapes had been drawn aside, the windows exposed and the whole room was bathed in afternoon sunlight.

"Can I come in?" she asked hesitantly. She wore her usual green tee shirt with white shorts and slippers on her feet. Her hair with streaks of reds and blonde was still short in a wispy cut framing her freckled nose face.

"Yes," he murmured.

"Where do you want me to sit?"

A matching chair sat separated from his by an end table. He gestured towards the chair. "You can sit there."

Puakea knew he was nervous about this moment, and intended to be especially tactful, but when she saw his face in the light, she simply uttered, "Wow."

"Wow?" He turned to face her. "Is that your reaction? You're not going to even pretend I look normal?"

"Well, I guess I should, but I'm so tired of walking on eggs with you."

"What do you mean?" he frowned.

"I have told you every single boring story about my life. We have never addressed what happened to you because I was so afraid you would kick me out of here, and that would have been worse cause I wouldn't be able to see you anymore."

"So what do you think? Go ahead. I know you have a zillion questions." He braced himself waiting for her reaction.

She moved her chair so she could get a better look as she studied his face. He wore a loose, long-sleeve tunic top and navy blue sweat pants. The right side of his face was as she'd remembered, but the left side was where most of his injuries lay. Scar tissue ran from the top of his forehead down over a corner of his left eye, stretching it so that it drooped with the cheek area, tightened by the scarring which continued down to his chin and further on to where his neck met his shirt. She was sure there was more damage done, but his clothes covered the rest of his body. He watched her nervously as her eyes moved over him, up and around and back to his, still stunning, eyes of blue.

"Hmm," she pondered.

"What?" he cringed.

"I thought it would be worse."

"Now, you're just trying to be nice," he glowered at her as she continued to stare.

"Can I touch it?"

He sighed irritably. "Go ahead."

She knelt down on the floor next to his chair, reached out her right hand and moved the tips of her fingers over his face, almost reverently.

"Does it hurt?"

He held his breath while she touched him. "Not the way other places do," he answered glumly. This was the first time anyone, other than the medics, had physical contact with him. Her face was closely level with his as she stroked it.

"I've had grafts done on my face. There were second degree burns there. They say it could have been worse. But what's worse than this?"

"It's fine Dee," she said softly. As she knelt in front of him, she grasped his hands and looked into his eyes. She brought them to her cheek, then laid her head on his lap, and gently whispered, "It's okay."

10

PUAKEA CAME EVERY DAY AFTER that—with a hint from Dee that he would welcome it. Over time he eventually, slowly, gradually told her about his ordeal. It was too hard to talk about all at once. So, she gathered and pieced together the puzzle of his life over the past two agonizing years.

He had traveled all the way by plane, then helicopter and finally by ambulance to arrive in Pittsburg, Pennsylvania where a Burn Center and Trauma Unit were housed under the same roof. It was new at the time, but specialized in treating severe burn victims like him. The staff consisted of 24-hour in house trauma surgeons, skilled critical care physicians and a full complement of highly skilled nurses and technical personnel who were trained in burn services.

Dee Crown had the best care that money could buy. And much was spent on this excellent facility. But all the money and skills in the world could not keep him from the pain and suffering he endured.

His wounds mostly on the left portion of his body included second degree burns on his face, later referred to as a dermal injury. The deeper the damage done, the greater the layers of skin were affected and the higher the degree of diagnosed burn. The worst area on Dee's body, the part which received the third degree burns was on his upper left area, his shoulders, arms, chest and neck. Sweat glands, hair follicles, and blood vessels were all affected. To avoid infection and other complications, skin grafts were taken from the right part of his body to beef up not only his face, but all the third degree areas. Operations, pain, and more pain...but his body survived, and his mind fell into a deep depression.

After the operations, came the physical therapy to avoid the contracture of his limbs; thus increasing flexibility in the burned areas. This was ongoing until the present time. A physical therapist still worked with him three times a week to keep the movement in his upper body and legs which had thankfully received just superficial burns.

He was in excruciating pain after these treatments, but they worked to keep him limber. He received them in the mornings. The only time Puakea had seen him was when he was exhausted in his bed soon after his therapy.

"Okay, today's the day," she announced at ten one Saturday morning.

He lay in bed when she came bursting into his room. By this time, his mom welcomed the presence of their Palolo neighbor who seemed to have made great strides in improving the fluctuating moods of their son.

"What day?" he groaned, squinting from the sunlight when she drew the curtains open.

"We're going out today."

"No way," he grunted.

"Come on. You promised."

"I did not. I said maybe and definitely not today."

"Why? Do you have something earth shaking to do?" she inquired with sarcasm.

"Puakea, leave me alone."

She said no more and proceeded to take all the covers off his bed. "Come on Dee, it'll be fun. Besides, I want your company. Please."

He opened his eyes and stared at the pleading girl. Sometimes he forgot how pretty she was. He'd *"grown accustomed to her face. It almost made the day begin...her smiles, her frowns, her ups, her downs were second nature"* to him now. The Lerner and Loewe tune from My Fair Lady came to mind at the moment. Now he was surely losing it.

He made her go downstairs, and forty five minutes later, he joined her in the kitchen. She was leaning over the counter, talking to his mom. Mrs. Crown was so pleased to see him dressed and actually willing to leave the house. She had prayed for this day and felt so grateful for Puakea's influence.

She tried to hide her elation, "So, I guess I'll see you kids later. I have a lot to do today. I've got to go down to the mall and get some things." She headed for the door before they did and closed it behind her.

"Did she say 'kids'?" Dee remarked.

"Oh, they're all like that—parents, I mean. Mine do the same no matter how old we get. Don't get your feathers in a ruffle, Old Man. I like being a kid, and I'm never going to grow up."

He smiled slightly, "You, know, Puakea. I think I believe that."

She stopped for a moment to look at him. He was wearing soft cotton beige pants and a loose, long-sleeve blue tunic shirt again. Apparently he had a whole wardrobe of the tops. They were specially made light cotton shirts that didn't cling to his body and had been ordered, probably by his mom, in every color.

She glanced at his face—one that she was so used to now—and marveled at how she barely noticed the change anymore. Perhaps, she told herself, it was through the eyes of love that she saw him. And if she cared to admit it, perhaps she had from the first day they met. It was different now, though—much deeper for her.

She shook herself out of her reverie, at the risk of revealing too much and said, "Okay, time to go. You ready to get into my old Dodge. It's a good thing there's just the two of us, cause I don't have a back seat."

"Why not?"

"Well, where else would I put my surfboard?"

Dee shrugged his shoulders, raised his hands up, and followed her out. He slowly approached the faded 1953 Dodge with limping gait. His legs had not been burned severely so he was ambulatory, but his torso area which had been affected slowed his movement.

They drove to the end of the road in Palolo Valley, past the residential section where the road was muddy and not as paved. The Monkey Pod trees were scattered on the hillside like fluffy umbrellas and shrubs of green covered the mountains. This area was dense in vegetation, more of a tropical forest atmosphere, due to the increasing moisture of the mountain rain. She brought out a basket from the car and Dee followed a short ways behind her.

He was still weak and not anticipating a long hike. Puakea knew this, but had planned for the occasion with a short trek. She found an opening off the trail that led down to a stream, not unlike the one in her back yard. The area was shaded by surrounding trees, yet covered by a lush grassy carpet in a park like setting. Puakea knew it was private property, but she had been here before and the owners were almost never in the vicinity.

She spread out a blanket on the grass, and Dee plunked down to lounge on it, watching her as she brought out the food in the basket. They ate the corned beef sandwiches and potato salad with soft drinks as they relaxed under the shade of the trees. He laid back and looked up at the cloud formations, enjoying the soft breeze that swished through the valley.

"Ah, I haven't done this in so long. Thank you, Puakea."

"See, all you had to do was get out. I knew it's just what you needed."

"I guess I won't be able to see Waikiki again."

"What are you talking about? There's shade there too. We can go there tomorrow."

"You think? I don't know."

"We could even get you one of those wet suits and you can paddle around on your board."

"Maybe. We'll see."

They did just that the next day. He was limited to time in the sun, but they found an umbrella and sat under a coconut tree. When it was time to go in the water, he changed into some long shorts, a long sleeve tee shirt, and a baseball cap to protect his face. They went to an area where there were tourists galore, so he wasn't as self conscious about his attire. They paddled around for awhile, but the pressure on his chest when he lay on the board caused increasing pain, so they had to stop.

"You're just not ready yet. Your body needs to heal more," she said, trying to keep him from being discouraged. He was cringing in pain and she knew he felt more than he was letting on.

Dee changed back into his tunic shirt and cotton pants. They had already packed the car with their surfboards and returned to the beach to get the rest of their gear.

"Dee, Dee," cried a female voice behind them. They turned to see a group of girls who were sitting on the sand. One of them stood and hurried over to them. She wore a leopard skin bikini that barely covered her tall, trim golden body. Her long hair flowed out of a visor cap, and she pulled the dark glasses she wore on top of her head.

"Oh, no," he groaned under his breath. "Luana, how are you?" he said in a louder voice. She hugged him and kissed his cheek and looked up into his face.

"Oh, Dee I'm so sorry." I never knew how bad it was. I tried to call, to come over to see you. No one would let me through. I assumed that was your choice. Is this why you wouldn't see me?"

"Is what why?" he asked, well aware of the answer.

"Your face."

"Uh, Luana, this is Puakea, we have to go now. We're late. It was nice seeing you."

"But…" Luana was not given a chance to finish. She stood there and stared at their backs as they walked to Puakea's car.

He was quiet all the way home. Puakea did not try to engage in any banter. She was well aware of the gloom that settled over him. He got out of the car, mumbled a quick thank you and got his board out of the car. She left him in the driveway, wanting to make him feel better, but knew it was not the time.

She called him and was told that he couldn't come to the phone. When she went over to the house, his mom apologetically explained to her that he did not want to see anyone.

"I'm so sorry, dear. I'm sure he'll come around. He's just having a hard time right now. I'll have him call you when he feels better."

Lilinoe had resumed her duties at the Crowns a few weeks ago. Puakea had no more excuses to be in their house. She had just been there on a social basis, now that her mother was back at work.

He never called, making it clear that he did not want to see Puakea again. It wasn't fair, she thought. One chance meeting with *that girl* had seemed to annihilate all her efforts to bring him out into the world… not only that, but it destroyed her dream to become an integral part of his life.

Kanoe

Kahana Valley

Kahana Valley

LOCATED ON THE NORTH EAST O'ahu, between the districts of Ka'a'awa on the south and Punalu'u on the north, this rare stretch of coastland brings the mountains down to the sea, so that the windward side of the Ko'olau mountain range is visible just a short ways from the pounding shore.

Kahana Valley is especially fertile due to its heavy rain that waters the shoreline trees and nurtures their growth to spectacular heights of sixty to a hundred feet. Amongst them are *casuarinas*, evergreens commonly known as ironwood trees with drooping slender twigs, resembling pine needles, *kamani, hala* and *hau* towering over the natural tropical setting, and majestic *coconut* trees in a park like setting located closer to the streams.

This was an area referred to as an *ahupua'a,* a stretch of land from mountaintop to ocean, forested, farmed and fished originally by Native Hawaiians: a managed unit that integrated the three biological resource zones, the upland forests, the agriculturally used land below, and the coastal zone into a sustainable human support system.

Ownership in Kahana reveals a long history of complicated land plots that passed from chiefs, to commoners, to Chinese owners, to a Hawaiian *Hui* or group who through 2500 conveyances, showed a record of bought and sold properties until Mary Foster owned most of the eight square miles of the valley by 1920. The land was leased to various groups of people, but stayed in the Foster Estate until later when

Hawai'i became a state and Kahana Valley was usurped by eminent domain.

1

1949

"Mommy, please don't leave me. Take me with you. I promise I'll be good."

"No, sweetie, you have to stay with Puna. I'll send for you. You can be with me someday. Not right now."

Kanoe hung on to her mother's dress, a blue linen traveling suit.

Her mother looked especially pretty. She always did to the little girl. The fragrance of her *pikake* perfume filled the air. Over the years, when she was left alone, she would huddle in her mom's closet to smell this same scent on her mother's clothes. It was the only thing that made her feel safe. Her mother had left her alone often.

Now all those clothes were packed in a suitcase. "Kanoe let go of my dress, you're going to ruin it, and stop that wailing. I'll come back someday. You'll see. You don't want Mommy to be unhappy, do you? This is my big chance. I'm going to marry Billy and then we'll send for you."

"Why can't you be happy with me, Mommy?"

"Because I can't, that's why. Now let go and give me a hug. Puna will be here to get you in a few minutes."

She was five years old and didn't understand. Kanoe stopped crying and hugged her; she thought if she closed her eyes and hung on tight enough then her mommy might change her mind.

Her grandmother walked in to the small apartment they lived in. "I can't believe you're doing this to her," she said.

"Mom, don't make this worse. She's already upset."

"You're right. I've already said what I've had to say. I won't make it worse."

"Kanoe, Sweet, come with Puna. I'll send someone to get your things later. Come, my darling girl. Puna will make you safe and we'll be fine."

And that's what she did. She made everything safe for the little girl who'd lose hope of ever seeing her mother again.

Margaret Kanoekahawai (the mist of the valley) Hunter is what she had been christened. She had never been called any other name except Kanoe since birth. She'd never known the father whose name she carried. When her mother left with an enlisted man in the army, it was Puna Maggie who came to her rescue—the woman whose first name she bore—who became both father and mother to her.

They lived in one of the few houses in Kahana Valley where her grandparents, Eli and Maggie Punahele, had come to lease their land and where Eli made his living as a *taro* farmer. He had passed away a few years before her birth leaving Puna alone. Puna was the shortened version of *kupuna*, one of the Hawaiian words for grandmother. Their home was a small faded brown, two bedroom structure with a porch on the front and a large yard that surrounded it.

The edges of the yard were filled with colorful fruit bearing trees that her grandfather had planted over the years to make sure there was always enough to eat—three towering *papaya*, two shade bearing *mango*, five *breadfruit*, a small *loquat* and ten varieties of *banana*. Tall *coconut* trees edged the corners of the yard, some growing at an angle from the impact of the wind and others growing straight up towards the sky. Kahana's heavy rains kept everything watered green to enable the trees to thrive on the land.

Kanoe waited and prayed for her mother to claim her until she realized that she would never return for her. There was no correspondence or any phone calls, and no one knew where she was. They weren't even sure if she had married. It was as if she had dropped off the edge of the earth. As a little girl, Kanoe finally lost all hope of seeing her again. There was a pain of abandonment that would follow her for years, but she never lacked for love, nor was she deficient in playmates.

She played with country children who had great freedom in exploring the mountains as well as the ocean and all the fun it entailed. Spear fishing, hunting for shells and glass balls, making forts and swinging through the rainforest trees in Kahana Valley, they took for granted the beauty that surrounded them.

A house of four boys lived less than a mile away in Ka'a'awa. They were the Irish-Hawaiian Kelliher family named after New Testament Bible characters and called by the Hawaiian translation of each: Makaio (Matthew), Maleko (Mark), Luka (Luke), and Keoni (John). Their mother and father were sticklers about their grammar. Makaio and Keoni slipped in and out of pidgin when it suited them, but Luka and Maleko would not cooperate. They went the way of their peers and annihilated the English language.

In age, Kanoe was only older than Keoni, but held her own when it came to keeping up; she could fish, and swim and swing from trees as well as all of them.

In exchange for fruit in her garden, the boys would take alternate turns mowing Puna's yard with her old lawnmower, and in return, she'd bake cookies for them or give them a few coins for doing so.

2

"KANOE, LET GO OF DA side. You can't come wit' us. Deyah's not enough room," said Maleko as he pushed Kanoe off while she was trying to hoist herself onto the small boat in the middle of the stream that emptied into Kahana Bay. He dunked the little girl's head under water while he tried to pry her loose.

His brother, Makaio standing on a bridge that arched over the stream, dove in, pulling her to the side of the stream. He left her to hang on to a long branch, swam out to the canoe, pulled himself up, yanked Maleko out of his sitting position and tossed him into the water.

"I evah catch you doing dat again, I'm gonna drown you for good. Now, go ovah to Kanoe and tell her you're sorry."

"Sorry, Kanoe," said Maleko grudgingly as he swam over to her with his brother behind him.

She hung on the branch and didn't say a word, knowing he wasn't sorry and had been forced into his apology.

"You okay?" asked Makaio.

"I'm okay," Kanoe answered.

She was eight years old at the time and Makaio, eleven. There were other incidents to follow where she needed protection, and he was the one who looked after her.

Kanoe was treated like a sister to the four brothers, not always an advantage when they didn't want girls around. Makaio was her self appointed protector and quietly made sure she was not bullied. The others tended to forget and were tempted to give her a bad time when they wanted to blow off steam, but, Makaio would yank them into line. They all feared him. Being the oldest, he was the tallest in stature and definitely, not one to be challenged.

As children, they ventured into the sacred land of Kahana and hiked the trails, caught *'o'opu* fish and tadpoles in the rivulets, and made floating devices to navigate the streams. They were rarely supervised and some of the boys were a little too eager in their adventures. Once, Maleko got hurt trying to devise a Tarzan like rope across the stream when the rope broke, and he fractured his jaw on a rock. He was rushed to Kahuku Hospital that day, and told his mother that he had a bicycle accident. No one ever squealed on him. They were all afraid that their freedom would be curtailed.

"Did you hear the news, Makaio?" Kanoe asked him one day when they were on the beach watching the sea turtles swim by. "I've been accepted at Kamehameha." She was soon to be thirteen in a few months. It was a magnificent Kahana day. The ocean was a calm aquamarine as the sun sparkled on the waters.

"No, I knew you been trying to get in. So, you finally made it."

"Yes, my Tutu is so happy. She really wanted me to go there."

"Well, at least you'll be with Hawaiians and not get all snooty on us." Makaio was sixteen at the time and a football player at Kahuku High School. His English was improving and he was conscious now of putting his "th's" together.

"Oh, that is one school where I heard they make sure you know your place. I'm kinda nervous about being the new kid and all," she said.

"You'll do good. Even though you don't look Hawaiian, just remembah not to show 'em you're scared. They can smell the fear and you going be picked on. It even happens at Kahuku. I see some of these *haoles* come in and they're toast when anyone notices dey can't take it."

"You don't pick on them, do you, Makaio?"

"Nah, das not my style. You know dat, by now."

She looked at him, now. He was over six feet and had grown in brawn as well as stature with the muscular neck of a football player, developed to protect himself from heavy hitters. Three of the brothers were fair in complexion and reflected their *haole* roots, but Makaio had all the Hawaiian genes manifested in his appearance with the exception of an aquiline nose from his Irish father.

His mere presence was intimidating for most. Kanoe was one of the few who knew he was the one with the marshmallow heart. She had always favored him and now, developed a little bit of a crush this first year as a teenager.

"No, you're right Makaio, it's not your style and that's why I love you."

He raised one brow and looked at her then. "I mean that's why you're my favorite," she corrected herself.

He laughed then and looked out at the ocean. "C'mon, the sun's coming out. Let's go swim." They dove in the ocean with the sea turtles as they swam with their heads bobbing in the aquamarine waters of beautiful Kahana Bay.

3

MAGGIE PUNAHELE TAUGHT THIRD GRADE in the small school of Ka'a'awa Elementary. Prizing education for Hawaiians, she not only taught in school, but tutored, free of charge, a handful of children every year who were not getting on in their lessons. She made learning fun for them, incorporating games and rewards of gold stars into her teaching. Kanoe was, on many occasions, included in these sessions. Most of the children loved coming to Mrs. Punahele's modest home where she baked delicious treats to reward them after their studies.

Puna's dream for Kanoe was to receive an education at Kamehameha. She had her apply every year, praying and hoping her *mo'opuna* would be accepted at the school for Hawaiian children, refusing to be discouraged from all the unsuccessful attempts. When Kanoe finally received her letter of acceptance for her seventh grade year, Tutu was elated. Kanoe tried to share in her enthusiasm, but she knew her life would change… and it did.

Kamehameha was a different world for her and took adjusting. She entered into the Preparatory School that was now on Kapalama Heights and could only enjoy her country life on weekends and on holidays, leaving Kahana very early each weekday morning and returning late in the afternoon. Four others rode with her in the carpool that different parents shared. Puna paid them once a month for her granddaughter's transportation.

There were rules and regulations and lunchtime etiquette that she had to get used to. She was continually reminded, along with the other students, how fortunate she was to attend that very special school. The rules, although seemingly harsh, had instilled a certain standard that was lost on many, but the values of Puna Maggie were reinforced, and Kanoe held fast to them, intent on learning how to fit in. Putting others first was constantly stressed, and all the manners and customs that were emphasized were a part of this creed.

Kanoe was so terribly shy at first that she found difficulty in speaking out in class or joining others on social occasions. Puakea Flynn was the one who reached out to Kanoe after two months of a lonely existence at Kamehameha.

"So, how come you're so quiet?" asked Puakea of her one day.

"I don't know. I guess I don't know what to say and when to say it."

"I wish that were my problem. But I guess it's kind of tough being new and all. Just hang with me and I'll introduce you to everyone. I'll let you in on a secret. No one really wants to hear about you. They're more interested in how you listen to them. All you have to do is ask a question or two and they'll take over from there. But you can't just sit back and say nothing. You'll stand out like a sore thumb and then the bullies will come after you. "

"Someone else warned me about that. I guess I forgot."

She took Puakea's cue and began to find her way around the seventh grade and this new culture she had landed in. Boys wore white shirts and khaki pants. The girls wore street clothes that were modest and never included a dress without sleeves. On special occasions, like Founders Day and song concerts, they wore white. Lunch was a formal occasion, eight to a table with a boy-girl-boy-girl formation. Students were designated as host or hostess and waiter or waitress, and usually a faculty member was present at every table. Each boy pulled out the chair of the girl to his left after grace was sung in Hawaiian or English. This protocol started with the students from the time they were in first grade. Seventh grade was the year that included the largest enrollment of new students. Kanoe was amongst the crop that arrived that year.

After a period of adjustment, her grades started to improve, and through Puakea's guidance, she became socially acclimated. The boys were just starting to get interested in girls at the time and particularly interested in the new girls who had arrived. Kanoe was not noticeable then. She was awkward, shy and still appeared as a girl from the country amongst the boisterous thirteen year olds. She was petite and fair, and like Puakea, favored her paternal *haole* roots in coloring.

By the time, she reached ninth grade, she blossomed in a different way. The boys and girls were separated by two different schools. The boys were missed by the girls. All the fun, mischievous antics and focus of attention went out of the classrooms. Now, it was much more serious and the distraction of boys was removed. Another crop of new students were added that year.

Kanoe experienced a growth spurt in body and height. She lost her pre-pubescent awkwardness, and her hair grew thicker, flowing in blonde streaked waves over her shoulders. She was still subdued and quiet, but her warm dimpled smile became her trademark. She had an air of serenity now that appeared to exude a quiet confidence. It was not what she felt inside, but no one knew that.

Her country home life had changed. The two oldest Kelliher boys were gone. Much to his family's pride and fervent prayers, Makaio would be going to Notre Dame in the fall, a lifelong dream of his father's. Maleko had enlisted in the Navy after graduation.

She had said goodbye that summer to Makaio when the teenagers gathered for a bonfire on the beach one night. She had just turned fifteen.

"Well, Kanoe, you gonna write to me when I'm away?"

"Yes, Makaio. You'll have to write first to give me your address."

"Okay, then, I guess it's up to me." He watched her as the firelight flickered across her face, realizing that Kanoe had turned, in such a short time, into a rare beauty. It was the first time he noticed. He considered her to be still too young, but he wondered how she had changed overnight. Perhaps she had always been that way and he hadn't recognized it until now.

When they stood up to leave that night she went to hug him goodbye. "Watch out for those boys, Kanoe. Protect your heart."

"Okay, Makaio. You take care and I'd tell you the same about the girls, but I think you'll be fine."

"I'll be fine Kanoe. I'll be fine," he said as he hugged her.

In her junior year, Kamalu Krieger was the boy who captured Kanoe Hunter's heart. He was her age and had come into ninth grade with the new crop of students. Excelling in every sport, he'd been the noticeable one and well known at school. Kanoe was not one to drool over boys, but she did notice when the other girls did. Everyone talked about Kamalu.

He saw her at a basketball game he played in. He was poised to make a free shot and turned towards the audience for a moment. His eyes connected with hers, and he was shaken by her dimpled smile—so shaken, that he missed the basket. The team won anyway, no thanks to Kamalu, but that didn't stop him from looking for Kanoe after the game. He found her in the crowd as she was exiting the Kekuhaupio Gym.

"You owe me one," he said as he tapped her on the shoulder.

"Me?" she simply asked.

"Yeah, you."

She stood there with a puzzled expression. "Why?"

"I missed that basket because of you."

She didn't ask why again. He introduced himself, and she told him that she already knew who he was. They walked out together, and he asked where she was headed. She was spending the night at Puakea's and they were going to a party afterwards. He showed up at the party, and they ended up talking all night.

They were inseparable after that. Kamalu's parents had both attended Kamehameha and married two years after graduating. He was the oldest of five children, well adjusted, and handsome with strong Hawaiian roots. He fit his uniforms well and carried himself with a swagger that exuded confidence, but he became clearly smitten with the quiet girl who played as a child in Kahana Valley.

Kanoe was wary at first, cautious in guarding her feelings and knowing that he could have his pick of any of the umpteen girls who cheered him on at all his sports events. Kamalu had to work to prove his worthiness in her eyes, but after several months of his earnest pursuit, she succumbed and trusted him with her heart.

After almost a year of being the most envied couple on campus, with strong approval from her grandmother and both his parents, they broke up after a minor disagreement. He had been awarded a basketball scholarship to Oregon State which he'd chosen over other offers. She would be attending San Mateo City College and wondered why he had turned down San Jose State's offer which would be closer to her. He got defensive, which created a rift between them and the next day, he told her that they should probably rethink their relationship. She was forced to agree; he changed his mind several days later, but she was already too hurt to take him back.

A month later, Kanoe was boarding at Senior Cottage and Kia would be going to the Senior Prom with Kamalu. It was heartbreaking for her and she did not get over him for a long time. It almost felt like the day her mother left her so long ago. She remembered Makaio's parting words to her the night before he left. She had failed to take his advice.

4

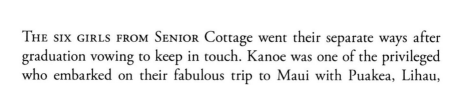

THE SIX GIRLS FROM SENIOR Cottage went their separate ways after graduation vowing to keep in touch. Kanoe was one of the privileged who embarked on their fabulous trip to Maui with Puakea, Lihau, Keala and seven boys. That one trip helped her break free from her shyness and it was life changing for them all.

Kanoe waited a year before she left Hawai'i. She went to work at the newly opened Polynesian Culture Center in La'ie about ten miles from Kahana Bay. Not her Puna's dream student, she had gotten by with average grades at Kamehameha with a few B's thrown in, but she waited a year before she was transported in the fall of 1964 to a whole different world in Northern California.

One of Kanoe's classmates, Missy Kalahea convinced her to apply with her at San Mateo City College. Missy had relatives in the Bay area and was planning to room with two other girls. Another girl joined them; so eventually there were five girls from Hawai'i stuffed into a two bedroom apartment near the Hillsdale Mall, at the bottom of the hill from the college.

Missy was a fun loving, attractive girl with thick ebony hair and eyelashes to match, tall and willowy with olive coloring that contrasted in every way with Kanoe's appearance and demeanor, but they had always gotten along and were in the same section at school. Cassie

Carpenter and Kulamanu Drake had just graduated from Punahou. Cassie, a fair haired *haole girl* was a serious student who was determined to go on to a University eventually.

Kulamanu was very stunning with a *hapa haole* mixture of seven nationalities, Hawaiian being one of them. The fifth girl who had hopped on board the last minute was an acquaintance of Cassie and lived near her in Manoa. She had come from Roosevelt. Her name was Kalani Smythe, another *hapa haole*, also a serious student, easy to get along with and eventually well liked by all.

They managed to get an old '54 Plymouth for two hundred dollars by putting their allowances together which they named irreverently Kukailani and used it for their primary transportation to school. None of the girls came from affluent homes. Their families had to make ends meet just to put them through school and the rent split five ways helped all of them.

The school was located on a hill overlooking San Mateo County. The times called for formal dress and an unusual culture for the girls from Hawai'i. The Kamehameha girls were used to it, but none of them were prepared for the ice cold weather. When they ran out of things to wear, they just wore trench coats. Missy was famous for hers. She sometimes wore her shorty pajamas under her coat when she ran out of clothes or was too lazy to get dressed for school.

They each took turns cooking for a week, and those who were not up to preparing meals, did cleanup instead. But things were fairly amiable during the first few months, and the five different personalities seemed to meld into a compatible routine. It didn't take long for boys to invade their humble home. They were everywhere. Their apartment building included many who were attending the same school, and more and more people were added to their environment as the weeks went by. Studying was almost impossible with all the traffic that went through the apartment.

Many were curious about the island girls and found them to be different from most. Missy was the life of their home, and everyone basked in her comfort zone. Kanoe loved the change; it was the first time she had lived with anyone besides her Puna. The first year, she got acclimated to the Bay Area, the culture and the curriculum at school. She went home for the summer and returned in the fall for her second year with the same roommates. Missy had stayed in San Mateo for the summer and held on to their apartment which they all pitched in to keep.

During the second year, one day at the end of October, she was approached by someone in the hallway. "Wanna come to a party this weekend? My best friend and I are giving it at my house."

He stood a whole head taller than she was, blonde streaks in his light brown hair with a Roman nose and dazzling green eyes, slanted at the edge that were rather dreamy in a sensual way. She noticed sandals on his feet which were unusual and that his hair was longer than the crew cuts worn by most of the guys at school. He had "surfer boy" written all over him, and she thought of it as a plus, unlike the preppies who wore sweaters and suede shoes.

"My parents are away and we're doing kind of a theme party for Halloween."

"So, what's the theme?" she asked.

"Uh, a Toga Party," he replied with a smile that made her toes curl.

She looked at his Roman nose and Grecian styled hair that curved around his ears and said, "Of course." *How fitting.*

"Of course, you'll come?" he questioned.

"No, I was referring to the Toga theme."

"Hmm. Come on. It might be a change from your usual Hawaiian *lu'au*. I'm hosting, but I'll have someone pick you up. Oh, by the way, my name is Bailey Benson. And you're Kanoway?"

"Um, Kanoe like fish and *poi*." She couldn't believe she said that. *Not cool, not cool at all.*

"Oh, sorry. I rehearsed your name several times before I spoke to you and even then I got it wrong. I even found out where you live... next to the Hillsdale mall right?"

She was taken back at all the information he had about her, but told him she would go. He reached out for her hand and held it in his—long lashed eyes mesmerizing her for a moment. "Paul Henley will pick you up. I've got your number too. He'll call before he comes." He'd definitely done some research on her.

She was hesitant to go, but a boy Kulamanu had been dating told her that Bailey was a great guy and had come from "good stock" whatever that meant. The girls had fun getting her ready for the party. Missy helped her put her hair up into a "Helen of Troy" style that was teased up with hair entwined around a rubber band and a curled pony tail at the back with wispy tendrils falling around her ears. They found a white sheet and tied it over one shoulder with a costume jeweled clasp. It was then belted with a cord that pulled the bodice snug and hiked the sheet up so that a wide slit showed a fair amount of one of her pretty legs. On her feet, she wore brown sandals. When the doorbell rang, she was ready to go.

Paul Henley was one of those *instant-friend-kind-of-guys*—he was likable on the spot—wide grin, twinkling eyes that emanated friendliness and someone that even babies would love. Not exactly gorgeous, he had sharp features, a beak nose and a chin that was a bit too small, but that made Kanoe even more comfortable with him and relieved that he would be the one escorting her.

He talked all the way over, making her feel at ease, telling her about the Bay Area, explaining that he was brought up in Burlingame, an affluent city in San Mateo County, known for its Victorian architecture with a significant shoreline on the San Francisco Peninsula. He gave her a little history lesson on how it was named after a prominent diplomat and the getaway town for many wealthy San Franciscans who sought a better climate for their second homes. He didn't use the words *wealthy* or *affluent* for the sake of modesty, but she got the picture as he drove through it on their way to the party and pointed out his own elaborate Victorian home.

They headed to the exclusive town of Hillsborough, which shared the same zip code with Burlingame, but was located a few miles east of the bay—home to some of the most prosperous people in America with tree lined streets and a minimum space by law to ensure exclusivity. There were no apartment buildings or multi living structures in this area—strictly single residential homes. Many of them were palatial. Bing Crosby lived in one of them and Bailey Benson lived in another one.

Paul turned his blue corvette into a circular driveway surrounded by towering oaks, pines, and redwoods that were illumined by low outdoor lights, exposing their sprawling branches and framing a three story home that appeared to be built in a semicircle to accommodate the driveway.

They walked up the wide steps through an open door into a marble floored solarium, surrounding a winding staircase that led to the upper floors. No one greeted them until they walked through the vast living room to the covered patio that overlooked the Olympic sized swimming pool.

They were late, and the party was now in full force with all the guests in Roman attire, lounging on large pillows that had been spread across the floor. There was a long low table set with scrumptious fare, roasted turkey, lamb and beef, platters of cheese with bowls of fruit piled high with lots and lots of grapes cascading over apples, pears and tangerines. Silver goblets spilling over with wine were lifted in toasts as the guests clinked them together. Pillars had even been erected throughout the patio to simulate a Roman bath.

Bailey sat amongst the pillows with a girl on each side of him as he fed them grapes in between sips of wine. His goblet contained a strong Mai Tai at the moment—one of many he had ordered from the toga clad bartender. On the right side of the room, there was a band of lutes and eerie music, reminiscent of the old Theda Bara movies with professional dancers dressed in flimsy fairy outfits flitting across the room.

Kanoe didn't know what to think. She felt like she had been transported back in time, a bit wary, but also largely impressed with the authenticity of the scene before her. Paul went to change into his outfit and she was left alone standing there. Bailey spotted her and bounced up from his lair of pillows, leaving the two lovely maidens to fend for themselves. He managed to hang on to his goblet and almost stumbled into Kanoe. She had to prop him up for a moment.

"Kanoway, you're here." He made a sweeping gesture, "Welcome to Rome."

"Thank you," she replied. "It certainly looks like something from a movie set. What a lovely home you have," she commented, attempting to sound light hearted and carefree.

He was now draped over her like one of the cascading grape clusters in the fruit bowls and she found herself face to face with bloodshot green eyes gazing at hers. "Wanna see the rest of it?"

"The rest of what?" she asked.

"The rest of the house, silly." The word *house* was almost a slurred *housh,* but she tried to ignore that.

"Okay," she agreed, trying to slip out from under the cascading body draped over hers. No such luck. She became like one of the white Roman pillars while he leaned on her as a crutch to give her the tour of his impressive abode.

After a walk through the gigantic kitchen and dining area, then back through the spacious living room, maneuvering the stairs was quite a feat. She almost lost him for a moment as he stumbled in the middle of their ascent, but they did make it to the second floor. He pulled Kanoe into one of the bedrooms, plastered her against the wall and started kissing her as spiderlike hands moved everywhere.

Am I just the biggest stupidest lolo that ever lived? she thought as she slipped out from under Bailey—then pushed him away. He was strong and a whole head taller than her, but so inebriated—no, not just inebriated, falling down drunk—that it was a little easier to literally dump him on the floor.

"Hey, Kanoway, that wasn't nice," he said attempting to get vertical again.

By that time, she had scurried from the room, down the stairs to look for Paul who had now joined the rest of the party by the pool. One by one, the toga clad people were jumping or pushing each other into the pool. Now, it looked like a real Roman orgy, and Kanoe was starting to panic. She was trying to get Paul's attention, when someone picked her up and jumped into the pool with her as he held her in his arms. It was Bailey. How he got there so fast in his state of mind was beyond her. They were on the shallow end of the pool, and he held her against the edge, practically devouring her face with his mouth. She didn't want to make a scene, but did anyway.

She screamed her head off and then punched him so hard that he went underwater. Her only hope was that he was truly drowned and dead forever. Kanoe scrambled out of the pool in her soaking toga which had completely unraveled by now, looking pretty much like a wet sheet, which it was. She spotted a pile of large white towels, reached for one, and wrapped it around her body.

She walked up to Paul Henley and said in a shivering voice, "Paul, I will withdraw the last of my life savings, $129.24 from my bank on Monday if you will drive me home right now."

"Aw Honey, you don't have to do that. I'll take you home and come back. No problem." And he did.

"Maybe the name Kanoway fits you better. I truly mean that as a compliment," he said as he winked at her and then drove off into the night. That was the end of Kanoe's first Halloween in Hillsborough, one of the wealthiest suburbs in America.

5

KANOE BUMPED INTO BAILEY THE next Monday in school. He was waiting for her outside her English Class. "I have to talk to you," he pleaded.

"Bailey, I have nothing to say to you."

"Please give me a minute to apologize."

"Okay, you've apologized. Now I have to go or I'll miss my bus down the hill.

"Let me take you home and we can talk on the way."

"No thank you. I have to go now," she said, moving around him to walk down the hall. She walked quickly and then almost ran the distance to her bus, mainly to put distance between them.

He tried calling her for days and left message after message with her roommates. She would not take his calls. He attempted several ways to communicate with her after that—waited for her outside her classes, stalked her in the hallways and almost made a pest of himself in his self appointed mission to speak to her. He even showed up at one of her P.E. classes watching her volleyball game from a distance. Kanoe avoided him like the plague and kept her eyes on the ground, rushing past him wherever he happened to be.

She told Missy about it when she got home one day. "What am I going to do? I can't seem to shake him. It's getting ridiculous; I'm starting to dread going to school."

"I think you should let him have his say. Talk to him. Maybe if you do, he'll lay off."

"I don't know. It could get worse," Kanoe pondered.

"Try it and if it doesn't work, me and the roomies will go beat him up after school," Missy laughed. "Or we'll run him down with Kukailani." The thought of it made Kanoe laugh too.

Her opportunity came a few days later as she stood waiting for the bus that she caught every day to take her to the bottom of the hill. Bailey approached her once again. "Kanoe," he called. This time he pronounced her name right (like fish and poi) which he had now rehearsed over time. "Can I give you a ride home?"

He prepared himself once again for another rejection, but she surprised him by one word, "Okay."

"Okay?" he questioned.

"Yes, thank you. That would be fine."

Bailey was almost speechless, but recovered quickly and knew he had to get her to his car before she changed her mind. He wore a winter down jacket with hip hugging jeans that fit snug against his long legs and was still the only one who wore sandals in school. His blonde hair with dark roots was parted over to the side and fell over the back of his neck in waves that were not straggly, but soft and fine. She thought for a moment that if he were a girl, he would be described as beautiful—not that he was feminine, but with the fairness of presence that sprung from the pages of a Greek anthology. When she looked into his dreamy green eyes, she was brought back to reality. They were the same eyes that were glazed over while he pawed her at the disastrous Toga Party.

She had second thoughts as he opened the door to his car. He noticed her hesitation. "I promise, you'll be safe with me. I just want to talk to you."

She slipped into the passenger seat and they drove off down the hill towards her apartment. When he stopped the car in a space below her building, he rested his hand on the steering wheel and looked straight ahead.

"Well, you wanted to say something for weeks, so here's your chance," said Kanoe.

"Now I don't know where to begin. Well, I guess I do, so here goes," he began, turning his face towards hers. "I was really looking forward to having you there that night, but got carried away with way too much to drink before you came. Some of the things I did at my party, I don't even remember. Paul clued me in to all the vague parts and I felt like a first class idiot when I put the pieces together. I wanted so much to make a good impression on you, and I blew it big time and I'm so, so sorry."

She smiled at him for a moment. "Yep, first class idiot would describe what you were. You got any more words for yourself?" He knew she was teasing him now and he had a ray of hope that maybe his apology was penetrating her resolve.

"Look, if I promise never to drink in your presence again, will you let me show you what a prince I can be by taking you out again?"

She sat there for a moment staring at him. He waited nervously for her verdict. "No more funny stuff?"

"Promise. Scout's honor. You wouldn't believe it, but I made it all the way up to Eagle Scout, badges and all."

"Nope, I wouldn't believe it," she said smiling again.

They agreed to meet again for a safe day date; that one led to another day date and finally to a whole bunch of night dates. He took her to a place near Half Moon Bay to an exhilarating high speed car race where specially built cars raced at up to three hundred miles an hour. On another day, they met two of his friends with rifles up in the San Mateo Mountains where she learned to shoot a twelve-gauge shot gun. He had a motor scooter which he picked her up at school with one day. She rode behind him as they drove to the top of a mountain with snow where they rolled up snow balls and threw them down into a valley. He was quite creative in his attempts to impress her with the fact that he was the good prince and not the *first class idiot* that she had remembered. He kept his word about not drinking and kept a respectful distance from her.

Of course, it all began to work—lulling the Hawaiian girl from Kahana into a sense of secure wonderment at the difference in his demeanor. She could not help but become entranced with the sheer uniqueness of his courting. One minute they were in their grubby clothes roughing it through the mountains and the next thing they were dressed in their most formal attire attending a concert of the Christy Minstrels at the Fairmont Hotel. He was going all out for her and she wondered why. Actually, she wondered out loud one night.

"Why me?" she asked him after he had given her his first heart stopping kiss as they danced to Frank Sinatra's "Where Are You?" in an out of the way nightclub lounge near Hillsdale.

She had used her fake I.D. that night. All five girls had managed to change their driver's license to the legal age status. A friend of Missy's had done it for a small price.

"What do you mean?" he asked as he pulled his head back to look at her.

"You could have any girl on campus. Why did you pick me?"

"Love at first sight. That's what it was?"

"Hmm. Love, huh? Wish I could say the same."

"Let's sit down and talk about this." They went back to their booth in a far corner of the room. "Why can't you say the same?"

"I meant love at first sight. I guess it's taken me awhile."

"So, you do love me, Kanoe?"

"Yes," she smiled, "I *think* I do."

They were sitting side by side and he put his arms around her and gazed intently into her eyes. "Well, that's progress. I'm going to make sure that you do. But that's pretty good for now," he crooned in a sexy voice and kissed her as she melted in his arms and was almost sure by then.

6

A CHRISTMAS DINNER AT THE Bensons was quite a night for Kanoe—the second occasion that she stepped into the immense Hillsborough home. No toga party theme here—this time it was all about Christmas—lights, lights and more lights in every color and shape from the circular driveway up the wide steps and into the mistletoe doorway.

Large evergreen trees were arranged and decorated with a different color scheme in every room—a formal white with crystal snowflakes and angels in snow in the foyer, a sugar cane candy tree tied in large plaid and polka dot ribbons in the dining room, an elegant international one with dolls and small ornaments from all over the world in the living room, and two trees in the covered patio decorated with miniature toys and a variety Santa's elves with electric trains that ran around the bottom through a miniature Christmas village.

On the mantelpiece over the massive fireplace in the living room was a Nativity scene with Madonna and Child surrounded by shepherds, wise men, cows and sheep with a bright star shining over them. The display was lifelike in miniature form; each character carved out of wood with a different expression on its face.

They were greeted by Charlotte Benson, Bailey's mother, who gracefully swooped into the room like a scene from "The Loretta Young Show" in a sheer flowing gown of soft emerald green chiffon. She was blonde and dazzling with a flawless face and Bailey's green eyes tinged by tiny creases near the edges.

"Why this must be...you'll have to say your name for me so I can pronounce it correctly," she said. Kanoe voiced her name with a nervous smile and went forward to shake her hand. "How wonderful to meet you. Welcome to our humble home."

Kanoe was just reacting to the *humble home* bit when another tall elegant being walked into the room in a black tuxedo. She knew instantly that this was Bailey's father whom he seemed to resemble in height and almost identical features. He was tall, dark haired with streaks of silver and a demeanor that definitely fit *the Lord of the Manor* mode.

After her introduction to him, he said, "Well, well, all the way from Hawai'i to Hillsborough. This must be an experience for you."

She did not see Bailey wince, but he did and hurried her along to see the rest of the Christmas decorations as they headed for the bar area. Now he needed a drink. He had not indulged since they first started dating, but she was grateful when he offered her a glass of wine.

As if the fairy tale picture was not complete, in walked the fairy princess, Jacqueline whose name she insisted be pronounced in the French version like *Jhakleen*. "Ah, Bailey, here you are" she spoke in a breathy tone as if she hadn't seen him just an hour ago before he left to pick Kanoe up.

He rolled his eyes. "Yes, here I am an hour later, Jack," he addressed her in the name she hated. "This is Kanoe," he said as he poured himself another drink.

The rest of the guests arrived: his mother's two sisters and their spouses, his father's brother and his wife and the Benson matriarch grandmother whom everyone fawned over. There were various cousins all about Bailey's age: three girls and three ivy league boys, one from Stanford, one from Brown University and the other from Yale.

Bailey was clearly the renegade of the group, attending a city college in his sandals. Kanoe wondered why and chalked it up to his need to assert himself in some rebellious way.

All eighteen people were seated in the spacious chandelier lit dining room at the long Christmas table fit for a king. Red candles sat amongst elaborate decorations of evergreen sprigs, pine cones, colorful fruits, a variety of scattered nuts and garlands of red holly berries. The crystal glasses and silverware on scarlet napkins sparkled under the light of the candles and chandeliers.

Kanoe had never seen anything like it. She was awed, wide eyed and scared to death when she was seated at the end of the table on his mother's right side. Bailey sat on Kanoe's right and Jacqueline and her cousin from Yale sat across from them. His father placed himself at the other end with the matriarch.

There were several courses laid out by servers dressed in uniforms—for appetizers, goat cheese spread with herbs and olive oil, shrimp cocktail, a pink grapefruit ganita to cleanse the palate, then the main course: a scrumptious prime rib roast with popover style Yorkshire pudding, potatoes au gratin, and asparagus in butter. Cherries jubilee was later served for dessert.

Jacqueline sat eating her grapefruit ganita, an ice with touch of spice, spooning it out of a stemmed glass flute. "So, Kanoe, I hear you're the Hawai'i girl that Bailey's been dating. I don't think we've ever had one from your part of the world."

"My part of the world?" Kanoe questioned.

"Well, he's had quite a collection from other parts."

"That's enough, Jack," Bailey warned narrowing his eyes at her.

"I told you not to call me that. It sounds so masculine."

"So what other parts are we talking about?" asked Kanoe directing her question at Jacqueline.

"Iran, Germany, Finland, Russia, France. The French one was one of the longest lasting. I think about three months, wasn't it Bailey?"

"Jacqueline, I don't think your brother is going to tolerate this discussion any longer," her mother now warned. "But I do think it was the Finnish girl that actually beat out the French one."

"Okay, Mom. Kanoe doesn't want to hear this," interrupted Bailey.

"Oh, but I do," she replied.

"Change the subject, NOW," he commanded and Jacqueline put her napkin over her mouth to stifle a giggle.

"So, Kanoe, how do your parents feel about your being so far away from home?" asked Mrs. Benson

"Um, I don't have parents."

"Really?" Mrs. Benson had one hand over her heart after putting her spoon down. "I'm so sorry, my dear."

"Oh, it's okay. I never really knew them. My mom and dad weren't married and after I was born she ran off with an enlisted man. I live with my grandmother now in a wonderful place called Kahana Valley."

"I see." The hand was still over the heart. "And how large is your grandmother's estate."

"Oh, we lease the land. Not very large. We have two bedrooms." Then she added, "But plenty of room for the two of us."

At that point all conversation in Kanoe's direction ended. No one but Bailey spoke to her for the rest of the night. By the third course, she was treated as if she weren't there. She gradually noticed. They talked to each other, to others further down the table, but she was never addressed again.

Bailey's cousin from Yale started firing questions at him, so he was distracted for awhile. Kanoe sat there, feeling more and more invisible as the night wore on. She made one attempt to say something to his mother, but Mrs. Benson rudely began talking to someone further down the table as Kanoe spoke. Bailey did not notice any of this. They were to retire to the living room where after dinner drinks were served. By this time, she was so ready to go home, but had to endure the snubs even from the others. She kept wondering what she had said that could have been offensive or misinterpreted.

The goodbyes confirmed her feelings. She went to thank Bailey's mom first. "Thank you, Mrs. Benson. I had a lovely evening," she lied.

"Bailey, you make sure you drive carefully and be sure to come right back. Your cousins are spending the night and you need to visit with them.

"Mom, Kanoe just thanked you."

"Oh, did she? Uh, you're welcome…glad you had a nice time. Now, Bailey remember what I said."

"Fine, Mom. I heard you. I'll be back."

The drive back to her apartment took about forty five minutes. They hardly spoke. Kanoe didn't know what to say, and Bailey was a bit irritated with her silence.

"Thank you, Bailey," she said as they sat there in the car when they arrived.

He turned to her with his arm on the back of the seat. "Is something wrong?"

"Uh, no. I guess I was a bit overwhelmed tonight."

"Too many strangers, huh?"

"Something like that," she replied.

"Yeah, it's quite a lot to dump on you."

"No, no...not that bad." She tried to cover. "Just..."

"Never mind. I know. I have to get back." He leaned over to kiss her. "I'll call you later, okay?"

"Okay," she said. "Don't get out. I'll open the door." She pulled the handle down, opened the door, and rushed out towards the entry to her apartment.

Missy was the only one home when she got in. The other girls were out on dates. She saw that Kanoe was upset when she walked in the door.

"What?" Missy said. They all had a way of reading each other. It came with the territory of living together.

Missy shook her head and flopped on the couch with her. "Hard to talk about."

"Try," urged Missy.

She sat in silence for a moment. Then she spoke, "It was like "Guess Who's Coming to Dinner".

"And you were the 'Guess Who'?"

"Uh, huh," she nodded her head with big tears rolling down her face.

"Well, Kanoe, it's not like Sir Bailey sprung the 'Creature from the Black Lagoon' on them. You look perfectly presentable all decked out in your prom gown. Could you imagine if he brought somebody like me home in my shorty pajamas under my trench coat?"

Kanoe cracked a smile then. Then she laughed. Missy could always turn the direst situation into a joke. "I think it was my explanation about who my parents were. That kind of did it. His mother kept a straight face and then acted as if I weren't there for the rest of the night."

"What else?"

"His sister hinted that he collected foreign girls as a hobby. I happened to be the Hawaiian one at the moment."

"Ah, well, that might be a problem—more than the Mother from you know where."

"You could be right. There's only one problem. I think I was falling big time for him." Kanoe started to cry again.

"Then unfall for him. You need to assess before you give your heart away," said Missy, pulling Kanoe into a hug. "Do you know how to unfall?"

"Not really."

"You get your power back and stop putting all your eggs in one basket. Go cover your bases and start going out with somebody else. There are boys all around here. We've got tons of 'em beating the door down. Take one of them."

"It's not that easy."

"Well, who said it was? Life is hard and then you die."

"Oh, Missy, you do have a way of cheering me up. Okay, okay. I should have stopped when I saw the first red flag at the toga party."

"Well, better late than never," said Missy as she hugged Kanoe again.

7

KANOE DID NOT HAVE TO make a decision to break it off. Bailey stopped calling. He made himself scarce in school. No more stalking or hounding her through the halls. She caught glimpses of him, but he was clearly avoiding her. She had a hard time processing it all. She thought of Puakea one day when she wondered what to do. Puakea probably would have called him out and beat him up. She wished she could—wished she had that kind of gumption.

Her outward serenity did not serve her well now. It was just a matter of two weeks when someone informed her that Bailey had a new girlfriend—some snow bunny from Norway. Kanoe doubled over and felt the pain of it all one night and the next morning she remembered the advice her Puna had given her years ago when she lost Kamalu. "Feel the pain for a moment, then pull yourself up as soon as you can, straighten out your shoulders, hold your head up high and walk off into the sunset without looking back." And this is just what Margaret Kanoekahawai Hunter did. She moved on into the sunset once again.

She finished her second year at San Mateo with fairly decent grades, receiving an Associate Arts Degree which filled her undergraduate requirements. That summer she came home to the little house in

Kahana Valley with great appreciation in her heart for the beauty that surrounded her. She was home and happy again. She walked the trails and explored the valley anew with a genuine appreciation for it after such a long time away.

Everything seemed so tall and towering: the ironwood evergreens that touched the sky, the swaying coconut trees, the fruit bearing banana stalks, *'ohia'ai* further up with its fruit of mountain apples and light red bottle tufted flowers, sprawling *hau* and *kamani* trees, *ginger* galore along the paths, *ti* leaves scattered, and lush green everywhere. Even the rain was unique—warm and refreshing and the scent of it on the tropical forest area, so different from California.

Then there was the water of Kahana Bay and its changing colors, sometimes a clear aquamarine, other times blue brown after the rains and then the multiple layers of blue on bright sunny days. On certain days it gleamed glassy, on others rough with white caps, reflecting all of its many moods like a temperamental woman.

She went swimming on one of those glassy days with the sun glistening silver across the bay. Kanoe swam from one end to the other and circled back. When she got to the middle area again, she saw a familiar figure on the beach shaded by tall ironwood trees. He was shading his eyes from the sun and spotted her as she swam closer. He had no shirt on; only his blue Hawaiian print shorts. He dove in the water and emerged next to her.

"Makaio, no, I can't believe my eyes." Kanoe impulsively put her arms around his neck and hung on tightly. He kissed her thoroughly and she responded—a kiss that lasted perhaps a little too long to make up for the four years they had not seen each other. They were both embarrassed by their enthusiasm when they pulled back in the water. He still hung on to her while he examined her face. He ran his hand over it, trying to see what had changed and what remained the same. She was not the little girl he remembered. Her hair was wet and slicked back from her face with water dripping from her long eyelashes. She wore a turquoise bikini that matched the water beneath them, staring up at him wide eyed, not trying to hide the hero worship that she had felt as a little girl.

"You look great, Kanoe." He meant more. He wanted to tell her how lovely she looked to him, how he had missed her and thought about her over the years…but he couldn't. He did not want to lead her on. Makaio was like the apostle he was named after, who portrayed Jesus as the Lion of God. Makaio was fierce and yet protective of his own. He felt that way about the people around him as well as his country.

It was partly why, after finishing school at Notre Dame, he had enrolled in Officers Candidate School in Fort Benning, Georgia. He would be leaving for Viet Nam in a month. His father had been active in the Korean War—an infantry officer who had done well and was successful in his missions. Makaio wanted to follow in his footsteps.

OCS was a means by which the army could generate large numbers of junior officers during a time of increasing personnel requirements, particularly during wars. By 1964 OCS had been consolidated from eight different branches into two schools: Field Artillery OCS at Fort Sills, Oklahoma and Infantry OCS at Fort Benning, Georgia. OCS was divided into three phases. Trained by Tactical Officers for the duration, the first, eight weeks, was a repeat of Basic Training, but under more stress. The second, also eight weeks, was Advanced Infantry Training, and during the third phase, the candidates took turns filling the command positions in their training class, now as commanders.

Makaio had enlisted in basic combat training for eight weeks and entered the OCS program where he was further trained for twenty one weeks. He graduated as a Second Lieutenant with a twenty four month commitment to the Army in that status. He would be paid $241.20 a month, about $141.83 more than a PFC starting salary.

He had specifically steered clear of any romantic involvements, so he could focus on his commitment. But here was Kanoe, the little girl he had protected, now grown into an alluring woman and it would take a great deal of strength to stay away from her.

He had quickly removed himself from the water upon their initial meeting. "Sorry, Kanoe, I gotta go. Just wanted to say hello and welcome you home and see how you are and all that, but I have an event I need to attend. I promise I'll see you later."

She was standing in the chest high water when he left her. She had noticed a lot about him too. His hair was buzzed off, his body was perfectly formed, his face had grown fuller, but still handsome with dark brooding eyes and his pidgin English had faded, almost into a Southern drawl, but not quite. She watched him leave the water, his wide back to her as he headed for a towel to dry off. She watched him walk far down the beach near the fish pond and eventually through the trees until he disappeared towards the road.

Makaio had carefully avoided seeing Kanoe, but thinking about her was another thing. It didn't help matters when his family brought her name up and Luka could not stop talking about her.

All four brothers were home at the time. Maleko had just gotten out of the army and got a job at Matson Shipping. He had been deployed to Laos and just missed Viet Nam because he had enlisted early. Luka, who was Kanoe's age, had been away at Pasadena City College and Keoni was finishing his last year in High School at Kahuku.

The boys each represented a form of their mixed heritage. Makaio and Keoni were the Hawaiian versions with their olive skin, jet black hair, and dark brown eyes of their mother's. Makaio inherited the fine features of his father's and Keoni the more prominent Hawaiian nose from his mother's side. Luka had grown to be the tallest of the four, fair of skin with lighter eyes and chestnut hair, and Maleko resembled him more in a shorter huskier body type.

Their Irish Hawaiian father, Kelly Kelliher was their role model. As a fierce master sergeant in the army, he served as an infantry man in World War II and the Korean War. He had been firm with his boys as children, but also gave them great freedom in striking out on their own to become the men he had molded them to be. He needed to counteract their mother's coddling and worry over her boys. She tended to hover, but it was a trait she could never seem to lose, and they were all secretly attached to her in their own way.

Her name was Lia Kamanu Kelliher and she was the pure Hawaiian who had spent all her life in Ka'a'awa Valley. She and her husband had inherited her family home from her parents who had worked the Kualoa Ranch which had much of its land in Ka'a'awa. They had a four bedroom home up near the cliffs with a panoramic view of the ocean, renovated with two add-on bedrooms over the years to accommodate the growing family. The house was built on a plateau type lot which enabled them to have a front yard with a view. There was a veranda that encircled the front and sides of the house. Stairs led up the front door in the middle of the veranda.

The family would often gather here to enjoy the view and the coolness of the trade winds on hot summer evenings. That's what they were doing tonight. Their mother and father were conversing on wicker rocking chairs on the veranda, and the boys were drinking their beers sitting on the steps. Keoni was not supposed to be drinking, but he kept stealing sips from his brothers' bottles of Primo Beer. Ti plants hedged the veranda, and the fragrance of plumeria blossoms from nearby trees filtered the air. The sun did not set on this side, but they could see the color of sky-blue-pink scattered amongst the fluffy clouds.

"You seen Kanoe, yet?" Luka nudged Maleko on the same step they were sitting on. Makaio sat two steps above them and his ears perked up.

"No, I heard she just got back from the mainland," replied Maleko.

"Ho, man you wouldn't believe. She's somet'ing," said Luka.

"Nah, last time I saw her she was just one little girl." Maleko questioned him.

"Not any moah. I tell you I wouldn't mind..." Luka continued.

"Wouldn't mind what?" asked Makaio loudly.

"You know," answered Luka glancing up the stairs at Makaio.

"She's like a sister to us. What you talking about?" Makaio stared daggers at Luka.

"No, brah, she's like one sistah to *you*. I got oddah plans."

"Fohget your plans. She's off limits," Makaio spoke in a steely voice.

"You ain't biggah dan me any moah, Makaio, so don't be bossing me around."

Their parents had not been listening to them until they heard the raised voices.

"What's going on here?" asked Lia.

"Makaio's trying to boss me aroun' again."

"Makaio," warned his mother.

"Stay away from her," he said under his breath to Luka and walked up the stairs into the house.

8

OF COURSE, MAKAIO'S WARNING JUST made Luka want to defy him even more, and he embarked on a mission to pursue Kanoe. It wasn't all that successful, but he was relentless. Kanoe's phone did not stop ringing, and he parked himself on her doorstep on a daily basis, trying to get her to go out with him. She finally set him straight one night. They were sitting on *her* steps this time.

"I don't understand it, Kanoe. Why won't you go out wit' me?"

"Because, Luka, I don't want to give you the wrong impression. I've tried to tell you that, but you won't listen."

"What's wrong wit' me? You know deyah plenty of girls who want some of dis action."

"Well, go out with *them*," she said looking at the frustrated expression on his face. "Luka, I think of you like a brother. Besides my heart belongs to...oh never mind. Just promise me you won't pursue this. You're just wasting your time."

"Who you talking about?" He studied her face now.

She had slipped, but she decided to throw caution to the wind and tell him. "Makaio," she almost whispered.

His face turned red and he stood up on the lower step, then proceeded down to the grass and faced her. "Lost cause, you know. He doesn't feel the same about you and he's leaving. What a waste, Kanoe. You coulda had me, but what can I say. I gotta go."

He walked away from her, and her vision was blurred by tears that slipped over her cheeks. *Lost cause.* Those words remained behind as Luka left her sitting on the steps of the small cottage in beautiful Kahana Valley where the green mountains met the bay of sparkling blue waters.

Kanoe had an understanding for Luka's plight. She felt the same way about Makaio's unrequited attention. She could not explain her need to see him, except that she knew he would be gone soon. All she wanted now was to connect with him somehow with a lasting impression.

She had seen him running on the long stretch of Kahana Bay followed by a long swim across the ocean. Kanoe assumed he was training to keep in shape for his deployment that would take place in a few weeks. She watched him now on a daily basis, hoping he did not see her hiding amongst the pines, trying to work up enough nerve to approach him.

One day, Kanoe couldn't stand it any longer. She waited till his run took him where she stood under the pines and ran out to join him. She was wearing her bathing suit under a tee shirt and caught up with him, running beside him. He stopped to catch his breath, bending down to put his hands on his thighs. "Kanoe," he said, panting from the run.

"Just keep running. I'll run with you," she offered. "Don't let me break your pace.

"Okay," he agreed. They ran to the end and back, not talking, but trying to concentrate on their cadence on the sand.

"I'll swim with you, too," she offered again when they stopped near the fish pond and river edge at the south end of the bay. She pulled her tee shirt off, wearing her same turquoise bikini and dove in the water to the left of the pond as she tried to match him stroke for stroke across the bay.

They finished where they started and stood in the shallow area in chest high water, now out of breath. At least she was. He was used to it.

"I've watched you for four days, now. I thought I'd join you today," she said.

"Four days, huh?" His eyes were piercing hers, but not warm, almost suspicious.

"Yep," she replied. *Now what?* She thought.

"Why?" he asked..

"I'm embarrassed to tell you."

"Okay, then we'll change the subject," he said looking away from her out at the horizon.

"You've clearly been avoiding me, Makaio. I just wanted to see you."

"I thought Luka was camping out at your house?"

"Um no, I set him straight the other day."

"Hmm, well. I told him to stay away from you, but he wouldn't listen to me."

"You did, why?"

"I don't know. Maybe I knew what Luka had in mind and I didn't like it."

"Oh," she said. Then she blew it right out of the water. "I wish *you* had what Luka had in mind."

Makaio shook his head as if to clear the water out of his ears. "I can't believe you said that Kanoe."

"I can't either," she agreed.

"Take it back," he said knowing how stupid that sounded.

"I can't," she said. "It's already out."

"You're supposed to be a nice girl, Kanoe. You can't go around talking like that. What did they teach you up in San Francisco? Nice girls don't talk like that."

"Um, it was San Mateo."

"What?"

"I was in San Mateo, not San Francisco. Well, we visited the city once in awhile, but I was mostly in a Bay Area town about an hour's drive, depending on the traffic from San Francisco. I mean if you were driving during peak traffic time, it took sometimes two hours before you got into the city and even then, the parking was so bad, it was three hours before you could even set foot on the ground. We had a car named Kukailani; it was a '54 Plymouth, stick shift and it was awfully difficult maneuvering those steep hills in the city and…"

"Kanoe," he interrupted. "What does that have to do with the price of eggs?"

"Oh, sorry. I was just trying to explain the difference between..."

"No, you were trying to get off the subject."

"Makaio, will you please give me a break. I am so embarrassed right now. And you're right. I stand corrected. Nice girls don't talk like that. So, I'm going to leave you in the water right now and go home and hide my head under a pillow." She didn't give him a chance to respond and swam as fast as she could towards shore.

He was faster and swam after her... grabbing her ankle right before she stood up. She ended flat on her face under water. Makaio pulled her towards him; they were rolling in the shallow water now, then he pulled her back towards the deeper end and held onto her. "You're right, Kanoe. I was trying to avoid you, but..." then he dipped his head down towards her face, found her lips and kissed her until they were splashed underwater by a wave. It started to rain now, a big black cloud poured heavy rain over them, but they didn't notice.

"But what?" she asked him to continue.

"But, not anymore," he said and smiled in the rain as the two hugged each other and kissed for a long time where the rains watered the valley so the *kamani, hau,* ironwood and *hala* trees along the seashore could maintain their greenness, basking in the much appreciated nitrogen that only rain water could dispense in beautiful Kahana Bay.

9

Makaio's resolve to stay away from Kanoe was instantly dissipated on that day. They were inseparable after that. They had two and a half weeks and spent every minute they could together. Most of the time they were at her house with Puna Maggie's best wishes and consent as she watched the two fall in love during their time together.

Kanoe kept up with his need to keep in shape, running and swimming with him on a daily basis, hiking through the trails of Kahana, seeking out waterfalls and mountain pools to kiss and indulge themselves at every opportunity. He barely left her side and she would not have it any other way.

Every boy she had ever encountered paled in comparison to Makaio. He was her dream come true and she could not imagine giving her heart to anyone else as fully as she committed herself in those two weeks. She realized that she'd always loved him as a child, but this was so different. They got to know each other in a whole different way as if they were starting anew.

Makaio on the other hand, proceeded against his common sense to encourage what developed at the time. It threw him off kilter and damaged some of his resolve to keep to himself and maintain the strength he needed for what was coming up. His weakness prevailed and he could not leave Kanoe's side for an instant. He was attracted to her beauty, her serenity that he had always admired and now to her steadfast love. He let her dream and make plans for their future together, but felt extremely guilty throughout it all, knowing that they were just the dreams of a star struck girl that may never come to pass. He finally told her on their last night together.

He sat on the sand holding her in front of him as they looked out at the moon sparkling silver across the bay. "I'll write to you every day, Makaio."

"I don't think that's a good idea, Kanoe."

She turned around to look at his face. "What do you mean?"

"I mean, we have to stop this now."

"Makaio, you're scaring me."

"I should have told you this sooner. I think I let this get out of hand."

"This? Is that what you're calling us? This?"

"I'm sorry. I don't have the words for what I want to say."

"You love me. You must. I know you haven't said it in so many words, but surely I can't be that blind to what we've shared."

"Kanoe, I'm going on a very dangerous mission and I can't get bogged down with love. I've been in training to become a killer, Kanoe. Do you have any idea what that means? It has nothing to do with moonlit nights or runs on the beach or a pretty girl that makes my heart beat faster than usual. I'm going to have to lead men in combat and there are so many question marks about what that means. I can't be thinking about you and I can't promise you anything."

Don't cry Kanoe. Don't let him see how much he's hurt you. Just take a deep breath and deal with this or you'll lose him forever.

"I'm still going to write to you every day," she turned to him and kissed him and those were some of the last words she said to him on a moonlight night as the light rippled across Kahana Baby.

10

MAKAIO WAS SCHEDULED TO GO with one of the first battalions to enter Vietnam. Amongst his commanding officers were seasoned veterans of World War II and the Korean War. Most of the infantrymen were volunteers, committed to God and Country, with high ideals about demolishing the "bad guys" and with the mindset of fighting for the right cause. Their predecessors in the previous wars had proven the might of the best country in the world and they were sure they would prevail. They had just completed training, were optimistic about their skills, their superior weaponry and had great confidence in the people in charge. The majority were high school athletes or those who came from working class, blue collar homes that were patriotic and stood up for the ideals of the American dream.

They were prepared in theory and in classes about the ways of their enemy, but few knew the language, the actual experience of the territory they were to undertake or the keen tenacity of their skilled adversaries. Their transport ship from South Carolina maneuvered through the Panama Canal, to the Pacific Ocean landing a month later in Qui Nhon in Central South Viet Nam. Their destination was An Khe, forty two miles west of Qui Nhon where their base camp was located.

Makaio was now referred to as Second Lieutenant Matthew Kelliher who was trained last minute by sergeants in airmobile-air assault tactics. He and two other lieutenants were plugged into spots vacated by commanders who were pulled out for other reasons. So he had spent another seven weeks training in a crash course in airmobile expertise for what had taken others fourteen months to endure. After all that training, he was switched last minute to command a platoon on the ground as an infantryman.

Much later, the assessment was made…that anyone who had the experience of the war in Viet Nam was never the same again. Nothing in any of his training prepared Makaio for what he was to experience. It was a whole different exercise to have mock villages and jungles and to jump out of a helicopter onto a training field in Georgia than it was to actually undergo the horrors of the actual guerrilla territory—the smells, the humidity, the jungles, the malaria, the snakes, the language barrier …and the killing. No one in his platoon had ever killed another human being, but that would soon change and then killing and death became a familiar experience like taking a walk through the park— except this time with a kind of jaded adrenaline that was so unfamiliar to the common man.

The two companies in his batallion were at first able to trump their enemies in a few skirmishes. They did manage to have that feel of victory, but soon after that it fell apart when he lost man after man either to malaria or horrendous deaths that were unspeakable in his sight. The first kill was like a "right of passage" to many. Makaio's first was to save a comrade, and he did not blink at the thought. After awhile it became easier as he fought to keep his men alive.

After two months in combat, they were near the La Drang River when all hell broke loose in Makaio's world. He saw three of his men go down as they were blindsided by five combatants from the enemy's patrol. One of the infantrymen was hit in the neck next to Makaio. He picked him up to carry him to safety where a helicopter was waiting. As Makaio dragged his comrade across the tangled brush, he heard a sound pass right near his ear and his last thoughts before everything faded to black was of Kanoe's face with lashes wet from salt water in the midst of Kahana Bay.

"Kanoe," he cried and then nothing.

NANI

※ ※ ※

KALIHIWAI VALLEY

Kalihiwai Valley

On the Garden Isle of Kaua'i, the northern most island of the Hawaiian chain, a verdant green valley named Kalihiwai lies nestled on its north shore. The valley, named appropriately, is the Hawaiian word for *river's edge* because its base is located at the edge of a winding fresh water river that empties into a bay, perfect in its half moon shape with waters that change with the tides from aquamarine, to turquoise and deeper shades of cerulean blue. Steep lava cliffs frame each side of the sparkling white sand beach scattered with tall ironwood trees.

The entire valley covers an area of 7.4 square miles which includes approximately a square mile of water. Its wet location enables the river to be navigated into the far reaches of its basin where a forest of giant Australian tree ferns, fan palms, towering Malay apple trees and strawberry guava shrubs leads to the five tiered Kalihiwai Falls. The watershed of the valley is fed by streams that meander and flow from two mountains: Namahana to the northern left and Makaleha to the southern right where the native forest rises up to misty peaks.

Most of the population in Kalihiwai was concentrated toward the beach end of the valley. Before 1946, the area had been more of a thriving community with taro farms and rice fields, irrigated by the abundant water from the valley. A school and three stores served the district as Japanese, Filipino, Chinese and Hawaiian families lived off the land by fishing and farming.

The laid back life in the quaint community was drastically changed in 1946 when struck by its first major *tsunami* with two waves reaching as high as forty five feet. The north coast of Kaua'i was especially battered. Lives were lost, numerous homes destroyed all the way to end of Ha'ena, and people had to rebuild and start over. Some structures were gone forever.

Eleven years later, the next disastrous *tsunami* pummeled the north shore of Kaua'i obliterating the beautiful community of Kalihiwai once again.

1

MARCH 1957

THE LARGEST *TSUNAMI* TO HIT the island of Kaua'i occurred on the day of Nani Banta's thirteenth birthday. It was a school day and four of her favorite classmates from Kilauea School had come home with her to celebrate.

Nani's home in Kalihiwai was situated a short distance up the river that flowed into the bay surrounded by cliffs on each side. Her house had been renovated after the '46 tsunami. It was small, yet functional, but not where the family spent most of their time when they could be outdoors, surrounded by one of the loveliest settings on the Garden Isle. Shaded by ironwood trees and lava rocks that kissed the river's edge, the home sat on a slope and stood out because of its color—an unusual butterscotch hue that her father had painted a few years before.

She and her ten year old brother, Lopaka, shared a room in the two bedroom bungalow. The kitchen and living room flowed together into one spacious area with a tiny hallway that led to the bedrooms. The family of four shared the same bathroom, and happily cohabitated in their small quarters.

Nani's grandfather Banta was the son of a Filipino family who had immigrated from the Philippines a generation before. They had been recruited to work on the rice plantation located up the river and built

109

their home in Kalihiwai. Her grandfather married a Hawaiian woman a few years after he had arrived to work in the fields. Her name was Mileka Mahoe whose family lived on the farthest end of the north shore of Kaua'i in Ha'ena. Robert "Bobby" Banta, had been their only child and spoiled from the day he was born, especially by his Hawaiian mother.

Her spoiling did not affect his disposition, however. He was a lovely man with a twinkle in his eye and fell head over heels for a *haole* girl of French extraction named Yvonne Dubois who had come to Kaua'i as a tourist in 1941. She had traveled all the way from New Orleans as a young girl with a church group and never returned. Kalihiwai had been her home ever since.

The Bantas struggled monetarily, surviving on *'opelu* fish from the river, *akule* from the ocean and avocado fruit from three trees, sweet potatoes and vegetables they raised in a small garden in the back of the house. Bobby made his living by fishing up and down the north shore. He sold his fish to neighboring markets and neighbors in the valley. He also worked as a part time gardener in one of the big estates in nearby Hanalei.

Even though Yvonne had come from a comfortable home in New Orleans, she never regretted her decision to make ends meet with Bobby. The sacrifices she made were worth it to her. They had built a life together, and she was content with her husband and two lovely children; she would not have had it any other way.

Nani, the Hawaiian word for *beautiful*, born by Caesarean section and, unlike most babies who scrunched their way through labor, had been a flawless newborn, without wrinkles or redness of skin. She was simply beautiful and thusly named. She had matched her name in appearance throughout her childhood and possessed a contagious effervescence of life. As a result, she drew people, adults and children alike, to her warmth, her vibrant nature with laughter that was always bubbling to the surface.

At thirteen, she had dark brown hair that she still wore in pigtails, a heart shaped face that reflected the mixture of the French in her olive green eyes, the Filipino/Hawaiian copper brown skin, small flat nose and full, lush lips that often turned up into a radiant smile.

That's what she was doing today—laughing in a small boat that was a bit overloaded with the four other girls who had joined her for her birthday. Nani was doing the rowing, and they were just returning from meandering up river where they had picked some strawberry guavas. Before their expedition, they shared a special meal for a special occasion—bologna sandwiches and Exchange Orange Ade poured from a pitcher followed by vanilla ice-cream and sponge cake without frosting.

The girls wore bathing suits and were in and out of the river, diving from the boat. Two of them were in the water at the time. The boat had come to stop while Nani rested from rowing the big load. She noticed the stream rising at a rapid pace and a rolling effect that made the boat go up and down.

She heard shouting and looked up to see several people on shore yelling at them. Then she saw her mother with a frantic look on her face, screaming with fright. Yvonne, wearing shorts and a Hawaiian shirt, tumbled into the river in her attempt to reach them. Nani, now aware of her mother's unusual alarm, dove in the water to meet her half way.

"Nani, we've been looking all over for you. I thought you were swimming in the ocean," her mom panted when they finally met in the middle of the stream.

"Mom, what's wrong?"

"I'll tell you when you get to shore. Have the girls get out of the boat and swim to the other side of the river bank, so you can get that boat out of the water quickly. Now, hurry."

She swam rapidly back to the boat, notified the girls who promptly dove into the water. By that time, the river was lined with people waving them in. She rowed the dingy to the edge of the bank and threw the oars to the side.

"Leave the boat there, we have to go," screamed her mother.

The five girls were now shivering as they sat on the ground. Nani's mom brought them towels, but had no time to get them their dry clothes. She herded the girls up the mountainside; they followed obediently, well aware that there was some kind of emergency. The rays from the sun were fading now. It would be dark soon. Nani realized they had stayed upriver longer than usual.

"Mom, tell me…what?" cried Nani as they were being herded like a bunch of mountain goats.

"Tidal wave," her mother shouted, still out of breath in her panic.

The girls exclaimed in excitement, not fear yet, but more exhilarated by the adventure of being together at the moment.

"Where are we going?" she yelled as her mother pulled her arm up the hill.

"Daddy's waiting for us on the cliff. He's there with your brother and some other people he had to help out of their homes. We've been looking for you for two hours…"

Then they heard the noise before they saw what was behind it—an ocean sound unlike any other. The tide had receded far back from the shore as they were hiking upward, and now, it seemed as if all the water from the Pacific had come to cover the valley. In the short time they had abandoned the boat, the river had risen high above the banks with a rolling motion that reflected the underlying movement and pressure that was now building up.

They reached the top of the cliff where people were gathered in fright. Her dad yelled out, "Thank God." He rushed forward to his daughter and hugged her tightly. "Nani girl, where you been?"

"I was up stream, Daddy, with the boat."

"Ho man, I tell you. You scayahed da you know what outta me."

"Sorry, Daddy."

It was not quite dark yet. The sun was starting to go down when everything went crazy as they watched from the cliffs, but there was still enough light to see the phenomena.

The water receded, exposing the rocks, sand and coral in the bay as *'alamihi* crabs scrambled for safety. Then the water came crashing in, covering a large portion of the area at the base of the river and homes closer to the bay. After it rushed in, it flowed out with a giant undertow, sucking out debris and floating wood which they realized were parts of houses that had already been demolished. The ebb and flow of the high tides, later calculated to be the highest of all the areas hit from Alaska down to South America, brought massive destruction to the area. In rushed the water covering and battering the homes or anything in its merciless path; then taken back out in pieces to the ocean. The tides would bring the objects back into shore and pound them again.

Exploding sounds up river turned out later to be the destruction of the Kalihiwai Bridge, the only means to connect the fifteen mile strip of the north shore. People were stranded everywhere as a result.

Technically, the onslaught was not a tidal wave that hit, although most islanders referred to it as that. Its correct term was *tsunami*, defined as a cataclysm resulting from a destructive sea wave caused by an earthquake. This one had originated with the third largest earthquake to occur anywhere in the twentieth century with a magnitude of 8.3, south of the Andrean Islands in the Aleutian Islands of Alaska.

The impact of the earthquake and its many aftershocks caused the *tsunami* to flow in strong underwater ripples as fast as 600 kilometers an hour, moving from Alaska, through all the coastal areas of the western shores of British Columbia, Washington, Oregon, California and hitting the Hawaiian Islands with a heavy impact. The *tsunami* slowed its speed as it neared the shores, so it did not hit as one big wave—causing its pressure to recede in a sucking motion and come back with powerful force as it flooded the area, especially the northern coast of Kaua'i.

Unlike, the one that hit in 1946, lives were not lost, due to the improvement in technology and buoys strategically placed, enabling residents to be warned ahead of time. A seismograph in Alaska was triggered and within six minutes of the earthquake, centers from Alaska to Tokyo were warned. After an hour, the epicenter was located; tide observers in the path of the *tsunami* were alerted, enabling local authorities to calculate the approximate time of its arrival.

This warning saved lives in 1957. Compared to the *tsunami* eleven years before, none were lost. There were seventy five homes and two hundred fifty people left homeless from the destruction that occurred in the fifteen mile strip from Kalihiwai to Ha'ena.

Nani's family were one of those, losing their home and all they owned including the small dingy boat that she had rowed up the river of Kalihiwai on her thirteenth birthday of March 9, 1957.

2

"Oh, Lihau, I can hardly believe it. I made it. I actually got the vote."

"What vote?" asked Lihau as they were walking from their sophomore biology class at Kamehameha towards the Girls School Auditorium.

"For song leader. I'm going to be a song leader!" exclaimed Nani, as she hugged her books tightly to her chest, an elated expression on her face.

"Wow. Good for you Nani," said Lihau as she smiled at her friend. "Of course I'm not surprised."

"You're not?"

"No. I knew you'd make it.

"You did? Oh, Lihau, you're such a good friend. I just had no idea whether I'd make it or not."

"Oh, oh, there they are," sighed Lihau.

"Put your head down and eyes on the ground," said Nani as they walked quickly, joining the rest of the girls who were filing into the large building.

Lihau nudged her. "Did you hear that, Nani. They're calling your name. Quite a few of them. It's like a chant."

"Shhh, Lihau. Don't look at them."

They were walking to the right of the school's Boy School battalion assembled in the Konia field next to the auditorium. It was always a daunting sight for the girls to behold.

Kamehameha was the first school in Hawai'i where the JROTC (Junior Reserve Officers Training Corp) had been instituted through the passage of the National Defense Act of Congress in 1916. Under the act, high schools were authorized the loan of federal military equipment and the assignment of active duty military personnel as instructors. Title 10 of the US code stated its purpose: "to instill in students… in secondary educational institutions the value of citizenship, service to the United States, personal responsibility, and a sense of accomplishment."

Although Kamehameha was considered a civilian school, the ROTC program was incorporated on a full time basis at the Boys School. They were provided with rifles, sabers, medals to denote rank or promotion, navy blue dress uniforms for special occasion, khaki uniforms for everyday use and even play uniforms for other activities.

At the time, the staff assigned to guide and teach the cadets military procedure included an infantry major and captain, two sergeants, three master sergeants and an infantry specialist. The staff's purpose was to teach leadership, obedience, self control, discipline, and military strategy with the goal of instilling the desire for these young boys to become upright citizens in their communities. Whether they carried on their careers to one of the three branches of the armed services was not necessarily the goal, but many were groomed for this purpose and it was not uncommon for them to head in that direction.

The cadets were formed according to their four companies A, B, C, D and another one designated for officers and the Drill Team. All of the officers were boarders in their last year of school and a senior girl was chosen as a sponsor for each company to march with them on formal occasions.

At the head of the command stood the battle group commander with the title of Cadet Colonel. Other officers included three staff sergeants, five cadet majors, a cadet lieutenant colonel, and five first lieutenants who were distributed throughout the ranks. Each company had a captain at its center along with various platoon leaders.

The boys at Kamehameha were given a sense of pride in this military atmosphere. The boarders, like Hekili, were taught to be meticulous in their hygiene, and all aspects of decorum. Their rooms were kept neat; they ironed their own uniforms, polished their brass, and were aware of a sense of order on a continual basis enabling them to carry this discipline later on to their private lives as so many of those in the armed forces were known to do.

The battalion was *at ease* when the girls walked by and not called to attention yet. Hence, the cat calls and Nani's name amongst them. Lihau heeded Nani's advice and quickly accompanied her into the auditorium.

The Cadet Captain from B Company watched them scurry across the field. He was not calling out to Nani, but he watched her out of the corner of his eye. He had observed her that way for a year now. He was a neighbor of hers in Kaua'i—not an immediate neighbor, but just a few miles away in Hanalei Valley. The first time he saw her was a year ago when they boarded a plane together as they returned to their homes for Christmas. They were seated on different sides of the aircraft. He was certain she hadn't noticed him.

In 1860 Kamehameha IV signed the Act to Regulate Names which was eventually repealed in 1967. Hawaiians were to take their father's given name as a surname and all children born henceforth, were to take Christian names or English names as a first name. Hawaiian names were transferred to middle names. Therefore most Hawaiian names were middle names. It was a law that many kept, but some slipped by the notice of government officials. At Kamehameha, the students were allowed to use their middle names, but most of the student body went by their English names at the time.

The Cadet Captain in question, Hekili Schmidt had been named James Ku'iikaikakahekilimekalapauila Schmidt. The name was run together, but actually, broken apart, should have been Ku'i ikaika ka hekili me ka lapa uila. This long name was translated simply as *thunderbolt*, a sign of strength in his family tradition, but also the circumstances that surrounded his birth in a thunderstorm. He used a portion of the name: Hekili (Thunder) and it followed him throughout his four years where he resided in Kaleopapa Dorm at Kamehameha.

In spite of his Hawaiian background and his home in the taro fields of Hanalei, Hekili Schmidt did not look Hawaiian. He was six feet two inches tall, blonde with light brown eyes and the chiseled features of his

German ancestors. Only his name reflected the Hawaiian blood that was passed on to him through his maternal grandfather and his paternal grandmother. Both parents were of Hawaiian-German extraction. The German dominated his features. In a Hawaiian school, it was a handicap at times, but Hekili was well liked amongst the boys and held his own in the military aspect as well as on the football field.

He would be graduating this coming year, and after attending Officer Training School during the summer, he was now leading a company. Actually, at the moment, he was *not* leading his company. He was watching Nani walk across the right side of the field.

The platoon leader next to him, Kevin Kalua who was also his best friend, nudged him. "Time to play soldier. Who you looking at?"

"Nobody," he responded too quickly.

"Ah, I got your nobody," Kevin sneered looking in the girls' direction.

Hekili turned around and called the troups to attention.

When the cadets got to the auditorium, the girls dressed in white had already been seated on the left and right side of the auditorium. The boys were assigned the middle section with the freshman class in the balcony area. The occasion for this particular weekly Friday afternoon assembly was a pre-pep rally. The football team was introduced. Hekili was one of them. He would be playing wide receiver this semester and was called up on stage with the rest of them.

The new cheerleaders, five guys in white and the five song leaders were also featured. Nani was one of the pretty girls who came on stage as their names were called. She ended up standing in front of him. He was just a foot away from her and inhaled the scent of her hair that smelled like *plumeria*—probably because she had two blossoms pinned in her hair. He studied her again without moving his head, glancing upward to the back of her head all the way down to her flat white shoes.

A simple white shirt-waist dress with short sleeves hugged her bodice and flared from the waist to below her knees. Most of the girls wore the same thing with slight variations. She was of average height, a compact figure with legs that were especially well formed. But it was her face that shone with a smile which radiated warmth. Her hair framed her face in wisps and dark curls that would have been ordinary on anyone else. Hekili did not view Nani Banta as ordinary.

Hekili continued to gaze at her as she stood there. She looked nervous in front of the audience, so her natural reaction was to glance at the players behind her. Her eyes landed on Hekili. She smiled and he froze. Her eyes up close were twinkling and crinkled at its edges. Pools of olive green lined with caramel gleamed at him. Add to that the smile of an angel and he could not look away. It was just a moment, and she quickly turned around.

The next time he saw her was her debut on the football field. She didn't seem nervous then. She was definitely in her element as she and the four other girls led the cheering section in all the songs. "Imua", the standard school song was being played by the band. "Imua Kamehameha e, a lanakila oe". The girls were dressed in glossy white outfits that hugged their bodies with blue pleats in their skirts, reflecting the school colors.

Hekili was not playing on the field at the time. He sat on the bench, trying to watch the game, but sneaking glances at the song leaders when he could. The last time he looked, her skirt was twirling around her legs and her face beamed up at the cheering section. He had to look away as if a bright light had blinded him.

In their game a couple weeks later, he had played rather well, catching three touchdown passes that led their team to win against St. Louis. The song leaders wore leis and would give them to boyfriends if they were playing or to someone who did exceptionally well. Nani did not have a boyfriend, so after much cheering during the game, she walked over to number 45, the one printed on Hekili's jersey. She had been prompted by one of the other cheerleaders to reward Hekili for his contribution to their win.

He was surrounded by well wishers and had been decked with leis already by admiring fans on the field. Unaware of her presence, he turned around when she tapped him on the shoulder, and there she stood, smiling up at him with her radiance. She reached up to put her lei over his head as he leaned over to receive it, and she kissed him on his left cheek. She did not know his name, but wanted to give him tribute. "Congratulations. You were great."

Hekili stood there staring at her completely tongue tied, but did manage to blurt out, "Thanks."

"My name is Nani," she introduced herself and smiled up at him.

"I know your name. I..."

"I have to go, but I just wanted you to know that we're all so appreciative of how well you did." She turned to one of her friends who urged her to hurry towards the bus that was waiting to transport the boarders back to their dorm.

He watched her leave as she disappeared in a flurry of people and friends who were urging her towards the bus. Hekili held his helmet in one hand and lifted the other one, absently caressing the spot where she had kissed him.

There were many opportunities for him to approach her after that, but he failed to take the initiative. He watched her at all the games, noticed her at church on Sundays, observed her at dorm activities, glanced at her across the room at dances, tried to catch a glimpse of her walking to class when the boys came up for devotions on Wednesdays and peered around the auditorium for her at assembly on Fridays, but for the rest of his senior year, he never talked to her again. Nani Banta was unapproachable as far as he was concerned. In spite of the fact that she was two years younger, he decided that she was way beyond his spectrum of social possibility.

Nani had not noticed Hekili's interest or his long term observance of her every move. She had been caught up in her own world and enjoying it immensely. She was Kamehameha's golden girl who took advantage of all that was offered and so appreciated the opportunities. Landing in B section during her freshman year, she did fairly well in this college preparatory class. She managed to maintain her Citizenship pin which reflected good marks in effort and conduct and was on the academic honor roll for several semesters.

The year that Hekili graduated, she had been invited to every prom, military ball and anything that included dancing at Kamehameha. Nani had only one sky blue chiffon dress that she wore on almost every formal occasion. It was not something she worried about, and her dates never seemed to notice. They were much more interested in winning over the smile and affection of the pretty song leader.

She had not favored anyone in particular at the time, but enjoyed playing the field. Lihau was her best friend, and they were inseparable in school sharing the same dorm.

In her junior year, she was pursued by the football team's quarterback, Lee Ahuna whom Nani could not resist. She had fallen for him instantly and for a whole month could not think of anything else. He was a boarder from the Big Island, tall dark and more than handsome with his Hawaiian brown eyes and magnetic smile. She was the envy of all her peers and they were seen together, on the football field, at one dorm dance and whenever they could possibly be together.

However...one of her peers who had Nani on her radar was Kia Kea. She had seen the happy couple together and wondered about the good looking quarterback. At the conclusion of the final football game of the season with Punahou, Kia conveniently arrived on the field to give Lee Ahuna one of her store bought ginger leis and a chaste kiss on the lips. He was hers after that. Nani was dropped like a hot sweet potato, and Lee became completely smitten with his new interest.

Of course, the fickle boy did not realize that he was in the clutches of the school's major man-eater and reaped what he'd sown when he was also dropped like another hot sweet potato after a month of what he thought would be an always and forever relationship.

Nani recovered, especially when she heard that her first heartthrob had suffered the same fate that she did. She learned a lesson, though, and guarded her affections with caution after that. She would definitely not be a member of Kia Kea's fan club when they were thrown together at the end of their last year in Senior Cottage.

3

Returning home on a Hawaiian airlines flight in the summer of her junior year at the age of seventeen was such a relief for her. She had missed her family and not seen them since Christmas. It had been four years since the *tsunami* had devastated their home.

Nani was greeted at the Lihue Airport by her mom, dad and fifteen year old Lopaka who had grown almost a head taller than his father now. Her mom had sewn ginger leis for her homecoming and the fragrance that so reminded her of home filled her senses. They turned right on Kalihiwai Road and another right towards the gravel road where she lived. Her dad had replaced their old car with another one—this one was a 1953 Ford Truck; she and Lopaka rode in the back with her suitcases and her dad's gardening tools.

Because the Kalihiwai Bridge had been demolished, the road had been split in two. Their house was on the river side of Kalihiwai Road before it meandered towards Anini Beach. She and Lopaka jumped off the truck when it stopped in front of their almost new house. Bobby Banta and his friends had, slowly over the last four years, constructed it with materials that were donated and sometimes bought with the little money he had to rebuild. It was not as big as their former one, consisting of only one bedroom. The smaller house had worked out for them, since Nani had been at Kamehameha most of the time. Her brother was designated to sleep in one of the two large *pune'es* in the living room. Nani would be sleeping on the other one when she arrived.

Not that she minded. She was just so glad to be with her family, even though they were squeezed into such close quarters. The most luxurious thing about the house was the kitchen, featuring a new sink, a gas range for cooking and a large refrigerator freezer that had been donated by the people who owned the estate that her father worked on. They had never owned a freezer before and were now able to store the fish, poi, and vegetables from their restored garden as well as fruit from trees along the river that were all wrapped and sealed tight for future meals.

The outside of the cottage was no longer a butterscotch color, but stained with a gray finish—not the most impressive house on the river, but definitely home for Nani, and the place that made her heart sing in Kalihiwai Bay.

She and Lopaka spent the whole week enjoying their valley— swinging on the rope across the wide expanse at the mouth of the river, body surfing on the pristine waves of the bay, and sitting in the sand until the moon came up over the ocean. Her dad had constructed a two man canoe for them in addition to his new fishing boat that he used for the family's livelihood. One day, Nani and her brother paddled far up the river and hiked along the trails to a fresh water pool and waterfall where they jumped off the high rocks into the icy cold water. Along the way, they picked mountain apples and the strawberry guavas that were used for their mom's special cake she baked whenever they were in season.

A week after Nani arrived home, the neighborhood *hukilau* took place in Kalihiwai Bay. People from the community attended and helped with the launching of an enormous net that was to be stretched out in a large area in the middle of the bay. The day began when the *kilo* (lookout person) stood on the cliffs on a spot watching for the large schools of *akule*, a silver mackerel with bulging eyes, as they swarmed towards the rocks. A conch shell was blown and the net was launched by two fishing boats that extended it across the bay.

A *hukilau* was an ancient Hawaiian fishing method in which a large net was laid in the ocean with lengthy ropes extending to the beach tied to each end. Long leaves, or *lau* in Hawaiian, which are bound along the length of the ropes, flutter in the water and help scare the fish into the net as the community pulls (*huki* in Hawaiian) the ropes, stretching the grid, gradually bringing the net to shore.

The holes in the mesh were large so that the smaller fish could escape, but small enough for the bigger fish to be trapped. Two boats set the nets from each side. About sixty people were involved as they pulled the large net to corral the fish. It was quite a production, an old Hawaiian practice that took many hands to stretch the netting— children and adults alike, but all basked in this proud tradition. When it was over, each family would take home their portion in a *pa kini,* a container for the fish.

Nani and Lopaka were half standing underwater in the sand and half treading water as the tide came in, at the far end of the net, where it was stretched out to the left of the bay near the rocks. She saw a familiar face on the other side of the net, but couldn't quite place him.

Hekili was home for the summer from his first year in Bemidji State University, a lakeside campus, located in the city of Bemidji in northern Minnesota, often registering as the coldest spot in the nation with its 30 below 0 temperatures. He had been there on a football scholarship with another classmate, and after two weeks at home, happily soaking in the warm blue waters of Kalihiwai. His friend, Kaulana, who lived in the community, had invited him to the event; it did not take much to persuade him to take part in the all day affair.

"I'll be right back," said Nani to her brother as she left her post at the far side of the net. She wore an old navy blue Kamehameha tee shirt that covered her two piece palaka bathing suit. She swam partially on the surface and then underwater over to the middle of the net.

Hekili's heart almost stopped when she popped up beside him... like a Polynesian maiden from a South Seas movie...with a tee shirt. Her hair was shoulder length now and slicked back wet from her face where long eyelashes dripped with salt water. "Hello," said Nani, trying not to sputter from the water in her mouth.

"Hello," he said with a surprised expression on his face.

"I know you, but I don't know from where."

"From school at Kamehameha. My name is Hekili."

"Ah, I thought you were familiar," she tried to recollect as she smiled at him in her friendly manner. "What are you doing here?"

"I live up the road in Hanalei. We're neighbors."

"I'm Nani."

"I know who you are, Nani." He frowned for a moment. He didn't want to remind her, but he did. "You gave me a lei last year at a football game."

"Oh, my goodness. You must think I've got marbles missing. Of course, I remember…now. You're the one that made all the touchdowns against…?"

"St. Louis. It was the St. Louis game." He had stopped scowling and attempted to match her friendliness, anything to keep her by his side a minute longer.

"Where do you live?" he stammered.

"Right there around the bend in the stream," she pointed behind her.

"Ah, I knew you lived close by." *I know everything about you, Nani and you can't even recall my name.*

"You did?"

"Well we have friends in common. I heard your name mentioned once."

"Hekili, Hekili. Now there's a name. What's your last name?

"Schmidt."

"Well, we can be friends now Hekili Schmidt and I promise I will never forget your name," she spoke earnestly and started to move away.

"Don't go," he said quietly.

"I have to. My brother is giving me the stinkest eye right now, cause I'm not holding my end of the net up. Bye, Hekili, I'll be seeing you around. We're practically neighbors." She gave him her radiant Colgate smile and promptly disappeared like a sea nymph under the clear turquoise water of Kalihiwai Bay.

He watched her go while his heart broke a little, so upset that he hadn't said more to keep her there—something witty, something profound that would make the first time she spoke his name memorable.

Five years would pass before Hekili Schmidt saw Nani Banta again.

4

Nani's senior year was exciting, as Kamehameha triumphed in winning championships in football, basketball and other sports. The senior girls and boys won their song contest. Her grades were acceptable, and she made friends and gathered fans especially amongst the boys.

She cherished her time at Senior Cottage and it was here where she grew to know and love Puakea, Kanoe and Keala. Keala was definitely her favorite person of all time and she marveled at how blessed she was to be in her presence. They were kindred spirits in a way—free with their musical laughter, both possessing expressive faces that exuded warmth and an appreciative outlook on life. They had been boarders together and knew each other socially, but bonded much more as friends at Senior Cottage. Kia was another story. Nani was still reeling from her own experience with her, and then Kanoe's followed it. She wasn't thrilled with Kia. And of course there was Lihau, her sidekick, to whom she was devoted.

Nani Banta graduated as a proven product of Kamehameha. Princess Pauahi would have been proud of her. She possessed all the qualities that Kamehameha intended to produce in its departing girls. She had been appreciative of her opportunities and embraced them with positive enthusiasm. She had pushed aside her homesickness and counted her blessings. She had never taken anything for granted, the fine meals, the camaraderie of dorm life, all that she learned in her classes, the thrill of song leading, and of course, the many friends she would carry in her heart for a lifetime.

Her parents had saved for months just to attend her graduation. She knew that, but wanted them there so much that she let them take on the expense. Her mother had brought her leis of ginger and the special *mokihana* of Kaua'i. Her dad was so proud of her and beamed as she walked up to get her diploma. Lopaka did not attend, but she understood that it was not financially possible.

Most of the graduating seniors were able to have elaborate celebration parties, but Nani just appreciated the presence of her parents who had truly sacrificed over the years and provided her with clothes, shoes and affordable things to make her life comfortable. She had been able to have her school expenses paid for by Kamehameha due to their monetary situation and all they had lost in the tsunami.

Nani could not afford to go away to college. She would have applied for scholarships, but even the scholarships, in her mind, would have been a burden on her family with the other expenditures involved.

One of her teachers had arranged for a job interview at Honolulu City Hall, to register voters for the upcoming election. She had gone home to Kalihiwai and returned in September to take on the clerk's position that was eventually offered her. She and a girl from school, Helene Awai, were able to get a small studio apartment in Waikiki. They joined their meager salaries to pay their rent. It was kind of an adventure for Nani and the first time on her own. Helene was employed as a waitress in a high end restaurant and, on occasion, was able to bring home leftover food from work.

Nani caught the bus to work located on the corner of Punchbowl and King Street. The unusual historical building was the site of the offices of the Mayor and City Council—a three story structure built around a large open court area where the registrar's office was situated. People from all walks of life came to register. It was a key election that would change the course of Hawai'i politics. Many came as proud Americans with the privilege of voting in the fiftieth state for the first time.

Nani met both gubernatorial candidates who had come in to register: William Quinn, the incumbent Governor and John Burns who would govern Hawai'i for the next twelve years. Nani did not realize at the time that she was in a historical setting precipitating, what some would consider, an "electoral avalanche" for the Democrats.

Preceded in 1960, by the election of John Kennedy, they would take over Hawai'i, now in its third year of statehood under the American flag. 200,441 voters turned out. The majority overwhelmingly gave their support to the Democrats who eventually came to rule every facet of Hawaiian politics, taking over the legislature as well as the National arena. Congressman Daniel Inouye won the first full term seat in the United States Senate.

Nani Banta registered and dealt with these voters who turned Hawai'i, for better or worse, into a Democratic majority.

A month after working at her job, she met a young man who was destined to change her life. She had provided him with the usual form to fill out when he came to register. He lingered awhile after signing his registration. "So, what time do you get off work?" he asked.

She looked up from the long counter she stood at. "Are you talking to me?"

"Well, you're the only one standing here. Yes, I'm talking to you."

She studied him then, taken back by his direct approach. By now she had encountered all kinds of people; very few surprised her. He stood tall over the counter; she noticed a muscular physique that was packed into a conservative blue suit, unusual in Hawai'i, unless one was in the business world. The weather was not conducive to suits, unless one was forced to wear them in his profession.

He definitely looked *haole*, but that was not a given, considering all those who looked that way in her Hawaiian school. He reminded her of the determined football players she had known on the field— not so much in his physique, but his air of confidence and aggressive demeanor. His dark brown eyes were direct, piercing and somewhat mesmerizing.

Nani tried to think of all kinds of evasive coy replies, but she simply replied, "At five."

"I'd like to take you to dinner and I wish I had the time to give you reassurances that I'm not some masher or gigolo or someone who's going to cause you harm, but I have a meeting to make right now; so just tell me 'yes or no'."

"No," she answered and concentrated on organizing the papers in front of her.

"You sure? I was thinking about steak and lobster at the Tropics and I'd have you home in plenty of time to get your beauty rest."

Nani looked up and thought about the can of corned beef she was thinking of opening to go with rice—not that she didn't love corned beef, but all week long she had eaten it with poi, mixed it with tomato sauce and peas, in a macaroni and cheese casserole, and between bread and mayonnaise. Right now steak and lobster at the Tropics sounded wonderful. So, she sold her soul for the offer.

"Alright. I'll meet you here after work."

"I'm Jason Miller and you are?"

"Nani...Nani Banta," she replied with her trademark smile that made him almost melt in front of her.

5

NANI'S FIRST DATE WITH JASON Miller did not end there. A huge price was paid for that steak and lobster. Her life was not her own after that. Jason took over every aspect of each living, breathing moment of her existence.

Jason was a graduate of Punahou, Yale, and the school of advertising. He had studied law which enabled him to be quite articulate in anything he presented, but he gave it up for something he did well—publicity, sales and marketing. You name it, he could promote it. Jason's wealthy father had advanced him starter money for his successful advertising firm; his accounts were legion with clients beating at the door to boost their businesses.

Nani became Jason's favorite promotion project. He was so caught up in her beauty—the special "it" quality she had, and all the potential ways he could market her—that he was relentless in his intent to make her a unique commodity. The thing he loved about Nani—he eventually did grow to love her—was her pliability and her acquiescence in letting him mold her.

He paid for her modeling school, her clothes, her hair dressers, and put her on Hawai'i's cover girl list. She became the most sought after model for commercial print ads—for perfumes, jewelry, resorts and anyone who would pay enough to have her as the face for their promotion. He even had her enter the Miss Hawai'i beauty contest which was a disappointment because she placed third, unable to match her tall, voluptuous competition.

Jason Miller became Nani Banta's Mr. Higgins of "My Fair Lady" she thought years later when the movie came out. She didn't mind at first and rode the wave on which Jason guided her. She was famous, flattered and unwittingly became the *charm on his arm*. Surprising her one night after a gala affair, he proposed by presenting her with a stunning diamond ring the size of one of the bumbula marbles she and her brother used to play with.

Nani convinced Jason to come home with her to meet her family. She had announced on the phone that she was getting married, much to her father's consternation, but eventual capitulation after her mother soothed his misgivings. Jason was welcomed into their humble home near the river that emptied into the bay of Kalihiwai.

The Bantas did everything they could to put him at ease. They had draped a Hawaiian print table cloth over two folding card tables to make, what they considered, an elegant presentation. Their best tableware, a roasted turkey, and all the dishes one would have at Thanksgiving were served, even though it was the second week in May, two months into Nani's twentieth year. She was deeply touched by their efforts and knew that this dinner had set them back a bit. But that was what Hawaiian hospitality was all about, and so they sat down to the rare feast in the little cottage by Kalihiwai River.

Jason was not impressed. He completely overlooked their warmth, their welcome and their hospitality. All he observed was, what he considered, the squalor they lived in—not the beauty of Kalihiwai nor that of her gracious family. He had booked a hotel room at Kaua'i Surf and could hardly wait to get back to it.

The thing that concerned him now was how to pull off a society wedding to include these people in the middle of his critical blue blood family. He'd purposefully kept his parents from meeting Nani, and they were not informed yet of his impending marriage. His dad had descended from a long line of land owners accumulating their wealth as far back as Kamehameha III who had awarded Jason's great great grandfather Miller with land in exchange for his ministerial services. Jason's mother had come from more modest roots, but acquired all the ways of pomp and ceremony over the years—something he was sure Nani could also accomplish some day.

Jason did not especially enjoy the company of his family. The pressure to succeed was always impressed upon him and what drove every aspect of his being. This did not endear them to him, but his drive was definitely a result of their influence.

Thus, the elopement came about which he decided was a genius stroke on his part—no fuss, no muss and an enjoyable honeymoon to boot which all took place on the island of Maui without friends or family except for two busboys as witnesses.

They returned to a reception at the Wai'alae Country Club that Jason told her had been put together by a few friends, but completely orchestrated with all of the special touches needed by the groom himself. Nani was presented like one of the poster ads he had created. He picked out her dress, her shoes, her hairdresser and everything that made her a replica of Jackie Kennedy at the President's Inauguration Ball. Her parents were not invited…but his attended and were far from enchanted with their new daughter-in-law. The only good part about it was that they had the class and finesse not to show it. And thus, Nani Banta from Kalihiwai was launched into society as the trophy wife of Jason Miller.

The new fairy princess was installed in her castle, an enchanting home nestled by a stream in Manoa. She thought she had walked into a dream when she first entered it. Jason had bought it as a wedding gift to himself and his new bride, and it was the site where he planned to entertain on a regular basis.

The home was a two story white colonial with a circular driveway that wrapped around a fountain pond. Two large monkey pod trees spread out their limbs over manicured lawns that surrounded the dwelling on both sides. Nani had to pinch herself as Jason enthusiastically gave her a tour of the rambling four bedroom home. Their master suite was something out of a nineteenth century picture book with a four poster *koa* bed covered in white lace.

They were happy in their first year there. In spite of his heavy work schedule, Jason was an attentive husband. Some wives would have been smothered with his hovering, his dictates and the way in which he orchestrated Nani's life, but she was flattered by his attentions and eager to learn how to be a gracious hostess in his ever growing business world.

Everything came tumbling down the day she announced to her husband that they were going to have a baby. "Get rid of it," were the first words out of his mouth.

"What do you mean, Jason?"

"I said get rid of it. We do not have room for a baby in our lives right now. Maybe not ever."

"We have plenty of room. Surely you're not serious?" she reacted, missing the meaning in his words.

"Don't worry about it, I'll find a doctor. It'll probably be on the mainland somewhere. Actually, I just thought of one I heard about in Washington State. You'll go there."

"No, Jason. I'm not going anywhere. I'm Catholic. I'll be excommunicated from my church. Besides, I would never do a thing like that."

"You are going to do what you are told and that's that Nani. I don't want to hear another word about it."

It would be the first time that Nani defied Jason's wishes. She refused to honor him in this edict, and she paid mightily on a daily basis. He was clearly frustrated knowing this was the one thing he could not force her to do. As the months went by, he grew more and more remote.

His seething anger was escalated by the fact that after seven months along in her pregnancy, she had gained almost sixty pounds. Nani's short stature did not carry this weight well. She had developed an appetite for food to feed an army, and in her depression, eating seemed to be the only thing that made her happy.

Jason did not hesitate to show his disgust for her. He ridiculed her, called her names and made her feel like "a big fat pig", a label he gave to her in a moment of anger.

Her home became a prison, no longer the site of hospitality and entertaining. He was too embarrassed for anyone to see his obese wife. When he finally decided to starve her, by removing all the food in the house, she could take no more. All her maternal instincts kicked in, and the months of verbal abuse had finally made her just as angry as her husband. This was a whole new emotion for the laughing carefree bubbly girl from Kalihiwai. Nevertheless, it fueled what followed next and propelled her to withdraw all her money from her savings account, pack her bags, call a taxi and finally board a plane for Lihue Airport on the island of Kaua'i.

She had not told her family anything except that she was coming home for a visit. Her father met her at the airport in his old Ford Truck, and she was delivered to the safe cocoon of the cottage at the river's edge in Kalihiwai Valley.

6

AFTER TWO YEARS OF COLD, wind, snow and sleet, Hekili Schmidt had enough of life in Minnesota. He abandoned his scholarship, his football career and life in America to come back to the peaceful valley of Hanalei. Hekili had a decision to make when he returned.

He descended from three generations of farmers who produced the best taro in the islands. Rice fields were also present to take advantage of the irrigation provided from one of the largest rivers in the state: the Hanalei River. The river was one of five main rivers that flowed from the high peak of Mt. Wai'ale'ale dividing Kaua'i into its various districts.

Hekili had been raised in a home on a road which led far into the low lying valley that simulated a patchwork quilt of various shades of green. It was here where his father and uncles returned every day from hard work in the fields to their family compound that consisted of several structures. Hekili's home was the largest which consisted of three bedrooms and housed his parents and four brothers. One of his uncles dwelt in a lean-to shack by himself as a confirmed bachelor, and another uncle lived with his wife and family of three boys in a two bedroom house. It was a world of men.

Hekili's mother, Hannah Schmidt was the one who had enrolled him at Kamehameha when he was accepted in seventh grade. His father was not happy about losing another hand in the field to a useless life in the big city, but his mother prevailed. The youngest son of the Schmidt family embarked on a road that eventually led him right back to where he started. This was the dilemma he was faced with when he returned from Minnesota. He was also faced with possibilities of being drafted into the military.

He had been surfing in Hanalei Bay when he ran across a schoolmate of his, Jackson Akana who had graduated a year ahead of him at Kamehameha. He told Jackson that he had to find work somewhere on the island and did not want to return to the taro fields to make a living.

"Come wit' me," said Jackson. "I going be one cop. I just got in. Dey got two openings, but you gotta pass da mustahd."

"Wow. That wasn't exactly what I had in mind, but I'll think about it."

It took him two days to consider it. He talked to his Mom first. "I think it would be good for you, Son," Hannah encouraged. "Your Kamehameha background has prepared you. You won't know if you don't try, but let's keep this under wraps until you get it. We'll face your father with the news then."

Once Hekili decided, he went all the way with a wholehearted determination. This endeavor would also solve the draft problem that he wanted to avoid. The more he learned what was required, the more he decided that he was the man for the job. He put in his application for the Kaua'i Department of Personnel Services, then took the written exam and passed. Then he filled out the personal history questionnaire and was called before the Oral Interview Board.

Having passed the muster there, he went through the process of initial background review, the suitability assessment, and the final background investigation. All this led to receiving a pre-conditioned job offer which also entailed other assessments including a polygraph, psychological review and a major physical examination.

During the interviews, background checks and assessments, he was drilled on his social competence, teamwork potential, and all the abilities—adaptability, flexibility, and conscientious dependability. Other factors considered in his make-up were impulse control, attention to safety, integrity, ethics, emotional regulation, stress tolerance, decision making, judgment, assertiveness and persuasiveness.

Hekili's military background, his leadership, and discipline on the football field at Kamehameha had prepared him to pass with flying colors. After a year, he had also completed his probationary period which included all that was required for the Police Academy and the Field Training Officer Program. If he wasn't totally fit before that, he was in top shape after it.

Hekili would be one of a small group of police officers who'd staff and patrol the three Kaua'i Police Department sectors between the Olohena Road in Kapa'a district extending to Ke'e Beach at the northern most end of Kaua'i. The district encompassed Kapa'a, Anahola, Kilauea including Kalihiwai, Princeville , Hanalei, Wainiha, and Ha'ena.

Hekili was well suited to his job. His easy temperament, patience and reliable integrity allowed him to keep cool under pressure. He had already handled petty crimes of the district: speeding, reckless driving, theft, and disorderly conduct.

He did manage to keep a middle aged Nebraska tourist from strangling his wife because she was reading the map incorrectly, but she eventually refused to press charges. That was probably the most violent incident so far. This was not a major crime district, but he was kept busy nevertheless. Wherever there were people, there would be crimes of some sort.

His co-workers took to the soft spoken Hawaiian who looked *haole*. He had never taken on pidgin in his articulation. Kamehameha had wrung that out of him, and his mother was an avid corrector of her boys' ability to speak the English standard. His brothers often wondered why she bothered. They always slipped into the broken speech of their peers when they were outside their home...but not Hekili. Cursing or foul language were exempt from his vocabulary.

At the age of twenty three, he had somewhat shaken his shyness with girls. Having been raised in a compound of eight boys and his two uncles and father, he had not had the opportunity to be comfortable with women. Being segregated in a boys' school didn't help matters either. He had dated a few girls in college, and spent time with some on Kaua'i, but they were definitely not his comfort zone.

His memory bank kept one girl hidden in its parts. She would slip into his daydreams every once in awhile and sometimes in the darkness of his sleep. He had spoken just a few words to her that would not even constitute a complete sentence…but, in his mind, he felt that he had known her all his life.

Hekili was devastated when he heard about her marriage to Jason Miller. He ran into his friend Kaulana from Kalihiwai and was informed just a week ago.

"So any news about the Banta family?" Hekili had asked him casually. He was off duty and had stopped to get something to eat at one of the stores in Hanalei when he ran into Kaulana.

"Not much. Lopaka joined da ahmy aftah he went graduate from school. So, da mom and dad got nobody in da house."

"Ah, what about the girl?" *The girl?* He couldn't even say her name.

"Oh, yah. Nani. She got married last yeeah to one big shot."

"Who?" asked Hekili, holding his breath trying to keep his shock from surfacing.

"I dunno. Some rich guy from Punahou. Imagine a girl from Kalihiwai. Nani's okay d'ough. She's one of da good ones. I t'ink she even ran foh Miss Hawai'i befoah she went get married."

"Hmm. Didn't know that," said Hekili absently, now tuning out as he tried to recover.

That was the gist of their conversation a week ago. He was still recuperating from the news. Shaking himself out of his reverie as he drove home, he wondered why he was hit so hard… but he was. And it would take awhile for him to figure out why.

7

A MONTH AFTER HEKILI DISCOVERED the news, Nani returned to Kalihiwai. No one, besides her parents, was aware of her homecoming. It took a week before she finally shared her situation.

"So, Nani, how long can we expect you to stay? You know I would be happy to help out and come to Honolulu when you have the baby," her mother offered at the breakfast table that morning. Her dad sat there with them, reading the morning papers.

"I'm not going back to Honolulu, Mom."

Her father put down the newspaper. "What?"

"What?" parroted her mom.

"I'm not going back. I left my husband for good."

They both had the same stunned expression on their faces. Nani sat there and explained. She left nothing out, in spite of the humiliation it caused her.

"He tried to starve you?" her mother almost screamed as she held her hand to her chest.

"Son of a bitch," her dad yelled. "I'll kill him."

"I wish you would," said Nani staring out into space now.

"No," that's not the answer," said her mother wanting to kill him herself.

"So, can me and Baby stay here?" asked Nani.

Bobby Banta pulled his daughter out of her chair and sat her on his lap as he used to when she was a little girl. She was a big girl now. A really big girl, but he didn't mind. She laid her head on his shoulder and nuzzled his neck.

"Don't worry, Baby. Yoah Daddy's heyah."

"Thanks, Daddy," she sobbed as she burst into tears and cried for a long time on the shoulder of her beloved father who had nurtured her and would continue to do so in the house by the river in the valley of Kalihiwai.

Nani loved her mom and dad, but her favorite person in the world was her Tutu Mileka who lived in a three bedroom home near Ha'ena Caves. The house had also been damaged in '57, but renovated and still standing in a cozy setting on a little dirt road nestled against a hill.

Tutu was riddled with arthritis and not able to get around the way she used to. She was almost eighty years old, had lost her husband twenty years before to heart failure, and lived alone ever since. She had never really been alone, because she had friends who loved and cared for her whenever she was in need. Tutu had inherited the Mahoe family home where she was raised as a child. She moved there from Kalihiwai when her husband died.

Tutu Mileka had informally adopted many a waif over the years. Her house was always open to the down-and-out and anyone who needed a safe harbor. Many of those who had grown up and gone their separate ways continued to keep in touch with her, never failing to remember her on special occasions. Nani was probably more like her than anyone. They both shared that special light that endeared them to many.

Nani wanted to see her. She begged her dad to let her drive the truck the few miles to Ha'ena from Kalihiwai. Her baby was not due for another month. She had seen a doctor in Kapa'a and was told that she was doing as well as expected. The doctor was somewhat concerned about her weight, due to the danger of toxemia, but he did not want to alarm her at this late date. The baby had dropped down, but seemed to be on schedule for the following month.

Getting into the driver's seat of the truck was difficult, but she didn't want her dad to see her struggle, so she made sure she left when he went to take his shower after work. The truck did not have adjustable seats, and her protruding belly was pressed against the steering wheel when she finally seated herself. She had to shift gears, and that was a problem with the pressure on her abdomen, but she finally got going and managed to get on the main road to her Tutu's.

When she arrived a half hour later, getting out of the truck was another problem, but she also managed that and waddled slowly towards Tutu's door. Her grandmother had not had a phone since the *tsunami's* onslaught. She had always wanted to reconnect one, but kept putting it off for eight years, so she was not expecting Nani's visit. Her home was surrounded by greenery in every tropical variety—large banana trees, giant birds of paradise, *papaya*, *mango* and avocado trees scattered amongst shrubs of *hibiscus* and *plumeria* flowers in every color. The house was surprisingly modern with its beige color and sage trim and a porch with a rocking chair to overlook the garden.

"Ah, no. What you doing heyah? I t'ought you was in da city."

Nani had not had a chance to tell her she was home. "No, Tutu, I'm home. Long story. Had to tell you in person." She put her arms around her and hugged her tightly, as snug as she could with her belly in between that was now starting to move with the baby's kicking.

"Auwe, da baby. I fohgot. You going have a little *keiki*."

"Yes, Tutu. The baby is almost here. Well, it's here," she said pointing to her stomach, "But not...you know."

"Yeah *ho'ohanau*. "

"Right. Oh Tutu, I have so much to tell you and don't know where to begin."

"Come, come sit down and put yoah feet up. Oh, Baby. Yoah ankles are swollen."

"I know, I'm a wreck." Nani sat there feeling like a bloated balloon. With tears spilling over her cheeks, she once again told her story.

"Dis is one bad man."

"I know that now, Tutu. I just feel so stupid."

"No worry, Baby. Everyt'ing's going work out. I got one idea," she said as she put her shriveled arthritic hand on her granddaughter's.

"What?"

"Plenty room heyah. You come live wit' yoah *tutu*."

"You think?"

"Yep. No room wit' yoah folks. Baby can have his own room heyah."

"His?"

"Or hers. We figah dat out when da *keiki* comes."

"I like that idea Tutu. You sure?"

"I need da company and oh, I would love to have a baby in dis house again."

"Okay, then. That's what I'll do," said Nani happily, now smiling with hope.

She stayed awhile. They went through the house and tried to figure out the rooms that she and Baby would take. The house was the perfect size for all of them and she was so much happier and thought how ideal it would be to live with her grandmother. They spent hours together. She ended up having dinner there after cooking a couple of omelets served over rice and a tossed salad on the side. When she left, it was about ten at night, and she had no way of calling her parents whom she knew would be worried by now. She bid Tutu goodbye and promised to come back in a few days.

Nani's lower back was aching now, and she thought it was due to sitting all night in a chair. She drove the old creaky truck onto the main road, and as she headed towards Hanalei around the curves near the cliffs of Lumaha'i Beach, it started to rain—not just rain, but heavy rain—rain that all of a sudden started to pour down in sheets. She had a hard time seeing the center line and as she was trying to adjust her vision, a tree limb fell on the truck.

She stepped on the brakes; the truck skidded, spun around and careened over the cliff. Everything happened at once, and she didn't have time to think until all motion had ceased. She found herself still sitting upright, facing forward. The truck had landed with its rear up on the back of the cliff and its front on a plateau like ledge that had broken its fall. If she had not landed in that particular spot, the vehicle would have toppled over the cliff to the rocks below.

She was still in deep trouble. In the process, the sharp pains that shot up her back were now excruciating. She was battered all over from the impact. In addition to that, she was sitting in a wet puddle that seeped onto the floor. It was not water from the rain. Her water had broken in the process and she had now gone into labor.

Hekili was almost ready to end his shift when he got a call to check out some kind of crash that had been heard from a neighboring house near the Lumaha'i area. He assumed it was all the noise from the storm that had just commenced, but decided to verify it anyway. He drove through the area that was still riddled with rain and noticed a tree limb in the middle of the road. He got out of his car and dragged the limb to the side of the road. As he did, he peered over the cliff and saw the truck.

He immediately got on his car radio and called for backup from the Fire department and emergency vehicles in the area. Hekili slowly skidded by foot down the slippery slope until he reached the truck.

He managed to pry open the door on the passenger side. What he saw sped his adrenaline up even more. Only two words tumbled out of his mouth.

"Oh, shit."

Lihau

Ha'iku
Maui the Valley Isle

Ha'iku, Maui

THE ISLAND OF MAUI IS the second largest in the Hawaiian chain, dominated by two volcanoes—Kahalawai which forms the West Maui Mountains, and the magnificent Haleakala of East Maui, the world's largest dormant volcano. The vast crevice of land that connects Kahalawai and Haleakala lent to Maui's designated name as "The Valley Isle".

Ha'iku lies within the north eastern shore and the upcountry of the island of Maui scattered with towering eucalyptus trees, lush greenery, grassy ranch lands and country roads sprinkled with bright colors of tropical flora growing wild amongst exotic foliage. Ha'iku's rolling hillsides graduate to elevations as high as 1,500 feet, intersected by valleys or gulches where running streams flow and rain forests are inundated with heavy rains to maintain its plant life.

The rugged oceanfront is dominated by dramatic cliffs and very little access to beach areas, except for the proximity to the town of Paia and the blue waters of Ho'okipa Beach. Ha'iku is just south of the curvy road that winds its way with views of waterfalls and steep ocean cliffs on every turn to the storybook town of Hana.

Planting of pineapple in 1860 and the eventual erection of a cannery in 1904 changed Ha'iku from an isolated community to one that attracted workers to harvest, manage and process the crop. In 1876, an elaborate ditch system was constructed to transport water from Ha'iku to the sugar plantations seventeen miles away in Wailuku.

The country setting became the home to the affluent as well as those who were just getting by, but they all enjoyed the peaceful commune with nature and the vivid beauty of this tropical paradise.

1

"DON'T CRY," LIHAU HEARD A voice say.

She sat in kukui grass with her face buried in both hands until she realized she was not alone. She looked up to see an older boy who had crouched down beside her.

Lihau removed her glasses, wiped them off on her pinafore dress, and put them back on so she could see the intruder. "Who are *you*?" she asked. They were almost face to face now.

"They call me Makena," he replied. "I'm Jesse's son." Jesse was their new gardener; he had taken the place of the man who had moved back to the Philippines.

"Oh. Then you just moved in?"

"Yeah, we live in the cottage over there. Do you live here, too?"

"Uh, huh," she nodded.

"What's your name?"

"Lihau. I'm seven years old," she answered as if that were a part of her name.

"Well, I'm twelve," said Makena to verify *his* statistics. "Who made you cry?"

Lihau sat with her chin resting on her knees, now. "Some kids. They're gone now."

"What'd they do?"

"Can't talk about it. I gotta go in now." Lihau dusted her dress off.

"Well, sorry you feel bad." Makena stood up now. He held out his hand to assist her. She grabbed it and he pulled her upright.

"Thanks," she said, then started to walk away.

"See you around, Lihau,"

"Yeah, see ya," she said as she walked back towards her house.

A variety of ginger plants—red torch, yellow blossoms, and the ones with white delicate flowers surrounded the path she tread on the way to her house—a sprawling ranch structure that stood against a wall of eucalyptus trees, its branches brushed by the wind after another heavy rain pour.

She entered the quiet domicile. No one was home at the time. The housekeeper, Fujinoko had driven to Pa'ia to get groceries. She was the only person Lihau saw on a regular basis. Lihau walked through the back into the spacious kitchen equipped with modern appliances and enough counter space to prepare meals for an army. However, there *was* no army...there was just Lihau.

She opened their refrigerator and retrieved a bowl of sliced mango; then walked past the high beamed dining and living room with enormous floor-to-ceiling glass windows that framed the eucalyptus trees outside and the rolling hills of grassland beyond. She walked down the long, long hallway past four bedrooms before she got to her own at the end of the corridor.

Fujinoko had already cleaned her room—not that she had to do too much. Lihau was a very fastidious little girl at the age of seven. She prided herself on order. Her shelves were lined with dolls in glass cases—dolls from all over the world—a colorful geisha from Japan, a Dutch maid from Holland, a can-can dancer from Paris, a Chinese Princess, an African washer woman, an English queen...on and on around the room they were placed.

But the only one she played with sat on her four-poster white canopied bed in a special place in the middle of her pink laced pillows. Her name was Mele and she was Lihau's only friend. Mele was an infant sized, dark skinned doll with long jet black hair with the kind of roots that could be brushed often. She had an entire wardrobe that she wore on different days; sometimes she was changed several times on the same day. But no matter what she wore, she was Lihau's Hawaiian doll and her best friend. Mele was the only one she talked to.

She sat Mele at the little table they shared together and took the small chair on the other side. She put her bowl of sliced mangoes on the table, picked up a piece as she savored the taste in her mouth and told Mele about her day.

Lihau could not share with Makena what went on today. It was really nothing new to her, but so humiliating—not that the word was in her vocabulary, but it described her constant dilemma when confronted with other children as well as the few adults she encountered.

Victoria Lihau Leng had been born in Honk Kong to Thomas Hotung Leng and Mary Kamalei McKinnon. The word Lihau sounded Chinese and the reason why Thomas let Kamalei choose the Hawaiian name which translated to *gentle cool rain* or *moist and fresh like dew laden air* in reference to the climate in her mother's hometown of Ha'iku.

Thomas Leng was an elegant Eurasian with aristocratic roots on both sides of his British Chinese origins. His maternal line stemmed from the original British colonialists who had aggressively changed Hong Kong from a rocky underdeveloped mountainous terrain to a thriving global trade metropolis after it was claimed under Queen Victoria in 1840 and ceded from the last dynasty of Imperial China. Thomas's father, who was associated with this change, held a prominent position as a paid Chinese liaison between the British and the resident Chinese. He was also related to the famous leader of the Hong Houses, well known sites of business, influential in consumer goods, trade and manufacturing.

His family background helped Thomas to acquire a key place in Hong Kong society and enabled him to be front and center in its political realm as well as a successful financier. He had traveled to Honolulu in 1941 and then to Maui to meet with a business associate. In the middle of the bombing of Pearl Harbor, he found himself stranded there for two months, unable to get passage back to Hong Kong. It was at a place in Lahaina, Maui where he first laid eyes upon Kamalei McKinnon.

He was forty years old at the time, never been married, and yet pursued throughout the world as one of the elite's most eligible bachelors with droves of women at his beck and call. Kamalei, a lovely *hapa haole* in her early twenties, had been in a group of friends, known to members of the band who were playing at the Pioneer Inn. She was summoned on stage to dance the hula to a superb rendition of one of Charles King's songs.

Thomas Hotung Leng was never the same. He pursued her with the same determination he put into his business deals. In two weeks he had whisked her far away from her home in Ha'iku to Honk Kong where they were married.

Kamalei had to make quite an adjustment to the fast paced world of finance and ambitious aristocrats, but quickly learned the customs of both British and Chinese alike. She had a crash course in her education, prompted and taught by Thomas Leng's paternal grandmother. His own mother had not been of much use in that department—never quite accepting any woman in her son's life—and certainly not open to a Hawaiian *nobody* from the hills of Ha'iku.

Three years later Lihau was born in Hong Kong to what should have been a home fit for a princess. Unfortunately, the princess was not the dream baby her parents expected. She had all kinds of ailments as an infant that kept her mother and nannies worried round the clock. Much to her father's disappointment, she did not resemble her picture perfect parents in any way.

Lihau was born with one eye that was positioned to look inward. In her first two years she had numerous exams and was diagnosed as having a severe vision problem. She eventually had an operation to correct the one lazy eye, but at three years old, was forced to wear glasses to enhance her sight. Her almond shaped eyes were an unusual color, almost turquoise, with a tinge of gray around the iris, so they were uniquely luminescent in color, but could not function without corrective lenses.

Lihau's plumpness, which remained with her past the age of *baby fat,* did not help to enhance her physical appeal, nor did it endear her to her critical father who was all about image in his world of refinement. Her mother loved her, nevertheless. Kamalei, however, was under constant pressure to leave Lihau in order to accompany her world traveling husband.

Thomas Leng owned homes all over the world—a luxury apartment in Hong Kong that encompassed a whole floor of a high rise building, another one in Paris, a villa on the French Riviera, and a New York suite. As a gift to his wife who inherited her family dwelling when both parents passed away, he built a rambling six bedroom house next to the one where she had lived in lovely Ha'iku, the land of her roots—the place Kamalei continued to think of as her home.

When Lihau was five, her mother moved her there without a hint of regret on the part of her father. Lihau barely saw him after that. He was like a phantom figure who had only visited once in the two years she had been in Ha'iku.

Kamalei was raised by her grandmother who recently passed away; her father had worked in the pineapple plantation in Ha'iku. He and his wife both died from influenza within three months of each other while Kamalei was away in Hong Kong. She had inherited the two bedroom house on the large piece of Ha'iku land before Thomas built her dream house.

She wanted Lihau to be brought up in her homeland and had every intention of being there on a frequent basis, but Thomas kept making excuses to keep her in Hong Kong or by his side as he traveled. Most of the time, the little girl was home alone with Fujinoko who became her housekeeper, nanny and surrogate mother.

Fujinoko barely spoke English, but she and Lihau developed their own communication which was adequate. This relationship and her mother's sporadic visits were the only sources of nurturing for the lonely child.

Lihau sat on the frilly chair near the side of her bed and dressed Mele in a new outfit, thinking about what had preceded her crying bout. Four boys who seemed to be a couple years older and a little girl about her age were playing on a rope on which they had secured an old tire they were using as a swing. The rope had been tied to a sprawling mango tree in a place near an open field where many of the kids gathered and played ball as well as other games. The field was adjacent to her property, and she would often watch them play there. She had worked up the nerve today to join them as they laughed and took turns on the swing.

One of the boys turned to her and said, "You like try?"

"Umm, okay," she almost whispered.

One of the other boys yelled, "No way, we ain't going have no four eyes on our swing."

"Yeah, she might break da goggles she's wearin," said another boy.

"Moh like coke bottles dan goggles," said the fourth boy.

"Plus she's fat. She going break da swing and den what we going use aftah dat," said the first boy who objected.

The little girl who was about her age, didn't say anything. She just put her hands over her mouth and laughed out loud.

Lihau ran away from them without saying a word until she got into her yard where Makena found her crying. It was summertime and there was no school. Lihau liked school. She was very smart and she liked to learn things, but anything that brought her together with other children was often torture for her. She had encountered this kind of teasing before, even in school.

She told Mele all about her day. Mele understood. She was her best friend.

2

MAKENA LAU LIVED WITH HIS dad, Jesse in Kamalei's two bedroom childhood home which was now designated to the caretakers of the property. It was luxurious compared to what they had occupied before. Makena's *haole* mother left his father when he was three years old and never returned to the islands. She had come from California to Maui and married what she thought was the man of her dreams. That lasted three years after she had given birth to their only child.

She was eventually disillusioned by the poverty they lived in and found that her husband was not what she wanted for the rest of her life. So, she took the first offer she received and ran away with a man who could satisfy her needs. Her husband had begged her to leave his son behind, and she had no qualms about that. Apparently—none at all—for they never heard from or saw her again.

Makena barely remembered her now. He so appreciated living in the wide open spaces of the five acre parcel they called home. His dad taught him the art of caring for all the plant life in their charge— pruning, trimming, fertilizing, weeding, watering, cutting down the ever growing plantation grass, and mowing the expansive lawn that they kept trimmed and manicured.

Jesse, the son of a Hawaiian mother and Chinese father who worked the pineapple plantation in Ha'iku, was a man of few words. Makena loved him and had no complaints about their life together. Jesse lived in Ha'iku as a child and wanted to return to the area. A friend of his had recommended him for the job at the Leng estate. They had lived in a shack in the city of Wailuku on a busy street behind a supermarket where cars and people were constantly in their midst. Ha'iku was heaven to both of them.

Makena observed Lihau over the next few weeks—a strange child he thought—always dressed in starched pinafore dresses, socks, and patent leather Mary Janes as if she were going to a birthday party with her horn rimmed glasses that made her look older than her seven years. Wherever she played—if that was what one could call it—she carried her Hawaiian doll.

Makena was not big on sentiment at the age of twelve, but something about this little girl pulled at his heartstrings. He was well aware by now, that her housekeeper was the only adult who watched over her. At first he thought the lady was her mother, but she wore a uniform every day, just as his father was expected to wear his army greens when he worked.

"Dad, where are the owners of the big house?"

"The Lengs? Thomas and Kamalei Leng are the people I work for."

"I've never seen them."

"They're mostly in Hong Kong, but return on occasion."

"Is that little girl theirs?"

"Yes, I think her name is Lihau, poor thing."

"Why you say that?"

"Oh, I don't know. I feel sorry for her all alone in that big house."

"She's not alone. She has that lady with her."

"Yes, I guess you're right, but it's not the same."

"The same as what?"

"Boy, you've got a lot of questions tonight, "Jesse said, smiling at his son over the dinner table in their small kitchenette. "The same as having a mother."

"I don't have a mother, and you don't feel sorry for me."

"You have a father and sometimes I do feel sorry for you."

"Ah, Daddy, I'm fine," said Makena, still curious about the little girl.

The next time, he saw Lihau, she was crying again. He didn't have to ask her *why* this time. The same kids were standing by the ranch style fence that surrounded the property, jeering at her. She held Mele in her arms and tears were running down her face.

"Four eyes, bubble eyes, can't even catch flies. How now brown cow, you're a sow, bow wow," sang one of the boys who was now on such a roll with his rhyming genius that he did not notice the tall Hawaiian twelve year old behind him, nor did he notice that his laughing audience was silent now.

His name was Kapali and the other little girl called his name out to warn him. Too late. Kapali was lifted high above the ground by the collar of his shirt. He was choking, now face to face with the older boy. Makena did not say a word as he slapped him once on the left cheek, then on the right, then on the left and on the right again.

"If I ever catch you teasing her again, you die," said Makena. "Understand? Don't speak. Just nod your head," he said as Kapali now started to turn blue, choked by his collar.

Kapali nodded as well as he could. Makena dropped him to the ground. He lay there choking, sputtering and muttering under his breath. "Say you're sorry to Lihau," Makena commanded.

"Sorry," Kapali said still choking on the ground.

"No. You get up and look her in the eye and say, 'Lihau I'm sorry I hurt your feelings and I'll never do it again." Makena prompted. "And act like you mean it."

Kapali brushed himself off, rubbing his neck now with his right hand. Then he spoke the words he was instructed to use.

"Now...do the rest of you think you're going to be mean to Lihau again?" Makena addressed the group of the young hoodlums.

"We were just having fun with her," said the little girl.

"Look at her, does she seem like she's having *fun*?" spat out Makena.

They all glanced at her sad face where the tears had dried. The other four shook their heads. "Sorry, Lihau," the little girl was the first to speak. The boys followed suit and repeated what had now become the mantra for the moment. They all turned to leave with the injured boy who was still rubbing his neck...probably thinking about how he had just escaped being murdered in the fields of Ha'iku amongst the eucalyptus trees and ginger plants everywhere.

3

Lihau at seventeen years old was a junior at Kamehameha now. Two years ago in her freshman year, she had arrived in her dorm for the first time to find her roommate unpacking and getting ready for orientation. "Are you Lihau?" said the pretty girl in her cozy room with its simple furnishings.

"Uh, huh," replied Lihau.

"I'm Nani," said the girl, her voice bright and enthusiastic as she got up from bending over her suitcase. She walked over to Lihau and, instead of shaking hands, put her arms around her and hugged her tightly. "I'm so glad to meet you and I hope we'll be really good friends," she said cheerfully with a radiant smile.

"Oh, I hope so too," Lihau smiled blissfully, and from that moment on, the two ninth grade girls contracted to be the best of friends for life. What Nani did not know was that she was Lihau's *first* friend…ever.

She was not Nani's roommate when they began their junior year, but they were in the same dorm and always together in one room or the other. It was Nani's second year as a song leader. Nani was popular, well liked and, because Lihau was her best friend, Lihau reaped the benefits. She was treated kindly, with respect and often included in whatever activities involved Nani.

As a result of her high scores in testing and her former grades transferred to Kamehameha, Lihau had been placed in A section, the same one as Kia Kea. Having made the honor roll every semester, Lihau excelled in most of her subjects, absorbing her lessons like a sponge. Kamehameha was good for her. She thrived on being in the social environment of girls and felt herself gradually emerging from her shyness.

Devoid of any athletic ability, the one class Lihau hated was PE. She felt clumsy, self conscious and useless when it came to doing anything that put her brain together with the activities of her body. The most humiliating aspect was the assignment that divided the girls into two categories: All Stars and No Stars. The No Stars hated their status and were practically ignored by the PE teachers. Kia Kea was an All Star, of course, and excelled in every sport she played.

Lihau, by now, had lost her roundness and the excess weight that followed her well into her pre-teen years. She now had the early stages of a decent figure which was slowly developing into something that she felt was not that bad—especially after all she suffered over the years for her mild obesity. She had stopped binging on sweets which had been her only reward to make up for her loneliness. Being at Kamehameha helped that void, and her eating became more balanced and sensible. She was fair skinned, having little access to the sun in Ha'iku, and actually had a waist now. She still wore her glasses, but that no longer mattered, for there were others who did the same.

No one was ever aware of the wealth she had come from. Boarders were only allowed a certain amount of clothing and their styles were also limited with all the dress codes at school. Lihau was just another girl at Kamehameha and that was fine with her. She was no longer a *non-person* as she considered herself for her first fourteen years. She was somebody now—she was Nani's best friend.

Lihau and a girl named Jenny Kamako from her section had been designated to take their Trigonometry class during last period at Boys School. They were two of the few girls who had been able to transcend the boundaries between the two campuses. Any other girl would have been thrilled, but Lihau's feelings of inadequacy were multiplied by this assignment. She did manage to do well—actually more than well when she started getting A's on a continual basis. The boys were her counterparts in A section, and a few began to notice her genius which was becoming evident.

A boy named Connor Kahana started talking to her one day after class. "Where's your friend?" he asked as she walked down the hall towards the stairs that led up the hill to the Girls School.

"You mean, Jenny?" He nodded and walked beside her now. "Oh, I think she's dropping out to take another class."

"So, you going be the only girl down here, by yourself."

"Yes. Not my choice, believe me," she said as the first words burst forth from her mouth in the presence of a boy at Kamehameha.

"Ah, poor thing. I'll walk you up the stairs so you won't be so lonely."

And that was the beginning of her friendship with Connor who was in her eyes the kindest boy she'd ever met since Makena. They were just friends. She knew he had no other interest in her, but it was one more thing that added to her security in school. Connor came from the Big Island and boarded in Liholiho Dorm where A company cadets stayed

Since the Trig class was the last period of the day, Lihau was sometimes able to see the boys gather on Mawaena Field and line up for their Hui scrimmage teams which were designated according to companies. Most of them were boarders. They had Hawaiian names and colors for each team that were worn on their tee shirts when they played: Company A—**Mo'i** (supreme) green; Company B—**Eleu** (alert) red; Company C—**Imua** (forward) yellow; Company D—**Kilakila** (strong) gray, and the team for battle group staff, drill team and band **Ali'i** (chief) were blue. These teams played their seasonal games against each other in the spirit of competition. Baseball was the sport of the moment. The green, red, yellow, gray, and blue tee shirts could be purchased by all students at the school store. Even the girls wore their favorite company's shirt.

It was the spring of Lihau's junior year. Junior prom was on the horizon, an event Lihau dreaded with the dilemma it presented her. She would have definitely avoided the whole thing, if it weren't for all the pressure put on her by her classmates. It was all anyone talked about. She was going to work up the nerve to ask Connor, but he casually mentioned that he already had a date.

"Going to prom?" he asked one day.

"Uh, no, I don't think so," Lihau answered, half way hoping he would ask her.

"I am.

"Oh, that's nice," she replied keeping a blank expression.

"Hey, I know what. Maybe you could double date with us. I have a friend who hasn't asked anyone yet. Lemme talk to him.

"That's alright. You don't have to do that, Connor."

"I know, but it would be fun having you there."

Lihau had no idea what he meant by that and decided not to ponder it after her mild disappointment, which she was used to by now. She did end up going to prom with one of Connor's friends, but she'd rather have gone to a torture chamber of a Laos prison camp than have to endure that nightmare again.

The first red flag she encountered was the minute her date arrived at her dorm to escort her. He took one look at Lihau and threw the lei he had around her neck without the customary kiss. He really didn't have to kiss her, she thought—not passionately, ardently or anything like that, but surely a nice peck on the cheek to go with the thick red carnation lei would have sufficed.

She was dressed in Nani's blue chiffon, a bit tight around the waist and too loose for her in the bust line—definitely not the dress to go with a double red carnation lei. (Nani borrowed another dress for the night and graciously loaned Lihau her only prom dress). One of the girls had helped Lihau style her hair in a teased bouffant to make her resemble Jackie Kennedy, but instead of the ravishing first lady, she looked like something that would have attracted a swarm of bees or small tarantulas. Plunk her horn rimmed glasses in the middle of the effect to complete the unruly look, and she became a sight to behold.

Her date, Leroy Aki, behaved even worse at the dance which was held in the usual place at the Prep School dining hall. They were with Connor and his beauty from Punahou, a blonde vivacious, chattering socialite, whom Leroy paid more attention to than his Jackie Kennedy date in blue chiffon and red carnation. She knew that the only reason why Connor asked her to dance once was out of sympathy for her and irritation at Leroy who never danced with her at all.

In spite of her high academics, intelligence and wisdom in some matters, Lihau Leng could not think of a thing to say all evening. She was almost grateful to the verbal socialite who took the attention away as her audience of three ended up listening to her endless stories, some of which were entertaining, and *all* of them about herself

4

Lihau went home to Ha'iku for the summer a couple months after her first prom. She was not pleased to hear that her father would be there. She had seen Thomas so seldom over the years that she barely knew him. Her parents did not come to the Kahului airport when she arrived. Fujinoko was sent to pick her up, but that was not unusual.

When she entered the door of the Ha'iku home, her mom rushed to greet her. "Ah, Lihau, Lihau, I'm so glad to see you." Kamalei hugged her tightly and then pulled away to examine her. "Let me look at you. My, my, how you've grown! I wouldn't recognize you. You look so, so… wonderful." Then she hugged her again.

Kamalei was even more elegant, now dressed in her traditional Chinese attire—this one in lime brocade—a high necked short sleeved *cheongsam*. Her hair was drawn tightly back from her face in a severe knot revealing her flawless face tinged with color that showed her elation.

She saw how much her daughter had changed—no longer the plump, little girl with her inadequate blankness stamped on her face. That was an unkind memory of her only child, but Kamalei was pleased with the girl who faced her now. Lihau wore a simple puffed sleeved dress that flared out from what was clearly a waist now. She noticed that her daughter had the clear fair skin of her husband's Eurasian ancestors, and that her light blue eyes behind her glasses had a brightness Kamalei had not seen before. Lihau's hair had grown a bit, past that Jackie Kennedy beehive she had worn two months ago to the disastrous prom, and fell naturally almost touching her shoulders.

Kamalei wiped a tear from her eye and hugged her daughter again, not able to get enough of her or to veil the guilt she had carried over the years. She had not wanted to leave this child to fend for herself. That was not the way Kamalei had been raised. But she had to choose her fate and…it had been her husband's wishes that she'd succumbed to.

Recently, she had questioned that choice even more. Over the last year, she'd expressed her need to be with Lihau in Ha'iku. She had threatened to leave him, and to appease her, he had relented and allowed her to come home. Thomas felt his wife slipping away from him, and suspected that she meant it this time. There had been other times. He knew Kamalei had been aware of his intermittent affairs over the years—but surely he had reasoned—she could not have taken them seriously.

Thomas lived in a bubble that encased him in having the world his way. His wife was a part of that world. She would not be going anywhere. Not without him. He needed a break from the fast paced demanding life in Hong Kong, and life in peaceful Ha'iku would be a reprieve. What Kamalei did not know was that Thomas Leng had acquired enemies over the years.

He had been involved in a few shady deals that involved opium trade, not uncommon when connected with Hong Kong's free trade, but Thomas had taken a cut in transactions as a liaison where he acquired payments that were beyond what either buyer or seller received. In addition to his notorious business deeds, he had insulted certain prominent members of China's elite when they were refused entry into some of the clubs which he had spearheaded for his business ventures. He had also offended communist refugees when he put a halt to their activities and exposed them for strikes they organized for dock workers. There were other reasons why he attracted the disdain of many, and he made sure they were all kept at bay.

His wife was unaware that the small entourage with whom he constantly travelled was not a contingent of business associates; they were bodyguards. Their briefcases were not full of important papers, but contained machine guns and high powered weapons that could be easily assembled at a moment's notice.

Wherever Thomas traveled, the guards were with him. They always had a hotel room adjacent to his with connecting doors. They were not large imposing men, but average looking Chinese citizens in business suits who had been trained by the best in martial arts, weaponry and defensive skills that, if tested, could annihilate an entire army... or at least incapacitate a large portion of its members.

Thomas realized that the safest place in the world he could land right now would be in the secluded haven of Ha'iku. He decided not to bring the *entourage*.

He greeted his daughter at dinner, having been on the phone all afternoon and well into the twilight time before they had their meal together. Thomas usually dressed formally. Tonight, what he wore was informal, but elegant—a white dragon silk suit with high split neck and Chinese button knots down the front.

"Victoria, how are you?" He inquired, using her first name with which she'd been christened after the Queen who had originally claimed the territory of Hong Kong.

"I'm fine Father." That was the only way she was allowed to address him—not the European, *Papa* or Americanized *Dad* or *Daddy*. He had always been *Father* to her.

Kamalei stiffened at this formal exchange. Surely her husband could find some kind of show of affection for the child he had hardly seen in her seventeen years of living. She was trained to overlook this sort of thing, but watched her daughter's face the whole time.

"I have been keeping up with reports about your studies. I see your grades are really quite adequate. Of course we'll never know how they would compare with the Central School in Hong Kong that I would've preferred...but your mother insisted on... what is the name of that confounded school for indigents?"

"Kamehameha, Father. I am happy there. "*I have friends for the first time in my life.*

"Well, happiness is not what life is all about, is it?"

"What is life about?" she inquired tilting her head to receive the reply she already knew the answer to.

"It is about building success, in becoming acceptable to those who count, those who can promote that success and make you a respected person."

"A respected person. Hmm. I'll have to think about that." She knew she was exposing her cynicism and planned on reining herself in any minute now.

Her mother attempted to save her. "Lihau, tell us about school and all the friends you've made."

"I have a friend named Nani. We've known each other for two years now. She's a song leader, very pretty and so good to me."

"Where is Nani from?" inquired Kamalei trying to stay on what she thought was a safe subject.

"Kalihiwai in Kaua'i."

"What does her father do?" piped in Thomas.

"He's a fisherman and I think he does gardening too."

"He does this for a living?"

"Yes, he does. Nani said he works hard to put food on the table for them."

He glowered at his wife. "You see what happens when she is sent to a school like this. She is consorting with daughters of fishermen and such—a disgrace to us. You're fortunate you only have one more year in that place, Victoria. I would take you out now if it was not too late. But know this, I will have first choice when it comes to picking your university, and I'm not even sure if the best one's in the United States."

Kamalei glanced at her daughter with a look that signaled two things to her—one was not to react and the other was that she had her sincere support. Lihau got the message and remained silent.

These excruciating dinners continued and Lihau learned to dread them. She so wanted to go back to being the lonely girl of Ha'iku—anything but the torture of her father's presence.

One night he announced that he was planning a dinner party for the following week. "Victoria, we are having prominent people from Maui and a few dignitaries from the Honolulu area. I have made a list and there will probably be a hundred in attendance. Your mother has been instructed to make sure that you are looking your best. She will get you the proper clothes and whatever it takes to make you presentable. You are not to wear those God-awful glasses at the affair. Is that clear?"

"But Father, how will I be able to see?"

"It's not how you will see that's important, but how you will be *seen*?"

"Thomas, I think that is an unreasonable request. She can't possibly function without her glasses," protested her mother.

"It's not a request, Kamalei, it's a command. She should have been fitted for contact lenses years ago. Surely with all the money I've allotted for her, you could have seen to that."

"Well, we can certainly arrange that later, but one week is not enough time."

"I have an idea," suggested Lihau. "Maybe I could just stay in my room during the party."

"This discussion is over," warned her father. "Kamalei, it's your job to see to her appearance and you *do* know how I want that to go." He stood up, threw his napkin on the table and stormed out of the room.

The Ha'iku party was in progress with caterers and serving people dressed to the nines, sparkling crystal, polished silver and enough candles lit to start a bonfire. The island's elite were there in addition to governing politicians, Hawaiian royalty, diplomatic dignitaries and major business owners from O'ahu who had flown in for the special occasion. Lihau stayed in her room until she was summoned by her father. She thought maybe he wouldn't notice her absence, but he did, not because he missed her, but because he had already made the point to have her there.

She actually looked rather stunning, in a black form fitting strapless gown that made her look years older. Her hair had been set in large rollers by a personal hairdresser and make-up artist who had come to the house a few hours before. After a facial, moisturizers, and all it took to transform her face, her hair was styled, teased back from her face, pinned up on the sides, and curled back to flow over her shoulders. Her mother, elegantly dressed in a red brocade *cheongsam*, had come in to her room to see the transformation. She was very pleased.

"Ah, Lihau. You look wonderful."

"Am I acceptable, now Mom?"

"You've always been acceptable to me, Lihau."

"Thanks for saying that."

"I'm not just saying it. Lihau, I mean it." Kamalei said this with tears in her eyes. She seemed to have a lot of tears lately. The last thing Lihau wanted was to make her mother cry.

"He's still serious about the glasses?"

"Yes, Lihau, I'm afraid he is."

After Lihau finally decided to join the party, things went well for about fifteen minutes when she could stand still in one place. But maneuvering across a room was another thing. Her long gown and three inch heels did not help matters much. She was coaxed by her mother ahead of time to introduce herself to their guests. Taking a deep breath, she stumbled her way through the crowd greeting people, and managing to pick up a glass of champagne here and there for fortitude. The fortitude did not last long when she introduced herself to the same group of people three times, not recognizing their blurred faces when they moved to a different part of the room.

She did this with others, until one of the rude ones finally said, "You know, Lihau this is the third time we've met. We know your name by heart now."

Whoops. She just hoped her father would not get word of this. They were seated at dinner at round tables in the large tented patio. She could not see her food, nor could she gage the distance of bringing food from her plate to her mouth. Pieces of filet mignon, green salad and mashed potatoes ended up on her lap. Her father *did* notice this because he was seated across from her. He quietly stood up from his seat and beckoned her away from the table.

"Victoria, we are going to have to take a vacuum cleaner to your dress if you don't stop spilling things."

"I'm sorry Father. I could do a lot better if I had my glasses on."

"Absolutely not. Just excuse yourself and don't eat anymore." So, she ate no further and headed towards another glass of champagne.

Lihau went into more panic when it was time to dance. She certainly wasn't expected to dance was she? A full piece orchestra had been hired and several young men and old alike came to ask the attractive girl with food stains all over her pretty gown to dance. Well, that in itself was a disaster. She not only tripped over her gown, but stepped on toes, eventually losing her equilibrium when some exuberant middle aged man twirled her across the room where she landed on the floor, putting a halt to her attempt at dancing.

The final faux pas occurred after her fall on the dance floor when she hurried to exit the room and bumped into a tuxedoed waiter bearing a tray full of champagne flutes. The tray toppled; all twelve glasses were tossed up in the air, and champagne went flying everywhere finding a home on the family's priceless Oriental rug. One nearby lady screeched as if a tornado had hit her, when it was actually just a small amount of champagne that landed on her dress.

Thomas stood in a group of people observing the fiasco and Lihau's eyes connected with his. She remembered the phrase *If looks could kill…* and she immediately headed towards the entry door and out into the cool clear night. She removed her heels and ran down the path into the darkness; then plunked down on the grass, rested her elbows on her knees, face in hands, and cried her eyes out…the eyes that were not wearing her horn rimmed glasses.

"Don't cry," she heard a familiar voice in the dark.

She sucked up a heaving sob and looked up to see a tall figure there. That's all she could see. Then he brought his face down to hers as he squatted in the grass. Ten years ago, he had done the same thing.

"Makena," she whispered

5

Makena Lau had not talked to Lihau Leng in a long time. He had been her champion those many years ago. She had seen him often before she attended Kamehameha when he worked with his father on the property, and once in awhile, he would stop to chat with her.

When he was fourteen, he started playing football; so most of his time was taken up with that and other sports including basketball and track. Then when Lihau was twelve, he graduated from Maui High and went away to school on a football scholarship at the University of Colorado. He had been away for five years and had just returned a week ago. Unlike most college students, he did not have the money to come home for holidays or summers.

Jesse had worked hard and drove his son to better himself. He did not want him to end up in his profession. It was Jesse's gentle coaxing and encouragement to do well in sports as well as school that enabled Makena to succeed in attaining a scholarship. He finished with a degree in engineering. Undecided what he was going to do in the future, for now, he was happy to be home in Ha'iku.

"There, there, nothing could be that bad," he said in a soothing tone.

"It's ss...so bbad that I ccccan't ev..en ss..see *you*."

"What are you talking about, Lihau?"

She pulled her gown up over her face and wiped her eyes, then blew her nose on her dress. She didn't care about anymore decorum at this point and was feeling like a complete failure, so why not let it all go and act like one. She stopped crying and felt a little better now. All she saw was a blur in the dark, but well aware it was Makena—Makena her hero of so many years ago. She had just about worshiped him for his rescue then, and now...

She looked up and put her arms around his neck from her sitting position and practically pulled him down to the ground where she was sitting. She had sipped on quite a few glasses of champagne to fortify her for the evening's events which was the reason why she did the next thing in her desperation. She kissed him when she finally found his lips in the dark and something nice resulted from her daring deed ... he kissed her back.

Makena held Lihau for a moment and rubbed his hands over her back. "What happened tonight, Lihau?"

"Oh, Makena, I made a complete fool out of myself. My father wouldn't let me wear my eye glasses, and I couldn't see a thing. I kept introducing myself to the same people, then I dropped food all over my dress; I went to dance and tripped over my skirt and somebody twirled me across the room. I went crashing down on the floor, and then I hurried out and bumped into the waiter, and all the champagne glasses went flying...and then my father..." she paused for a moment.

"What?" Makena asked, trying so hard not to burst out laughing.

"My father looked at me like he wanted to kill me, and I ran outside and here you were."

"Ah, Lihau. You've certainly had a night of it." He attempted again to sound grave and knew he must not laugh now.

"Yes, I have. And on top of it all, I will die of embarrassment tomorrow morning when I realize I had too much champagne and made you kiss me."

"Now, don't add that to everything else. You didn't make me kiss you. I wanted to."

"You did? Why?"

"Because I just did that's why. And I enjoyed it."

"Then do it again," she petitioned.

And he held her face in his hands in the dark and kissed her again right there under the stars in the garden of the house in beautiful Ha'iku on the Valley Isle of Maui.

6

WHEN MAKENA SAW LIHAU AGAIN, she was wearing her new contact lenses. It had taken a week to get used to them, but she was fine now and felt much more confident about her appearance. She wavered about that, though. She hated that it was a condition required for her father's approval. She was really not happy about his presence in *her* house.

She had a car now and her driver's license for a year. Lihau suspected that her mom, out of guilt, had sent money to Fujinoko to purchase an automobile for her sixteenth birthday. She and Fujinoko had gone to a Used Car lot in Wailuku to purchase it. She picked out a black MG sports car and learned to work the stick shift in a week. She had to return to school a week later, so this was really the fifth time she had driven it. She had gone to the small town of Pa'ia and cruised around Makawao, but that was all.

She almost bumped into Makena when walking down the stone path of her house towards the driveway. He was startled to see her and surprised at her appearance in the light of day. She wore white shorts with a blue scoop-neck tee shirt, her thick black hair swinging in a pony tail and her long legs looked pretty darn good, thought Makena. This was the first time he had seen her eyes so clearly, and he was caught up in the aquamarine color that stared up at him from long thick lashes.

Now that she had her new eyes on, Lihau could examine him too. Five years had certainly changed him. He was twenty three years old now, standing tall, muscular from his football training, raven hair falling over his forehead and brushing the back of his neck. She recognized her twelve year old hero in his warm brown eyes and now remembered kissing him, feeling a flush across her face.

"Wow," he blurted.

"Wow, what?" she scowled.

"Wow, you, that's what," he grinned as he gazed into her eyes.

She smiled and cocked her head to the side, "Really?"

"Really."

"Wanna come with me?" she invited.

"Where?"

"Anywhere, but here."

"Okay," he easily replied. "Lemme tell my dad and I'll be right back."

He returned in a few minutes, changed from work clothes into shorts and a yellow tee shirt that read *Pineapples Rule*. "Okay, I'm ready," he announced. She was leaning against her sports car and he reached over and opened her door for her. The top was down, so he hopped over into the passenger seat.

"Where to?" she asked.

"What about Hana? Let's go to Hana. Haven't been there in years."

"Okay. That sounds great." She put the car in first gear, bumped forward a bit, shifted into second, then third and took off. He wondered how long she'd been driving, but decided not to say anything, admiring her legs as she maneuvered the car.

The MG wound around the country roads until they reached the Hana Highway, turned right and headed for Hana. They drove awhile, and Makena told her to make another right after the next bridge. "I wanna show you something," he said. You've probably been here before."

"Makena, I have not been anywhere but Ha'iku."

"Amazing. How could that be, Lihau? You've lived here since you were...what seven?

"Five," she answered.

"I guess Fujinoko wasn't up to taking you around?"

"Not really. We pretty much went to the market and back to the house. Then there was school of course, but Ha'iku was it for me as far as Maui 's concerned."

He thought about that for a moment, feeling some anger at her situation and her parents' neglect. "Well, we'll have to fix that. This'll be our first stop. I want to see this place again. You feel up to a small hike?"

"Sure." *Anywhere with you, Makena.*

After they turned by the bridge, they stopped the car and secured the canvas roof in place. He waited for her to join him, grabbed her hand and started walking. She liked that simple gesture and didn't want to read anything into it. No one had ever held her hand to go anywhere.

They followed a short path to a grassy park and continued on for about ten minutes beside a stream. When they reached Makena's destination, there below them was a magnificent waterfall which he explained was Lower Puohokamoa Falls. The water dropped from the cliff where they stood, cascading down more than a hundred feet over steep lava rocks into a dark pool of water.

Makena stood with his hands on her shoulders as they peered down into the waterfall, crashing over the rocks below. "Cool, huh?"

"Wonderful," she said as she put her right hand over his. He turned her around, looked at her for a moment, and kissed her, the most romantic kiss she had ever received there on the cliffs overlooking Puohokamoa Falls near the road to Hana.

He held her hand again down the path to their car and they continued on their journey. For two hours they drove, making a couple stops to see the spectacular views. There were curves with splashing waterfalls on the right that ran down sheer lava hillsides, and to the left were crevices with steep ocean cliffs that met an unusual variety of black, red and white sandy beaches. In other places, fields of *taro* patches and agricultural vistas could be viewed from the winding road as well as the vast Pacific Ocean that stretched forever towards a far horizon beyond.

At one point when they stopped, peering down towards the ocean, Lihau stood and let the trade winds blow through her hair as she raised her face up to the radiant sun. She had never been happier. She pondered— all this had practically been in her own back yard for the twelve years she had resided in Ha'iku—and no one had bothered to bring her here. She thought of the little homely girl who could barely see without her glasses and all the loneliness that surrounded her... again, tears came to her eyes.

"What's wrong, Lihau?" asked Makena.

"Poor Makena. You always seem to be asking me that question. Every time we see each other, you see me cry. Do you realize you're the only one who has?"

He shook his head. "But why now?"

"It's a different kind of crying now. They're tears of happiness. Thank you, Makena for coming with me." She turned to face him as she said this.

"You're welcome," he smiled. He put his arms around her, holding her snug against him, gazing into her sparkling blue eyes and once again, he kissed her there on the site overlooking the steep ocean cliffs on the road to Hana.

They had a wonderful day in Hana. They went to a Japanese Market to get food for a picnic, sat on the black sand beach at Wai'anapanapa State Park strewn with *hala* trees and ate their lunch, then went swimming in the ocean. Lihau had a one piece bathing suit under her clothes and Makena went in with the shorts he wore. The hot sun dried them off in no time as they sat and talked and talked about so many things—another first for Lihau.

She had never shared much about herself with anyone. As close as she was with Nani, she had not been the one to confide. When she conversed with Makena, she did not get maudlin or speak of her life in Ha'iku. She certainly did not want to incur his sympathy again...but he could read between the lines. It wasn't sympathy he felt, but admiration for her courage.

Of course she admired him for just about everything. No problem there. Her knight in shining armor got better and better as the day wore on. She was deeply in love by the time the sun went down.

They saw each other often during the summer of Lihau's seventeenth year—always in secret to avoid her father's disapproval. She would join him at night after her parents were asleep, and they'd walk in the dark and kiss under the moonlight. He'd meet her in the day at the end of the driveway after work with his dad, and they'd go for long leisurely drives.

She was braver to take on the roads of Maui with Makena at her side. So they drove, and Lihau saw Maui for the first time in all the years she'd been here: around the crater rim of Haleakala, down to the south shore of Kihei to the location of Makena's name sake at the end of the road and over to Lahaina, exploring the harbor and swimming in the crystal blue ocean as they watched dolphins in the distance.

It was a wonderful magical summer and Lihau's heart sang with happiness for the first time. On their last night together, Makena presented her with a gift wrapped in a silver package.

She breathlessly opened it and could not believe what she saw. There in a tiny velvet box was a sculpted silver ring. "It's a promise ring, Lihau." I want you to know that you have my heart now and that is a reminder.

"Oh, Makena. I think I'm going to cry again."

"That's okay, I'll always be here to catch your tears," he testified, and then he kissed her again for the last time that summer before she left for her senior year at Kamehameha Schools.

7

LIHAU, FOR THE FIRST TIME, was homesick for Ha'iku as the days droned on at Kamehameha. She had no heart for Kamehameha now. She just looked forward to Makena's letters and realized how much easier it was for him to express his feelings through letters.

One of the letters read:

Dear Lihau,

Received your last letter and glad to hear you're doing well and that you miss me. I think of you often and count the days before Christmas when I can see you again.

I never told you this, but I think I've loved you for a long time. I watched you as a little girl and wanted so many times to reach out to you, but you know how guys are, we get caught up in our own lives and my interest in sports was everything to me. Besides, you were way too young and not ready for me. We've still got a big age gap between us, but as time goes by, the less that matters.

I hope we can plan a future together some day. It's probably too soon to talk about such things, but I'm going to find a good job to make that future more secure.

After hearing about your parents and what they want for you, I sometimes get discouraged, but maybe we can cross bridges when we come to them.

Over the years I've watched you bloom like one of the flowers in my dad's garden…strong and beautiful and sweet. Now, I'm sounding like a sappy poet, but I also want to say that I admire your courage and your resiliency to have almost raised yourself into a wonderful girl.

I love you more than you know,

Makena

Lihau had nothing to do but study. So she did—determined to do well in her last year. She waited for every letter that arrived promptly on a weekly basis. She and Nani still hung out together and attended all the usual school functions. She couldn't keep up with Nani's fans; Nani was kind to all and never seemed to favor anyone special.

When Lihau went home for Christmas, she was relieved that her parents were not there. Fujinoko was aging and barely kept track of her, so she could be together with Makena whenever she wanted. She had dinner with him and his dad the night before Christmas and the three of them sat down to a wonderful meal of orange duck with yams and fruit salad that Jesse had cooked for them. He was so nice to her as they talked and laughed, and she envied the warm home life Makena had.

"My dad likes you," he said when he walked her home.

"I like him. You're so blessed, Makena. You've had the love of a good father."

"You're right. He's been great—making up for my flaky mother, whom I can barely remember."

"Well, we can't have it all, can we?"

"Someday I will and I hope it'll be with you. Maybe we can have a bunch of kids and make up for all that we've lost."

"That would be great, Makena. I can hardly wait."

They talked about their future together that Christmas as if it was inevitable, and Lihau grew to finally have a ray of hope in her life.

Lihau did well in her studies for the rest of the year and was suggested for valedictorian, but another girl was chosen instead. She enjoyed her time at Senior Cottage, not doing terribly well in the domestic activities, but felt a real kinship with Keala who put all of them under her umbrella of love. She had been in the same class with Kia for four years and the only thing she could say about Kia was that she was consistent. She continued to treat Lihau as a *non-person* as if she simply did not exist, even throughout their time together at Senior Cottage.

Makena agreed to make the trip for her senior prom and accompanied her in a black tuxedo, looking very debonair and handsome. Lihau was so proud of him. She also looked especially lovely in a print aquamarine taffeta gown, a designer's creation her mother had sent from Hong Kong. Her hair had been curled to flow down over hers shoulders, and Lihau Leng looked better than she ever had. The Ha'iku couple kept their eyes on each other as they danced the night away at Lihau's last dance as a Kamehameha teenager.

Graduation came and went. Tearful goodbyes were said by all…well not all, but some of those whom Lihau had befriended: Nani of course, Keala, Puakea, Kanoe and a handful of others. Lihau bid Kamehameha a final farewell and came home to Ha'iku. She reflected on how her time at school had changed her life, and she was grateful for the refuge she found there when she had needed so much to have a family.

But she was glad to be going home to Ha'iku…now that she had Makena.

8

AT THE END OF JUNE, she joined Puakea, Kanoe, Keala and eight boys on their visit to Kihei, Maui and had a wonderful time, never experiencing that kind of group camaraderie before. They had so much fun, just being teenagers wild and free without adults. She and Keala went on the Haleakala trek with three of the boys to watch the spectacular Maui sunrise; then drove down to her house where Fujinoko prepared them breakfast. All were impressed with her elegant home. She was a little embarrassed about the fuss they made over it, almost wide eyed with envy. *If they only knew the price she paid for living there, she thought.*

Of course, she and Makena continued to see each other and were reunited happily, making plans for their future and finding great comfort in being together. Lihau had been accepted to Princeton and was expected to go there in the fall. If she had her way, she would stay in Maui, but even at eighteen, her life was not her own.

Her parents arrived in July with her mother feeling more guilt about not attending her graduation. Thomas again, needed to get away from the pressures of Hong Kong. He had run into some close calls with threats made on his life. Solitude at Ha'iku would serve a double purpose. He was losing control over his wife and it would be a good time to plan his daughter's future.

"I don't want to go to college," she announced to her parents at dinner the night after they had arrived in Ha'iku.

Her father looked at her as if she had called him a foul name. "Nonsense, Victoria. You have no choice. You are going to go to Princeton. I've decided. Besides, you've been accepted and that's it."

"I don't want to go," she said, looking at her plate as she forked another piece of broccoli.

"After all we've done for you, Victoria; you sit there and defy me in front of your mother." Thomas's eyes moved to his wife across the table who was also concentrating on moving her broccoli across her plate.

"What *have* you done for me?" asked Lihau, just throwing caution to the wind this time.

She'd never seen her father turn colors. His face flushed into deep maroon. "Victoria, go to your room. I will not tolerate such obstinate behavior from you."

"Okay," she replied calmly, put her napkin on the table and moved her chair back to rise.

"You sit right, there young lady."

"But you said…"

"Sit," he almost screamed…well, bellowed in a manly way.

He stood and walked to her side of the long dining table, pulled his hand back and slapped her across the face. Her mother gasped and rushed to her side. "Enough, Thomas, enough," she yelled. "Are you alright, Lihau?" she whispered. Lihau nodded her head in shock. She did leave the table then and ran outside.

Thomas realized he had gone over the edge, but he was not used to being challenged especially by such a mouse of a person like his only daughter. She would have to learn who was king here.

Lihau ran to Makena's house and threw herself on him when he opened the door. He came outside with her and they huddled together as they walked into her yard. She sat with him on the grass, crying once again. Then, she told him what happened.

"I don't want to leave you Makena. I don't want to go away again."

"I don't want you to either, Lihau. We'll think of something." He tried to soothe her rubbing her back and shoulders and then he kissed her to calm them both. The kiss and embrace they shared was the first thing that Thomas witnessed when he had come out into the night to look for Lihau.

"So, *this* is the reason why you don't want to go to college? The gardener's boy, Victoria? How obscene can you be? Get up off that grass or I'll pull you up myself. "He was talking in a controlled manner now which, to Lihau, was even more ominous than the yelling she had previously experienced. She scrambled on to her feet to stand.

Makena stood up also, towering a few inches over her father. "Sir, I…"

"You are not even fit to address me. Tell your father to pack his bags. You are both leaving this property tonight."

"No," protested Lihau.

"No," came a voice from behind them. It was Kamalei. "Thomas come inside. I need to talk to you."

"Kamalei, are you defying my orders? What is happening here? Has everyone forgotten who I am?"

"No, Thomas. Come inside. We can talk about this reasonably." Kamalei went to put her hand on his arm and he brushed it off; then relented and followed her inside the house.

"Oh, Makena, I've made such a mess of things. What are we to do?"

"It's alright, Lihau. My dad and I have a place we can go to in Wailuku. His sister has a big house. We can stay there until I figure things out. Do you want to come with me?"

"I wish I could. More than anything in the world, but my father is a dangerous man, Makena. I should have thought of that earlier when I opened my big mouth."

"Don't blame yourself, Lihau. What you said to him was mild compared to what he had coming. I'll get in touch with you somehow, I promise." He kissed her once more and disappeared into the night.

Lihau was afraid for her mother that night. She heard a lot of shouting at the opposite end of the house. They were in the master suite, and even though secluded on the other side, she could hear the voices.

"You hit your daughter and you may as well as have hit me...because I felt it even more than she did."

"Well I can always accommodate you there," he said standing in a supercilious position. Kamalei sat on an ottoman next to their king size cloud of a bed. She looked up at him and saw what she had avoided seeing all these years.

"I'm not afraid of you any more, Thomas. You've taken the most precious thing from me in the world—my child. She is eighteen years old now and I have seen her maybe ten times in her life. How stupid was I to let you keep me away from her."

"She's not like us. She needed to be secluded."

"Oh, my. You've actually come out and said it. I suspected you thought that, but to say it brings the whole ugly reason to life." She sat there disgusted, not only reacting to what he'd said, but at the revelation that she had failed to see what was behind her separation from her daughter all these years.

"Thomas, you gave me this house as a gift to improve my land and to give me a wonderful place to come home to. I appreciated that so much and remember how happy it made me. The house is in my name and therefore, I am asking you to leave. I don't want to be your wife anymore. I will never forgive you for convincing me to leave my daughter. She needs me now. And I don't need you."

She looked at him and thought he was going to burst a blood vessel, the blood rushing from his neck to his face. And then he took a deep breath and seemed to calm. "If I go, you will be cut off from everything I own. I will make sure that you and Victoria are penniless."

"So be it, Thomas. You must do what you think is right." He headed toward the door of their suite and just before he reached it, Kamalei spoke again, "Thomas, her name is not Victoria. It is Lihau." And on that note, he slammed the door behind him.

Kiawe

Makaha Valley

Makaha Valley

LOCATED ON THE LEEWARD SIDE of O'ahu's west coast of scattered Kiawe trees where pristine blue waters of the Pacific meet the rugged mountains of the Wai'anae Mountain range, Makaha Valley is situated in a secluded area enhanced by its dry, hot climate and spectacular sunsets.

By the middle of the 1800's the Wai'anae Coast included the communities of Wai'anae Kai, Kamaile, Makaha, Makua, Ma'ili, and Nanakuli.

The Valley encompasses approximately 5,000 acres. Its history reflects a roadmap of ownership—originally under the stewardship of Hawaiian chiefs, it was then sold to a shipyard company and subsequently acquired by prominent nobility who converted it to a privately owned ranch. When the property eventually passed on to the heirs of the ranch, they chose to lease the land to sugar plantations, coffee growers and Chinese rice farmers. By 1902, due to the conflict that arose between the heirs, Makaha had become the corporate property of the Wai'anae Plantation.

Seven years before this, the O'ahu Railway and Land Company had established a railroad that included Makaha and continued its tracks all the way around Ka'ena Point to Kahuku. Constructed by Ben Franklin Dillingham to enable parcels of land to be sold in Ewa Beach, the railroad provided easier access to that side of the island, and its service lasted until the end of World War II. During this time, travelers were able to make a two hour trip to Wai'anae instead of the tedious thirty five mile horseback ride. Thus, the peaceful country isolation of the Wai'anae Coast was diminished.

Sugar became priority and water—the precious source of the plantation's survival. The sugar moguls had seized almost total control over the Wai'anae coast water—hoarded and dispensed sparingly to the rest of the population. The water issue became a major one and even the Wai'anae Plantation found itself suffering from a severe drought. Their effort at digging a tunnel into the base of Makaha Valley finally produced a major flow of water from the other side of the island. By this time, it was too late and the corporation was out of funds, forcing its stock holders to liquidate in 1946.

A Chinese investor by the name of Chinn Ho, on the heels of the liquidation, came in and formed an informal partnership called a *Hui,* closing a deal to purchase 9,150 acres of land for the sum of 1.25 million dollars. Some of his ideas were controversial, but he became a well loved source to people who needed housing. In addition, to beachfront properties, he parceled out land that the residents could afford and as a result, the population of Makaha grew.

Hawaiians as a race prevailed in Wai'anae. They originated there, serving the chiefs, working the livestock on the ranches, harvesting the sugar cane on the plantations, and eventually, many were able to acquire their own land after the War. Other people came—the Filipinos, Japanese, Chinese, Portuguese, Samoans and *Haole* (Caucasian). Many had been recruited to work on the plantation and later, came those who were attracted to the prospect of affordable housing.

Because of the area's isolation in the early years, even their Chief and Governor, Boki and his wife Liliha were considered beloved renegades who did not choose to conform completely to the outside world. This attitude continued over time with the residents who chose their own independent way of life. Friendly, warm, and hospitable, but somewhat territorial, they remained a culture unto themselves, appreciative of outsiders who behaved as *guests* and disdainful of those who did not.

1

Summer 1955

THE FIRE ENGINE ARRIVED AS the children hid behind a hedge. They were crouched down and huddled together watching, wide eyed, as the firemen turned off the siren of the shiny red truck and began to disembark. Flames and smoke were billowing out of a large discarded oil drum. Kia, the oldest of the group, pressed her forefinger to her lips to quiet the group as they observed the men unwind the hoses and connect them to a fire hydrant nearby.

The four Wai'anae firemen continued to douse the flames, but also perused the area to see if they could detect the culprits. They had been here before—perhaps not in this particular spot, but to other burning trash cans. There seemed to be one every week now. They were determined to find the perpetrators.

The children were so intent on watching the firemen that they'd overlooked the unmarked police car that just arrived and parked about fifty yards from where they huddled. Eleven year old Kia was the eldest of the children. There were two boys, Keoki and Lono, both nine year olds, and Keoki's little sister Kaleo who was seven. It was Kaleo who gasped when she turned around and saw the big policeman standing behind them.

"Oh, oh," she whispered.

The uniformed officer, a large imposing Hawaiian, towered over all four children when they looked up from their hiding place. He glared at them with a stern expression.

"Kia did it," blurted out Kaleo, her lower lip trembling with the rest of her body. Keoki shoved her to quiet her. Kia started to run, but it took the policeman all of a few heartbeats to catch up with her as he grabbed the neck of the tee shirt she wore. The four were herded into his large black Ford and slid into the back seat.

Two firemen walked over to the police car. One of them leaned down to look through the window. "Nabbed em, ha?" he said, frowning at the children.

"Yep," replied the cop. Even got a witness to testify." Kaleo lowered her head; the others stared daggers at her. Keoki nudged her again.

"You keeds have no idea what a pain in da you know what you've been to us," scolded the fireman and then turned to the cop, "Well, I hope you t'row da book at 'em. A few years in jail oughta straighten em out."

The children did not see the policeman wink at the fireman. "Serious business. I'll shuah try my best," he said as he started his engine.

After questioning them, the officer discovered that he knew Keoki and Kaleo's father. When he delivered the brother and sister to their door, he had a serious talk with him. Then he drove to Lono's house and went through the same routine with his parents.

Kia sat stone faced in the backseat, trying to hide her fear. The policeman did not say a word as he drove down a long street in the middle of Makaha Valley. Kia had reluctantly given him directions to her house located on another dirt road that veered off the main one to the right. The car stopped in front of a large lot surrounded by *mango* trees. A mock orange tree appeared to be growing in the middle of the foundation of a house, causing it to slant precariously to the right as if it were going to topple over.

Several disabled cars were strewn on the lawn area, one of them on blocks. An open garage to the right of the house appeared to serve as a workshop with car parts and tools piled in disarray. There were three men sitting in the garage area, drinking beer and laughing as the cop drove up. One of them, a stocky Hawaiian-Portuguese man, shirtless in shorts, quickly changed the expression on his face and put his can of beer down as the officer approached. The two friends who sat there also stopped smiling.

Kia, who had been instructed to stay put, watched from the back seat. The police car was parked on the road a few yards away from the house. She couldn't hear the conversation—just read the body language of the officer and her father. Her eyes were on her dad the whole time as he shook his head. She noticed his frown deepen.

The two men finally walked towards the car. "Kia, I'm turning you ovah to your dad now. He's convinced me that he'll deal with you. Keoki's dad is my good friend. If he wasn't, you'd be on your way to da bad girls' home. You cost da city a lotta money." The officer shook his head as he said this and headed towards his car.

Kia walked into the house. Two small bedrooms were separated by a living room and the kitchen area. An old worn-out brown couch sat in front of a large radio console in the living room where yellow and brown linoleum—scuffed and peeling—covered the floor. The same linoleum continued into the teal green kitchen with an overflowing sink of dirty dishes and beer cans. A red plaid, plastic cloth covered the chrome dining table in the corner next to a shattered window that had been repaired with black electrical tape.

Kia was fearful of the fact that her father had not spoken to her. She went to her room which lay at the left end of the lopsided house. A dresser of drawers, a night stand and a Chantilly covered bed made up the sparse furniture that tilted with the sloping floor caused by the invading tree. She sat on her bed for almost an hour before her father finally came in. She was aware that he had been waiting for his friends to leave.

2

KIA'S NAME WAS A SHORTENED version of Kiawe, after the algaroba trees that grew abundantly on the Leeward Coast of O'ahu. There was a story related that missionaries had planted the trees with its large thorns to encourage the natives to wear shoes on their bare feet. But quite to the contrary, the unique Kiawe became one of the principal shade trees of Honolulu and was found to have many uses.

Although native to Puerto Rico, South America and the Caribbean, the Kiawe tree had been brought over from Paris by the first Catholic Priest in the islands. From one tree, planted in a corner of a church yard, there descended a hundred fifty thousand trees enhancing a vital part of the island terrain particularly the dry coast of Wai'anae. The heavy wood from the trees was utilized for fence posts, floats for boats, a preventative for land erosion, a source for charcoal, fuel, fodder, and protein ground from its pods and seeds.

Kia was the only child of Takako Fujimoto and James Kea. Takako's homeland of Fukushima, Japan, originally a castle town was renowned for its silk production. Takako's parents had farmed a small plot of land in Fukushima and raised flowers and their own vegetables. When they were recruited to leave Japan to work the plantations in Wai'anae, they were able to save some money and establish a nursery business on land that they leased deep in the valley of Makaha. Both her parents died before Takako married.

Takako also passed away, due to a mysterious lung disease, when Kia was two years old. Her husband, Jimmy had been married to her for only three years. He grieved for her when she died, but moved on to a lifestyle that was not conducive to another marriage, or for that matter, to raising a child.

Jimmy had now been single for ten years. In and out of trouble over the last two years, Kia had become a growing burden to him. When he thought about it, which was rarely, Jimmy acknowledged that his unconventional lifestyle was perhaps a deterrent to keeping his daughter on the right path. He made room for Kia as long as she didn't interfere with his activities.

Jimmy raised cockfighting roosters and their counterpart hens which were bred for the favorite undercover sport among Wai'anae locals. He did not personally enlist them in the sporting arenas, but sold them to various entrepreneurs who would enter them in the gory events that were held once a week in an undisclosed ranch in the valley. The roosters were kept in cages, fed special diets, and bred to be fighters. The minute some of them were hatched they came out scrapping and had to be separated from each other except when they were prepared for the ring. At the time Jimmy had fifteen hens and twenty roosters in separate cages.

Kia's job, even as a young child was to help feed them at a scheduled time; she learned early to keep her hands gloved and away from their sharp beaks. Having experienced numerous incidents resulting in bleeding fingers, she soon discovered how to avoid being injured. Her father did not coddle her and thought the best way to learn something was to figure out the consequences through trial and error.

Located in the bathroom was a first aid kit. Kia was also instructed at a young age how to tend to her wounds. She knew that crying or calling attention to her ailments was never rewarded with sympathy and that she got more strokes for being tough and self sufficient. If she was sick, she would get the thermometer out, and if she was running a fever, that was the only excuse for staying home from school. She calculated early to heat up the thermometer by artificial means until Jimmy caught on to her.

Her father was actually a gregarious man who loved the camaraderie of his friends and his job as a freelance mechanic which he conducted in his garage. A product of foster homes with a lack of understanding about family life, Jimmy had no idea how to raise a daughter. Without a blueprint for this, he saw to her care as he looked after his pets... minus the encroachment of a cage.

Father and daughter cohabited in Jimmy's world of cockfighting, cars, drinking beer with the guys, sometimes hunting for wild pigs in the mountains and fishing on the shores of Wai'anae. Kia could come along if she wanted to, but much of the time, she was allowed to run wild and do her thing. That was fine with her, and she found all kinds of activities to keep her busy while her father attended to his interests.

What surprised everyone around her was the fact that Kia was a brilliant student in school. It was discovered early by her teachers, that she had been gifted with a keen intellect that led her to excel in learning. Her sharp memory combined with an analytical mind enabled her to shine in almost every subject. Jimmy had been informed of her abilities on a regular basis. His only reaction to this was relief that she managed to avoid trouble in school. He had no understanding of what potential her genius could have on her future, nor did he ascertain how to encourage her academic development. Thus, they both continued over the years, attaching little significance to her scholarly achievements.

Unfortunately, Kia used her savvy to create all kinds of mischief to keep her mind active. She was successful in coaxing other children, mostly the boys in the surrounding neighborhood, to get involved in her ventures. Starting fires, not an original idea of hers, was something she did for excitement. Her father owned a bag of old golf clubs which Kia put to use in an innovative way. She and her friends collected golf balls from a nearby driving range. She figured out how to slit the balls, fill them with lighter fluid, put a match to them, and using a club, to hit them off into the hills igniting fires amongst the dry brush as they all waited for the fire engines to arrive.

During World War II, much of the Wai'anae Coast had been utilized by the United States military as a strategic spot for their maneuvers and storage of ammunition. At the end of the war, the area resumed its charm, but some of the bunkers and barbed wire remained. Kia and the boys discovered explosives that were left over from these maneuvers.

They'd explore the off limits military areas in Makaha Valley, find old hand grenades, take them apart, make their own bombs and set them off. One day, they almost blew themselves into oblivion because their timing in running from the explosives had not been accurate. It was a close call for Kia, and she escaped with a few burns which she took care of on her own without her father noticing.

Even though today's incident was something minor she concocted out of boredom, it was the first time she got into trouble with the law. She knew her father would be furious. He had always lived under the legal radar and expended great efforts to keep it that way. Kia was not looking forward to the consequences.

Jimmy stood there as he entered the doorway to her room. "Kia, I dunno what to do wit' you. Dis is bad. I wish I could give you a good lickin' like I used to when you was one small girl, but you gettin' too old foh dat, so I gotta t'ink of somet'ing. Stay in yoah room until I do." That's all he said as he turned around and closed the door behind him

Kia would have preferred a lecture to these unknown consequences that she pondered all night and into the next morning. She was not afraid of her father. He had always been fair with her with a few temper flares over the years. Not an affectionate man, he had seen to her needs, but basically left her to her own devices. Although not a priority with him, Jimmy loved Kia in his own way. Just as he cared for his roosters, he had fed, sheltered and protected her somewhat over the years. She had been fine with that, never knowing any other kind of life.

He came in the next morning and sat at the edge of her bed. "I t'ought about it last night and here's da plan. You getting too old foh dese kind of pranks. Maybe I not up to raising one girl. You missed out on yoh mom and I figahed I could pull it off, but I can't and I t'ink you need somet'ing else."

Kia was informed that Jimmy had called his only living relative, Aunty Mapuana, his father's younger sister, now aging in her seventies and the last person who had nurtured him after he'd lived in a series of foster homes. Mapuana lived in a housing project in Kalihi. Kia pleaded with her father not to make her leave her beloved Makaha. She cried and begged and promised all kinds of things, but he packed her bags and dropped her off in Kalihi one day.

All he said to her was "Be good," and left her at the door of a woman Kia had only met once in her life.

The housing project was not exactly the best environment for Kia either. In fact, she felt more like the caged roosters at home and continued to rebel on a daily basis. To protect Kia from the elements in the area, Mapuana made her come into the apartment every day at four o'clock. There was nothing to do, but homework and listen to the radio. She was miserable because of it.

Kia ran away twice and played hooky from school several times. Mapuana, a stern Hawaiian, no-nonsense lady, had raised her own children with an iron hand. She had no idea how to handle this unruly child and thought of giving up—finally notifying Jimmy who came to see her after the last incident.

"Next time you gonna go to da bad girls home and dey going lock you up and t'row da key away. One moah time Kia and dat's it. You bettah straighten out if you know what's good foh you."

"I'm sorry, Daddy. I'm sorry. Please let me come home and I'll be good."

"Kia, I can't handle you. Youah too much *pilikia*." As he said this, he turned around and walked out the door of the small apartment in the middle of the housing project.

Kia stared at the closed door after her father walked away, and something happened to her that day. Her heart turned to stone, reeling from what she considered her father's ultimate betrayal and abandonment. The carefree girl, who had laughed and played in the valley of Makaha on the shores of the Wai'anae Coast, was changed. She dried her tears and determined, from that day on, never to cry again. She resolved to conform to all that was required of her to get along in the world. But she would never again trust someone to look after her. She would do it herself, and someday, she would be free again. As an eleven year old girl—the day her father walked out on her—she had advanced beyond her years.

Kia attended Dole Elementary School and, in spite of her previous truancy and disciplinary matters, continued to excel in her classes. Her academic abilities easily enabled her to succeed in each course. Kia's sixth grade teacher noticed this right away, aware of her recent problems, but recommended that she try out for Kamehameha School so that she could attend the following year.

Bernice Pauahi's will stipulated that priority be given to a percentage of applicants who were indigent or orphaned by the loss of a parent. Kia qualified in this category. With her father's permission and Mapuana's cooperation, Kia passed the test, the interview and all the requirements needed to enter Kamehameha in her seventh grade year. Because of their financial circumstances, she was awarded a free ride. Her tuition, meals, books, room and board were paid for by the school. Kiawe Kea was now enlisted to board with a group of children from seventh and eighth grade.

3

BECAUSE OF THE LACK OF space on campus, Kia's seventh grade dorm was located off campus. The large converted mansion stood on an impressive site surrounded by abundant shade trees and lush greenery, flourishing from the rains and damp climate of Nu'uanu Valley. The girls were bussed a few miles up to the main campus on Kapalama Heights each morning. It was here that she met Keala Kalia who became her first roommate and would remain her friend for life.

Kia had run with the boys in Makaha Valley whom she found more adventuresome and conducive to all her aggressive activities. She had never been inclined to befriend any girl in particular. Having had no interest in dolls or dresses or playing house or all the things little girls include in their world of make believe, she was a tomboy with a capital T, but found her prepubescent years somewhat confusing.

Her body was producing the usual hormones, changing in ways that were strange to her. She had no mother or parental guidance during these changes. As an undernourished waif, she wore tee shirts and cut off jeans, but had now developed a waist and curves that terrified her. After shopping at a local thrift store, Aunty Mapuana had purchased four oversized dresses that were altered to fit Kia by the time she started her first day of school. She had never worn a dress in her life. Her awkwardness clearly showed, but she was not alone in this dilemma which many girls were trying to adjust to at her age.

Kia was drawn to Keala's friendliness on the first day when she entered her dorm room. "Hello, my name is Keala." Kia sat on her bed to rest for a few minutes after she had unpacked her clothes. Keala had come late from the airport upon her arrival from Hilo, a town on the Big Island of Hawai'i.

Kia glanced up, did not smile, but said, "Mine's Kia."

Keala's big brown eyes sparkled in a face that featured a cute turned up nose and perfect bow shaped lips that spread into a radiant toothy smile. Well rounded, already developed with ample hips, Keala was short in stature with the dark olive skin of the Hawaiian. Kia was sitting on her bed and Keala plunked down beside her.

"Don't look so sad. We only have six more years and then we'll be out of this joint," said Keala, laughing and watching Kia's face.

Kia looked up at her and almost smiled, but couldn't. "What are you so happy about?" she asked.

Keala reached over and tapped Kia's hand. "C'mon you gotta smile." She nudged her and said, "You can do it." Kia just sat there looking at the floor.

"Don't worry. My mother told me that life is what you make it and things are going to get better." She elbowed her again and said, "You know why?" Kia looked up and raised her right eyebrow. Keala laughed, "Because I'm going to make it better. We're going to have fun."

Keala kept her promise to Kia for the next six years. They started off in a seventh grade dorm room, the waif from Makaha Valley and the warm jolly girl from Waipi'o Valley who brought light and love and a glimmer of happiness into Kia's life.

They were inseparable during seventh grade and remained close as the years went on. Keala gathered people and made friends wherever she went, and Kia trusted no one except her. Keala was the only one of their peers who could make Kia laugh, share her secrets and to whom she gave her loyalty, but within Keala's wide circle of friends, Kia refused to participate socially. As the years went by, she was considered reclusive, aloof and perceived as uninterested in anyone but herself.

Kia had come to seventh grade as a plain, bedraggled tomboy from Makaha Valley, but by the time she reached the age of fifteen in her ninth grade year, she started to bloom in her appearance. Her hair, which had always had possibilities in spite of its shortness, had grown out to a shoulder length jet-black sheen and, her body had taken on proportions that most girls envied. It seemed like she had sprouted overnight into a tall, long legged, well endowed thoroughbred. Kia's family traits were evident in her long lashed almond shaped eyes of her Fukushima heritage with a light hazel tinge from her Portuguese ancestors. These same contributions also lent to petit features, high cheekbones and flawless skin without a single blemish in her pubescent years.

The only trace of Hawaiian blood lay in the coloring of her golden olive skin, and of course, her tall stature which she inherited from her father. Her beauty did nothing but provoke jealousy amongst the Hawaiian teenagers who were all struggling with their own insecurities. Kia's remote detachment endeared her to no one—except Keala who would not let anyone berate her in her presence.

Kia excelled easily in her studies at Kamehameha with a natural ability that seemed almost effortless. Not only was she an honor student, but a fabulous athlete to add to her stature. Tennis and volleyball were her favorites, but she did well in everything else.

The boys, who were hardly aware of her in seventh and eighth grade, definitely noticed her the summer after she returned. By then, they had separated into a military Boys School below the Girls School at the top of the hill. She was selective in her choice of whom she honored with her attentions, but for some unknown reason, she seemed to choose the boys who were usually associated with other girls. This added to Kia's unpopularity, but her conscience never bothered her regarding the matter unless Keala brought it up.

"Kia, I worry sometimes. Everyone's talking about you. Don't you care what they say?"

"What do they say?" she asked.

"That you are encroaching on other people's territories."

"Keala, if these territories are someone else's, they need to confront the boys who ask me out and not blame me for their betrayal. I can't keep track of who's connected with who—or is the word *whom*. Anyway, it's their problem not mine."

"But you're my friend and I have to defend you. What will I say to them when they talk about you?"

"Just say, Kia is my friend and I can't say anything unkind about her. Then move away. I would do the same for you." Keala would try to shrug it off; she talked to her more than once on the subject, but to no avail. Kia's reputation continued to suffer, but she chose the power it gave her over the need to be accepted, and that choice became her pattern as the years went by.

Kia now spent holidays and summer vacation in Makaha Valley, finally able to return home on these occasions. She had become a different girl and her time at Kamehameha had changed her. Jimmy was pleased that she did not seek trouble the way she used to, but he was not impressed with her new sophistication that made her out of place in his home.

One of Kia's seventh grade English teachers had taken her under her wing and spent time with her, improving her diction so that her pidgin was no longer rampant. She spoke with all the proper enunciation expected of an English standard school. Her change would have been alright with her father if she hadn't been affected with a new air about her that he couldn't quite pinpoint.

She had learned etiquette that was poured out on the boarders on every occasion which included three meals a day in the most formal circumstances. What he objected to was the fact that she seemed to look down on him, their house and his lifestyle. This was not verbalized blatantly, but in her mannerisms and her affectations.

As a result, he became ruder, cruder and more obnoxious in her presence. They had never been close, but as a little girl, she had not appeared to disapprove of him. He sensed her change by the way she looked at him when he ate meals with her at their modest table in the kitchen.

"Whacchu looking at?"

"Just watching you eat. Do you have to make so much noise?"

"So you t'ink you all high and mighty now dat you going school wit' all dem kanakas. I eat da way I always eat, so if you don' like it, you can eat somewheah else."

"I think I will," she replied and left him at the table.

This was just one of many incidents, but it set the pace for the hostility that erupted between them, and they avoided each other whenever they could. They were both too stubborn to even attempt a truce or find some way to compromise; the house became a quiet war zone when the two were in a room together.

Kia was not one to examine her faults as the years passed. She had learned to survive in spite of obstacles and had very little tolerance for those who could not take care of themselves in the same way. The principles she learned at Kamehameha about putting others first and the integrity of "the virtuous woman from Proverbs 31" that they memorized and repeated out loud every Founders Day in Bernice Pauahi Bishop's honor meant nothing to her. Kia's world was one of survival. The words *sympathy* and *empathy* were only those she knew how to spell, but rarely incorporated into her moral fiber.

It was no surprise by the time she arrived at Senior Cottage to join forces with the rest of the girls, that she had already alienated each of them in one way or another prior to their six week tenure. Luring Nani's football player away from her and going to the prom with Kanoe's boyfriend were just samples of her offensive behavior.

Keala continued as Kia's loyal friend and remained true to the fact that once she pledged her friendship to someone, she concentrated on her virtues. She was proud of Kia's accomplishments and had encouraged her over the years, attending her tennis matches, supporting her in her school work, praising her for her successes and complimenting her on her beauty. For that is what Keala saw, the beauty in people. Unfortunately, she was the only one who cheered Kia on.

Kia's awareness of her beauty, her academic ability and her athletic prowess were, in her mind, a ticket—out of poverty, away from her father whom she no longer tolerated and an escape from Hawai'i itself.

4

AFTER GRADUATION, KIA RECEIVED AN academic scholarship to the University of California at Berkeley which she attended for four years. In the middle of her enrollment, the campus was just beginning to become infamous for its protests over the Viet Nam War, its bohemian academics and the inflamed activists who were growing amongst its student body. All the riots, the intense opinions, the fervor and the anti-war philosophy went right over Kia's head. She had one purpose in going to school and that was to make enough money someday to enable her to climb the ladder of success.

Kia's refusal to care about those around her became a wall that insulated her from the sit-ins, the marches, and the drugs that were starting to pervade the campus. She did not join clubs, or sororities, or anything that smacked of group participation. Ironically, she left behind an island culture, only to become an island to herself.

Her professors, many of them extremely liberal in their philosophical bend, were impressed with her brilliance, her ability to write her required papers, and her knack in passing tests with superb scores. She never spoke in class, always sat at the back of the room, but when she was expected to give a talk on a subject, she delivered it flawlessly, often hiding the fact that she had little passion on the subject of her presentation.

Kia graduated with honors. Unfortunately, no one in her family was there to witness her success. Her estrangement from her father had become worse over the years, and her aging aunt never bothered to keep in touch. She had few acquaintances during her four years at Berkeley. Even in the dormitory which provided much more freedom than Kamehameha, her aloofness kept others at bay, and she never found another friend like Keala.

Alone in the world now as she'd always been, Kia did not ponder it, nor did she feel lonely. She was used to being on her own and that became her strength in the days to come.

She moved to San Francisco where things were still somewhat formal, but just starting to make a turn. Women dressed in fashionable coats, high heels, gloves and hats and, men wore suits and overcoats as they promenaded up and down the steep hills of the City by the Bay.

After graduation, Kia decided to take some time off to decide whether she'd go further with a master's degree. She started work in a spacious office of a high profile investment firm on the fifteenth floor of a building overlooking Market Street. She had rented a small one bedroom apartment on Geary Street with no views, facing the wall of another building, but when she walked out her door, she felt the excitement and pace and uniqueness of San Francisco.

Riding the cable car to her office was an experience that always presented something different every morning. Strange characters that boarded the tram included a variety of people who relieved the everyday boredom of going to work—people from every race, class and walk of life—the tourists, the businessmen, the glamorous elites, beggars, bohemians, beatniks, hippies and the blue collar workers. It stirred something in her to notice a different world —a far cry from the small valley of Makaha which she rarely thought of now.

Kia presently worked at the main desk of a firm with thirty investment brokers—young men on their way to creating financial gain for their clients in stocks, bonds and corporate entities. She applied for the job with the intent to learn and digest the climate of money making—chosen because she presented a reflection of beauty, style and class to their prestigious clientele. No one suspected that her roots were what they were—only that she had come from the islands and that her heritage included a Hawaiian mixture which enhanced her exotic image.

The management of the large firm did not encourage the front desk to present a picture of warmth and a casual down-home quality. Success and power was its facade, and Kia handled that well. Her posture, elocution, and style exuded what they wanted their clients to see. She had been handpicked along with the other girl at the desk— both the picture of formality and sophistication.

Kia learned at an early age to become a chameleon adjusting to each situation from the time she left Makaha to go to Kamehameha. She had become an actress on a stage to rid herself of her former life—not in order to become acceptable to others—but to attain a standard for success.

5

"So who's the Pineapple Ice Princess at the desk?" asked Mario Lorenzo as he seated himself in the conference room with one of his brokers.

"Well, at least you've surmised she's from Hawai'i," answered John Carlton.

"That much I got. She didn't seem interested in passing the time of day. All business and mostly ice."

"Her name is Kia and she's not there to give you the warmth from the islands. We train 'em that way—unless she offended you."

"No, no. No offense taken. Just wondering."

They quickly got back to business as charts were laid out, portfolios spread and their discussion began. Always at his best when he met with Mario, John conscientiously did his homework, making sure he prepared for answers to anticipated questions along with any visual aids he could present. Mario Lorenzo had a reputation. His bank account was hefty, but the means by which his money found its way there was a mystery. Of course his broker was called upon to make it multiply under no small pressure, but John had lived up to Mario's expectations—so far.

Dressed immaculately in a three piece suit, ebony hair slicked back from his forehead, Mario sat back and listened to John's presentation.

Expressionless, and hard to read, he gave no indication as to what he was thinking. John was used to this, but always squirmed inwardly, because of the slight intimidation he felt about this powerful man.

"Don't try to snow me Carlton. I've done my own homework. What you just presented to me is crap. That company you so diligently tried to sell me is going under in a matter of months."

"What are you talking about? All the figures point to its success. Its ratings, its P/E ratio and the management has had a fine record of success."

"The CEO happens to be a nemesis of mine. He's been under my personal surveillance for some time. "If you had really done your homework, you would have discovered that he's heavily indebted to loans from a company that my corporation happens to own. He's embezzled millions and falsely reported earnings. As soon as the public hears about this, and they will shortly, the stockholders will pull out and the price of its shares will hit rock bottom. That is when I will consider buying before I announce that the company will be under new and improved management with a merger that includes one of my most successful entities

John sat there with his heart beating out of his chest. A trickle of sweat ran down his pale face. "I'm so sorry, Mario. I didn't know."

"Well now you do," he said as he began to rise out of his seat.

John stood up at the same time. "How can I make amends for this grievous error?"

"You can tell that ice berg at the desk that my car will pick her up tomorrow evening at her place of residence. I want her dressed and ready by seven o'clock with a smile on her face."

"But,"

"No buts, John. I'm sure you can arrange it."

Mario Lorenzo walked out the door of the conference room. He passed the girl he had just spoken of at the desk, glancing in her direction briefly. She was on the phone and made eye contact when he walked by. She had no expression on her face, not even a departing smile.

Kia was bathed, perfumed and dressed in a simple black sheath that fit snugly against her body, wearing spiked heels, an imitation diamond

necklace and matching earring studs when her doorbell rang at exactly seven pm. Her hair was pulled back in a French twist, and the only make-up she wore was a touch of apricot lipstick applied lightly to her full lips. She did not have a smile on her face when she opened the door to a man dressed immaculately in a black suit.

Kia had been railroaded and almost blackmailed into accepting this assignation. John Carlton had pleaded and cajoled at first and, then when his mild threats of possibly terminating her position did not move her, he proceeded to bribe her with the prospect of doing all he could to move her up in the ranks—the ranks being the opportunity to become a broker herself . She knew he did not have the power to do that, but he promised to do everything he could to bring this about including paying for her courses and opportunity to get her license.

So, there she stood reluctantly as she grabbed a black wool coat, the only one she owned, and proceeded out the door of her modest apartment. The driver, who spoke very few words except to greet her, opened the back door of the sleek black limousine which she entered. She seated herself on plush leather upholstery and did not say a word until they arrived at the Fairmont Hotel. She was somewhat nervous when she discovered their destination. After being escorted to an elevator that brought her to the top floor, she was relieved to know that it led to a restaurant and not an unsavory hotel room that she had suspected would be the calculated intention of this night's plan.

The driver spoke to the maître d' and left her as she was escorted to a private table with a spectacular view of the city. The familiar man, whom she had encountered the day before, stood to greet her. He was finely dressed, also in black, but in an elegant Continental style suit that showed off his physically fit body. He was of average height, dark complexion–what some would consider handsome in a slick polished way, probably in his late forties and exuded power just by the expression in his eyes. She had barely noticed him this morning, but was now aware of his penetrating gaze which moved over her body and examined her from head to toe. She had no hint that he approved, except for a lift of his eyebrow and tentative smile that appeared at the corner of his lips.

"Ah, Kia," he said as he rose to greet her. She moved forward as he did simultaneously. He grabbed her right hand in both of his and kissed it lightly in a debonair style that surprisingly did not offend her. She smiled hesitantly as he moved behind her to seat her on the chair opposite him, intentionally positioned to take advantage of the spectacular view of the city of San Francisco. A tuxedoed waiter appeared magically with a chilled bottle of Dom Perignon and filled the champagne flute to the right of her place setting.

"To a special evening which I hope you'll enjoy," Mario said as he raised his glass to her. She lifted hers and actually did smile then. And that is how their evening began.

Mario Lorenzo turned on the charm. By the second course of their scrumptious dinner which he had ordered for both of them, she found herself, relaxed and somewhat comfortable with the efforts of this powerful man. His attentiveness increased as he focused on her life; Mario subtly asked questions about her career goals, interests and background. She purposefully dodged the latter, relating her educational accomplishments and a small glimpse of her life in Hawai'i.

In turn he regaled her with stories on numerous subjects, but skimmed over his personal life as she had with hers. By the end of the evening, Kia was well fed with more than enough champagne to make her head spin. He put his hand to the small of her back when they emerged from the restaurant and kept it there as they entered the elevator. The champagne had not numbed her awareness that she was probably expected to pay for this expensive night—something she was definitely not planning to do—future or no future. But Mario surprised her when he walked her to the entrance of her modest apartment building, kissed her hand lightly and thanked her for a lovely evening. She stood there watching as he walked back to his sleek black limousine.

6

THAT WEEK, KIA CAME HOME from work to a plethora of flower arrangements which had arrived at her door on a daily basis. Her small apartment overflowed, with roses in every color, some she had never seen before. On the following Friday, she received an elaborately wrapped silver package. When she opened it, she unfolded a black velvet box. In it was a diamond necklace—a replica of the artificial one she'd wore on their first date. She read the simple note that said:

Wear this on our next evening together.
My car will pick you up at six on Saturday night.

The limousine and driver again appeared at her door as scheduled and whisked her off to a destination away from the city over the Golden Gate Bridge. She finally arrived almost an hour later due to the after-work traffic at a quaint restaurant overlooking the water in the small town of Sausalito. When he greeted her at the door of the restaurant, Mario was pleased to see that she wore the diamond studded necklace. She was draped in a gray silk dress gathered at the waist, softly covering her knees. Its bodice hugged her curves and, in spite of the chilly weather, exposed her broad shoulders. With her hair worn down, framing her exotic face, he thought she looked exquisite. The restaurant was warm with a blazing fire and he helped her off with the light gray shawl that matched her attire.

When they were comfortably seated, she gazed down at her fluted wine glass, then looked up at his dark hooded eyes and said, "What do you want, Mario?"

Not much surprised this jaded man, but the abrupt question caught him off guard. "The pleasure of your company...for now." He smiled as he said this and stared into her almond eyes, waiting for her response.

"Well, that you have...for tonight," she replied. Kia reached down into her clutch bag, brought out the black velvet box and laid it on the table. She put both her hands behind her neck and unclasped the necklace she wore, put it in the box and handed it to him. "You asked me to wear this tonight, so I did. However I can't accept it, but I thank you for the very extravagant gesture."

Mario tried to mask his inward reaction as his eyes glazed over. "I am sorry to hear that, but I think I understand."

They did not mention the gift again, talking over their wine and dinner as the soft jazz music played in the background. Kia learned a little bit more about him. He told her how he had married at an early age to give his son a name. The girl he had married was Irish, a great strike against her in his strong ethnic family who had come over from Sicily during the war. The family was happy when the marriage broke up after five years. He had been separated from his son for ten years and then reconciled with him when he was a budding teenager. Mario had brought him into his business ventures, grooming him to become his heir some day.

Kia listened to Mario, sipping her wine with the music in the background. When the evening was over, she realized that she had actually enjoyed herself, losing some of her suspicions, but still cautious when he leaned over and kissed her good night before finally escorting her out of the car. As kisses went, it was conservative, respectful and not entirely unpleasant. She smiled as she entered her apartment alone with the onslaught of fragrance from the roses.

Mario poured himself a strong dose of brandy which was situated in a mini bar in the limo. He thought about the girl he had just said goodnight to. What he had not told her, among other things, was the fact that she was almost the exact replica of a woman who had played an important role in his life fifteen years before—a woman with whom he'd developed a lifelong obsession. Lorena was her name. She had the same exotic features as Kia, the same tall voluptuous body, the same distant air about her and… he had loved her. *Loved her* was too simple a phrase—he had worshiped her. In all his dealings with women—and there were many over the years—she had been the one woman he could not get over.

Their relationship had been volatile from the first; the more she fought him, the more his obsession grew. Nothing he did in his attempt to win her over would satisfy her. She was as elusive as a butterfly in a field of flowers, and he could never prevail in the assurance of her loyalty. All of it was fleeting, but she excited him as no other woman had. When she died in a plane crash with the lover she had left him for, he was almost relieved. The sight of Kia, each time he saw her, brought it all back to life. He suspected he was playing with fire, but surely history would not repeat itself.

He was not devastated on his next date with Kia when she told him that it would be the last one for them. In fact he took it in stride, and decided that it was for the best before things got out of hand. At least that's what he told himself in order to move on in another direction.

7

AT THE TIME, SEVERAL EVENTS were taking place in San Francisco. It was the year when thousands of hippies descended on Haight Ashbury causing chaos everywhere including changes to the formal attire and prerequisites for proper deportment that symbolized the reserved culture of the city. It was also the year that The Cannery was reconstructed.

The former warehouse, originally built by Del Monte in 1907 as a fruit and vegetable canning plant for the California Fruit Packers Association, was the site of the largest peach canning facility in the nation. The deteriorated building, no longer of use, was saved from demolition by a private entrepreneur. The Cannery became the country's first and most innovative historic building re-use project when it opened the same year Kia had moved to Geary Street.

One Saturday, on a windy Spring San Francisco day, Kia took the cable car down to the bottom of Columbus Avenue to Del Monte Square to explore the Cannery renovation which so many had raved about. When she arrived, she was not disappointed—so impressed by the red brick structure. Creating a European touch of old and new, the unique marketplace featured a variety of unique shops, boutiques, and restaurants with delicious smells that permeated the walk and singing minstrels who entertained the lunch crowd. She meandered through, purchasing a long multicolored scarf which she slung around her neck as she proceeded out of the area towards the wharf.

Seagulls perched on docks and seafood aromas wafted through the air. Ocean vessels of every kind cruised along or were moored in the water—bay cruises for tours and whale watching, sport fishing boats, and a recently docked cruise ship. Several kiosk type booths with shelters had been set up by vendors selling a variety of food—crab, oysters, abalone and fish from the ocean.

As she passed one of the vendors, Kia heard a voice calling to her. "Bella, Bella, cara mia."

She glanced over to see the pleasant smiling face of a young man with twinkling brown eyes that lit up as he spoke. He was dressed in a simple black tee shirt that hugged his muscular body, a white soiled apron tied around his waist, faded jeans and a canvas hat scrunched sideways on his head, reminding her of the Bowery Boys from the old movies on television. He stood there mimicking the motion of someone stabbing his heart, held his hands over his chest, briefly closed his eyes and then looked at her again.

She couldn't help but smile at his engaging attempt to draw her attention. As she did, his eyebrows knit together and, in a dramatic gesture, he softly said, "Marry me."

An unusual way to make a sale, she thought; somewhat embarrassed, she started to move away. He stood on one side of the shelter with another young man in attendance. He leaned over and said something to him, removed his apron and scurried around the structure to catch up with her.

"Don't leave me," he pleaded.

"Does that work?" she questioned as she tilted her head for an answer.

"Does what work?" He now stood just a foot in front of her.

"One of these days, some girl is going to take you up on that proposal."

"I swear to you, I have never said that to another soul, another woman, not even a young girl when I was starting to grow up and notice. Only you. You are the first."

Kia rolled her eyes upward and smiled. "Okay, if you say so." She tried to step around him, but he kept trying to block her way. He could not stop staring at her face. He had not even noticed the rest of her. She was covered in winter clothes from head to toe—the colorful scarf draping her neck, a black knit winter coat, leotard stockings, and sensible walking shoes.

"Let me walk with you, I will be your guide." He continued to stand before her with pleading eyes, reminiscent of a cocker spaniel begging for food.

"You're working. What would your boss say?"

"I am the boss. Sort of. It's a family thing."

"Look, I have no idea what you're about, but I don't know you and I have to go," she said as she finally stepped around him.

"My name is Enrico. That's all you have to know. You can call me Rico as my friends do. I come from a family that owns businesses everywhere. I'm just helping out today," he said as he quickly fell into step beside her. "What's your name?"

"Kia," she replied as she picked up her pace.

"Oh, no... Kia, Kia, cara mia." He held his hands up high in a gesture of praise.

"Okay, any more of that stuff and I *am* going to walk away." She stopped and turned to him. The sun shone on her face and he was mesmerized by her long lashed almond eyes, flawless complexion and features that were just as alluring to him in her perplexed state.

"Alright, alright, I promise not to get carried away by your beauty, your eyes, your face, your..."

She put her hand up, palm out and said, "That's it. I'm leaving."

"No, no, I promise. I'll keep my admiration to myself. Just let me walk with you."

"Aren't you cold? It's freezing out here," referring to the thin tee shirt that she didn't want to notice hugging his broad chest, exposing firm biceps and muscular forearms.

"I am used to this weather, but you're right. I'll be back in a minute." She watched him hurry back to the kiosk, talk to his co-worker again and return to her side as he zipped up a brown leather jacket. He had removed his hat and looked so much better, even though his chestnut waves were in disarray.

Combing a hand through his hair, he announced, "There, now I can spend the rest of the day with you. I'm all yours." He winked and grabbed her free hand, clasping it in his as if they had known each other forever.

Kia was amazed, more at herself than at the exuberant, walking, talking specimen of a man by her side. She could not believe she had been enticed so quickly into doing something that was so foreign to her cautious nature. The more they walked and the more he related stories and facts of interest about the wharf, she grew increasingly comfortable with her decision to give a complete stranger the pleasure of her company for the day.

Her serious reserve fell away as she found herself laughing, responding to him and pleasantly engaged in his warmth. They had lunch in the famous Alioto family restaurant started years ago by a widow who needed to make ends meet after her husband died. Rico related this tale to her as they ate mouthwatering Dungeness crab grilled to perfection, accompanied by a crisp tossed green salad. Kia allowed herself one glass of wine, and Rico, she knew, refrained from having more as a gesture of respect.

She had taken her coat off. Rico held his breath, as he admired her even more in her form fitting turtle neck sweater that tapered down to her small waist and a fitted knee length skirt. He distracted her with stories to hide his need to stare and take in her beauty and all that went with it.

Even he could not fathom or explain to himself how the short span of time with her left him completely captivated. Well aware of her reserve and aloof demeanor, he sought to coax a rare smile—considering it a gift each time it occurred.

"So, Kia cara mia, tell me your story."

She stiffened for a moment. "What story?"

"Anything you want to tell me. Where you're from. What you do. What you like. What makes you happy. Anything."

"Well, that's quite a lot. I don't know where to begin."

"You can start with your birth and go forward twenty what years?"

"Twenty three," she answered.

"Hmm, I've only got two years on you. Okay, tell me about the day you were born. What kind of baby were you? Did you smile more then? Were you happy? Tell me about that."

Kia laughed and leaned back, then her face clouded and she looked for the words that would tell him what she could and omit the parts that were still painful to her—the events she wanted to forget. She would skip her childhood completely. She remembered for a moment. It wasn't too long—not that many years ago when that little girl had wreaked havoc in Makaha Valley.

She could not even reconcile now what she had strived so hard to change. Was there a trace of that tomboy who fed the roosters every morning and made a hobby out of starting fires? No, she told herself—that girl started to fade when her father sent her away and finally put to rest when she could not return to his home without resentment. She would grieve no more for that little girl. She was all grown up now—sophisticated, polished, cleaned up—no one need know about that Kia of Makaha. She didn't exist.

"I'm from Hawai'i, went to a private high school, to Berkley after that, got my degree in business, came to San Francisco about a year ago and work in an investment firm." She sat back in her chair and looked out the window that faced the wharf and the fishing boats.

A moment passed as Rico studied her. He knew there was more and could have questioned her further, but he sensed that her past was something she did not want to visit. For that matter, he felt the same way about his.

"Kia, you are way too serious. You need to lighten up and have fun. Come with me today and I will show you how." And he did. Not only did she succumb to his charm on that blustery spring day, but she allowed him to take over her days from then on.

That one chance meeting led to many others. They gradually became inseparable in their free time. Kia was caught up with his growing admiration, his wit, the energy he spent on bringing out a whole new side of her. He was her opposite and yet they balanced each other in their compatibility—Kia as a captive audience and Rico in his constant need to bring out that rewarding smile of hers. Keala had been the only other person she had responded to in this way. Now there was Rico.

After two months, they were madly in love. Rico had fallen from the beginning. It took Kia longer. This was a first for her. She had never let anyone penetrate her wall of reserve. He showed her sides of San Francisco she had never seen. She met some of his fishermen friends on the wharf who invited them out on fishing boats to explore the bay and all the surrounding sights from a whole different view. They rode cable cars everywhere and drove in his pick-up truck when they had to travel out of town across the Oakland Bridge or the Golden Gate to Marin County. Rico had the charm of a young laughing boy. His enthusiasm and zest for life was contagious.

And yet, in spite of all the moments spent together, they had each avoided talking about their lives before they met. She knew little about his family, except that he worked for his father now and been brought up by a single mother who lived in a small town in the Bay Area.

He came over every day to her small apartment, bearing all kinds of food dishes instead of flowers. "I'm going to get fat with all this food you're bringing," she said one day.

"I would love you anyway," he said. He spoke of his love often, ever since that first day they met. She smiled and put her hand on his, sitting across the table in her small kitchenette.

"I love you too, Rico." She had felt it for weeks, but it was the first time she said it.

He repeated his mantra, "Kia, Kia, cara mia. I am a happy man today." He stood up and pulled her from around the table to sit on his lap. "You finally said it. I knew you couldn't resist me, but you finally said it."

She punched him playfully and nestled her head on his shoulder. "Yes, I finally said it." He kissed her passionately then, caught up in her final assent to become his, and in the next few hours, they submitted to what they knew would be inevitable.

Afterwards, they lay on the double bed in her small bedroom facing Geary Street. With a dazed smile, he held her in his arms as she laid her head on his chest. "Remember the first words I said to you, when we met?

She lifted her head and looked into his mesmerizing brown eyes and the contented smile on his face, "What words?" she asked, but she knew the answer. She had remembered it often when she thought of him.

"'*Marry me*' I said. I mean it now and I think I meant it then."

"Oh, Rico, you didn't even know me, then. You barely know me, now."

"I know enough, my Kia. Enough to want you by my side for the rest of my days."

"I never wanted to get married."

"You'd never met me before," he said as he kissed her soundly to ward off any doubts.

"You're right. I never met you before."

"Say yes, Kia, you would make me a happy man."

"Okay, Rico. If you think it'll work out, I will be your wife someday."

"Someday soon," he said. "The sooner the better." Then he kissed her again and proceeded to remove all her doubts.

8

KIA RECEIVED A PHONE CALL from Rico on a Thursday night a month from the night he proposed. "I have to do some work, but tomorrow, I will pick you up and we are going to drive to Napa Valley. My father wants to meet you."

"I thought he lived in the city?"

"He does, but he spends much of the summer at the family place, just another one of his many projects. I finally told him I met a girl I want to marry. I haven't seen him in awhile; we had only a minute to talk, but he wants me to bring you up there. I'll tell you more later when I pick you up."

Kia hung up and sat on her small sofa with her feet on the coffee table staring into space. There was so much she did not know about Rico. For that matter, she had told him little about herself. She had shared some things about her work, her studying to become a broker, all the events that went on at the office—other mundane things about her present life, some facts about her time at Berkley purposefully avoiding the subject of her past in Hawai'i.

But neither did he reveal anything more about his background. Oh, she had a lot more facts about his work at the wharf, his fishing experiences and lots of amusing anecdotes that entertained her to no end about his adventures with his friends…but nothing about his family.

When she thought about it today, she had missed something that was vital to her future. She did not even know his last name.

Kia had taken a small overnight bag with her to work and waited for him outside the tall building of her investment firm on Market Street. She spotted Rico's black pick-up truck and slid into the front seat when he leaned over and opened the door for her. In spite of the traffic that was waiting to get past them, he kissed her long and tenderly.

"I've missed you," he simply said.

"We've only skipped one night," she replied dreamily smiling. "But, I missed you too."

He drove through the heavy afternoon traffic that would delay their trip across the Golden Gate Bridge as he held the steering wheel with one hand and hers with the other. He eventually let go to shift gears. Half way through the trip, she noticed how nervous he seemed as he quietly concentrated on the road.

"Tell me about your father, Rico. You never talk about him. I don't know what to expect." She wasn't sure if she imagined it, but his face seemed to darken and take on a tense expression. He swerved to avoid something in front of him on the road and she thought that must have been the cause.

"My father is a gentleman. He is much more polished than I am. He will like you and show you the utmost courtesy, hospitality and charm."

"And what if he doesn't like me?"

"Then he will still show you the utmost courtesy, hospitality and charm."

"Then I won't know if he does or not."

"Very few know what my father is thinking, and to me it doesn't matter."

Somehow, she knew that it did, but she refrained from adding to the tension that she clearly saw on his face. They drove listening to classic Italian music as he pointed out all the points of interest along the way, distracting her from all the questions she had intended to ask.

He turned the truck off the main highway onto a road that narrowed to two lanes. Now in the heart of Napa Valley surrounded by trees and shades of green, the hustle bustle of the large city seemed to faded away.

After a few miles, Rico veered down an even narrower road that ended at a gate framed by an elaborate arbor.

A sign read *Casa de Tranquilidad*, and Kia realized that they had arrived. Rico got out of the truck to open the gate with a key that he produced from his pocket, returned to his seat, and drove through the long driveway, almost a half a mile in.

The sun was just starting to fade as twilight set in when they made their final stop on a circular brick driveway located in the front of a sprawling hacienda type structure—more Spanish in nature, framed by its red tiled roof, a mixture of stucco and brick on its façade, hanging bougainvillea pots and a sheltered portico that surrounded the front. Summer flowers in bloom bordered the house in colors of fuchsia and lemon yellow. The sweet fragrance of white honeysuckle permeated the air as they walked up the four layers of red brick steps in front of the entrance.

Rico grabbed Kia's hand when they approached the Spanish red double doors. He turned to face her, "You ready for this?" She nodded her head and smiled tentatively. She had no idea what to expect when they left on this venture, but surely not these elaborate surroundings which they were about to enter.

"If you feel any discomfort at all, I promise we will turn around and go back to the city. Everything will be fine."

A stout matronly lady in a simple frock tied back with an apron answered the door. "Ah, you're here," she said greeting them with a smile.

"Antonia, how are you? You look as gorgeous as ever." He planted a kiss on her cheek and hugged her. "Antonia is my father's housekeeper, but more like family to me. Antonia, this is Kia, the love of my life."

"Well, it's about time. So glad to meet you, Kia. You'll be happy to know that this is the first time Enrico has brought a girl to this house. Welcome, welcome."

He gazed at Kia and winked, "The first time and the last." Then he looked at Antonia. "You know what I mean. The last girl I will bring anywhere." It was an off-hand remark, but in that single moment, Kia was completely assured of the sincerity in his all encompassing love for her.

From the front entrance that led into the main house, they walked through a delightful courtyard. The immense living room was simply furnished with a mixture of Italian and Spanish décor, enhanced for comfort with large white cushioned furniture and colorful tapestries on the walls. The room faced a patio viewed through floor-to-ceiling glass panes framed with Spanish framed arches.

Seated on the patio with his back to them, was a man at a small table with a glass of wine in his hand. He seemed to be preoccupied with papers in front of him and did not hear them when they stood at the doorway to the large open area overlooking Napa Valley and the grape vineyards that stretched over a hundred acres.

"We're here," Rico said once again. The man turned to greet them with a smile on his face. Kia froze in motion.

"Kia, this is my father, Mario Lorenzo."

9

WHEN KIA RETURNED TO HER home the following evening, she told Rico that she was not feeling well. He wanted to stay and take care of her, but she tactfully reassured him how much she preferred to be alone. She explained that she thought she had the stomach flu and that she would end up being terrible company for him. He did not pursue the matter, kissing her at the door and promising to come over the next day.

She tossed her overnight bag on the floor, rushed into the bathroom and threw up everything she had eaten in the last few hours. She was well aware that she did not have the stomach flu. Her nerves were shot, her stomach queasy and she was breaking out in cold sweats. Kia showered, letting the warm water drench her body; then dried off with a towel, put on a flannel nightgown, got into bed and pulled the covers over her head. Eventually, she eased the covers back and stared up at the ceiling.

She was certain of one thing—that this had been the worst weekend of her life, in spite of all the luxury, the breathtaking scenery, the fine wine, the elaborate dinner, Rico's lavish attentiveness and Mario's genteel hospitality. The worst—bar none. She tried to reason her overreaction to it, but nothing seemed to pacify her. It had been a veiled nightmare from beginning to end.

She knew by Mario's immediate response that she was the last person he'd expected to see at his son's side. Even though, for an instant, she thought surely Rico would have mentioned her name before coming—apparently not. Rico seemed to have a habit of forgetting to mention names.

Mario had recovered quickly, masking his face with the cool aristocratic demeanor of a man who's in charge. He played the role of everything Rico had predicted… the charming host with courtesy, charm and hospitality. But she knew behind that façade, there was something different, something that showed up in his piercing gaze that never seemed to veer from her, all during their excruciating dinner conversation of polite inquiries and witty remarks. Even during the tour of the vineyards and corresponding winery, his charm had not eluded them, but she knew better.

Rico had not noticed a thing. He was completely oblivious to the underlying tension, noting later, during their drive home, how much she had seemed to impress Mario. "See, I told you everything would be fine. I think my father was pleased with you, certainly with your beauty. He could not stop staring. But not to worry, he is a connoisseur of women. He knows a thoroughbred when he sees one."

Mario sat on his patio sipping wine looking out at the vineyards that stretched before him. Twenty four hours ago he had been a different man. He had been sitting on the same chair at the same table overlooking the same scenery until… he was faced with what consumed him now.

What are the odds that this could happen? He was used to odds. He was used to winning. He was used to getting his way in every way, but one. He had not taken the rejection of this simple girl lightly. Planning to lay low for awhile, he'd made up his mind that he'd pursue her again, perhaps from a different angle. Once, set on a goal, there had been nothing to stop him in the past. This was not part of the plan. He admitted he had waited too long.

During the visit, Mario had watched her, studying her like a piece of art. That's how he thought of her—exquisite, fine lines, brilliant colors, alive and vivid. He had his fill across from her at the dinner table, dressed in white with a simple strand of pearls, which he knew were not real, around her neck. Her skin still flawless, her face, the expression of ice: high cheekbones, long lashed almond eyes that revealed her shattered nerves as they darted in every direction, but his. For some reason this pleased him. He relished that he made her nervous, giving him an edge of power over her. He worked to increase that every minute he was in her company.

This was the girl of his dreams he had pondered, not a sentiment that was familiar to him, but one he found invading his thoughts, his work...his life. He was seething now and had to do something about it. He always took action to soothe his frustrations.

When Rico told him he had met the one he was going to marry, he was skeptical, but detached. In his own way he was fond of Rico who had only been a part of his life for ten years now. Although, the boy admired and sought to emulate Mario, they were unalike in every way. Rico talked like Italians, hung out with them, took on their manner, and put on the culture like a second suit. But he was not anything like Mario. He was soft like his Irish mother—warm, sensitive, caring—all the things that attracted Mario to her and all the reasons why he eventually left her.

Very few understood the nature of Mario's business. He used many of his ventures as a front for certain illegal activities—activities that bordered on the fringe of San Francisco's organized crime which dated back to the 1930's, still active in gambling, racketeering, money laundering and, now the emerging drug business.

Mario was the liaison for some of these activities. He invested large sums of money that had been laundered through various schemes to flow into legitimate companies that were up and coming and doing well on the stock market. Some of the money had been used to open successful businesses, and some of the enterprises were established in other states. He had entered companies in other people's names, getting cash under the table for his expertise. Even his vineyard was acquired through a shady operation that he picked up in a foreclosure after the original owner had been sent to prison.

Friends were rare in the business. Enemies were rampant. Mario had to watch his back constantly, and anyone who threatened it, lived to rue the day. He was ruthless in meting out punishment for betrayal. Many a dead body lay *swimming with fishes* as the mob cliché so aptly described. Cunning, lethal, brilliant in manipulating, and a sociopath without conscience were the terms to describe Mario Lorenzo. He was dangerous to the extreme…especially when he could not have what he wanted.

10

KIA HAD NOT HEARD FROM Rico. Two weeks had passed since the Saturday evening he had dropped her off at her apartment. She tried to reach him by phone every day, several times a day, and received no answer. She was frantic with worry. Imaginations ran rampant in her head. Had he tired of her, had he changed his intentions toward their relationship or had something terrible happened to him? All thoughts eventually led straight to Mario.

On the Monday of the fourth week, she went to work, waited for John Carlton to go to lunch and slipped into his office to look at his files. She found the one she wanted—Mario Lorenzo's business investments, his trust account and all the records he had with their firm. She finally found several phone numbers, closed the file drawers and hurried back to her desk.

That evening when she got home, after dialing the third number, Mario actually answered the phone. She wasted no time. "Mario, where is Rico?"

"Ah, I was wondering if you'd call. Would you like to discuss this in person?"

"I'd rather not. I just need to know where he is. I haven't heard from him in two weeks."

Mario sensed the distress in her voice. He thought he'd torture her a moment. "Maybe he's tired of you, Kia. You know how that is. Some people just move on in their relationships. Don't take it personal. It could be nothing more than that."

"Is that it, Mario? Did he tell you that?"

"Not in so many words, but I was told he had 'other fish to fry', if you would pardon an expression used on the wharf."

"Rico wouldn't just walk away. He would have said something to me."

"You know how these things go; people move on. They don't always like to be hampered with explanations. Why, come to think of it…you did the same thing to me."

"Is that what this is about, Mario…you and me? I didn't walk away without an explanation. I told you that I couldn't see you anymore."

"Well, yes. You did do that…didn't you? And then jumped immediately into bed with my son."

"It wasn't like that Mario. I had no idea he was your son. I would never have considered seeing him if I knew."

"Then why *did* you stop seeing me?"

She hesitated and softly answered, "Because I didn't want to lead you on."

A silence followed. "I see," he finally said.

"I'm sorry to bother you, Mario. If something horrible had happened to him, you would've told me. So, I guess it's as you say, 'He had other fish to fry'."

She didn't say goodbye. She just slowly placed the phone down on its receiver.

Two months later, a newspaper article in the San Francisco Chronicle was brought to her attention by John Carlton of all people. He showed up at her desk, "Kia, have you seen this article. It's related to Mario Lorenzo, the client you went out with several months ago."

"I'm not interested in anything to do with Mario Lorenzo," she said, going back to concentrate on the work at her desk.

"I'll leave the paper on your desk. It's actually not about Mario. It's about his son." John put the newspaper down and walked away towards his office.

Kia pounced on the newspaper as soon as he left. On the inside of the front page, was the article:

Wharf Merchant Arrested for Murder

Enrico Lorenzo, 25, held without bail in San Francisco County Jail after being arrested under the suspicion of first degree murder. Several witnesses came forward to testify in an ongoing investigation into organized crime that Lorenzo was the hired hit man to kill Carlo Carlucci on a fishing expedition in the San Francisco Bay. Trial to be held six months from today.

Kia could read no further. Her heart pounding in her chest, she once again broke out in cold sweats and headed down the hall. She threw up everything in her stomach and dry heaved more as she bent over the toilet of their office restroom.

In addition to the horrendous news, she went to a doctor two days later and had her nagging suspicions confirmed—she was four months pregnant with Rico's child. She had lived in denial for weeks and had not acknowledged all the symptoms. Life could not get any worse. Or could it?

She soon found out it could. Her morning sickness eventually subsided. In most cases, it was known to last for just the first trimester, but her nervous condition had prolonged it for another month. She had no idea what she was going to do, but went into survival mode and made her plans accordingly. She hid her condition from her co-workers as long as possible and it wasn't hard, because she had lost so much weight.

The baby started to move after the first day of her medical exam. The cold ice berg that developed over the years in Kia Kea's heart had begun to thaw. And from that day on, she grew to love the life growing in her, vowing to do everything to keep it. She would not give it up as she had been advised by her doctor.

After the initial shock of the loss of Rico in her life, and the onset of her pregnancy had passed, she looked forward to the birth of her baby, determined to set up a life where she could raise her child. She started to show in her seventh month and informed her boss who eventually notified her co-workers. Some objected to her working the front desk, so she started wearing a wedding ring to ward off any disreputable slurs that could occur.

Kia eventually passed her exam for her investment broker's license, pleased to accomplish this as it gave her an incentive to plan for her financial future. She decided to wait until her baby was born to embark on her new career, but in the meantime, she worked to learn how to acquire a potential client list for the future.

She seemed to be coping until the day that Mario Lorenzo walked into their investment office and almost bumped into her as she was returning to her desk. He stopped cold in his tracks when he saw her. His eyes went right to the protruding bulge under her maternity blouse. She was now in her eighth month. He was speechless and did not stop staring until John Carlton arrived to greet him. Kia quickly sat down to answer the phones that were now ringing, and John escorted Mario to his office.

Kia made sure she was not at the desk when he finished his appointment with John, taking a lunch break soon afterwards.

A week later, she received a letter from Rico.

> ### Dear Kia,
>
> *I know you have given up on me and I don't blame you. By now, you have heard the details of my arrest. I would do anything to turn back the clock on this horrible nightmare. There are so many things I want to tell you, but I don't think they would help. I have confessed to my crime to avoid a long trial and to receive a break in my sentence, I will be given twenty five years to life to be served in San Quentin State Prison at the end of this week.*
>
> *I was informed through the grapevine that you are with child. I assume it is my child. No, I take that back, I know it is my child. Therefore, I have directed my attorney to set up a trust fund for you and the baby to use as you need and to plan for the future.*

It is a considerable amount and will not do me any good in here.

I want you to know one thing, Kia, I will always love you and I have from the first day we met. I wish I could explain all this, but I don't understand it myself. You can forget about me now, but always know that I would have had it different and wanted only a future with you.

God bless you cara mia and take care of our child,

Rico

He still loved her, was her first thought. *He hadn't abandoned her* was her second thought. And she had lost him forever to what? So many questions unanswered. A range of emotions followed in the wake of Rico's letter—anger, betrayal, sadness, hopelessness and finally grief. She grieved especially for the illusion that she had trusted to be real. She could not fathom the reasons for his crime and the secrets that lay behind it. Reading the letter over and over on a daily basis, she was now positive that Mario had everything to do with these circumstances.

11

RICO SAT IN HIS CELL, soon to be abandoned for another one in San Quentin. He was at the lowest point in his life, going over all the events that led to his incarceration and the life sentence imposed upon him.

The day after he had dropped Kia off at home, he received a phone call from his father. "The time has come for you to be a "made" man in our organization. There are threatening circumstances that can bring down the collapse of our business and affect hundreds of people involved. You've been selected to prove yourself and take on the ultimate sacrifice. You'll be protected and nothing will occur to affect your life. Just this small deed and you'll not be expected to do another one. You will receive further instructions by one of my soldiers and I will contact you later."

This was the initial one sided conversation with his father. There would be others. All of it led up to the one simple horrendous act that Rico committed for the sake of his father, the business and as he had been notified "the hundreds of people involved" that would be adversely affected.

Rico was informed that he would be doing away with a very bad man—a man who had every intention of ruining his father, and as Mario had later implied—one who was intent on ending Mario's life. Rico had no other choice, but to show his loyalty to the man he loved. He remembered himself as a young boy who had yearned for his elusive father and how he had finally come to be a vital part of his life.

And so, on a bright Summer day, he undertook a fishing trip with Carlo Carlucci—a middle aged friend of his father's, someone he had known since he was a teenage boy who had graciously accepted his invitation to join him—a man who trusted him. They had taken one of his father's boats, a fishing trawler, one of his finest out into the middle of the bay where Rico Lorenzo dispatched one bullet into the back of the head of Carlo Carlucci —who, just seconds before, had worn a happy smile on his face—looking out towards the ocean and the city that lay beyond it, enjoying the bright sunny day on San Francisco Bay.

Rico had been convinced that he was undertaking an honorable deed right before he shot the gun, but he knew the instant he did… that it was the worst mistake of his life. Even now, he could not forgive himself. A priest had come to him a week ago, heard his confession and urged him to admit to his crime as evidence of true repentance, no matter what the consequences. The priest told him that he was absolved of his sin by God, but he would have to pay the price to the state and its edicts. And so his decision was made and the consequences would follow.

Rico had no inkling, not even a suspicion as to the real reason why his father had manipulated these events.

12

KIA'S BABY BOY WAS BORN on Christmas day a few days earlier than expected. She had experienced a fairly easy labor as births go—only six hours and her eight pound nine ounce squalling little boy came into the world. She loved him from the first moment she saw him and could not believe the full head of hair on his head, reminding her so much of Rico and his curly chestnut locks. This was not a day to be sad, so she counted her blessings for the healthy, hungry baby that lay before her. She named him Christian Kalikimaka Kea to celebrate the blessed day of his birth,

True to his word, Rico had set up the trust fund he promised and a monthly income followed by a check from his attorney. Kia had arranged her small apartment with a crib and changing table and all the accoutrements that a newborn would need. People from work had showered her with gifts at the hospital, and she packed them all into a taxi along with her baby as they headed home.

She had taken a leave of absence and now, after a week, was somewhat adjusted to a routine schedule. Kia put the baby down to sleep after breast feeding him, tiptoed into the bathroom, shed her nightgown and got into the shower which she enjoyed as the hot water soothed her tired body. She stood there, soaped herself down, taking her time and emerging about twenty minutes later. She toweled dry, sprinkled her body with powder and her favorite after bath cologne, walked from the bathroom with the towel draped around her directly to her closet, put on a housecoat, dried her hair and padded softly over to check on Christian.

Her heart stopped beating for a moment and her body froze in mid motion. Christian was not in the crib. She almost screamed, but as she stared in horror, noticed a piece of paper the size of a postcard propped up against one of the small stuffed animals in the baby's bed.

*Do not call the police if you want to
see your baby again. You will be contacted.*

Kia dropped the note and covered her mouth with both hands to stifle her wrenching sobs. She was just about to pick up the phone to call the police when it rang. "A car will be by to pick you up in an hour. Do not contact anyone," said a muffled voice and hung up.

Kia could hardly contain herself, nerves again on edge, dealing with a thousand thoughts, but one intention…to get her baby back. She suspected who was behind this plot, wavering between extreme anger and abject terror. But she managed to get dressed in a blue turtle neck sweater and slacks to match, followed by her winter coat and comfortable walking shoes.

She grabbed her keys and purse and rushed downstairs to the front of her apartment to wait. She was not surprised when the same limousine that Mario had sent almost a year ago showed up next to the curb. Mario was not in the limo. The driver got out to open her door and handed her a blindfold.

This time she was asked to sit in the front seat so he could make sure she followed instructions. She did not have to be told to put on the item she had been handed. She strapped it around her eyes. The driver started the limo, and they were on their way to their destination. They rode for about an hour, probably south, she thought because she had not detected any of the main bridges. They finally stopped, and the driver assisted her from the limo. He grasped her elbow escorting her up the stairs towards a door that was opened for them, and then up another long winding stairway into a room where her blindfold was finally removed.

Mario stood before a fire, dressed in a casual white embroidered, long sleeve shirt and ivory linen slacks. On his feet were soft white loafers without socks. Kia thought it was unusual attire for this occasion until he spoke.

"Do you want to see your baby Christian again, Kia?"

"Yes, please, please Mario, I'll do anything you ask."

"Marry me," he replied.

Keala

WAIPI'O VALLEY

Waipi'o Valley

SOME REFER TO WAIPI'O VALLEY as "the most beautiful place on earth". Situated on the Hamakua Coast, on the northeastern shore of the Big Island of Hawai'i, the vast stretch of land is intersected by Waipi'o River which flows into the ocean at the beach. Its grand majestic cliffs, some as high as 2,000 feet, frame the valley base extending one mile wide and six miles deep. The shores of black sand and lava rocks are kissed by the deep blue Pacific at its edge, and hundreds of waterfalls cascade down the mountains after heavy rainfall.

At the far end of Waip'io Valley stands the island's tallest waterfall, Hi'ilawe which pours 1300 feet from lava cliffs. The fertility of the valley is reflected in giant ferns, an array of tropical foliage, sprawling hibiscus bushes, exotic orchids, a large variety of ginger, an abundance of fruit trees and towering ironwoods near the ocean.

Once the home to thousands of Hawaiians and many rulers of Hawai'i, Waipi'o was referred to as "The Valley of the Kings" and noted as the most fertile and productive valley on the Big Island of Hawai'i. It held a cultural as well as historical value to the early Hawaiians as the site of *heiaus* and caves where many kings were buried. King Kamehameha I fought his first naval battle near Waipi'o before he embarked on his mission to conquer all the islands.

Like the fate of Kalihiwai, it also had been a thriving community of churches, schools and restaurants with a post office and a jail until the *tsunami* of 1946 swept large waves far back into the valley, devastating many structures and driving most of its population from its shores. Just a handful of the population remained in the area, destined to be without the modern facilities such as piped in water, gas and electricity because of its remote location.

1

August 1951

THE SADDEST MOMENT OF HER life was the day she stood on Waip'io's black sand shores watching the canoes as they spread her father's ashes in the deep blue ocean that happened to be calm as glass that day. Members of one canoe, which included her mother and two older brothers, spread the ashes. Four other canoes scattered orchid lei and plumeria flowers that were gathered from the fertile valley farther inland.

She was seven years old and too young to accompany them. She could barely see the process, but some of the flowers washed into shore. The little girl stooped and stumbled over the smooth rocks to pick up a floating *plumeria*. It was then that she cried tears that never seemed to stop for the rest of the day.

It was a time to cry, and no one made her ashamed of it—for her father would be missed by many. She loved him more than anyone… even her mother whom she adored. The little girl was the favorite of his six children. He had never said the words, but she knew in her heart that she was. Today she was inconsolable, but she would carry his love within her for the rest of her days, and the strength of this knowledge fortified and enabled her to become the warm, loving girl which she grew to be.

Keala'iliahi—fragrance of the sandalwood—was named after the precious wood of the forests of the Big Island that were plundered and preciously hoarded to exchange with the many foreigners who prized this rare commodity. The fragrant tree was referred to by Hawaiians as *la'au'ala* meaning "sweet wood" named for its aphrodisiac and herbal medicinal properties.

She was never called by her full name, unless her mother was angry with her when she had misbehaved. She was Keala to everyone, the youngest child of the six Kalia children. Keala Kalia—it had a ring to it—and she was proud of it ever since she could remember. Keala was one of the few people, along with her immediate family, who could claim to be of pure Hawaiian heritage. Her family was the second generation of Kalias who lived in Waipi'o Valley and among the handful of residents who stayed to rebuild after the tsunami of 1946.

John Kalia worked hard to support his family by the living he made from the lo'i (taro) fields that had been in his family since his grandfather had come to Waipi'o. He had inherited the land as a reward from his father because he was the only one of his brothers who took pride in it as a growing boy.

Taro is a popular multipurpose staple in Hawai'i. Its leaves are used as a vegetable in making *laulau*—pork wrapped taro leaf. Taro roots or corms are cooked, pounded into paste and thinned with water to make *poi*, referred to as "the Hawaiian staff of life" and main staple for many natives. The corms can also be boiled, baked, steamed or fried like a potato.

The wetland taro was predominant in Hawai'i and grown in rain fed areas where running water covered the roots of the taro plant. The *lehua maoli* was the name of the kind of taro the Kalias harvested, the favored variety for making *poi*.

Although taro takes six to twelve months to grow, their fields were alternately ready at different times of the years. Because of the ample amount of rain in the valley, they did not have to wait for a particular rainy season to begin planting. Two fields could each be planted at different times so that harvest time for one field was planting time for another. Some of the young green leaves from a plant could be harvested at any time and the rest left to grow.

Her father was an expert at this, and it became a family affair. Keala had already learned how to pull weeds correctly soon after the first planting and right before harvesting to protect the quality of the plants. The work was tedious and back straining.

Unaware of his weak heart, John Kalia, who had never been to a doctor in his life, died of a heart attack in the midst of harvesting his crops. His two older sons Panoa, seventeen and Kala, sixteen—the same boys who spread his ashes from the canoe—were the ones who found him lying face down on an embankment and carried his body home.

Besides the two boys, the others ranged in age. There was another boy, Kalani at fourteen and the girls: Keahi, ten, Kalena, eight and Keala, the youngest who was seven years old. They all had Christian first names, but were addressed by the Hawaiian middle names with which they were christened.

The Kalia family lived about a half mile into the valley in a home with a corrugated tin roof, built high off the ground as if on stilts, but fortified by strong beams that kept the heavy rains from reaching the main floor. The area below was cemented like a patio, but used as a work area for sorting taro and leaves that would be taken to market. A stream ran by the house. Its ice cold water was used as storage to refrigerate any goods they needed to be kept cold in nets they pulled up by their cords.

Wooden stairs ran up the side of the house to the top floor where three bedrooms, a small living room and a kitchen area were individually partitioned off. A wood burning stove was the only means of cooking available. They had no electricity, and oil from *kukui* nuts from nearby trees was used for burning lamps to light the house at night.

A small bridge over the stream provided access to a path that led to an outhouse; a few yards away a bamboo enclosure had been built to surround a shower area constructed to pump water from the stream. There was no hot water, but once a week, a large tin tub was brought out to the cement area below their house. Water was heated on the stove in the kitchen, hauled down and poured into the tub so that members of the family could take hot baths in shifts.

The family knew no other life. They did not feel deprived, nor did they complain about their primitive conditions. They were unusual in the fact that they were all grateful for what they had, and they loved their lives in the beautiful valley of Waip'io. Not only did they love the valley, but they loved each other, in spite of all the different personalities that inhabited the house. They were taught to look after each other as children, and the older ones were to protect and take care of the younger ones. Everyone looked after Keala.

They all had, what Keala would reflect on in her later years, a deep Christian faith in God. Because of it, they thrived with the strength and fortitude to accept gracefully what life had to offer them. They were taught at an early age that God would "never leave them or forsake them" and that he could be depended on no matter what. They were not religious about it nor were they pillars of virtue, but love reigned in their home as they looked after one another, sharing whatever they had with their neighbors.

They worshiped upstream in another Hawaiian house, where the Ka'ape family lived. The older couple held Bible studies on Wednesday nights and a form of church service on Sundays, either outside in their lawn area or crowded on their living room floor. The eight Kalias were included in their congregation of twenty people, and it was here that they were reinforced in their faith on a weekly basis, singing old Hawaiian hymns, reciting scriptures and taking turns leading the services.

The children would have to walk up the steep, rocky road to the top of the rim of Waipi'o to a little town called Kukuihaele and attend school in a small building or "one room schoolhouse" which accommodated all ages. At the time of John's death, all six of them trudged up the steep winding road to school.

Sara Kalia, their mother, was the rock of the household. Keala looked like her more than the others. She had large brown laughing eyes and a lovely expressive face that warmed the world around her. Everyone wanted to please Sara, and in spite of her warmth and smiling demeanor, she was the disciplinarian in the family. She was the one who formed their values and reinforced their Christian faith. They all went along with whatever she said including her husband. John had been a quiet man who worked the fields, encouraged and trained his children in their work, but left the rest to Sara.

She prayed to God about their circumstances when he died, and her prayers were answered not more than two weeks later. A man named Manu Makua, who had been attending the Ka'ape services on Sunday, approached her there and offered to come and work the taro fields for awhile until she got more help.

The "for awhile" stretched into a period of two years until Manu eventually convinced Sarah to marry him. By then, the children were used to Uncle Manu, and all of them grateful for his help. At the time he married their mother, he had already become a part of the family and realized the children needed more than work and school. Manu introduced *playtime* to the Kalias and decided that after noon on Saturdays, unless there was an absolute necessity, all work should cease until Monday morning.

Manu, ten years younger than Sarah, a jolly, fun-loving man, brought music and life into their home. A collector of the *'ukulele*, he even designed and made them on his own. He taught the children how to play the instruments, originally introduced by the Portuguese to the islands. On Friday and Saturday nights, they'd sing, taking turns as they made music with the tapping of spoons, blowing handmade nose flutes and strumming the *'ukulele* while the girls danced the *hula*. Keala became a natural at the *'ukulele*. From an early age, she possessed a crystal resonance to her alto voice and learned to dance the *hula* with grace and poise.

Before he married Sara, Manu lived deep in the valley in a two room shack with a large plot of land around it. He had inherited money from the estate of his grandfather and was allotted cash set up through a trust fund. He raised horses and a couple of mules and would still tend to them in between his work in the taro fields. Manu also had an old Ford automobile he kept at a friend's house in Kukuihaele, and he would take the children three or four at a time to ride into Honoka'a for various events. There was a movie theater there where Keala got to see her first Betty Grable movie—such a thrilling experience for her.

Three years after they married, it was Manu who helped Keala apply for Kamehameha and paid for her to fly to O'ahu to take the test for seventh grade boarding. Keala was accepted after tests and interviews, and like Kia and Nani, she fell in the "indigent orphan" category, in which a portion of the applicants qualified to become accepted.

2

KEALA ADJUSTED TO KAMEHAMEHA SCHOOL like a fish to water. She walked into it with awe and appreciation for all that was offered. She thought her first dormitory in Nu'uanu was like living in a mansion unlike any she'd ever seen—running hot water, toilets that flushed, all the food she'd never eaten and people her age she could befriend. The world was her "oyster" as the old cliché propounded, and Keala was the pearl in its midst.

She had already developed a full figure—buxom, well rounded hips and short of stature. Her shape might fluctuate, but it was her face that stayed the same throughout the years to come—large rust-brown dreamy eyes, framed by long curling lashes, a not too flat turned up nose, full kewpie doll lips and high cheekbones in a face surrounded by an array of black natural curls which she wore shortly cropped.

As early as seventh grade, Keala was well liked amongst the girls as well as the boys. She could not stand to see anyone out of place. She did not just pick the well liked people to befriend, but with her keen antenna, reached out to those she sensed were lonely or ridiculed or left out of groups. She was the mother bear that enveloped the outcast as well as any others who needed a cheerleader in their camp.

Keala was the only one who loved Kia Kea and that is because she saw through her cool façade early on in their first encounter as roommates. She was the one who heard Kia cry at night when she thought Keala was asleep. Instead of addressing Kia's problems, she just showed her love, hoping that in feeling it, Kia would change—much frustration there—but she continued undaunted as her friend.

The boys adopted her as a kind of "den mother" and she became privy to their circles, often giving her ear to their wondering stream of thoughts about girls whom they had just recently discovered in a whole new light. She often found herself surrounded by them as they included her in their bull sessions, asking about this girl or that girl, and whether they would stand a chance which usually meant nothing more than a glance from the chosen one.

Keala had a contagious laugh that bubbled from her diaphragm and rose up into bursts of delightful sounds. She could always be detected walking down a hall or playing on a field with this laugh, and it warmed the presence of those around her,

When she transferred to Girls School, even though separated from the boys in ninth grade, she still managed to maintain contact within their ranks. They sought her out especially on Sundays after church and she was the girl who received the most "callers" as she was beckoned from her dorm to meet with them in the breezeway of the porticos of Konia where the Girls School was located. None of these were romantic encounters, although some wished they were, but she knew how to deal with them platonically and understood how to keep them as friends, more meaningful to her than fleeting entanglements.

Keala joined Kanoe and Puakea in C section and did manage to get on the All Star Team in P.E. excelling particularly in volleyball, even though she was short in stature. Out of all her friends, Puakea was her favorite and in spite of her short fuse, Keala loved her feistiness and laughed at her antics on a regular basis.

She was the only one who got along with all five girls when they finally got to Senior Cottage and had to constantly defend Kia—not her favorite pastime.

Keala could not afford to go to college either. She had not planned on it and knew that she needed to return home to Waipi'o to help out with the family's income. So, after the girls in white said their farewells to the school that made a favorable impression on Keala's life, she did just that: she returned to the place where the ocean kissed the shores of the black sands and the waterfalls cascaded down the steep cliffs of the fertile green valley of beautiful Waipi'o.

She was pleasantly surprised, upon her return home after graduation, when she was given a graduation *lu'au* where all the neighbors in the valley were invited. Many of them brought food to share. The Kalia family had spared nothing in the production of this festive occasion where long tables were set with ti leaves, wild orchids, red *hibiscus* and a buffet of *laulau, kalua* pig, *lomi* salmon, sweet potatoes, platters of fish from the ocean, chicken long rice, *poi* and *haupia* for dessert. Everything except the long rice came from the valley. The pig, sweet potatoes and hot items were cooked in an underground pit or *imu* with heated lava rocks.

Manu and the boys serenaded them with *'ukuleles* and sang in blended harmony. Keala danced a solo to Kawohikukapulani and sang a duet with her brother to Pua Mae'ole, John Kamana's rendition which the Senior Boys had just a few months ago sung to win Kamehameha's Song Contest. The celebration ran for several hours on a Saturday afternoon and ended when the sun finally faded to twilight in Waipi'o Valley.

A short time later she joined her classmates in Maui which included four of the boys whom she had been close to since seventh grade. She was the *'ukulele* player of the group and led them in singing every night or wherever they gathered as a group. As the cohesive ingredient of the "Maui Gang", she was the one who made sure everyone got along and loved their time together. The fond memories of this trip would stay with her throughout the years.

3

As a young girl, Keala was taught how to weave *lauhala* (hala leaf). She and her sisters would collect the long sinewy leaves in the early morning from the *hala* trees close to the ocean which would be cut from the trees or gathered from the ground. These tended to be the best kind for weaving because they'd been cured by the sun and the salt wind. Sometimes, they picked some of the newer leaves and dried them in the house or outside in the sun for two weeks. Older ones were too brittle and lost their pliability for plaiting. The leaves that were dried inside produced a darker shade and the ones that were bleached in the sun were lighter.

After being washed in the ocean or stream, each leaf was stripped of its thorns on its edges in a tedious process with thumb nails or a knife moving in the direction that the thorns were pointed to avoid getting poked. The base and tips of the leaf were cut off; then stored in a damp location, usually in the lower level area of the house, dried but still kept damp for pliability and cut into strips with a special razor type needle that Manu made for each of them. A towel was used to cushion the needle that pierced the leaf, and the lauhala was pulled straight through using the finger to gage the width of the strip.

At last the strips, some thin, others wider were woven into a variety of things—hats, wallets, head bands, purses and large tote bags that were later sold at different venues. A family project, when Manu arrived on the scene, was to weave mats for the house. Eventually there was one in every bedroom and a large one for the living room.

Weaving *lauhala* was a tedious chore, but somewhat relaxing and certainly satisfying when the product was finished. It was a time when the girls and their mother could sit together and socialize. There was a certain type of skilled dexterity needed for the craft, requiring patience and the ability to keep the fingers moving quickly in the process making the more advanced weavers the masters of their trade.

Keala, with much practice in her background, became one of these. Her work was exquisite, and she chose the thinner strips for finely woven articles, particularly the much in demand headbands and wide brimmed (*ka'e*) high crowned (*ipu*) hats referred to as *papale lauhala* for the *paniolo,* the Hawaiian cowboy. The hats had replaced high crowned felt hats and were light and well ventilated.

Keala and her oldest sister Keahi brought their *lauhala* goods to market at one of the impromptu rodeos being held in the town of Honoka'a. Cowboys came from all over the area to compete, many of them from nearby ranches and the bulk of them from the gigantic Parker Ranch that covered a large portion of the island.

After Manu dropped them off in his old Ford car, the girls were set up in a booth next to a food concession. Other vendors were there selling their wares— Hawaiian quilts, feather and *kukui* nut leis, *koa* jewelry and other items. Both girls wore their Sunday best—long *mu'umu'u's* and *lauhala* hats or *papale lauhala*. Keala wore a high necked red and black print with a wide brimmed hat and Keahi wore blue with a smaller, more fitted *papale*.

Keahi was the serious one in the family of six. She tended to mother the rest of her siblings, even her brothers who were older. She had no favorites, but she was her mother's helper and took on the household chores without any instruction. She and Keala were complete opposites, but they loved each other in spite of it. Keahi tended to censor Keala's spontaneity, but Keala just ignored her and did whatever she wanted anyway. Keahi was an excellent *lauhala* weaver, and her specialty was the large bag used by many for carrying their *hula* instruments.

They watched three men approach their lean-to-tent which sheltered two hat racks with mirrors attached and two long tables with more hats and Keahi's bags. They sat at the tables weaving headbands. Keala looked up and put on one of her radiant smiles.

"Ah, *paniolo*," she crooned, "and such handsome ones at that." Her sister elbowed her as she said this. "Can I interest you in one of our top of the line *papale lauhala* made especially for you in the beautiful valley of Waipi'o?" urged Keala. She stood as they approached and reached for several hats that were on racks behind her.

"All da way from Waipi'o huh?" said the tallest one of the lot.

His raven hair was long, parted in the middle and tied tightly back in a braid; a long sleeve, blue and white *palaka* shirt fit snugly over broad shoulders. There were Hawaiian words for his paniolo attire. He wore the traditional *kelamoku* denim knee breeches over his long legs with rawhide leggings or *likini wawae* that covered the tops of heavy *kama'a puki,* buckskin boots. His light eyes were almost a pale green, but looked as if they could change colors depending on the light of day. Fine handsome features that did not reflect a Hawaiian heritage were camouflaged by dark skin, probably a result of the sun.

"I am Miguel Cardoza from Waimea," he said puffing himself up "And these two guys are da greatest cowboys in da land—Justin Kometani and Lance Shimabukuro or "Shima buckaroo" is what we call him, and we all happen to be looking foh somet'in' to put on our heads."

The other two wore identical outfits like Miguel's. They were both of Japanese descent—Justin was not as tall as Miguel, but taller than Lance who was wiry and well built. They all had belts with shiny buckles that differed in design. Lance wore a bandana on his head. Miguel pulled one out of his pocket and so did Justin.

Keala stood in place and shook all their hands enthusiastically which Keahi thought was highly improper. "I am Keala Kalia and this is my sister Keahi"

She watched Miguel and Justin put their bandanas on their heads. "Now why are you putting those on?"

"Because we weah 'em under ouah hats and if we try on hats, we gotta do 'em wit' da bandanas," explained Miguel. Keala moved to the side of the tent to find bigger hats to fit around the bandanas. She brought several out for them to try on. They stood there in front of the mirror that was attached to the hat hooks trying on several. Miguel did most of the talking while he flirted with Keala.

"So what else you going gimme if I buy one of yoh hats?"

"Oh, a smile and a thank you, and if all three of you buy hats, I'll throw in a *lauhala* headband for each."

"What about a kiss for a lonely *paniolo*?" asked Miguel.

"Oh, I can't do that," laughed Keala with her famous laugh that held nothing back.

"What about a phone number, then?"

"We don't have phones in Waipi'o."

"Then how'm I going take you out?"

Keala laughed again and tried to help him adjust an off white, fine woven hat which he had tilted to the side. It had an adjustable chin strap which she tightened. He grabbed one of her hands as she did this. "Did you hear me?"

"I'm trying to ignore the question which I'm sure you're just teasing me about."

"Now what makes you t'ink dat?" He was still holding onto her hand.

"I have a feeling there is a whole crowd of girls who are standing in line for you. You don't need one from my valley too."

"She got you wiyahed," said Lance. "He's got 'em lined up alright."

"Dat's enough outta you, Shima."

Keala laughed again and pulled her hand away. "See, I knew it—handsome boy like you. Now, tell me which one you like."

"You're the one I like," said Miguel.

"I meant the hat. Oh my, I think you have to get the white one. It fits you perfectly, and the girls will never leave you alone after that."

"Yeah, da white one. Den I can look like...who's dat sissy guy who sings in da cowboy movies?"

"Roy Rogers. Yep, that's the one or was it Gene Autry? He sings too," confirmed Keala with a gleam in her eyes.

"Nah, it's da king of da cowboys, Roy Rogers, dat one."

"Okay, nuff already," said Justin. "I'm getting' dis one," he said as he handed Keala the money for a two-tone beige *lauhala*. "Lance what you going do?"

"I dunno, it's between dis one and da oddah one."

"Make up yoh mind, we gotta go," said Justin impatient to leave.

"I t'ink I'm getting two of 'em," said Lance.

"Oh, that's wonderful. I'll give you a hat box for one of them," gushed Keala.

"Nah, I'll just carry one and weah one."

Keala clapped her hands after the two handed her their money. She turned to Miguel.

"Okay, I'll be da king of da cowboys," Miguel agreed as he put his money in her hand. "You sure a kiss doesn't go wit' da sale?"

"Oh alright, you caught me on a good day," she smiled and tiptoed up to kiss him quickly on the cheek. Not quick enough, because he turned his head instantly and caught her lips with his, as her knees went weak while her sister stood there in shock.

"Keala Kalia," Keahi yelled. It was too late. Keala was caught up in the kiss that made her head spin and curled the toes she was standing on.

"Wow, dat was sometin'. I'll buy annodah hat for anoddah one of dose."

Keala knew she should be embarrassed, but she just let loose with her bubbling laughter and actually batted her eyelashes, "Well…"

"Keala, that's enough," said her sister.

"Oh dear, I think I've done it now. I'll never hear the end of this," she said looking into those light green eyes, then sideways at her sister.

Miguel stood there staring at her. "Where'd you get such beautiful eyes?"

"From a wonderful man who passed away when I was seven years old," she replied candidly.

"Sorry 'bout dat," he said continuing to stand in front of her. "But I could drown in em."

"Yeah, well we goin' drown you in da ocean if you don't say goo'bye to dose pretty eyes, right now," muttered Justin.

"Okay, okay. Everybody got deyah hats and we're off." He turned back to Keala. "Bye, good lookin'. I guarantee you, we'll meet again."

"Aloha," she sighed smiling into the eyes she felt she could drown in too.

"I'm in love," said Miguel as they walked away.

"Yeah, I t'ink dat happens about once a day at da rate you going," grumbled Justin,

"What about once ev'ry five minutes," piped in Lance. "Geez, Cardoza, don't you have enough fillies in da corral. You want annodah one panting aftah you. Besides she's not yoh type."

"Whachu talking? You dunno what's my type."

"She's too…Hawaiian."

"No such t'ing," said Miguel as he put his new hat on his head.

"Well, you know. You got all dem oddah types. Dis one is too… you know."

"She's not…," attempted Justin.

"Not what?"

"She's not built like da oddah ones."

"Mebbe I'm changin' my tastebuds. I'm tiyahed of da skinny ones. Besides, if you don't eat enough, you tend to get grouchy. Da skinny ones got too much mood swings. Dey always ticked off about one t'ing or anoddah."

"Yeah, well I got one feeling deyah usually ticked off about each oddah," said Justin.

"Okay, nuff about da stupid fillies, it's givin' me a headache," said Miguel, as he nudged Justin to the side. They picked up their pace and headed towards the rodeo. Lance was scheduled in half an hour for his bull riding event.

4

Miguel Cardoza was the son of Portuguese immigrants whose families had come to Hawai'i at different times. His mother Alma Andrade was related to the first group who had migrated from Portugal's island of Madeira in the late 1800's. Her grandfather had come to work in the sugar plantations along with the Japanese and Chinese immigrants who were paid ten dollars a month, a room and a small allotment of food which, by their standards, were fine compared to the poverty and political upheaval from where they came. Alma was raised in Kalihi Valley on O'ahu, attended school at Kalakaua Intermediate and graduated from Farrington High School.

At the age of nineteen, she made a trip with friends to the Big Island and met the famous Andre Cardoza, a transplant to the Parker Ranch from San Francisco. He was forty at the time, well established in the *paniolo* world and had come with others in 1913 to work the ranches at a young age. She was very pretty with the light eyes of the Madeira Portuguese and became swept up in the charm of Andre's world. He had been well seasoned by then, sown all his wild oats with women galore, ready to settle down, as well as mesmerized by Alma's quiet beauty.

When they had their one and only son five years after their marriage, he became his father's pride and constant companion. They both doted on him, but everywhere Andre went, there was his little *paniolo* at his side. Miguel, named after a Mexican vaquero and friend of Andre's, learned both the good and bad habits of his father. They looked alike, talked alike, and had the same swaggering gait. Andre Cardoza taught his son all the skills he knew about riding, roping, and everything there was to learn about the handling of steers for profit.

The word *paniolo* came from the word, *Spanish* or *Espanol* after the Mexican *vaqueros* who were recruited in 1832 to work at the Parker Ranch bringing their flamboyant lifestyle with their expertise in handling long horn steers.

Decades later, it was Andre and his Portuguese friends who came to add their skills to the growing ranch business. He settled in the town of Waimea, and during World War II, when 20,000 troops invaded the town after signing a lease with the manager of Parker Ranch, he was among the cowboys who took part in their first rodeo competing with soldiers from Montana and Wyoming.

Andre was a keen craftsman in the making of mounts called tree saddles which were crafted especially for Hawaiian cowboys. The saddles were created to be fully submersed in the ocean when the *paniolo* would swim their cattle out to the awaiting boats and return back to shore again. A minimal amount of leather was used so that the sea water could just run right through the saddle due to its attached leather skirting which kept it from soaking up water. Andre's saddles were comfortable, minimal and designed to fit almost any horse. And even though it took him awhile to make them, they were in demand and enabled him to earn the extra money which he saved over the years along with his pay check to buy land of his own.

He started off with a half an acre and built a small three room shack. Then he accumulated another acre and, with the help of his friends, built a more substantial house. By the time Miguel was ten years old, the Cardozas had their own working ranch with five acres, several heads of cattle and a corral of the finest horses. All of Andre's skills paid off, and he accumulated more as the years went by, grooming his son to take over the business and teaching him everything he knew about ranching.

Miguel had no desire for any other life and even added a few skills of his own to the mix. He was employed on the Parker Ranch as a teenager and became an expert at rounding up wild *pipi* or bulls. It was dangerous work that required the best horses that were trained to work with him in split second teamwork with much needed speed and stamina for the challenge of roping and capturing these bulls on rough terrain.

On their own ranch, Andre taught Miguel the training and shoeing of horses and the importance of keeping them from being injured on the lava terrain. He learned in his training that horses needed to rest and reflect in between certain tasks, and that they excelled when they were given a short respite in between their duties and rewarded for any signs of obedience. Because their horses were cooperative and well trained as baby colts, people stood in line to purchase them from the Cardozas.

The next time Keala saw Miguel was at another rodeo in Waimea where the Second Annual Event was being held. They had another booth there, but her sister Kalena had also come with them, so Keala had more free time to roam around and watch the events. She saw Miguel's name on the program for Bare Back Horse Racing and made a point to watch his event. She noticed he was wearing her hat and watched him glide to home stretch as the winner. There were other events she slipped in to watch. The rodeo was held in an outdoor arena with theatre style bleachers on one side.

She watched Lance win the Bull Riding event with amazing tenacity, Justin place second in a Barrel Race and all three of them win the Team Roping. She felt she had to attend the last event, the Po'o Wai U. It was the one rodeo exercise unique to the Hawai'i *paniolo* where the rider, with the help of his horse, tied a bull to a tree fork, similar in shape to the base of a sling shot. Miguel won this event as he managed to lasso a bull, strap him to the tree and pull the rope taut within the shortest time span. This was an old custom used on the ranches in the early days and a dangerous, tedious way to round up bulls on the wide open plains of the Parker Ranch.

As Keala watched Miguel win this event, she clapped and cheered. She thought he looked like a character from the movies—not Roy Rodgers—but more like a wild Indian with his long hair, whirlwind speed, magnificent strength and the skill of a horseman born to the saddle. She wavered about going to say hello, but every time she saw him between events, he was surrounded by women. *Nope, better not,* she thought and went home that day with more thoughts of the handsome *paniolo.*

5

A month later, Manu persuaded the family to perform in the annual *lu'au* that the farmers were putting on in Waimea. A wealthy rancher had offered his ranch for the affair, and a large tented area had been set up on a grassy lawn. They all wore their Sunday best again which was the tutu *mu'umu'us* for the girls and *aloha* shirts for the boys. Keala had three she owned; this afternoon she wore her blue and white which she referred to as her "Kamehameha mu'u" because of the school colors.

The three boys were living independently on Manu's property. They still helped with the taro fields, but also worked on breeding, raising and training Manu's horses. They built and added two rooms to the small shack he owned to make it livable. None were even close to getting married. Their love of the valley kept them from going too far.

Bringing their *'ukuleles* and sweet singing voices, the family of eight walked up the steep hill on a Saturday afternoon to meet one of Manu's friends who had a truck to transport them. They piled in the back of the truck as Manu and Sara followed in his car. Windblown and happy to be together, the grown up children sang all the way to Waimea from Kukuihaele, the small town on the edge of beautiful Waipi'o Valley.

The occasion included hundreds of people from all over the Hamakua Coast and the town of Waimea, also including some who traveled from

Kona. These were people who worked the *'aina* as taro farmers, flower, fruit, vegetable, and coffee growers, and just simple people who planted their own gardens to survive.

The Kalias were the scheduled entertainment along with another group who were known for their musical talent. They started on an upbeat chorus with the songs of the islands *Hilo March, Molokai Nui Ahina, Maika'i Wale No Kaua'i, Maui No Ka Oe, Beautiful Ilima* as the audience sang along with them.

Then the traditional songs were sung in Kalia family harmony: *Akaka Falls, Across the Sea, Ahi Wela, Akahi Ho'i, Kaulana Na Pua, Ke Kali Nei Au, Hi'ilawe,, Pua Ahihi,* and *Puamana.*

The three girls danced to *Waikiki* a wonderful version of Andy Cummings song; then Keala danced a medley of two *haole* renditions: *To you Sweetheart Aloha* and R. Alex Anderson's *I'll Weave a Lei of Stars for You.*

"Deyah her," said Lance sitting next to Miguel at a table five rows back from the stage.

"Who?" asked Miguel as he looked up from the *kalua* pig and *poi* he was in the process of devouring.

"Da *papale* girl. You know da Hawaiian."

"Wheyah?" said Miguel looking around the room.

"On da stage. She's dancing."

Miguel glanced up at the stage and saw her. His heart slammed into his chest, and her smile made him go all soft inside. It was what hit him during their first encounter—and here she was again, gliding across the stage like a Hawaiian princess.

> *I'll weave a lei of stars for you*
> *To wear on nights like this*
> *Each time you wear my lei of stars*
> *I'll greet you with a kiss*
> *The moon is filled with jealousy*
> *Shines on our rendezvous*
> *For when you wear my Lei of Stars*
> *The fairest one is you*

Keala's sparkling eyes, which were enhanced by make-up, were flirting with the audience, and the radiance of her smile entranced them as her hands gracefully told the story.

Miguel left his *kalua* pig and moved behind Lance's sister, Gwen, who was seated four people down from Miguel and Lance. "Could I borrow your lei?" he asked her.

Their Japanese mother, Haruko had an unusual preoccupation with the medieval legend and named her oldest son Arthur; Lance was short for Lancelot, and then there was Guinevere who shortened her name to Gwen. Haruko's husband, Mr. Shimabukuro, put a stop to the nonsense when she insisted on naming their ranch *Camelot* and promptly cancelled the order that she had put in for the sign that was to hang over the entrance to their large property.

"What do you mean *borrow* my lei?"

"I mean could you *give* me your lei and I'll owe you one, or I'll pay for it right now."

She wore a double ginger that she loved, but she saw the look on Miguel's face. "Okay, you'll owe me one then," she said as she pulled the lei off her neck to give to him.

He put the lei around his neck as he watched Keala and waited for her to walk off the stage. Her brothers and Manu continued to play, and she exited after she bowed to the audience to much applause. Miguel followed her with his eyes; then jumped up from his seat in pursuit.

When he caught up with her, she smiled up at him and said, "The Paniolo, how nice to see you."

"Come wit' me," he blurted out, grabbing her hand and leading her outside the tent towards the stables near the corral of the large ranch.

"Where are we going?" she asked, laughing nervously, but anticipating she knew not what.

"I have to lei you?"

"You have to lay me?"

"I mean I have to give you a lei," he said.

"Why do we have to go so far for you to give me a lei?"

"Cause I have to give it to you properly."

"What are you talking about? We're going all this way so you can give me a lei?"

"Yes," he replied and he spun her around against the wall of the stables, took his lei from around his neck, put it around Keala's, pushed his body up against her and gave her a kiss that had them both panting when he was done.

"Well, I guess I see why we had to..." she stopped in mid sentence when he angled his head and kissed her again."Wow," she finally stammered.

"Yep, dat was a 'wow', alright. Where da heck have you been. I've been looking everywhere hopin' to run into you."

"Um...I saw you a month ago."

"What?"

"I went to the Waimea Rodeo. I saw you win the bareback race and I watched you tie the bull to the tree. That was really exciting."

"Why didn't you come talk to me?"

"Too many fans around, and besides..."

"Besides what?"

"I don't know. I just decided not to."

"So, when can I see you again?"

"I don't know," she said. "Probably not a good idea, Miguel, I'm not really your type."

"And what is dat?"

"I don't want to put anyone down. Just be satisfied with that. Okay?"

"Can't," he replied and bent down to kiss her again.

She heard someone calling her from the direction of the tent. It sounded like Keahi. "I gotta go," said Keala. She gave him her bright smile again. "Thank you, Miguel for the lovely lei. I'll keep it forever." She kissed his cheek and turned to run towards the tent.

6

KEALA WOKE UP ONE MORNING in the small bed that she had slept in all her life. The three girls had shared the same room for years, but Keahi and Kalena moved into the boys' room now that they were out of the house.

An end table sat next to her bed and a set of dresser drawers which Manu had crafted out of koa wood stood against the wall where a bamboo framed mirror was hung. Her mother had sewn her a green and white Hawaiian quilt and pillows to match. She always kept her room organized and neat, a ritual from her dormitory days at Kamehameha. There were some things that were missing like electricity to keep the room lighted at night, but they each had lamps lit with the aid of *kukui* nut oil.

Keala stretched and put her feet on the *lauhala* covered floor. A recently built deck ran completely around the living part of the house on the second floor. Her favorite thing to do was to drink her Kona coffee on the deck before she started her day. There was always a tin coffee pot heated on the wood burning stove put on by the first person who got up. This morning she poured the aromatic coffee into her favorite mug, walked out to the deck in front of the sliding screen door of her bedroom and sat down in her favorite canvas chair.

Her double ginger lei was now wilting after two days of scentng her room with its unique fragrance. Their yard was filled with all kinds of ginger, but somehow this was special to her. She had not permitted herself to think about the handsome *paniolo*, but that lei seemed to symbolize his presence. She thought about the kiss they shared and a smile passed over her face. Then she quickly got up and slapped the side of her head. *Okay, that's enough, Keala, you have more important things to do than daydream about somebody who should be off limits.*

She remembered Justin's words "Nuff already", and went to brush her teeth after pouring water from a pitcher into a ceramic bowl that was set out on her dresser. She pulled a pair of jeans out of her closet with a long sleeve cotton shirt, looked in her wall mirror and brushed her short hair back. She applied lipstick to her lips, a ritual she could not live without. Today, she wore a bright red to go with the hibiscus she would pin in her hair when she picked it from a tree that grew next to the house.

Keala had not changed in appearance since high school. She was still short in stature, well endowed with round hips, more of a soft womanly figure than that of a girl at nineteen. Country girl or not, Keala paid attention to her appearance even when there was no one around to see her. It was a long time habit that made her feel good about herself.

She headed downstairs, picked a miniature red hibiscus and pinned it in her hair, then went to sort the *lauhala* she was going to strip and cut today to start making a hat. She was alone this morning. Her sisters had already left for Honoka'a with Manu and her mom to get supplies for the house.

Keala loved the luxury of solitude which was unique in a large family. While she stripped her *lauhala,* she hummed her favorite Hawaiian songs and concentrated on the task at hand. She was ready to weave a little before noon. After gathering her strips, she retrieved her favorite chair to sit under the shade of an avocado tree near the small stream that ran beside the house. Keala was in the midst of singing one of her favorite Hawaiian songs which sounded like a hymn, but was actually a sexy song about making love when she heard the clip clop of horse hoofs.

The sound got closer and she thought it might be one of her brothers who'd come to visit. She turned around and sitting there on a caramel colored stallion was Miguel. Keala stood up quickly dumping her lauhala strips on the ground.

"Oh my goodness. You're here."

"Yep, I'm heyah," he said dismounting from the immense horse that snorted and stamped his foot.

"How did you find me?"

"Wasn't easy. Had to stop at every house befoah I found dis one."

Keala stood staring at him, absolutely tongue tied in shock. He was here on her land in her territory in the Valley of Waipi'o. She couldn't believe it. He wore his long sleeve *palaka* shirt and blue jeans over brown leather boots. The hat she made sat tipped at an angle on his head and he looked like the vision of the daydreams she had tried to ward off in her mind.

Recovering from her daze, she went forward to greet him. "Well, then. Welcome to Waipi'o Valley." As she said this, she gave him the bright smile that he had come all the way to see as her eyes shined up at him.

"Ah, I was hoping to see dat smile," he said grasping her hands.

"Just for you," she replied. "Come inside and I'll make you something to drink and eat."

"Sounds good to me," he smiled, still grasping one hand as she guided him to the stairs that led to the second level of her house. "Where's your family?" he asked when she opened the sliding screen door to the living room.

"Oh they went to Honoka'a for the day."

"Hmm. We're alone then."

"Uh, yes, I guess we are." Her mouth went dry. "Okay, Cardoza, don't be getting any ideas," she said trying to pull away.

"Alright, I won't, but I t'ink I need a reward for comin all dis way." Then he pulled her closer and bent to give her a long luscious kiss.

Afrter a moment, she pushed away from him, flustered and trying not to show it. "Your reward is going to be a good lunch and something to drink. Now you have to promise to behave yourself."

"Okay, I promise. Maybe I just goin' have you for dessert."

He sat at their long family table admiring the hibiscus in her hair, as his eyes checked her out from head to toe while he watched her prepare tuna sandwiches and a small avocado salad. Then she quickly ran downstairs and returned with a cold bottle of Lucky Lager beer.

"Where'd you go?"

"I had to retrieve this from the stream. That's what we use instead of an ice box."

He liked that for some reason and was fascinated with the pioneer house, asking her all kinds of questions about their lifestyle without electricity and central plumbing.

"Unreal dis place. So you gotta finish yoah work or you wanna show me around Waipi'o?"

"Oh, hospitality comes first in this neck of the woods. I'll show you Waipi'o. You don't have to work today, either I guess."

"Nope, I decided to play hooky."

She laughed her musical laugh that made him warm inside and infused him with that strange sense of *coming home*—something he couldn't quite understand, but connected him with a feeling of well being.

When they were finished eating, she cleared the table, showed him around the house and all the contraptions they used to improvise. Miguel had been on the range and used to roughing it, but was impressed with a household that lived this way on an everyday basis. As they stood by her bedroom door, he noticed the wilted ginger lei on her nightstand.

"You kept it."

"What?"

"Da lei."

"Oh, that. I just forgot to throw it away."

"Hmm. I don't t'ink so. You wanted to remember me."

"Umm. I think it's time to go outside now."

He caught her hand in his when they reached the bottom of the stairs and they walked towards the outside area. She showed him a small fresh water pool that they had built a dam around to catch the mountain water and where they rinsed off on hot days. Then they walked over to the bamboo shower area where they bathed.

"So who rigged this up?"

"My dad did years ago and Manu improved it. He's the one who married my mom and saved us all. Actually he's done a lot of improvements around the house. He built the deck, put in sliding doors, and made a larger platform down below the house for us to sort the taro and hala leaves. Manu's an amazing man, and we're all grateful for him."

"So, you wanna get on my horse wit' me. We can see da rest from horseback."

"We do have horses too, you know. My brothers take care of them. I could go over and get one of them."

"Nope, I t'ink it would be more fun to ride togeddah."

She turned towards him to look at his face. "Hmm. More fun? You promised to behave remember?"

"No sweat," he replied. So, she mounted the brown stallion; then he hoisted himself up behind her, and they saw the rest of Waipi'o from horseback.

"By the way, the horse's name is Malasadas."

"Oh my, you named him after a pastry?"

"Yep, my favorite pastry and my favorite horse."

"Of course," she laughed again. "You wanna see the ocean or the waterfalls?" she asked.

"The waterfalls. I saw da ocean on my way in."

It took awhile to feel comfortable riding in front while he encircled her with his body. At first, she sat up stiffly, leaning forward. "Relax," he urged her, pulling her back against his chest where she finally nestled for the rest of the ride.

She showed him their taro fields, a wide spread of land where running water trickled through the elephant ear plants with a lush beauty of their own, sitting in rows waiting for their harvest in a month. Keala explained the process to Miguel and all the work it took to keep the weeds from strangling their growth progress.

"I've pulled weeds from taro fields ever since I was a young *keiki*. We all did. Never a day went by when we weren't working these fields in one capacity or another. Now that Manu has helpers, my sisters and I have more time to do our weaving, and my brothers take care of the horses at Manu's place which is our next stop."

They traveled up a wide path which was really a stream bed with running water. When the rains came, it was a full on river, but for now it was shallow, and the horse could easily clop through the water. They came to a high fenced area with smooth wires attached to posts around the perimeter. Keala eased down from Malasadas and went to open the gate to the property, which was not locked, but simply latched.

She waved them in and ran alongside the horse when a big Hawaiian, built like a heavy-weight prize fighter, approached them as they were arriving. It was Kala, her number two brother. He was dressed in jeans without a shirt exposing his massive brown chest.

"Kala, this is my friend Miguel Cardoza. He's from Waimea." She watched the two men size each other up. Miguel had a smile on his face. Her brother was either squinting from the sun or scowling. She couldn't figure out which.

"Cardoza, yeah, I've heard of you. I know your friend Justin. He comes down heah ev'ry once in awhile."

"Yeah we've known each other a long time," replied Miguel as he slid off of Malasadas.

"So how'd you two meet?" asked Kala.

"Umm," she smiled at Miguel. "We're old friends, but this is the first time he's come to visit."

"How'd you get heah, Keala?"

"We rode tandem," she said. "Now, Kala, I think you need to put on one of your best *aloha* smiles and welcome Miguel to the Valley."

Kala put on a smile that didn't quite reach his eyes. He followed it by saying, "Welcome to Waipi'o, Miguel Cardoza," and reached out to shake his hand.

He gave them a tour of the mini ranch and Miguel admired their horses while Keala pointed out the new barn that was being built to give them shelter. Kala sent them off with a cold drink and they headed towards Hi'ilawe Falls.

"I t'ink yoah bruddah doesn't trust me."

"Should he?"

"Of coahse," he smiled and tightened his arms around her.

They meandered through lush jungle trails along the hillside, through streams and rivers, observing waterfalls on the cliffs, ponds, colorful flowers, and native trees accompanied by the sound of exotic birds everywhere. The weather in the valley could change in an instant, but today it stayed sunny; Keala had prayed it would remain so. She wanted Miguel to see her homeland at its best.

He was enjoying the ride in more ways than one—patting himself on the back for suggesting the tandem ride, as well as enjoying the closeness of this soft joyful person whose smile made *him* smile and whose enthusiasm for her heartland helped him share in her pleasure.

They talked as they rode. She pointed out points of interest and exclaimed at everything as if she had not seen it before. Each time she wandered through here, she saw something new. He told her stories about his escapades with his friends, his love of horses and how he trained them; he talked about what a great man his father was and as they rode, they got to know each other better.

They reached a banked area, approaching a large stream, that they decided not to navigate, but they got close enough to see Hi'ilawe at a distance in its splendor as it fell a few hundred feet onto an upper pool, then slid and cascaded down the face of the cliff for another thousand feet.

They watched it for awhile, a magnificent sight that made the Valley of Waipi'o so unique in its grandeur. Miguel watched the waterfall tumble down the mountain and observed the expression on Keala's face—such a zest for life; her appreciation was contagious. He hugged her tightly and nuzzled her neck giving her such a chicken skin reaction that she almost jumped off the horse. Then he turned her face to kiss him and she complied gladly. He knew she had softened towards him and that made him happy.

He left her that day with another kiss and wrote down her post office address, when he realized it was the only way he would be able to reach her. After that, he wrote her a short note once a week, something she anticipated each time the mail was retrieved from the post office box in Honoka'a. One day, he arranged to have her meet him at the top of the hill and drove her to his ranch where she was taken to meet his family.

7

Alma Cardoza liked Keala immediately and fawned over her, sprinkling her words with her native Portuguese and serving homemade bread with butter and her famous Portuguese soup, a favorite dish in the islands. Keala's warmth was contagious, and Andre followed suit in his wife's affection for this congenial Hawaiian girl. They would have preferred someone from their own culture, but Andre decided there were no package deals in life. And besides…they were here in Hawai'i after all.

Miguel showed Keala *his* world—their stables, the horses, the three corrals, the large ranch house and its views of majestic Maunakea, the fruit trees in the circular driveway. Then he took her to a separate two bedroom house, which was his alone, where he lived and breathed and woke every morning to the Waimea sunshine or mist on certain days. Like her room, it was organized and neat, but filled with rodeo memorabilia, silver belt buckles, other trophies, one of his father's elaborate tree saddles displayed like a piece of art, pictures galore with every cowboy imaginable, but not one with any women. She wondered if he had hidden them for her visit, but appreciated it anyway.

On his living room wall was a painting of a cowboy and a little boy. At a closer look, she realized it was Andre and Miguel when he was about seven. They were wearing matching *paniolo* outfits with their arms around each other and two horses in the background. She loved it and told him so.

He pulled her to him and kissed her then. He thought how nice it was to have her there and noticed that the room was brightened by her presence. He kept kissing her until she gently pushed on his chest and moved towards the door to go back into the main house.

"Chicken," he teased her.

"That's me the big chicken," she confirmed.

"Okay, okay. Let's go see the folks. I t'ink dey like you."

"Well, good, cause I like them."

"Yeah, me too, I guess."

"Your mother called me *beleza* and she calls you *macaco*. What do those words mean?"

"Macaco means monkey which she called me since I was one small kid. I guess I climbed anyt'ing dat was tallah dan me."

"And *beleza*? What is that?"

"Beauty, cause dat's what you are."

Keala's family was not as enthusiastic towards Miguel. Her brothers came over for dinner at the main house one night and Kala started it. All eight of them were seated at the long family before a feast her mother had prepared. They had poi with fresh fish that was fried in a pan on the wood burning stove, avocado salad with vegetables from their garden. Panoa and Kala had caught the fish that day in Waipi'o Bay. Manu said the prayer before dinner and they all began talking and eating at once.

"So, Keala, you still seeing dat Cardoza guy?" asked Kala.

"Uh, yes, I am…once in awhile."

"I heard some bad t'ings about him."

"Who you talking about?" asked Panoa.

"Miguel Cardoza. You know him—da one who rides wit' Justin."

"Who's seeing him?" asked Kawai.

"Keala," replied Kala.

Two "Oh no's" came out of Panoa and Kawai's mouth.

"I don't want to talk about him," said Keala.

"Keala, he's kind of a snake in da grass," said Panoa.

"Girls comin outta hees eyahs," said Kawai.

"A lot of girls," said Kala.

"I don't want to talk about him," said Keala one more time.

"He's not da one for you," said Panoa.

Manu saved her and said, "She said she doesn't want to talk about him, so leave it alone."

They went on to other subjects, but Keala was forewarned. She was concerned about her brothers' words of caution, but could not discount the great effort Miguel took to see her. He had come down to Waipi'o all of five times now—not exactly a hop, skip and a jump from Waimea. He had to load up Malasadas in a horse trailer, attach it to his truck, park the truck at the top of the mountain, unload the horse, mount him to ride down the steep rocky incline into the valley and ride farther up a stream to reach her house. He made it clear what he was after. She was no fool. He got bolder and bolder every time she saw him, but he respected her screeching halts to everything. The more time she spent with him, holding him off was equally hard on her.

They were sitting on rocks by the stream one afternoon. "I t'ink I'm in love," he said again—this time to her.

She laughed and mimicked him, "You tink you're in love?"

"I'm all serious heyah and you makin' fun of my English?"

"Sorry," she said, trying to stifle her laugh.

"I talk like everybody else on da Big Island, except da *haoles* of coahse. You da one who's different. How come?"

"Ah, Kamehameha I guess…and then there's my mother. She hounded the girls and gave up on the boys."

"Well, getting back to da subject. Umm now where da heck was I?"

"You said, "You were in love, but you didn't say with whom."

"Now you making me mad and ruinin' my speech I was going give you."

"Okay, go ahead…"

"I'm sick and tiyahd of comin' down dis hill and I was wonderin' if you just might want to take a stab at livin' somewheyah else…wheyah it's cooler and not as much rain or maybe just as much, I dunno."

"What are you trying to tell me? You want me to live with you?"

"No, you can't jus' live wit' me. My maddah would have a fit. I meant mebbe we could get married."

"What?" she said turning towards him in shock.

"Well, what you t'ink I've been comin' around for. I would have stopped on the first run down dat stupid hill."

"Oh, Miguel, what a lovely thing to offer me. I love you too," she said and threw her arms around him and kissed him several times on his face.

"So, what's da verdict. Was dat a yes?"

"Two questions before I answer. Are you willing to forsake all others?"

"Whachu mean?"

"Other women have to take a hike. Can you do that? I hear it's a big habit with you."

"Not any moah. I only have eyes foh you," he said with a sexy look on his chiseled face. "So what's da oddah question?"

"Can I still go to my church?"

"We have to marry Catholic or my maddah's goin' have one cow and say hundred Novenas foh us…but you can go to yoh own church aftah dat."

"Then it's a yes Miguel Cardoza, for better or for worse."

He gave out a *paniolo* whoop and kissed her long and hard.

8

AFTER MANY OBJECTIONS, PROTESTS AND boycotting from her family, Keala finally got their reluctant approval. Her brothers were the most vocal and she had heard it all from them. Her sisters were doubtful, but looking forward to having their own rooms. Manu was the sweetest of them all and gave her a hug and sincere blessings for a long and happy life.

Her mother approached her one evening as she sat on the deck watching the stars that lit up the valley on an unusually clear night. "Hi Baby."

"Hi, Mama."

"Can I join you?" Sara asked as she sat in another canvas chair beside her.

Sara was fifty seven years old at the time, and looked a bit older than her years. Her hair was almost completely gray which she wore short and styled herself. Her face showed the wear and tear of the many years of working hard in the sunlit taro fields and the unending chores that it took to take care for a family of six. But her calm demeanor and steadfast spirit were still what carried all of them through their trials and joys. Her faith never wavered and she was their rock because of it.

"Please do, Mama. I've been wanting to talk to you. You've been awfully quiet in all of this."

Sara understood the "this" Keala referred to. "Yes, I have. I've been waiting for the right time to say things."

"Well, you can let me have it now."

"No, no Baby, it's not like that. I just want to make sure of certain things."

"Like what?"

"Well, are you prepared to take this big step? There are a lot of unknowns about this man. I am assured that he loves you. He even told me himself. I am confident that he will take care of you. He seems to have the means for that. But..."

"You're worried about his tainted past."

"Somewhat," replied Sara. "I've been married to two good men. There are some men who only need one woman and then..."

"There are others who need more attention than others, right?"

"Yes."

"It's too late, Mama. I love him and I'm going to try my darnedest with the help of our Lord and Savior to make it work."

"Then, Keala'iliahi I give you my blessings and I will never from this day forward say another word on the matter," promised Sara as she got up to give her youngest daughter a long meaningful hug.

"Forsaking all others, for better or for worse, in sickness and in health, until death do you part, in the name of the Father, Son and Holy Spirit." With those words Keala Kalia became Mrs. Miguel Cardoza—a happy, blissful day for both of them in the presence of a hundred people who saw them pledge their vows in a small Catholic Church in Waimea.

Hundreds more from Kona to the Hamakua Coast and even those who drove from Hilo showed up for the reception at the Cardoza Ranch. There were *paniolos* and ranchers, farmers and laborers, some of the big wigs from the Parker Ranch and everyone who was a friend of the bride and groom and their two families. The beer and wine flowed, the music was played by several groups, young and old alike danced merrily, and it turned out to be a festive occasion for all.

The Cardozas insisted on putting on the whole affair. They tented their front yard with a stage and dance floor and barbecue spits were going with *huli huli* chicken and the finest beef from the ranches around. The Kalias participated in playing their music in between Hawaiian country and Rock and Roll bands.

The bride wore a simple white. *tutu mu'umu'u* with a special lei of purple orchids interwoven with pikake and a *haku* lei on her head The groom was decked out in the traditional wedding garb which had originated with the *paniolos* of old in long sleeve white shirt, white slacks and a red sash. His hair was tied back in his usual braid, a lei of maile leaves around his neck and his head crowned with another *haku* lei, specially woven by Sara Kalia for the occasion.

They performed all the traditional things that weddings require— the cutting of the cake, the throwing of the bouquet, and dancing the first dance together in which they had eyes only for each other. Miguel was proud of his bride and thought she looked enchanting. He had no doubts that this was the girl for him.

Of course, there were many girls whose hearts were broken and couldn't believe that Miguel Cardoza had chosen his bride over them, but they were comforted by the hundreds of single men who attended.

One of the Parker Ranch big wigs gifted them with a three day honeymoon at the Kona Inn, and they left their guests behind as they drove off in his truck decorated with tin cans and leis, which he promptly removed when they got two miles down the road.

"Okay, Keala, this is when the fun begins," he said when they entered the room of their bridal suite.

Keala burst out in her laugh that bubbled forth with joy and exclaimed, "I can hardly wait." And the fun began.

9

THERE WERE GOOD TIMES TOGETHER. They loved each other more and more as they got settled in their two bedroom house. Keala added a feminine touch with a Hawaiian flair. The trophies and saddle and memorabilia went the way of the storage shed, and the house bloomed with Hawaiian quilts and spreads and pillows and flowers and lauhala mats galore. Miguel was fine with all of it. He loved his wife and whatever she wanted to do, he was willing. She gave him lots of freedom to work the ranch, to be with his friends and to ride the plains of Waimea.

He taught her to become an adequate horsewoman, showing her how to train the colts from birth to acclimate themselves to the world and their masters, a process called "imprinting". She learned to gently touch them in every part of their bodies to make the eventual training easier. After three months, she got them used to a halter as they were taught to "lead" or follow with a rope and a halter around their necks. Once the colts got adjusted and were a year old, they were ready to wear the saddle pad and a light blanket; then hitched to a post and trained to be tied up and obey commands.

She learned the process with two colts, one that was just born and another that was ready to take the saddle at two years old. She teamed up with Miguel with the task of riding the two year old for his first outing with a saddle. She had previously trained it to take the bridle —a headstall with bit and reins. Soon after, Miguel put her on the saddle while he walked and led the horse on foot. Keala manipulated the horse by her soothing voice, and her hands and legs as it learned to turn in different directions while Miguel handled the reins.

He gave this first horse that she trained as a gift to her to use for pleasure riding. Keala named it Waipi'o after her homeland. They had five acres on which she could ride and she loved the exercise every day as she viewed the peaks of Maunakea during her outings.

Her in-laws left them to themselves, but would have them for dinner once a month on Sundays. Miguel's mom was a firm believer of giving privacy to newlyweds in their first year, an old Biblical tradition.

Keala did not go back to her church in Waipi'o as planned. She discovered Imiola Congregational Church, a quaint historic place, the oldest church in Waimea where many Hawaiians worshiped. She found comfort there and convinced Miguel to come with her once in a while.

They called each other by their Portuguese names his mother had given them. He was Macaco to her and she was Beleza to him. Keala spread her joy amongst his family and friends. Their house was full of people who basked in the hospitality that was Waipi'o born. She never tired of cooking meals and sharing whatever they had to give. The luxuries of plumbing and electricity were not taken for granted by her, and he was pleased with her appreciation for everything.

All went well in the first year of wedded bliss and then it crumbled after a series of incidents.

One of the habits that he picked up from his father that she had not noticed until after awhile was the need to drink on a nightly basis. From the drinking, stemmed other things. He seemed to handle it well, so she was not alarmed at first. As a happy drinker, he was affectionate and loving with her, so she overlooked the downside until he started to feel the need to go out with his friends to his favorite watering holes until all hours of the night. It started on weekends and sometimes carried over to intermittent weekdays.

She went to look for him one night after waiting for him to come home and found him in a bar lounge. Lance was with him and several other people, but one of them was an attractive woman who was draped over Miguel like a *paniolo poncho.*

"Hello," she said to the woman. "My name is Keala," she introduced herself as she approached the bar.

The woman was clearly inebriated, kissing Miguel's ears while Keala stood there. "Get lost," she said to Keala as Miguel tried to undrape her from his shoulders.

"I've come to take my husband home. I think he's in trouble and you happen to be the trouble," said Keala as she pulled Miguel away from her.

"I guess I gotta go home now," was all he said as he followed his wife out the door.

Of course, he apologized all over himself the next day and vowed never to let it happen again...but it did. She caught him in compromising situations at parties, at restaurants, at the bars on several occasions, but the worst happened when she came home unexpectedly after visiting her family in Waipi'o. She was supposed to spend the night there, but decided against it and came home on the Borgward car that Miguel had purchased for her a few months before.

She opened the door and heard scrambling and voices in the bedroom. Her heart stopped and she stood in place. The first person to come out was a thin wisp of a girl with tousled hair wearing one of Keala's robes. Miguel walked out next just as disheveled with no shirt and his jeans.

"Surprise," she simply said as Miguel stood there in a stupor.

"Keala," he whispered.

"Miguel, you need to take this poor girl home. She looks tired."

After she got dressed, Miguel accompanied the girl to his truck and returned a half hour later. Keala was sitting on their couch, looking so sad it broke his heart.

"Miguel, remember that smile that you loved so much—the one that you said you could not live without. It's gone now and I can't seem to get it back."

"Keala, I..."

"There's nothing more to say, dear Miguel. I've loved you from the moment we met and I may love you until the day I die. But you broke your promise to me and my heart. Remember that promise?"

"Yes," he mumbled—his voice thick with grief.

"Say it so I'll know you didn't forget."

"*Forsaking all others*," he whispered. He even put the "th" together to make it clear.

"Ah, you remembered," she said with tears rolling down her face. "Keala, I..."

She held up her hand to stop him from saying more. "Miguel. I must go now. I came to you with nothing more than the clothes I wore on my back and that is all I am leaving with. You may pick up the car at the top of the hill and please do not ever go farther than that. I don't want any more memories of you in my valley."

"Keala, please, please just one more chance. I love only you. I'm so sorry."

"I know you are, my dear sweet boy who made me laugh and taught me how to love. I thank you for that," she said as she slid her Hawaiian wedding ring off her finger and put it on the coffee table in front of the couch.

He ran after her and chased the car on foot down the driveway. "Keala," he cried as she drove from the sprawling ranch in Waimea overlooking the hills of majestic Maunakea and headed towards the beautiful valley of Waipi'o.

The Gathering

The Aloha Breakfast

THE SIX WOMEN HAD RESPONDED to each others' stories as they sat at the long koa table in Keala's dining room overlooking the majestic mountain of Maunakea. They dined over omelets with brown sugared spam in the morning for Puakea's tale, corned beef sandwiches in the afternoon for Kanoe's tragedy, sweet sour spare ribs and rice for Nani's cliffhanger, French toast and Portuguese sausages the next morning for Lihau's drama, chicken salad for Kia's suspense thriller and a wonderful Hawaiian feast with *laulaus* and *poi* for Keala's domestic saga.

In between meals, they had gone horseback riding on the ranch, sightseeing along the Hamakua Coast, shopping in Honoka'a, long walks in Keala's neighborhood, a drive to Hapuna Beach and finally to the Waipi'o Outlook overlooking Keala's beautiful valley.

They had spent the last four days getting to know each other again in more intimate ways, and yet all six of them had unfinished stories. Keala's motive was to have them absorb the telling and to inspire a keen interest in each story. She did not expect what resulted—that they would each end their accounts in suspense and leave the listeners anticipating their conclusions. Puakea had started the pattern and they had all followed suit. They were now eager to share the rest.

Insisting that they help Keala restore her house to the way they found it when they arrived, the women spent the early morning, changing sheets, cleaning bathrooms and packing their suitcases. Breakfast was simple with pastries from a local bakery and freshly brewed Kona coffee. They were ready and Puakea was the first to speak.

Puakea

I GAVE UP ON DEE after that. It was sad and frustrating, and you know me, I hate being unhappy. So I moved on. I finally decided to please my dad and go to UH, surprised that the admissions people even looked at my transcripts which were riddled with C's and a few D's thrown in, but by some miracle, I got in.

You know, it was not really that bad. I actually started digging on some of the classes and tuned in for the first time. Just for fun, I decided to really learn something, so I studied hard to get A's. Now, did I ever do that in high school? No.

Another thing that was weird was being with so many people from different races. I didn't realize what a Hawaiian bubble we lived in at Kamehameha. I know everybody was mixed, but when you come right down to it, we were all Hawaiians. Now, I was there since first grade, so I was really entrenched in the bubble and my exposure to others was pretty much Waikiki and the paddling world. So that was mostly *haoles* and more Hawaiians.

The University was dominated by Asians which is what they're referred to now, but I started making new friends in this world. The girls were always dressed, not like me in the tee shirt and jeans or shorts when I could get away with it, but these girls were something else. They had the best hair styles and their clothes were immaculate. I exaggerate, but that's how I saw it. Plus, they seemed a tad smarter than everyone else and that started to give me a complex.

So because of the complex, I took it on as a challenge and started powering up to compete with them. Before I knew it, I was on the honor roll and started to ace all my courses. After two years of undergraduate courses, I picked my major. Now, being on the All Star Team in PE at Kamehameha had given me confidence in my athletic abilities and not to brag, but you all know that I was pretty good in that area. So of course, I chose Physical Education as my major and went on to graduate with that degree.

You're probably wondering about my social life which was so-so during that time. Guys were getting drafted and it was right on the edge of the Viet Nam War. Even with the shortage of guys, there were a few intellectuals interested in me, God only knows why, but they were and I actually found myself having heavy duty philosophical conversations with them.

But that's all talk and I much preferred the jocks who were scattered in my classes. I did date a UH football player. I wouldn't call it dating unless a beer at Charlie's Tavern or a bite to eat at Rainbow Drive-In is considered dating, but we were an item for awhile. And then there's all that trying to avoid the inevitable—and you know what I'm talking about—which became more and more expected as "free love" became the thing. So, I graduated from UH actually avoiding all that—by the skin of my teeth I might add.

In the meantime, my parents were really cool about giving me room and board while I went to school, and I did manage to keep my two jobs in Diamond Head to pay for gas and whatevers. That nice lady on Wilhelmina Rise died and left me ten thousand dollars in her will. I was flabbergasted when I heard the news from her lawyer, and it really helped as a nice cushion which went right into a savings account to collect interest. I more than worked for her; we'd become good friends.

I'd just graduated from UH and my brother Lanakila comes over for dinner one night. He'd been living in Waikiki and moving up the ladder as a fireman if you'll pardon the pun. We sit down to dinner, after saying grace of course, and he makes his big announcement—he's getting married. Well you could fill a barnyard with all the chicks my brother had in his date book, not that he actually had one, but I never dreamed he'd settle down. In fact I'd never seen him with the same girl after he broke up with Connie—that's his high school girlfriend— for more than a week.

"So who's the lucky girl," I asked,

"Connie, of course."

"Now how did you finagle that one? I thought she was done with you years ago?"

"She changed her mind. Actually, I changed it for her."

"Amazing," I said and my mother went all teary eyed and started gushing. My dad just kept eating.

So, the reason why I'm telling you this is it led to another big event—probably the biggest one in my life. Guess who came to the wedding? Yep, Thaddeus Crown himself. Can't tell you how floored I was when I saw him standing at the bar at their reception.

I had no idea what to do. Should I talk to him? I decided not to. I thought he'd avoid me if he saw me, so I turned in the opposite direction and tried to hide. I found out later that he was looking for me. He found me hiding at a table of old ladies I didn't even know. They were relatives of Connie's and were talking about all their aches and pains and operations. I tried to sound really interested like I was taking a course at UH.

"So, when did you have your gall bladder removed?" I asked one of them.

"Oh it was four months ago."

"So, did it hurt?

Stuff like that we were talking, and then I felt these hands on my shoulders. "Puakea, do you want to dance?" It was him and my heart just about slammed out of my chest when I turned and saw him.

"Well, I was…" I was going to tell him I was in the middle of this riveting conversation, but knew he wouldn't buy it, so I excused myself and got up from the table to follow him.

I have to tell you, that I just happened to be looking rather stunning in this blue chiffon dress—not unlike the one you wore to all your proms, Nani—which Connie chose for her bridesmaids. I was one of four and she had originally chosen this God-awful pink number which I tactfully talked her out of. "Pretty in Pink" was not me; I would have looked like some washed out *haole* and of course it was all about me, right? Connie has blue eyes and I told her that if we wore blue (which is my favorite color since I went to Kamehameha, but I didn't tell her that) that it would bring out the colors in her eyes. So she bought that and thus, I was looking pretty darn good when Dee came to ask me to dance.

We stood together on the dance floor and a Hawaiian band played "Who's Sorry Now?" Would you believe? But it was actually a good song to slow dance to and I slipped into his arms and we swayed to the music. He didn't say much and neither did I, afraid of breaking the spell which was really my dream come true.

When the dance ended, he spoke. "I need to talk to you." So, I followed him outside to this patio area where there were chairs at cocktail tables. What hit me was that Dee Crown, the recluse who wouldn't step out of his house forever was actually in a public place and not one bit concerned about dancing with me on a crowded dance floor. I looked at his face as we sat down and I thought he looked wonderful. The scars that ran down the left side had lost their redness and he was not as gaunt and thin as he was before. He was dressed in a dark suit for the occasion and his hair was longer. He was different and I was soon able to find how much he had changed.

"You look beautiful, Puakea," he said. So see, I told you that blue chiffon did the trick. Thank God, I talked Connie out of the pink.

Like an idiot I said, "Ya think?"

He started laughing and that broke the ice. "I've been trying to get up the nerve to see you again and figured you'd be sure to come tonight.

"Well, he is my brother."

"I know *that*," he said. "He asked me to be his best man, but I told him I didn't want to be on display...so he understood."

"You look great too, you know. You would have made a fine best man. So, why did you need nerve to see me? I'm in the same old place right up the street from you in Palolo."

"I know. I guess I thought you'd moved on and were married by now or something like that. I've been away for a long time."

"Well, I did move on. I got my degree from UH, so there. That's moving on, huh?"

"Wow. I'm impressed. You were always a brilliant girl. I had a feeling you'd be college material."

"Why wouldn't you see me four years ago, Dee?" I just decided to come out and ask him. This small talk was making me antsy.

"I was in a dark place. I'm not anymore."

"You hurt me."

"I'm so sorry, but I hurt myself worse. I missed you so much, but I was such a mess at the time."

"I never figured that you missed me."

"Every day for four years," he replied. Well that said it all didn't it? I was about to jump into his lap, but I kept myself under control.

"So, what changed you?" I asked.

"I went back to the burn center and had more operations. I had developed an infection from the third degree burns on my chest area. Then I went through more physical therapy and while I was in therapy, I met this guy who was worse off than I was. We got to talking and turns out he was this Christian psychologist who had been burned in a private airplane crash. I saw him every day in physical therapy and after awhile we started hanging out together. Long story short, he changed my life."

"Wow," I said trying to search for something in my college background that was an intelligent reply. Couldn't come up with it.

"You know that saying: 'I cried because I had no shoes and then I met a man who had no feet.' Well that was the theme of my life after that. This guy was so badly burned; face, body, everything and yet, he managed to stay positive every day. He'd always find something to be thankful for. And not only that, he was into making other people's lives better."

"We started going into children's wards in the burn center and taking them stuff like toys and games. They accepted us more because they knew we'd been through the trenches too. It was great. I became quite an artist, drawing pictures with them and making them laugh. Loved it and I'm still doing it today."

"I don't know what to say, Dee except that...I'm proud of you."

"Well, good. Cause I need that...especially from you."

I wanted to tell him he could have anything he wanted from me, but it wasn't the time.

"You'll be happy to know that one of the things I became thankful for was my mom. I've been trying to make amends to her ever since I discovered how much she sacrificed for me and all the patience it took. Dad too, but my mother stood by me no matter what."

"Oh, Dee. I'm so glad. Your mom tried so hard and I always thought she was a trouper. You were not the easiest patient."

"Are you seeing anyone, Puakea?"

"Nope, just waiting around for you to come to your senses."

"That's the best news I've heard in a long time," he said and a big fat smile broke out on his face. It was the most beautiful thing.

After that, one thing led to another and I became Thaddeus Crown's girlfriend. Well, I was so puffed up after that you couldn't touch me with a ten foot pole. Just kidding. Needless to say I was happier than a pig in you know what. So, then one thing led to another again and a year later I became Thaddeus Crown's wife.

And if I thought I was ravishing in that blue chiffon, you should have seen me in my wedding gown. My bridegroom could not wait to get me out of the gown at the end of my wedding and I thought it was such a shame because I just wanted to wear it forever. I came down to breakfast with it on my honeymoon and he just laughed at me. Imagine that? I still have it in mothballs to this day.

We lived with his parents for awhile. His father was rarely there and then sadly they got a divorce. He had just been away too much and she had started dating some guy. They divorced, and for some reason which still escapes me, we got the house. She went off with the guy to the mainland and married him, so there we were in Palolo Valley in the mansion.

Well, there was nothing else to do, but fill the mansion with children and that's what we did. We filled it with the pitter patter of little feet and the experience at Senior Cottage came in handy. I became a multi-tasking mother of four and followed in my mother's footsteps. Well, not quite. She's a lot nicer than I am. I named them all after places in Palolo Valley and started off with Tenth Avenue. No, I didn't name him Tenth Avenue, but my first born who is now a year away from forty is named Umi which you all know is the number *ten*. And I can tell you, he is a *ten* in more ways than one—so drop dead gorgeous and takes after his mother who snagged his father in that blue chiffon dress. I digress.

Anyway, I had one boy at each end with two girls in the middle: Umi, Ahe, Ipulei and Ka'au named after the crater. I was a little worried about Ka'au for awhile because he fit his name and ate a lot—kind of like a bottomless crater. All four got into Kamehameha to carry on the tradition and they're great kids if I must say so myself. I was like a mother lion ready to kick *okole* for anyone who dared to bully them, but they were fine. I did fly off the handle once in awhile, compared to my calm husband. So every night before they went to bed, I reminded them that they were having a happy childhood.

"What are we having, I would say?"

And they would all answer in unison, "A happy childhood, Mom."

It wasn't like I brain washed them or anything. They had the best childhood, between Waikiki, Kamehameha and all the love they had. Who wouldn't answer in that way? You wouldn't believe it, but my girls are calm, sweet and serene like Kanoe. I don't know where they came from, but I'm glad they didn't turn out like me. Neither of them beat up a single boy in school and that might be a good thing.

Now, Ka'au probably takes after his mother more than any of them. And like his namesake, he is a volcano ready to erupt. He's gotten into so many scrapes over the years that I had to keep a first aid arsenal just to keep from racking up doctor bills. I even learned to stitch up cuts. He's so naughty and he's all of thirty now, and I shouldn't say this, but he's my favorite. Dee would kill me for that because he loves them all equally.

Oh, and I now have four grandchildren, two boys from Umi and his Japanese wife, and two boys from Ahe who also married a fireman. Ipulei's not married yet, but goes with a boy who makes her cry all the time and I hope to God she *won't* marry him.

Anyway, all's well that ends well and that's the end of my story.

Kanoe

LUKA CAME OVER ONE RAINY morning and gave me the news. He sat me down on the porch and told me that Makaio was missing in action and presumed dead. I didn't handle it well. I collapsed into his arms and sobbed my heart out. It was the worst day of my life since my mom left. I remember watching the pouring rain falling on the steps. My tears were falling just as heavily and wouldn't stop. He held me for a long time and cried too.

His family was devastated. I don't know who took it worse—his mom or dad. I guess we all walked the country like zombies going through the motions of life. Even the beauty of Kahana seemed dark and dreary. The sun never shone as bright after that and the stormy winter weather matched our moods.

For weeks there was still no confirmation from the government about what had happened to him. They finally confirmed that one of the second lieutenants in his company had removed Makaio's tags. According to a report given to his family, a small group from his platoon had been moving fast over an incline. The officer saw Makaio get hit by enemy fire while trying to carry another soldier to safety. It was an impulsive move to take his tags and not the correct procedure on the officer's part. He had an attachment to Makaio and was so impressed by his bravery that he wanted the tags as a keepsake. Later, when medics went back to retrieve his body, it was missing.

The family was going to have a memorial service for him, but they held out longer and still had a slight ray of hope. I didn't. I think the length of time said it all.

Something else happened. The timing couldn't have been worse. My mother came home. I was twenty one years old and had not seen her since I was five. She just walked through the door as if she had gone to the store or something. I barely recognized her. Mom was thinner than I remembered with hair that was streaked with gray. She was smiling and cheerful, and I was a wreck when I saw her. Puna had gone into Honolulu to do some errands.

"Kanoe? Is that you? Oh my, what a lovely girl you are," she cried. I just stood there with my mouth open. She held out her arms, "Aren't you going to give your mommy a hug?" she asked.

"Um, no, "I said, "I don't think so."

She dropped her arms to her side and didn't know how to deal with what I just said. Thank God, Puna walked in then and took over. She was just as shocked. Mom told us she caught a bus from the airport that morning and wanted to surprise us. Well that she did. But for me it wasn't all that pleasant.

My grandmother, being the gracious person she is, was trying to deal with it as best she could. We only had two bedrooms and in my stupor, I didn't realize until later that I had to give up mine when she settled her bags in there.

Long story short, she ended up staying and it wasn't until two days later that Puna told me she would not be going back. So, there she was after all those years—the mother I had dreamed about and yearned for, right there in Kahana Valley—home to stay. She and my grandmother had long talks on the porch every night while I tried to make myself scarce. They seemed to be getting along. I heard laughter and sometimes the sound of my mother's crying.

After a week, Puna took me aside. "Let's go for a walk," she said. That was unusual. With her arthritis, walking was not her thing, but I went with her down the road until we reached the main highway and walked across to the beach, my favorite place in the valley. Puna and I sat in the sand and then she told me.

"Kanoe, your mother is very sick. She says she's come home to die. She has cancer."

314

I looked up at my sweet grandmother's face and she had tears in her eyes. In all the time I'd known her, I'd never seen that. I cuddled up close to her there in the sand of Kahana Bay and lay my head on her chest, just wanting to comfort her. After all these years, I realized that my mom was her only child, and no matter how badly she'd behaved, Puna still loved her as all mothers loved their children. Then why didn't I feel the same thing from my mother? And why didn't I want to give it in return?

"Kanoe, you have to put all your grievances aside and welcome her home. You just have a little time with her and you'll regret it later if you don't."

We went home that day with an unspoken understanding on my part and I did my best to fulfill Puna's wishes. My mother was not easy to love. She was selfish and sometimes demanding and never seemed to acknowledge the pain she had caused us by her absence in the past… but she *was* sick and grew weaker as the days went by. They didn't have the advanced treatment for the disease that they do now, so her chances of survival were almost nil. She was given medication for pain and I became her servant, waiting on her hand and foot, mainly to take the burden from Puna.

I was alone with her one night right near the end and she spoke to me for the first time about why she left me. "I'm sorry, Kanoe. I'm so sorry," she said.

"About what?" I asked her. I thought she was apologizing for being sick.

"For leaving you. I was so caught up in *him* that I could think of nothing else." She couldn't say his name, but I knew it was the man she had run away with. She shifted in her bed and I could see that she was uncomfortable, so I reached up behind her and straightened up her pillows. She was only in her early forties, and yet, she had aged with her illness and lost even more weight. She was no longer pretty, and I tried to see what features she had that belonged to me, but I couldn't. I must have looked like the *haole* father I had never known.

"Was it worth it, Mom?"

"No, Kanoe, it wasn't. Oh, maybe at first. I was crazy about him and he was so attentive for awhile. Then it all fizzled after a few years. He had a drinking problem—started going out with other women; then left me high and dry. There were others after him, but nothing ever panned out. I wanted to come home so many times, but I was so ashamed."

"Why didn't you write or call or something, Mom."

"I don't know, Kanoe. I wish I could give you a decent answer."

"Didn't you miss me...or Puna? What about her?"

"Yes, Kanoe. I missed you both, but I thought you'd be better off without me."

She seemed overtired with the conversation, so I didn't press her further. We never brought it up again.

Then one night, we heard a cry. I was sleeping on the *pune'e* in the living room where I had slept since my mom had come home. I heard Puna come out of her bedroom. We both rushed into her room. Her breathing was pretty raspy and different as she struggled for breath. Puna ran to the phone to call the doctor who lived about ten miles away in Malaekahana. It was awful to see her struggling like that, so I put more cushions under her shoulders and held her up.

"Kanoe," she cried and then I knew— it was different this time. She was trying to say something and I lifted her in my arms.

"It's alright, Mom. I forgive you. It's alright, "I said as I smoothed her brow. She relaxed then with a peaceful look on her face. "Go with Jesus, Mom," I said and I kissed her cheek.

She lay back, closed her eyes and whispered, "Thank you, Kanoe." And she was gone. I had not cried for my mom since I was a little girl... but I did that night. I cried all the tears that I'd held back for so long. Somehow it was cleansing and all mixed up with feeling sad, and yet, a relief to be able to cry out my grief. I had cried for Makaio and now her...and maybe that night, I was crying for both of them.

After all was said and done, she was cremated and her ashes spread far beyond the sand bar of Kahana Bay. The Kelliher boys came to help us. Luka, Maleko, and Keoni took me out in a boat with her urn while Puna stood on the shore with her friends and neighbors from Kahana Valley.

I certainly had my share of sadness during that time and prayed to God for some kind of joy in my life. After a few weeks, He brought it and my whole world changed. Makaio came back.

Puna and I had gone to a little church in the town of Hau'ula ever since I was a little girl. We never failed to miss a Sunday. The congregation was very small in number, but they sang Hawaiian hymns that filled the small area and shook the rooftops—always one of my favorite times. It increased my faith and filled me with comfort and hope. Probably a sappy thing to say, but it did.

So, it was on a Sunday morning, when I returned from church where I had once again asked God to take away my sadness. It was a magnificent day. The sun was shining. The mists were cleared, and there wasn't a single cloud hovering over the mountains. I put on my bathing suit to go to the bay where the ocean was glistening aquamarine and glassy. As I dove in the water, I started swimming from the middle of the cove towards the fish pond, and I stopped to turn back when I saw someone waving from the shore.

I swam closer to the beach, and then I recognized *him*. He was standing there like a vision of an angel from heaven. I started running in the water, and by this time, he was running towards me. We slammed into each other while I was still half way in the water. He was dressed in long slacks and an *aloha* shirt and had probably just been to church, but it didn't matter—nothing mattered at the moment as we both fell down in the water and embraced. I swear it was like something out of a movie—not exactly like *From Here to Eternity*—but almost.

He held me tightly and kissed me and kissed me and kissed me and I did the same to him. I have never been happier in my life and it was a long time before any questions were asked.

The answers to the questions came that night when we were all changed and dressed and sitting on the porch steps drinking hot chocolate that Puna made for us. He told me the story in bits and pieces in between kissing and hugging and running our hands all over each others' faces. I couldn't believe it. I just couldn't believe that he was really there.

He told me that he was unconscious with a severe head wound and unidentified when they found him alive on the same incline on which he had fallen. They were collecting the other bodies around him, and one of the medics saw that he was still alive. Apparently there was a mix-up. The medics who had gone later to retrieve him did not know about those who already had. He was rushed by helicopter to an emergency hospital in Saigon and in a coma for several weeks. When he came to, he had no memory and it was another few months before they could identify him. They didn't even know where he had come from to notify his family.

"The only name they called me was Kanoe," he said as he smiled at me.

"What?"

"Well, they kept asking me my name and the last thing I said when I was hit was *Kanoe*. So, it was the only word that stuck in my brain and all anyone heard me say for a long time."

I ran my hand over his face then. It was still so fine. I might be exaggerating, but it was absolutely beautiful to me. He was thinner and pale, but his hair had grown back and his body was still firm and strong. I did notice a haunted look in his face when he wasn't concentrating on me, and sensed there was a world he'd experienced that was filled with horror. I didn't want to question him more, so I told him about Kahana Valley and all the happenings there.

I probably don't have to tell you that it did not take long before we were married—actually as long as it took to get the banns posted. We wanted to please his parents and married in a tiny Catholic church in Punalu'u with a pot-luck reception in Puna's back yard. It seemed like all of Ka'a'awa and Kahana Bay showed up as the Hawaiian community came out in full force with their contributions of food and gifts which we were so grateful for.

Of course, the honeymoon was the best and lasted for years as far as I was concerned. We were very happy for a long time. We moved in to a small house of our own in Punalu'u where I could walk to Kahana Bay and look after Puna whenever I needed to.

I wish I could say the story ended there like in the fairy tales. But Viet Nam came to revisit Makaio in his dreams and everyday life for many years. His flashbacks caused him extreme anxiety later on, and he went through therapy for a long time. Loud noises and crowds would throw him into one of his fearful states and it took a lot to calm him down. He was eventually eligible for disability compensation which is given to wartime veterans. I went to work for Hawaiian airlines as a ticket agent and between the two incomes, we managed fine. We even got to go on trips through my airline perks and that was another gift to us.

But, you know, through all of it, I was just so grateful to have him alive and breathing, that just his presence in my life as my husband was worth it. He did *not* wish to have children and that was hard for me at first. I had always wanted to make up for what my mother didn't give me, but it was not to be. As the years went on, his brothers started their own families, and we got to have their kids whenever I was in the mood for nurturing which was quite often.

Keoni's youngest child who is now in his thirties was my favorite. His name is Billy; now that's a good Hawaiian name, but he was named after Keoni's best friend. Keoni had six children, so they could be generous in sharing one with us, and from the time Billy was a baby, he was mine. He was my gift from God to make up for my own lack and I think I got a little carried away with him. At least I had permission to and I was so thankful for that. He had his own room in our home and he just ended up staying most of the time.

I thought about how inadequate I felt at Senior Cottage with baby Bradley. Billy was my chance to prove myself. So I did and now he has babies of his own that come over all the time.

Puna eventually passed at a ripe old age, and by that time, I was ready for it. She had been through so many hospitals and all the indignities of a nursing home that she was primed to go. I was relieved for her at the time, but I will miss her for the rest of my days. She was my true mother in every sense of the word.

So, here I am without the usual success story. I did not finish college, one of my regrets. I did not have children of my own, but I raised Billy. My marriage had its difficulties, but I thank God for each day that I can be with my husband and for bringing him home to me.

Nani

"Oh shit," I heard as I was laying there in complete disarray, panting in between horrendous contractions, not to mention the cuts on my head and what felt like a broken arm as I was pinned between the steering wheel and the front seat.

So what did I say, when I saw this cop with his flashlight open the door. "You can say that again," is what I said and so he did, over and over again.

Now, that may have not been the most professional behavior, but this poor guy was reacting to the fact that the baby was definitely on his way out. Yes it was a *he*. Anyway, *he* was heading out and of course… guess who got to deliver the little guy? Me pushing and the cop doing the best he could between expletives. I had to forgive him for his language because this was not exactly in the line of duty, or written in the police academy training manual.

I won't go into the gory details. You can use your imagination, but there we were—talk about your cliff hangers—the truck actually hanging on a cliff with a baby squalling his head off. Stretchers and ambulance guys and cops had arrived soon after, but this cop deserved a medal. I couldn't see him in the dark, just heard his voice which was somewhat familiar although distressed.

I never saw him again because everyone else took over. The baby and I were whisked away to the hospital. I lost a lot of blood and I guess they were concerned about my hemorrhaging, not to mention the other injuries I had sustained during the accident. When all was said and done, I left the hospital with cuts and bruises and a broken arm. I guess I was lucky, but still in a lot of pain and wondering how I was going to care for my baby.

I heard the policeman had come twice to see how I was, but I was sleeping on his first visit and taken away for surgery the next time he came. He left flowers, but didn't leave his name, so I couldn't thank him properly.

So flash forward three months and....oh by the way, I named my baby Lumaha'i Miller after the cliffs on which he was born. So anyway, three months later, I am just ready to pull out of the parking lot of a small market in Hanalei and this guy comes up to my passenger window where Lumaha'i lay in his infant seat. Remember those days when we didn't have seat belts and babies weren't strapped in? I don't know how we all survived.

"So how you doing, Nani?" he asked.

I recognized him, but forgot his name again. It was the Kam School guy from the Hukilau. He was dressed in shorts and a cut off tee shirt looking so handsome I just sat there and stared.

"I'm fine, thank you. Now tell me your name again. I'm sorry, I keep forgetting. "

"Hekili," he said looking at me with a strange expression on his face. It looked like disappointment.

"Oh, now I remember," I said,

"I see you're all healed up, now. I was worried about you," he said and reached in and gently touched the baby. "That's a healthy baby, Nani. I guess he survived everything too. Glad to see it."

I sat there and stared at him trying to put what he had just said into perspective. Then I realized the news of my accident was all over town, so his comments weren't all that unusual after all.

"Well, take care Nani. I have to go to work. Oh, what's the baby's name?"

"Um, Lumaha'i," I replied.

"Goodbye, Lumaha'i. I'm so glad you're okay now," he said and walked to his car.

It took me the drive to Ha'ena, which wasn't all that far, to figure out what was what. When I did, I was so completely embarrassed and ashamed I wanted to cry. I sat there in the car before going into the house feeling like a complete idiot. I should have recognized that voice anywhere.

My mission the next day was to find him, so I had to do some detective work. I went to my parents in Kalihiwai to take Ha'i (that's what I ended up calling him) there. They insisted on seeing him every day. Either they came by Tutu's house or I went to theirs. I left baby there with my mom and walked up the road a bit to Kaulana's house. He was the one who had brought Hekili to the *hukilau* in Kalihiwai. I was so grateful he was home. Kaulana stood outside with me awhile as I drilled him on Hekili's whereabouts. He told me I could find him at the police station, but I didn't want to do that. So, he gave me directions to his house.

It was mid morning, and I figured Hekili worked on the night shift and might be home. I told my mom I'd be back and headed toward the Hanalei *taro* fields. I saw that there were three houses at the address and didn't know which one to approach, but I did notice the car he had driven the day before.

"Hello," I called as I got out of my car which was really Tutu's Nash Rambler she had loaned me. Three dogs were barking their heads off and two of them looked ferocious. The door opened at one of the houses, and a middle aged woman walked out as she shushed the dogs to be quiet.

"Is Hekili here?" I asked. I was wearing a plain blue sun dress which I picked out just for that day, hoping to see him. Thank goodness the sixty pounds I'd gained had mostly gone—not that I had a sixty pound baby, but I did manage to lose most of it between stress, breast feeding and all the exercise I was getting with that little boy.

"Yes, he is. What's your name?" said the lady who now had a smile on her face.

"Oh, my name is Nani. We went to school together."

"He might be sleeping. He had a late shift, but I'm sure he'll be glad to see *you*." She said this as if she knew who I was.

"HEKILI," she called loudly and he emerged from the house a moment later without a shirt, wearing shorts with his hair all tousled as if he had just gotten out of bed. It's strange because his hair was mostly blonde, and his mom looked so Hawaiian.

As I stood there, the expression on his face changed from sleepy eyed to something else. "Nani?" he almost questioned. "I can't believe it. You're at my house."

"Oh, Hekili, I have so much to say to you, I don't know where to begin." By this time the dogs were all over me. You know how it is when dogs are threatened and barking and growling, and then they find out you're a friend and they're all over you. Well that was them.

"STOP IT," he yelled and they went to immediate sitting positions with their tongues hanging out. It was amazing.

"Sorry, bout that," he said.

"Can you come for a drive with me?" I asked.

He stood there, and I can't explain it, but this really sexy grin spread across his face. "Sure, lemme put on a shirt."

Well, I tell you my heart was starting to beat after that and even more so when he finally got into the car. I drove past the fields and headed towards the pier on the water of Hanalei Bay. I never forget how radiant it was that morning with the rippling morning sunshine across the still water and a few waves in the distance. We sat on the pier with our legs dangling over. I don't know where I got the nerve to do what I did next, but I was so overwhelmed with gratitude towards him.

I turned to him and grabbed both his hands in mine and I kissed them. "These are the hands that delivered my baby. How can I thank you enough? I am *so* sorry, I didn't recognize you. I know you know how out of it I was that night, but it's such a bad excuse. I will never forget that soothing voice as long as I live, in between the swearing of course."

"I have to tell you that unlike every other guy on the island, I never swear. I don't know where all that came from. I guess I was scared." He chuckled at me and looked down at our hands which were clasped. He hesitated a moment and then said "I love you, you know. I always have."

"WHAT?" I said almost too loudly. I dropped his hands in shock.

"Nani, you were my dream." He gathered my hands in his again.

"I don't know what you're talking about?"

"The first time I saw you, you were fourteen on the same airplane going back to Kaua'i at Christmas. The next time I saw you was at school. I watched you everywhere. You were always surrounded by people and flitting all over the place. I had a major crush."

"Why didn't you say something?"

"I don't know. I guess I was lacking in something—maybe aggressive guy stuff. Whatever it takes to declare one's self. I didn't have it, until it was too late. When I heard you got married, I lost it. I really regretted not speaking up sooner. Course, maybe even that wouldn't have worked."

"Oh, I don't know about that," I said.

"Really?" He slanted his head with a kind of questioning look.

"Really," I confirmed with a Cheshire cat grin. "You know what I think Hekili?"

"What?"

"I think what you just told me is absolutely, positively.... wonderful."

He leaned over very gently and kissed my lips in the softest sweetest way possible, and I treasured it for the rest of the day. We talked for awhile and he told me more. When we drove back to his house, he didn't get out right away.

"So, what about this husband of yours?" he asked.

"History. It's a long story, but not a good one. We'll be divorced officially in three months. I filed with a lawyer in Lihue and I just want to get it over with.

"So, do you think it would be alright to see each other, or should I wait?"

"Oh, Hekili. I think you've waited long enough. Want to come over for dinner on your next day off?"

"That's tomorrow," he said.

"Then tomorrow it is," I said as I kissed his cheek.

The divorce took a little longer than I had hoped. Jason was being a real pill about it. He hated losing, and he wasn't going to go down quietly. He did not like the fact that I left him, but his upset was mostly about the money the courts decreed that he had to pay me and the baby. I had a great lawyer who made Jason pay his fee along with the monthly payments he finally had to fork out.

In the meantime, Hekili respectfully courted me and the baby. The three of us went everywhere together on his days off which meant lots of picnics and beaches with umbrellas. Ha'i loved him and showed it. He got very attached.

And when the divorce was final, I loved him and showed it and we were all about that. He surprised me one evening with a candlelight dinner at Coco Palms and a ring, and I could not say *yes* fast enough. He was and is the finest person I know.

Well, I tell you, after our barefoot wedding on the beach, we started right away on having babies, and poor Hekili... we ended up having four more children after that—one after the other. What did we live on you ask? Lots of love and fish from the ocean.

We have five boys all together. I gave up on waiting for my girl and that was okay with me. I loved them all and still do, but we had our problems which added all this gray hair on my head. You would think the sons of a cop would be angels, but they weren't. One had a drug problem; one landed in jail for six months; one went to Harvard on a scholarship; one got his law degree, and one is a beach bum. I won't mention which ones are which. You'll just have to meet them when everyone's perfect.

God did provide for us, sadly through Tutu's death when the kids were little. She willed us her house, her land and all the money she had been saving in the bank. I offered to share it with my brother, but he refused, knowing that Tutu was thinking of my ever growing family. So, we added on to her house making it into a larger home to accommodate the boys and that's where we live today.

In all of this, my husband Hekili has been a quiet, strong undaunted rock and I bless the day he asked me to be his wife.

Lihau

My father eventually had his way. He had never considered leaving my mother behind. The night everything blew up, he came to my room and spoke to me privately. He was very calm, conciliatory, almost civil, and tried to give me reasons why Princeton would be the best thing for me. When he heard my objections again, he gave the ultimatum.

I was powerless, or thought I was, to do anything else when he did. He agreed to keep Makena's dad on as long as I went to school. My father's keen abilities as a negotiator came into play. He promised to give Fujinoko a retirement package along with Makena's dad if I signed a contract to stay in school for four years and cut off all contact with Makena. I was not to return to Ha'iku until I finished. I wondered why this was so important to him and knew my welfare was not what he was thinking of. Later, it became clear that it was all about keeping my mother under his control...and also a way of getting rid of me.

A contract was eventually drawn up. I was eighteen at the time and could legally sign. My mother wasn't notified about our agreement. She thought I had reconciled with my father and that I had seen the sense of going away to school. So, with a stroke of a pen, I gave up Makena and all our dreams of being together.

I wasn't allowed to say goodbye to him. Even that was in the contract. And so, I left for a place that was almost six thousand miles away in a land I knew nothing about: New Jersey.

Young naïve and bitter about my circumstances, I felt nothing could impress me or open me up to recognize the advantages of being in such an impressive school, one of the top Ivy League institutions in the nation. But that would change and so would I.

I arrived at the impressive campus, scattered with Gothic architecture, and what they referred to as residential colleges where freshmen and sophomores were housed in dormitories with dining halls, libraries, study spaces, dark rooms and an array of other facilities.

I was housed with a Jewish roommate, named Lottie Daniel who had been there a year. She was amazing. She talked fast, walked fast and her brain was running on overload all the time. She either noticed I was a pushover or she didn't notice what I was. I could never figure it out, but she plowed through and organized my life. She led and I followed. What I did discover is that she had a heart of gold, but that was much later after I got accustomed to her agenda.

We ended up rooming together for three years and she was such a good influence on me. What I discovered through her is that I had a brain, and if I'd put it to use, I could derive great satisfaction from it. She challenged me to get A's and taught me how to study—how the mind worked and how it could process short term memory into long term memory through recitation. Mnemonic devices were her favorite ways of acing essay exams, and she taught me how to analyze professors, listening closely to their emphasis in classes and how to detect what their exams would include by keying in on the first one given. She studied professors, their egos, how to be sure to sit in the front rows whenever I could to show them interest, how to do extra credit projects and write papers with concise, meaningful articulation.

I thank God for Lottie Daniel. She would have been irritating for someone else, but she was just what I needed. I was lost and she just took over...in a good way. I majored in American Politics and maybe my Hong Kong roots kicked in. I was fascinated with the workings of government and the diplomatic arena—even joined the debate team and discovered that I could listen, think and talk at the same time. The courses were great—mass media, political law and psychology, foreign policy, public leadership, campaigns and elections and other related classes.

During my second year there, President Kennedy was assassinated. He had attended Princeton in his freshman fall, leaving due to an illness and had gone on to Harvard later. We grieved at Princeton with the rest of the nation. It was a horrible time for everyone. All my teachers were obsessed. The subject of John Kennedy was at the forefront of every lecture and class for awhile.

While I was there, I actually went through a belated growth spurt, shooting up to five feet eight inches, which was surprising. I guess the words "late bloomer" would apply to me. My hair got thicker and it grew down to my waist which was basically the style when the mid sixties came around. I was still wearing my contacts and I know I shouldn't even say this because of that proverb we quoted in school that says "let her own works praise her in the gates", but I was gaining confidence about my appearance.

Guys were starting to notice and I even started dating—nothing serious, but I did go out with a few Princeton Preppies. Most of them I met in my Political Science classes and we had a lot in common with our majors—good stimulating conversation, but nothing like what Makena and I had. Well, I take that back, there was one guy who almost had my heart beating for awhile, but it fizzled and he walked off into the sunset, probably with some other girl.

I was there every summer and never went home. I took classes to lighten my load for the fall semester and that helped, but I was literally in school without a break.

So the years passed and graduation came. Imagine, me graduating from Princeton University, one of the best schools in the nation? And guess who came to my graduation? Nobody—not a soul, not a single person I knew. I'm sure my mother would have come if she could, but she didn't. She had kept in touch through letters. The phone was so unreliable with the time difference and being available at the right time to receive calls in the dorm was too difficult. I never heard from my father. That was not a surprise.

After that, I had no idea what I was going to do with my life and my major. It was over and my contract was fulfilled. I was twenty two years old, going home to Ha'iku with a degree in my hand—so relieved and happy to be done with it all, but didn't know what to expect upon my arrival.

I realized the one person I *could* depend on was Fujinoko. In all those years from the time I was five years old, her English had not improved one bit. But I was sure of one thing and perhaps had taken it for granted all those years: she was the only person who was consistently there for me, and loved me in her own way. She was very happy to see me when she came to pick me up at the airport. Fujinoko was still petite, soft spoken, and was now showing signs of her age. We embraced and kissed each other when I arrived. She had never kissed me before but she did then; it was nice.

We drove home to Ha'iku...and there was my house, just as I remembered it. The eucalyptus trees looked even more immense, and the grounds were overflowing with more tropical plants. It was so different from New Jersey. The sound of the wind blew softly through the trees, and I was sure that the birds sang especially just to welcome me back. It was heavenly to be home.

The house had not changed one bit. It was almost as if time stood still and I had walked out the day before and just returned from an outing. I was back in the only home I'd known. Fujinoko fixed a special dinner for us that night and sat down to eat with me at the long formal dining table. I liked that. She didn't used to do that either.

That night when I went to put my things away, I was sorting out my clothes to hang, and there in the back of my closet was a large plastic bag. I uncoiled the tie on it and inside was a large box, so I opened it... and there she was, my Mele, the doll who had been my best friend. Tears ran down my eyes as I hugged her to my chest. So silly, but I know you understand what she meant to me. I even slept with her that night.

Of course, you're wanting to hear what happened to Makena. Where was he? Was he married? Did he have family now? Had he gone away? Believe me, all those questions were running through my mind.

I got up the next morning and walked into the garden in my nightgown and a light robe. I heard someone working there and moved in that direction. It was Jesse Lau, Makena's dad. I smiled at him and he dropped the shovel he was using and came over to greet me.

"Ah, Lihau, so nice to see you. Such a pretty grown up girl you've become," he complimented me with a warm smile that lit up his now craggy face.

We talked for awhile and I told him I had gone away to school and just graduated. Then I worked up the nerve to ask him. "So, Jesse, what happened to Makena?" I ventured.

"Ah, Makena. He's working for Maui Electric. He has a good job. He lives in Wailuku now, closer to his work."

"I guess he's married by now," I said. I was holding my breath so long waiting for that crucial answer that I thought I was going to turn blue.

"No, no, not Makena. Not married."

I sighed in relief and casually said, "Well, tell him to come see me when you talk to him." Jesse agreed, told me he was glad that I was home, and I went back into the house.

It took a week before I finally saw Makena. The doorbell rang; I went to answer it and there he was. He was dressed in work boots, jeans and a short sleeve work shirt. His hair was longer, his face tanned from the sun, and he stood there scowling at me which emphasized the lines on his face. But he was the Makena I'd longed for and such a sight to behold.

I was dressed in shorts and a sleeveless tee shirt wishing I had on my prom gown or something to make me more appealing, but I had no advance notice. "Makena," I said breathlessly, almost in a Marilyn Monroe voice, but not on purpose.

"So, you came home," is all he said.

I nodded and asked him to come in. He followed me through the living room as we walked through the sliding glass doors to the patio on the other side of the house. "Can I get you some iced tea?" I asked.

"Okay," he replied.

I went to the kitchen to pour two glasses of iced tea and returned to the patio trying to rehearse what I was going to say to him. I was really trying to buy time. He spoke first and didn't mince words.

"You left me," he said. He sat across from me at a round glass patio table.

"I had to," I answered.

"Why?" he asked.

"My father," I answered.

"We could have worked it out."

"It's complicated," I answered.

"I'm with someone now," he said.

"I figured you would be," I replied. "I thought you'd be married."

"No, not married," he said.

"I hope you're happy," I said.

"I was till you dropped out of the sky."

"Sorry, bout that."

"Are *you* with someone?" he asked.

"No," I replied.

"I have to go," he said.

"Okay," I replied. And that was it. I walked him to the door, and he left, without a backward glance.

All kinds of thoughts were running through my head—a lot of *if only's*. One of them was *If only I had been wearing my prom gown*. I just wished I had been looking my best. Maybe that would have made a difference...but maybe not.

Another week of toiling and trying to get over him passed, and then the doorbell rang again.

"Okay," he said. "I'm not with anyone now."

"Good," I replied. We stood there staring at each other. I did not look any better than I had the first time. I was practically wearing the same outfit. I couldn't help the smile that burst forth from me and was trying not to be too happy, but it was hard.

He was still scowling, but he reached out and pulled me into his arms and kissed me. I would say it was more of a devouring kiss—you know the kind that starts out gentle and then turns into a feast. We just went at it in the doorway and then realized that it was highly improper to be standing there like that. If we had kissed any longer, we would have ended up on the floor. Yes, it was that kind of kiss.

So, you're asking—did we end up together or was it just a devouring kiss? The answer is...of course we did, but other things were to take place before it happened.

We went back into the patio and he was still upset. He asked me the same question again.

"Why did you leave me, Lihau?"

"I'll be right back," I said.

I came back a few minutes later and handed him a copy of the contract. He sat there and read in silence. Then, he stood up and slammed the papers down. I thought he was going to leave, but he started pacing back and forth and I could see how angry he was.

"I can't believe you did this. Do you want to hear what I went through after you left?" He didn't wait for my reply. "No one knew where you went. It was as if you disappeared into thin air. Fujinoko had no idea and neither did my dad. The house was empty and not a soul ever came back to it. I went crazy. You never wrote; you never called. It was just as if *we* never happened. I waited a year and then I waited another year and then I thought that was it—that you were somewhere in Hong Kong. Four years, Lihau and not a word from you."

"It was a condition of the contract," I replied. "I couldn't contact you."

"You didn't even try," he stopped pacing as he said this.

"Makena, sit down and let me have my say."

He sat at the table, still scowling at me with a horrible look in his eyes.

"There were three people I had to consider who'd benefit by my sacrifice. I wasn't one of them. I didn't want to leave. However, I did not leave out of weakness. My father told me that my mother would be penniless, that your father would be out on the street and so would Fujinoko. As you can see by the contract, he promised to set them up for the rest of their lives if I agreed to his terms. One of the terms was never to contact you during my time away. He made sure I was not to return until I had a degree in my hands. Yes, he wanted to get me away from you, but he also wanted me away from my mother and out of his miserable sight. I was thrown out there in the world and it was a sink or swim situation. The only good part of it was that I did well at Princeton. That's where I went—not to Hong Kong, but to New Jersey where I stayed for four years."

"I have to think about this before I say anything more," he said. He got up and walked out again. I didn't follow him.

That night the doorbell rang, and this time, I looked a little better. I was dressed for dinner, probably out of habit. I wore a bright multicolored shift that showed off my figure and my hair was brushed for a change. He stood at the door and he looked pretty good too with his hair combed back, a blue *aloha* shirt and sexy jeans.

"Okay," he said.

"Okay?"

"Yeah, I guess it's okay. I hate what you did, but it's okay."

Well, I guess that was a start and believe me, it took awhile before it was really okay, but he admitted that I was *the sacrificial lamb* and knew that I suffered almost as much as he did. I never told him how well I adjusted to Princeton. That would *not* have been the thing to say—maybe another day on that one.

We began our courtship all over again, and *I* was the one who had to woo *him*, but it wasn't that difficult. He liked all the attention, and it was my turn to show him how much I cared. Makena had taken care of me as a little girl. He had soothed me and loved me and protected me… and now it was my turn. So, I did it gladly and one day a few months down the road, I asked him to marry me and he said "Yes".

Right in the middle of all this happiness, my father died. He didn't just die. He was murdered. The enemies he had accumulated over the years finally caught up with him. He was killed by an assassin's bullet as he attended a high profile social affair in Hong Kong. It happened in a flash. A silencer had been used and no one heard it in the midst of all the noise in the crowd. Even his body guards were taken by surprise. They never found the murderer.

I should have been sad when the news came to me, but I wasn't. Maybe later I mourned him when I pondered that there must have been something good in him that I had never been able to see. He was my father after all, and eventually, I honored him just for that fact alone.

My mother had to stay for a few months to get his estate in order, but she did not expect me to come to his funeral. I talked to her on the phone and told her I was getting married. She made me promise to wait for her so she could help me with the wedding.

When she came home to Ha'iku, I thought she'd bring back her valuables from Hong Kong, but she left them all behind. She wanted to start a new life without the memories. My mother did, however, return as a very wealthy widow.

We had a heartwarming mother-daughter reunion. I could tell she wanted to say so much about the mistakes of the past, but I said, "Mom, let's try to move forward. I understand certain things, and I've worked them out on my own. I know you've always loved me; it's all that matters now."

"I'll make it up to you, Lihau. I promise," she said.

"Are you sad about Dad?" I asked her.

"Yes, Lihau. I'm sad that he was not a better man. I'm sad that he was not a good father to you. But I am not sad to be home and that is what I've wanted for years and years."

My mother offered the master suite in the house to Makena and me as a wedding present. Actually, the house was the wedding present. She made plans with contractors to build another one on the same property for herself and Fujinoko. That would take awhile and we planned to live together until then.

What a wonderful wedding day that was. My mom, Jesse, and Fujinoko were the only ones who attended. That's all we needed My mother told me something that Makena said that day. She saw him before the wedding at his father's house to notify him that the pastor had arrived.

"My, my Makena, you look so handsome," she said as she straightened out the tie of his tuxedo. "How do you feel right now?" she asked.

"I can hardly wait," he said to her, and when she told me this, it made my heart sing. I was so touched.

"And so we were wed" as they say in the books. I became Mrs. Makena Lau in the back yard of our beautiful house in Ha'iku amongst the eucalyptus trees and the birds who were singing merrily as we said our vows.

Life was good after that. Makena worked his way up the ranks at Maui Electric and I got a job teaching Political Science at Maui High School. Would you believe? We always had weekends off and spent as much time together as possible trying so hard to have a baby.

My mother built her home which was a mini version of the large house except for a bedroom she designed for herself on the second floor. Fujinoko was given a suite on the bottom floor and took care of my mom until she herself took ill five years later. Then, it was my turn to take care of Fujinoko until she passed away. This quiet, humble woman who looked after a lonely, friendless little girl was truly the anchor in my life and I loved her until the day she died.

Ten years after we married, after much frustration and almost losing hope, I gave birth to a little girl we named Mana, which is Hawaiian for *miraculous*. She was a wonderful baby with lovely blue eyes. She did not inherit my disability, and her vision was the first thing we checked. It was fine. She was a joy and a delight from the moment she was born and she is thirty two now with two little boys whom I adore.

So, that's the story of the poor little rich girl who remained in her castle with the gallant knight that saved her, and they lived happily ever after...so far.

Kia

"MARRY ME," HE REPLIED AFTER I offered to do anything to get my son back. Well, I didn't. No, I walked away that night from Mario Lorenzo. It wasn't easy to do that. I had to pretend that I needed time to think it over and that was the answer I gave him before his driver took me home, blindfolded once again.

I was taking an enormous risk, but I gambled that they would not harm my son. Perhaps I wouldn't have if I'd known how ruthless Mario truly was. I counted on the fact that the baby was his grandson, and surely he was bluffing with his threat. I did not know then how he had set up his own son to go to prison.

What I did know is I had to buy time to think of a plan. It would take years of frustration with a huge hole in my heart before I could accomplish this. I wanted to go to the police, but Mario had assured me that this would mean instant death to my son, and nothing could ever be proved regarding his involvement. This, I believed, so I had to take another route.

I wanted to tell someone and there was no one I could turn to. I wavered back and forth about what to do. The days went by slowly and coming home was agonizing for me, particularly to the apartment where my baby had been removed. I kept thinking that Mario would change his mind, so I tried to think of all kinds of tactics that would move him. I called him and begged him to reconsider. He scoffed at me, "Kia you know what you need to do. Don't contact me until you're ready to give me what I want."

I couldn't eat or sleep or do anything to take pleasure from life. All I had was my job which is what consumed my time. I threw myself into my work after much agonizing, wavering back and forth about whether to throw myself under the bus by marrying Mario. No matter what, I couldn't do it. Something told me that it would be more dangerous to give in, so I prayed which I'd never done before and hoped that I'd find the right answer to it all.

Christmas was the worst time of the year for me. I hated that time of year and as the years went by, I started to lose hope that I'd ever see my little boy again.

I had been working as an investment broker for five years when I acquired one of my firm's most affluent clients. His name was Isaac Weiss and he was worth over a hundred million dollars. It was my job to increase these millions into millions more, and through a series of savvy investments which I advised him to make, his account was multiplying.

Investing is a tricky business, and it's not as if I had a magic wand or that I was more knowledgeable than others, but I did have a knack for studying companies that were solid with good management, reasonable price to earnings ratios and in the process of increasing in their revenues. It wasn't something others didn't know, but what I did gain that no one else did was his trust.

Mr. Weiss was a German Jewish immigrant who had come from a prominent banking family in Hamburg, Germany. His maternal grandfather had owned three castles where he visited as a little boy. Just before Hitler went crazy, Isaac was able to book passage on a boat to America. He had $5,000 in the sole of his shoes, and from this small amount of money, he was able to multiply it into what became his fortune. By the time he was sixty, he owned ten thriving businesses from barbed wire, to steel, to interests in American banks, oil companies and thousands of acres of real estate all over the country.

My job was to invest his income in stocks and tax free investments. We bought hundreds of bonds that gave high interest incomes from up and coming cities, mostly in California. I tell you all of this to make the point that he had money and behind his money were connections that became very useful to my cause.

He was sixty five when he became my client, and we had an association that lasted fifteen years. Mr. Weiss seldom spent his money. He was all about making it. When I met him, he had recently lost his wife, had no children and was basically alone. He was surly, demanding, impossible at times, and chewed me out whenever I made a mistake that cost him money. He rarely complimented me, but as time went on, we developed a trust that was mutual.

I made a decent amount of money through my association with him and acquired clients which included many of his wealthy friends. He rarely asked about my life because usually our dealings were mostly about him. But, one day he said, "Kia, there's something wrong with your personal life, and maybe you should tell me what it is."

I hesitated to talk about my situation. He said that he noticed that I never dated, that I was way too devoted to my work, that I seemed to have no life and certainly not any joy in it. I did not retaliate by reminding him that his life was not all that different from mine.

So, I spilled the beans—almost all of them, and he perked up and offered to help. Now, I did not realize that a person like this had connections to those who are connected in both high as well as low places. And it was the low places that eventually both he and I became most interested in when we put our heads together and mapped out a plan.

Mr. Weiss offered to hire one of the best private investigating firms in the city which consisted of a team of investigators who went to work on my case. It was through this investigation that we found out almost everything there was to know about Mario Lorenzo. All kinds of low-life snitches came out of the woodwork and were paid for their information. What was most shocking to me was what Mario Lorenzo had done to his own son.

Something in me was so full of rage and horror when the information surfaced. I could not fathom how evil a man like this could be. Then, more and more came out about all the murders he had participated in over the years. I had no idea how ruthless he was, and what scared me the most is that I wondered if he had actually carried out his threat to get rid of my baby. If he could set up his own son, I now knew he was capable of anything. This is the one mystery that hadn't been solved after months of investigation. Where was my baby?

As all this evidence was uncovered, Mr. Weiss wholeheartedly invested himself in my cause, and determined to see it through. I acquired a powerful ally in him.

I was a wreck one day when our receptionist announced that a Mr. Lorenzo wanted to know if I had time to see him. He walked into my office a few minutes later and got right to the point. "Kia, why haven't I heard from you?"

"I'm still trying to figure out things," I replied. "Is my son still with you?" I asked.

"I thought maybe you lost interest in your precious son."

As he said this, I thought of something that might buy even more time for me. It was risky, but I decided to say it anyway. "Maybe I have, Mario. You can keep him. I'm a career woman now. I don't have time for a child. He's got Lorenzo blood in him and probably more important to you."

He stood, walked up to me and said, "You're almost as cold as I am, Kia. That's why we'd make such a good team." He ran his forefinger down my cheek. It made my skin crawl. "I still want you, Kia, but you're going to have to come to me," he said and turned to walk out the door.

I couldn't stop shaking after he left and stood there trying to get myself together. When I thought about it later, there was something in that exchange that gave me hope. I can't explain what it was— something in Mario's demeanor told me that my son was still alive, and that after all the research we'd done on him, I didn't think he was capable of harming a child.

One day soon after, I met the man who was heading the investigation for Mr. Weiss. He made an appointment with me, and we decided to meet at a small eatery near Union Square. He was younger than I thought he'd be—dark hair, strong features, built like a linebacker as he filled out a suit that showed off his large physique. I always pictured private investigators as these wimpy guys who snuck around in corners with cameras waiting to find husbands who were cheating on their wives.

He soon let me know that he was no pushover. "Miss Kea, I'm Dino Palumbo and I needed to talk to you privately." We shook hands and his grip was firm and confident, but not enough to put me at ease.

He ordered coffee for both of us without asking me what I wanted, emphasizing that he was definitely in charge of this meeting.

"You're Italian," I commented.

"We're not all on the wrong side of the fence, you know. In fact, my ethnic background has enabled me in this particular case to enter *where angels fear to tread.*"

"How so?" I asked.

"I've been able to open doors to people who are willing to *sing* if you catch my drift." I did.

"And what have you found?"

"I know where your son is."

I almost fell out of my chair. "What?" I reached across the table and grabbed his hands squeezing them tightly. "Tell me," I almost screamed.

He didn't shake me loose, but looked down at our clasped hands and into my eyes. "Before I tell you, I want you to know that I think we have to bring law enforcement into this one."

"No," I shook my head. "No cops. He'll do something drastic if they're involved. "

"Well, we're going to have to do a lot of illegal things, not that we haven't already with all the bribes and snitches we've paid off," he said.

"Like what?" I asked.

"Like breaking and entering into a compound that is heavily guarded. If we use the law, we could go in with search warrants and do it right. "

"But how do we know which cops Mario has in his pocket?"

"I have a few trusted ones who I know are clean," he answered.

"But, it could get out to the others. You know what I mean?"

He nodded his head. "With the ones I know, I think we can do it. Look, you do want Mario to go down over this? He will always be a danger to you if you let him ride. If the law is involved, we'll have good solid witnesses to the fact of the kidnapping."

"You think you can do it? Then go ahead" I said. I had not let go of his hands until that moment. He looked almost disappointed, but for the first time smiled at me.

I met with him three times after that at different places where coffee was served. I know it was poor timing, but there was something going on between us. No brainer for me. He was definitely attractive and all those things that go with it: macho, cool, with an aloofness that was challenging. Plus, he was about to be my hero, working diligently on retrieving the most treasured thing for me…my son. Now, this was new for me; I hadn't even looked at a man since Rico. I didn't know if the feeling was mutual, until he showed up at my apartment one night.

I had recently purchased my very own apartment, now that I was making more money. It was a spacious loft on the fifteenth floor of a steel and concrete building centrally located in Pacific Heights with breathtaking views of the city of San Francisco and the Golden Gate Bridge. There were floor to ceiling windows, spacious light-filled, high vaulted rooms, a covered balcony with a master suite and large walk in closets. The building had lots of security with a doorman, an onsite manager and lighted parking with an expansive roof top deck.

I don't know how he got past the doorman, but I assumed that this kind of guy could get anywhere when he wanted to. It gave me even more confidence about his abilities. "What are you doing here?" I asked.

"Hope you don't mind, but I was in the neighborhood."

"Hmm, in the neighborhood, huh? Well come on in."

I offered him a drink, but he settled for iced tea. He looked around at the apartment and then brought his attention back to me, "Actually, I wasn't in the neighborhood. I had to fight traffic clear across town to get here. I just wanted to picture where you lived." It was the first personal thing he'd said to me since we met. Well, it wasn't all that personal, but maybe it was the way he said it.

We sat there in silence for a moment which was making me nervous, so I started babbling about my apartment and all the things in it which made me sound like a materialistic fool. He was sitting on a chair and came over to sit beside me on the couch and of course my heart took on an extra beat. The chemistry had now escalated to full throttle, but the conversation had nothing to do with it when he told me what the plan was.

"I have contacted a friend of mine at the FBI. You do know I used to be FBI, right?

"No, I didn't," I replied.

"Well, I assumed you had done your homework and checked my background in order to trust me for this work."

"I trusted Mr. Weiss. He's the one who hired you."

"Anyway, after much strategic planning between my guys and the Feds, they're ready to go in tomorrow and retrieve your son. He's located on a ranch in Cambria, a small beach town on the way to San Simeon, just west of San Luis Obispo. The snitch who gave us this information was paid a lot of money thanks to your Mr. Weiss. The FBI does not know about the money,"

"Who is he?"

"Mario Lorenzo's driver. He's received the money and will be taken to an undisclosed place to live with a new identity. If he's frugal, he can live comfortably on his funds for the rest of his life. You have a very generous benefactor. We could have squeezed this out of him the usual way, but Mr. Weiss understood that time was of the essence. The boy has been moved on a regular basis from location to location. But we're sure he's in Cambria now, Miss Kea."

I moved closer to Dino and put my hand on his. "You can call me Kia. That's what my friends call me." Well, we almost did something... but it wasn't the time. When I say did something, I thought he was going to break down and kiss me, but nope—none of that.

His quiet demeanor and the look in his eyes told me he was tempted, but he returned my hand to me and slowly rose to leave. "I am exceedingly grateful. Are you saying that I might see my child by tomorrow night?" I asked as I walked him to the door. He nodded.

I hugged myself, closing my eyes, trying not to be too happy because of all the things that could go wrong. Then I leaned up to kiss his cheek, "Thank you from the bottom of my heart, Dino," I said with tears in my eyes. I didn't realize until he left when I was leaning with my back against the closed door that I had called him Dino.

Well, if I was teary eyed then, you should have seen the tears that flowed from my eyes when my little boy stood at my door the following evening. I was a mess—a wonderful happy, elated, grateful, thanks-be-to-God mess, and a blubbering one at that. Imagine, calm cool, collected Kia who tried all her life to be the one who looked like she didn't care. Well, you wouldn't have recognized me then and I was never ever the same person again. It was like the *Grinch Who Stole Christmas*. My heart grew a few sizes larger that day.

He was the most beautiful sight to behold. Dino held his little hand and he looked so small next to the linebacker PI. His large brown Rico eyes and my nose, gazed up at me with such a sweet expression. I crouched down and tried not to scare him. "Do you know what a mommy is?" I asked him.

"Yep, but I don't have one," he replied.

"Well, you do now," I said and held out my arms. It was easy after that. It was like whipped cream, and smooth velvet pillows, and satin sheets and "raindrops on roses, whiskers on kittens, bright copper kettles and warm woolen mittens". My little boy was home!

There were two court trials that followed the blessed reunion and I was heavily involved in both of them. Mario Lorenzo was arrested and went on trial for murder, conspiracy to commit murder, kidnapping and a slew of other indictments that were slapped on him. Witnesses came out of the woodwork, including the driver who was hiding out under witness protection.

I went to San Quentin on a Sunday morning, and Rico reluctantly agreed to see me. He looked different—much buffer with a physique that showed he had been working out in prison. He had short buzzed hair and a face that was a road map of what he had probably suffered there over the past seven years. He wasn't the same happy boy I knew before. I didn't expect it, but it saddened me to see him. I still loved him. I was sitting on the other side of a glass partition in a partitioned cubicle, and we each had to speak through telephones.

"Kia," he simply said when he picked up the phone. He wasn't smiling and I sensed it upset him to see me. "You are still as beautiful as ever." My hair was long then, but I had it pulled back in a pony tail. I wore jeans, a turtle neck sweater and an overcoat, nothing special.

"Thank you, Rico. I'm so happy to see you."

"I didn't ever want you to see me like this. I wanted you to remember me the other way."

"It's alright, Rico. I'm still happy to see you. I have some news for you. Some of it is good, some not so good, but the good part is we might be able to get you out of here."

"I don't think that's possible Kia, mia." The old endearment warmed me. "There's no denying what I've done. We can't turn the clock back."

"Well, let me tell you what I have to say and we'll go from there."

So, I told him everything: how I had dated Mario a few times, how his father set him up to take a fall, the kidnapping of our son for five years and all the other terrible things Mario was involved in.

He sat there stunned, almost in a state of shock. Then he put down the phone; then covered his face with both hands and cried. I wanted so badly to comfort him, but I had to be strong and convince him to do what I asked next.

He picked up the phone to listen to me again. "Rico, I have a lawyer who is going to come to see you. He will be working to overturn your case. He'll probably tell you that it would be in your best interest to testify at your father's trial for the prosecution and tell them how he set you up. Then he'll start proceedings with his team to set you free. I am making good money now and will pay for everything, but I need your cooperation in this. I hope, after you think it over, it will all make sense to you."

He had not given me an answer. I knew he was too upset and needed to think about it. I put my hand against the glass to show him my support. He was still crying.

Long story short, everything fell into place. It took two years. Rico was an excellent witness for the prosecution, although emotions were pouring out of him when he faced his father from the witness stand. Mario could not look at him. Mario went to prison for life. He should have gotten the death penalty, but his lawyer fought hard to, at least, free him from this. I had no sympathy for him. He deserved everything he got.

Rico had an excellent team of lawyers that I had hired. I found out later that they were actually paid by Mr. Weiss when no legal bills were sent to my address. He was given credit for time spent in incarceration and released on probation, nine years after the date he was sent to San Quentin. Enrico Lorenzo was a free man when his son had just celebrated his eighth birthday.

It was a wonderful day when father and son were united for the first time. Rico loved him. We called him Christian, the name he had been given at birth. It took awhile for him to get used to it. He had gone by another name when he was under Mario's roof. Christian was the one who got Rico used to a normal life again. He had been in the hard cruel world of San Quentin and had to acclimate. His cousin kept his business going on the wharf for all those years. The boat was still there. I offered to help him financially, but he was too proud to accept help.

Getting along with his son was a lot easier for Rico than his relationship with me. We tried to establish something. After all, we'd loved each other once and we had a son. But time was not on our side. It just didn't work for us anymore. It was Rico who made the decision as he tried to explain it to me one day.

"Kia, I want my son in my life, but you and me we just..."

"What?"

"I'm a different person and I have to figure out who I am now. I can't do it with someone watching over my shoulder. We were great before, but I've been in another world, Kia and I don't want to be ashamed of it all. I have to start fresh and I want to set you free. I'm doing it because I love you and want what's best for you, too."

I was crying then. "I think I understand," I said.

"Does it seem like I have no gratitude after all you've done for me?"

"Not at all, Rico. I truly *do* understand." And I did. My heart was broken, but later, much later, it all made sense.

So, let me wrap up the next thirty years in a nutshell. That other Italian hunk, the private investigator, well you just knew I didn't bring him into my story for nothing. He waited for me. He was actually biding time until I was over Rico. He'd pretended to check in on a professional basis over the three years since Christian's return. Once in awhile a call on Christmas and special holidays, but nothing like, "Will you go out with me?" He always asked how Christian was; then he'd inquire about Rico and I'd say, "He's fine."

Then one day, I said, "Rico and I aren't seeing each other anymore. We've decided to go separate ways." I said something like it was for the best, and we would always remain friends and that he'd still see Christian.

And then, lo and behold, he said, "Can I come over?" Well that was something. And that something led to a lot of other things which led to… you guessed it—love and marriage, but we stopped there. No baby carriage. We tried, but it didn't happen and that was okay because I got a very romantic, macho, studly specimen of a husband who has trucked through the *for better or worse* with me.

He did not take over the father role, but was nevertheless a great influence in my son's life. Rico eventually married and had other children, so Christian had two households to be nurtured in. He grew to be a great man with integrity and honor and lived up to his name. Actually, Christian became a Christian and studied to become an evangelical pastor. He now shepherds a small church in—you won't believe this—the little town of Cambria, California. And because of his dedication, even his mother is now going to church on Sundays.

I forgot to mention that Mr. Weiss died fifteen years after I met him and his death made a huge impact on my life. A few days after his services, which were attended by half of San Francisico's Jewish community, I was asked to attend the reading of his will. He left a large portion of his money to various charities, but I was astounded to hear that he left the bulk of his estate to me. There was a line in the will that read, "She will know what to do with this money and will use it wisely. She was the bright light that came into my life and made it worth living."

I have to stop and wipe my tears here…because, as you know, I've never been anyone's bright light and I want to express something now. I was not a good person to any of you, except for Keala. I have no excuses, but I do want to say, that because of my bitterness towards my father, I built up a wall around myself and it was not a happy wall. It was cold and uncaring and self serving.

Do not think for a moment that Pauahi's legacy did not touch me. I struggled with my conscience for years and finally I came to the conclusion that the only way I could make up for my coldness was to give of myself and to become the servant that I was taught to be at

Kamehameha. I heard a saying soon after I inherited that money, "The time to be happy is now, the place to be happy is here and the way to be happy is to make other people happy."

The money which Mr. Weiss gave me was devoted to charities. I quit my job and worked tirelessly toward that end. It wasn't just giving away tax deductible money. I worked in shelters and soup kitchens and especially devoted myself to children's causes. I started a foundation which built a private boarding school for children who needed a decent break in life.

As Lihau reminded us, "Let her own works praise her in the gates," and I will stop here with listing my achievements. I just wanted you to know I've changed. I'm sorry for being so horrible, and most of all, I'm sorry for hurting anyone who is here today.

Keala

I WENT HOME TO WAIPIʻO and lived my life as I had before. Yes, there was sadness in me that never seemed to go away, but I prevailed. Like Puakea, I refused to let it mar my happiness, so I spread the joy, joy, joy wherever I went. Now you laugh, but it's the only way to get out of the doldrums. And as Kia noted, "the way to be happy is to make other people happy". No licking my wounds for me. I will admit that I stayed away from the *paniolo* scene and did not want to venture near horses again. I even avoided Manu's property where my brothers were training them.

I took up weaving with a vengeance and, as a family, we were asked almost every weekend to perform at different events. The Kalias were becoming famous on the Hamakua Coast, and I was "weaving my lei of stars" everywhere. I also made a point to give to my community.

It wasn't in big ways, but wherever I saw a need, I tried to do something about it. There was a family who was worse off than ours. They were a large family of nine who lost their father. The kids were running wild and the mother needed help. One day, I brought them some fish that my brothers had caught and poi that we had pounded from the taro corms from our fields.

They invited me to sit at the table with them. The table was covered with left over newspapers that they'd collected whenever they went to town. A two year old baby sat on his high chair and there were more newspapers on the floor around him. All the fish bones were thrown in the middle of the table; then wrapped up at the end of the meal. The family dog sat panting next to the high chair waiting for the baby to drop something on the floor. The dog and the baby had kind of a symbiotic relationship that continued after the baby cried to be let down from his high chair. He sat on the floor and let the dog lick the rest of the food on his face. It seemed to be kind of a routine. I wondered if I was the only one who noticed.

This family became a project with me. I brought the children home with me whenever I could and taught them how to weave. I put them to work and paid them with food or money when they helped me pick and prepare the *lauhala*. There were three older girls who were especially interested in weaving, and they all became adept at it. By the time I had my next craft event, we had quite a collection. Then I had an idea about selling them in hotel gift stores and tourist shops. I borrowed Manu's car on these occasions and took the girls with me to sell our wares. Before we knew it, we had a thriving business going.

I sent half of the boys to help my brothers with the horses and the other half to work in the taro fields. They made their choices in this. Of course, the goal was to help their mother with finances and to make them self sufficient and ready for the real world. The Kalia family had all learned this as we grew up; I was just passing it on.

There were needs everywhere and our family came to the aid of others whenever we could. Those who were sick and needed tending were my sister Keahi's *kuleana*. She was skilled in the use of Hawaiian herbs. My brothers helped wherever muscle or physical labor was needed. Manu was a blessing everywhere. He did anything he was asked. Perhaps he was our role model and we learned by his example. My mother was the hospitable hostess along with Kalena and welcomed anyone into our home.

No, I was not unhappy in this atmosphere. It was the life I knew. I was willing to return to it and be content. Miguel had sent a check every month to our post office box, and every month I sent it back to him. Pride is a terrible thing. I could have used that money.

The family went to perform at a County Fair that summer, and as I was dancing the *hula*, I heard someone calling my name. Then I saw Miguel at the back of the crowd, moving towards the stage. Thank goodness the dance was just ending, so I picked up the hem of my *mu'umu'u* and headed outside. My family covered for me, and my sisters helped me hide until we were sure he had lost sight of me. It was a silly thing to do, but I didn't want to face him. That was the only time I saw him, and it had now been eight months since our break up.

I was all settled into life in Waipi'o again and along came a knock at our door one late afternoon. There stood Lance and Justin.

"Oh my goodness, what a surprise," I said and welcomed them into the house. I sat them down at our table and brought them some fresh *liliko'i* juice to cool their palates.

"We brought you one gift, Keala," said Lance. "You need come outside to see it."

I followed them down the stairs and there next to their two horses was my very own horse...Waipi'o. Well, I tell you, I was speechless for a moment. I never wanted to set eyes on a horse again. I think that resolution came from the fact that I missed Waipi'o so much. She stomped her feet as she pawed the ground and shook her head up and down when she saw me. Ah, the tears started to flow then. I kissed her and hugged her and talked to her soothingly as I had done so many times before.

I think I even saw a little tear in Justin's eye as he and Lance watched this reunion unfold. Well, maybe not. I hugged both of them for the lovely gift, and then realized where my gift had truly come from.

"Thank you and thank *him* for me," I said smiling at them with tears on my lashes.

"Keala, you need to come home. Miguel is in bad shape," said Justin.

"Oh dear, is he sick?" I asked in alarm.

The two of them looked at each other with eyebrows knit. "Yeah," said Lance. "He's lovesick."

"Oh, there are plenty of girls to remedy that," I answered, staring at the ground now.

"You don't understand," said Justin. "He can't function wit'out you. He's drinking himself to death and he won't do anyt'ing else but moan and groan about you. It's sickening. You have to help him. You have to come back."

"Do you know why we broke up, Justin?"

"Yeah, I do," he replied.

"So, you are asking me to come back to *that*? Do you think so little of me that you would ask me to do such a thing?"

"No, Keala. Lance and me and da rest of da boys, we wouldn't ask dat?"

"Well, what are you saying?"

"Deyah's no moah girls now. He won't go neyah *wahines*. He just wants you."

"Oh, well that'll change. I think he's just taking a break."

"I sweyah, Keala," said Lance now. "No moah girls. He's done wit' dat."

"Well, I have to think about it," I said, slowly breaking my resolve.

"Come back wit' us, Keala," said Justin. "Please."

"You brought my horse all the way down here, and now I'm going to leave her again?"

"We'll come get her if you stay. Please, Keala, come."

You all know me. I was always a sucker for a sad story. It took awhile for me to think about it, well maybe at least two minutes. We took Waipi'o to my brothers and they put her in the corral with the rest of the horses. I told her I would come back. I was just going for a little while. So, there I went traipsing up the hill riding tandem on Justin's horse until we reached their trucks where we put the horses in the trailers. I drove with Justin, and we dropped Lance's truck and horse off at the ranch that almost became Camelot, but named something else now.

"Now what?" I asked as I sat between them on the way to wherever they were taking me.

"We have to find him," said Justin.

They stopped at two places before we ended up in a small bar just outside of Waimea. There was a jukebox playing Elvis' song, "Fools Rush In". Well, those were the very words he was singing as we walked in. I guess the real name of the song is "Can't Help Falling in Love" but the other title was more appropriate at the moment.

So here we are at the end of the afternoon; it's not even dark yet, and there's my husband with his head on the bar, looking like a drunk skunk or is the saying *drunker than a skunk*? I walked up to him and tapped him on the shoulder.

He lifted his head and looked at me. His eyes were bloodshot, he was unshaven, and his clothes appeared like he had slept in them for days. "Go away," he said. Then he put his head back down. I shook his shoulders. "Go away," he yelled. Then I started to walk away, and he lifted his head.

"You look like my wife," he stammered.

"I am your wife, you idiot," I said looking back at him.

"Keala, is dat you?"

"No, it's somebody else," I said.

"Keala, shtay heyah," he slurred.

"Did you say SHTAY here," I mimicked him.

"No I said shtay heyah," he said.

"Sounded like SHTAY to me," I said and then I started giggling and burst into full on laughter.

"Ah, Keala, you making fun of me, but God, I missed yoah laugh," he said and then put his head back down on the bar.

Well, it wasn't a hop, skip and a jump to get him out of that bar, but between the three of us we managed. I got his keys out of his pocket and followed them in his truck. Then we had to practically carry him into the house. He kept saying, "Whersh ma wife?"

When we got into the house, I couldn't believe it. It was a pig sty of the worse kind. There were newspapers, beer bottles, garbage and dirty clothes everywhere. It looked like he hadn't picked it up in months. The kitchen sink was piled with dishes and I even saw a humongous cockroach peer out from one of the food crusted plates. Unbelievable.

"What have you done to our home, Miguel?"

"It's not a home, it's a housh," he said. The guys had dumped him on the couch. "It's only a home wit' a wife," he said and passed out again on the couch.

"Just help me do one more thing," I told the guys. "Help me get him into the shower."

Well, that too was a mess, but we dumped him on the floor of the shower and I simply turned on the cold water. He yelled to bring the roof down, but I had no sympathy for him. I just ran that ice cold water over him until he was begging for mercy. I changed the filthy sheets and pillow cases on the bed while the guys got him out of his wet clothes. I heard him shouting all kinds of bad words, some of them in Portuguese.

After I gave them a clean robe to wrap him in, they dragged him down the hall and deposited him on the bed where he passed out for the rest of the night.

I must have spent the next six hours bagging up beer bottles and garbage, sorting dirty clothes, scrubbing the bathrooms, sweeping and mopping the floors, cleaning the kitchen and killing cockroaches. *Auwe noho'i e,* as my mother would say. I was exhausted and collapsed on the living room *pune'e.*

"Keala?" I heard a voice the next morning. "Is dat you?" Miguel was standing over me. I wakened slowly from my sleep of exhaustion.

"Were you expecting someone else, Miguel?"

"Keala, I canna believe you're heyah?" He literally dove into bed with me and started kissing me over and over again on every part of my face; then when he started running his hands all over me, I had to stop him.

"Miguel, stop it. We have to talk."

"Okay, but can I jus' stay and hold you while you talk?"

"I can't think like this."

"Please," he begged.

I relented, the sucker that I am, and was then. "Miguel, you have to stop this drinking."

"If you stay, I'll nevah touch annodah drop again."

"You mean if I SHTAY in the HOUSH," I said and burst out laughing.

"No, if you stay in our home," he replied in perfect English.

"What about the girls," I asked.

"Oh dat guy wit' da girls, he's dead and gone."

"Okay, I'll SHTAY," I answered and laughed my laugh that he loved so much as we cuddled on our *pune'e* in our home in beautiful Waimea overlooking the majestic mountain of Maunakea.

Miguel Cardoza was true to his word from that day forward. Now don't think he was an angel or anything like that, but I never saw him pick up another drink, and as far as I know, that guy with all those girls was dead and gone. You question, what more can a woman ask for? Well…help with all those babies who came every twelve months for the next six years. Would you believe this…girl, boy, girl, boy, girl and then the last boy came thirteen months after? Barefoot and pregnant—that was me. You would think a man would get sick and tired of seeing his wife look like a bowling ball for six years, but it was his idea, not mine. I would have stopped at one.

The kids who took after their mother were fabulous. The kids who took after their father were not so hot. Like Nani, I won't tell you who was who, but let's just say half of them almost drove me to pick up the bottle. Just kidding. Two of them made it to Kamehameha, two became *paniolo's*, one became a rodeo queen just for a summer, and the baby—he became a mama's boy. He's thirty one and the only one still at home. I never want him to leave. He and my husband are staying at Lance's ranch this week. Oh, and I have ten grandchildren so far, and I will always welcome more.

Miguel's dad Andre passed away ten years ago and his wonderful mother is still with us. They both welcomed me home with open arms when I returned and graciously traded homes with us when the babies came. As for my husband, he's my ever lovin' *paniolo*, getting a little creaky with age, still riding the hills of Waimea and worships the ground I walk on.

Epilogue

ALL SIX GIRLS HAD A common thread that they brought to the table—they had a shared experience at Kamehameha Schools and Senior Cottage; they each came from a valley of the islands with the heritage of their Hawaiian ancestors who had lived communally where the spirit of sharing and nurturing were the custom of the land, and they were individual survivors of whatever God brought into their lives. They loved and were loved in return, and they were all in their own ways, fine examples of Pauahi's legacy when she directed her trustees to carry out her will:

"To devote a portion of each year's income to the support and education of orphans, and others in indigent circumstances, giving the preference to Hawaiians of pure or part aboriginal blood

To provide first and chiefly a good education in the common English branches, and also instruction in morals and in such useful knowledge as may tend to make good and industrious men and women"

So, these good and industrious women who were instructed in morals, some with indigent circumstances and others who were orphans, were the beneficiaries of Princess Bernice Pauahi Bishop's generosity and kindness. They had not always lived up to her standards, but her example served as a creed that they carried with them throughout their lives.

Kia was the first that morning to depart. She had an early flight back to San Francisco. "I left an envelope for each of you with Keala. Don't open it until I leave and promise me you will all receive what's in it as a favor to me. I loved coming here to Waimea, and I thank you for listening to my story, but most of all for your friendship and all your sharing that I'll carry with me forever."

Kia was dressed in another Chanel suit and looked elegantly sophisticated as she hugged them each in farewell. A long black limousine arrived to pick her up, and then she was spirited away as she waved goodbye.

They went back into the house to drink their coffee and finish the rest of the pastries Keala bought that morning.

"Well, pardon me as I drive away in my fancy suit and my limousine and leave early to boot," said Puakea as she plunked down on a seat in her shorts and tee shirt.

"Now, now Puakea, I thought Kia's story was the best," admonished Kanoe. I've forgiven her. She's been through an awful lot."

"We've all been through a lot. Well, it's true, our stories don't read like *The Godfather,* but she got everything she wanted, including tons of money to keep her in limo's for the rest of her life. I don't think it was nice of her to boast about all that," sputtered Puakea.

"She wasn't boasting, Puakea. It was a vital part of her story," said Nani.

"Puakea, just face it, you've never liked her and maybe she's the one person in the group that you never will," sighed Keala. "But I think the conclusion to Kia's story was genuine and definitely changed her attitude about life."

"Let's open our envelopes," suggested Lihau. "I think it was nice of her to leave us a card."

"She wants us to open them at the same time," confirmed Keala. "So, on your mark...get set...ready, go."

They each slit open their individual envelopes and found a note that read:

Have fun with this and go ahead and use it foolishly.
With much love and fond aloha,
Kia

Behind each card was a cashier's check written in the amount of ... one hundred thousand dollars and paid to the order of their individual names: Puakea Crown, Kanoe Kelliher, Nani Schmidt, Lihau Lau and Keala Cardoza.

A silence permeated the room, and for some reason, they all glanced at Puakea. "I don't know why everyone's looking at me," she said as she held the envelope to her chest. "I love Kia. In fact...I consider her my best friend."

Recited by the Girls of Kamehameha Schools each December 19th on Founder's Day to commemorate the birthday of Princess Bernice Pauahi Bishop

Proverbs 31:10-31 (King James Version)

Who can find a virtuous woman? For
her price is far above rubies;

The heart of her husband doth safely trust in her
so that he shall have no need of spoil.

She will do him good and not evil all the days of her life.

She seeketh wool and flax and worketh willingly with her hands;

She is like the merchants' ships; she bringeth her food from afar.

She riseth also while it is yet night and giveth meat
to her household and a portion to her maidens.

She considereth a field and buyeth it; with the
fruit of her hands she planteth a vineyard.

She girdeth her loins with strength and strengtheneth her arms.

She perceiveth that her merchandise is good;
her candle goeth not out by night.

She layeth her hands to the spindle, and
her hands hold the distaff.

She stretcheth out her hand to the poor; yea she
reacheth forth her hands to the needy.

She is not afraid for the snow in her household; for
all her household are clothed with scarlet.

She maketh for herself coverings of tapestry;
her clothing is silk and purple.

Her husband is known in the gates when he
sitteth among the elders of the land.

She maketh fine linen and selleth it and
delivereth girdles unto the merchants.

*Strength and honor are her clothing; and
she shall rejoice in time to come.*

*She openeth her mouth with wisdom and in
her tongue is the law of kindness.*

*She looketh well to the ways of her household
and eateth not the bread of idleness,*

*Her children arise up and call her blessed;
her husband also and he praiseth her.*

Many daughters have done virtuously, but thou excellest them all.

*Favor is deceitful and beauty is vain, but a woman
that feareth the Lord; she shall be praised.*

*Give her of the fruit of her hands; and let her
own works praise her in the gates.*

Author's Note

THE WAIMEA GATHERING HAS BEEN the result of my return home to Hawai'i. There is so much to soak up in this wonderful culture, rich with characters and stories that inspired the subjects that have sprung to life on these pages.

I covered some of the history of Waimea in my book, *Lanikai*. The town was renamed Kamuela to avoid post office confusion with other places with the same name, but most residents and visitors alike, still refer to it as Waimea. I used to picture heaven as a place with rolling hills and green pastures, and I think Waimea is close to my vision of this with its aura of tranquility, and the reason why so many love it there.

I want to thank all the people I've talked to who have helped me with this undertaking including: Malia Tongg with whom I stayed in Palolo Valley, the women of Kahana Valley who hosted an event I attended, Chauncey Pa and Suzie Hanchett Swartman and their stories on beautiful Kalihiwai, Sue Wilson whose house I visited in Ha'iku, David Alama who introduced me to his awesome Waianae friends, and Bob Masuda our informative guide to Waipi'o Valley. I've included these particular valleys because I fell in love with them and wanted readers to feel the same. I see Kahana Valley every day and never tire of its beauty.

My sincere appreciation extends to my wonderful friend, Laurie Michaud, who also used her genius with *Kahala Sun*, and has now assisted me in *this* endeavor by fine tuning it with her special magic.

The same goes to my dear daughter, Kalei who was the first to read *The Waimea Gathering* and gave me the "thumbs up" to release it to the rest of the world. I send my love to Maile Trask, Rosemary Ahina Eberhardt, and Edie Smith Metzger for their friendship and for being my supportive cheerleaders in this process.

About thirty years ago, I met a young man from San Francisco, and we had a long talk about God's forgiveness. He shared a chilling story regarding something he did that he thought was unforgiveable. He had been released from San Quentin after fifteen years for the crime that Rico committed in Kia's story. Like Rico, he was ordered by his "mob" connected father to take a friend of theirs out on a fishing trip to execute him. He got out of prison because someone testified on his behalf and against his father. He lived in agony over what he had done and for being misled by a man he had admired all his life.

My reference to "Pauahi's Creed" is an expression to describe how her actions reflected what she believed in—that she led her life with humility and charity, relinquishing her opportunity to become queen in order to devote her time and eventually, most of her vast estate to better the plight of her beloved Hawaiians. She never had children of her own, but generations of them were blessed by her benevolence.

I've dedicated this writing to a true example of Pauahi's creed, my childhood friend, Bina Mossman Chun who has given everything that hospitality can offer including two Waimea gatherings in her fabulous home with twelve of my "forever" friends. Bina and her husband, Mike are the servant leaders who work tirelessly to make Kamehameha what it is today and are my role models for giving.

Using their maiden names when I knew them as children—the girls who attended the Waimea gatherings were Sybil Burningham, Leina'ala Blomfield, Mary Sue Brown, Maile Chinn, Kaliko and Nani Chun, Billie Cockett, Kaipo and Pua Kincaid, Karen Kneubuhl, Rowena Peroff and Melva Ward. Karen suggested I write a book about the gathering, which was such a memorable experience for all of us. I could not write about all twelve of them, so I made up six of my own and thus, *The Waimea Gathering* came to pass.

My other dedication is to the "Maui Gang" whose adventures are mentioned briefly between these pages. It's difficult to capture in words what we all experienced when we were just innocent (well some of us were) young teenagers out of Kamehameha that summer of 1962— a fabulous, fun-filled time with such enduring memories that the boys have managed to stay together for almost fifty years. David Alama, William Blaisdell, Jerry Gomes, Douglas Ing, Sam Kapu, Clement Souza and George West were the boys of the Maui venture. Mary Sue Brown, Nanette Mossman, Suellen Kahapea, and yours truly, Mahealani Harris were the girls that joined them. I should mention that Wright Bowman and Agenhart Ellis were supposed to come with us, but due to other commitments couldn't make it.

Wright Bowman, Jerry Gomes and Clem Souza have since passed away, much too soon with our heartfelt regrets. My prayers of appreciation are given in memory of these lovely friends who have been deeply missed by all of us.

Last but not least, I pay tribute with these pages to:

The Kamehameha Class of 1962

A wonderful close-knit class thanks to a boy I've known since first grade: Carl "Dutchy" Judd, our illustrious leader who keeps us well informed as our link between past and present and is another fine example of Pauahi's legacy.

I attended Kamehameha Schools since first grade, indoctrinated and exposed to its principles and edicts for twelve impressionable years. I hope I have done the school justice by these pages. It was not always my favorite place to be, but nevertheless, consciously or unwittingly, a few good things remain with me.

Me kealoha pumehana,
Mahealani Harris Shellabarger

Readers are invited to e-mail me at
mahe@booksbymahealani.com

Or visit my website at
booksbymahealani.com

Glossary of Hawaiian Words
Used in Context

ahe	Breeze; to blow or breathe gently; softly blowing; street in Palolo Valley
ahupua'a	Land division usually extending from the uplands to the sea so called because the boundary was marked by a heap (ahu) of stones surmounted by an image of a pig (pu'a'a) or because a pig was laid on the altar as tax to the chief.
'aina	Land; earth
akule	Big eyed or goggle eyed scad fish
Ala Wai	Fragrant water; place name of a canal in Waikiki
'alamihi	A common black crab
ali'i	Chief; name of a hui scrimmage team of the band and headquarters at Kamehameha and printed on blue tee shirts
aloha	Love; affection; compassion; mercy; pity; kindness; charity; regards; sweetheart; loved one; beloved; loving; greetings; hello; goodbye; farewell

Anahola	Land section in Kawaihau district in northeast Kaua'i
'Anini	Dwarfish, stunted; stream and beach in Hanalei district of Kaua'i
auwe noho'i e	Goodness! Alas! Oh!
auwe	Oh! Oh dear! Alas! Too bad! (much used to express wonder, fear, pity, scorn)
'awai	Rostrum; pulpit; speaker's platform; scaffold
'ehu	Reddish tinge in hair
eleu	Alert; name of hui scrimmage team for Company B at Kamehameha and printed on red shirts
Ewa	Crooked; plantation; beach area on West Oahu
Ha'ena	Red hot; burning red, place name of district and caves in Kaua'i
Ha'iku	Speak abruptly or sharp break; quadrangle and land section in east Maui
haku	To weave as a lei
hala	Pandanus or screw pine, native of southern Asia, a tree with many branches tipped with spiral tufts of long narrow spine edged leaves used in weaving mats, baskets, and hats
Haleakala	House by the sun; volcano and national park established in 1961, located in Kahului quadrangle on east Maui
Halekulani	House befitting royalty; hotel dating back to 1917 located on Waikiki Beach in the city of Honolulu, Oahu
Hamakua	District on eastern coast of the island of Hawai'i

Hana	Work; Road and district on East Maui
Hanalei	Crescent bay; name of valley, bay and district in North Kaua'i
haole	Caucasian; foreigner; white person
hapa haole	Half white; Hawaiian Caucasian
Hapuna	Spring; beach in Puako quad on the island of Hawai'i
hau	A lowland tree with rounded heart shape leaves and with cup shaped flowers of five petals that change in the day from yellow to dull red
haupia	Coconut pudding
Hau'ula	Red hau tree; land section in Kahana quadrangle on O'ahu
Hawai'i	Largest Island in the Hawaiian group and the name of the 50th State that encompasses the entire Hawaiian group of islands.
heiau	Pre-Christian place of worship
Hi'ilawe	Lift [and] carry; highest freefall waterfall in Hawai'i and one of the highest in the world located in Waipi'o Valley
Honoka'a	Rolling [as stones] bay; town in Hamakua quadrangle, Hawai'i
Honolulu	Sheltered bay; place name on O'ahu and capital of the state of Hawaii
ho'ohanau	To deliver a baby
Ho'okipa	Hospitality; beach and surfing area near Pa'ia, Maui
ho'opuakea	To appear bright; to shine

hui	Club; association; society
huki	To pull as on a rope; stretch; draw; reach
hukilau	Pull ropes; fishing with a large net with leaves fluttering around the edges to attract the fish
huli huli chicken	Chicken roasted on a rotating spit
Imiola	Seeking life; oldest church in Waimea established in 1857
imu	Pit or underground oven usually fortified by hot lava rocks
imua	Forward; name of hui scrimmage team for Company C at Kamehameha and printed on yellow shirts
ipu	High crown of a hat in this story; bottle gourd or container
ipulei	Container for leis; street in Palolo Valley
Ka'a'awa	The wrasse fish; land section in Kahana quadrangle, Oahu
ka'ape	Humble; servile
Ka'au	Forty; name of Crater in Palolo Valley, O'ahu, named after Ka'auhelemoa, a supernatural chicken in Palolo who flew to Helumoa
ka'e	Brim as in a wide brim hat
Ka'ena	The heat; land section, quadrangle and northernmost point of O'ahu said to be a brother or cousin of the goddess Pele who accompanied her from Kahiki
Kahalawai	West Maui mountains or Mauna Kahalawai; the Hawaiian word Kahalewai means *house of water* and another word for this mountain range

kahale	The house
Kahana	Turning point; place name for valley on windward side of O'ahu
kahekili	Thunder
Kahuku	The projection; village and land division on the northernmost point of O'ahu
Kahului	The winning; town and site of the main airport in Maui
Kaimuki	The ti oven; land section of Honolulu, Oahu
kala	Forgive
kalahea	To call out a pronouncement or proclamation
Kalakaua	Last reigning King of Hawai'i; after his death, his sister Lili'u'oukalani became the final monarch to rule Hawai'i when it was overthrown
kalani	The heaven; heaven; heavenly
Kalena	Karen
kaleo	The voice
kalia	A variety of sweet potato
Kalihiwai	Water's edge; valley and stream in north shore of Kaua'i
kalua pig	Pig baked underground with lava rocks and ti leaves
kama'a puki	Buckskin boots
Kamaile	The maile vine; land section on Waianae coast in Ka'ena quad. on O'ahu
kamako	Tomato

kamalei	Beloved child
kamalu	To forbid
kamani	A large tree found on the shores of the Pacific, with shiny leaves, white flowers and small globe like green fruit; the wood is hard and formerly used in calabashes
kanoe	The mist
kanoekahawai	The mist of the valley
Kapa'a	The solid or the closing; place name in Kawaihau district on Kaua'i
Kapahulu	Worn out soul; avenue in Honolulu that ends at Waikiki Beach
Kapalama	The lama wood enclosure; location of heights in Honolulu and site of Kamehameha Schools
kapali	The cliff
Kaua'i	The enumerable dark (heavens); referred to as the Garden Isle one of the islands of the Hawaiian group that make up the state of Hawai'i
kaulana	Famous; celebrated; renowned
kawai	Point
Kawohi- kukapulani	Sacred virgin standing in heaven
kea	Shiny, white mother of pearl shell
Keahi	The fire
keala	The fragrance; shortened version of Keala'iliahi
keala'iliahi	Fragrance of the sandalwood
Ke'e	Avoidance; beach and cliff west of Ha'ena, Kaua'i

Ke'elikolani	Middle name of Princess Ruth; State office building in Honolulu
keiki	Child
Kekuhaupi'o	The standing arched hau tree; name of the gym at Kamehameha Schools and named for the favorite warrior of Kalani'opu'u
kelamoku	Denim knee britches
kilakila	Strong; imposing; having poise that commands admiration
Keoki	George
Keoni	John
Kiawe	The algaroba tree, one of the commonest and useful trees growing in Hawai'i
Kihei	Cape, cloak; place name of village in Maui
Kilauea	Spewing, much spreading (referring to volcanic eruptions); place name in Hanalei district, Kaua'i
kilo	Lookout person
koa	Valuable wood from the largest of the native forest tree used for canoes, surfboards and furniture
Kohala	Place name for district in northwestern island of Hawai'i
Konia	Burned; building at Kamehameha Schools, maiden name of the mother of Bernice Pauahi Bishop
Ko'olau	Windward; one of two large mountain ranges on O'ahu
Kuhio	Beach at Waikiki; named after Prince Jonah Kuhio Kalaniana'ole

ku'i ikaika-kahekili me-ka lapa uila	Thunderbolt
Kukailani	Heavenly dung
Kukui	Candlenut tree; name of the nut from this tree
Kukuihaele	Traveling light (night marchers were seen here); village above Waipi'o Valley on the Big Island of Hawaii
kulamanu	Bird plain
kuleana	Responsibility; jurisdiction
kupuna	Older generation; grandparent
la'au'ala	Sweet wood; description used for sandalwood
Lahaina	Variety of sugar cane and sweet potato; poising or leaping; place name of former capital of the Islands located on the West side of Maui
La'ie	Leaf; land section in district of Kahuku, O'ahu
Lana'i	One of the eight islands of the Hawaiian Chain
lanakila	Victory (named in honor of Kamehameha's victory in the battle of Nu'uanu)
lau	leaf
lauhala	Pandanus leaf especially used in plaiting and weaving
laulau	Package of ti leaves containing pork, beef, salted fish baked in ground oven, steamed or broiled
lehua maoli	Favored taro for making poi
lei	Garland of flowers
lihau	Gentle cool rain; cool, fresh as dew laden air

Lihue	Cold chill; main city on island of Kaua'i
likini wawae	Buckskin boots
Liliha	Rich, oily; name of the wife of Governor Boki who became governess of O'ahu when he died and tried to start a revolt against Kamehameha III
liliko'i	Yellow fruit growing on a vine used for desserts and beverages
lilinoe	Fine mist, rain
lolo	Feeble minded
lomi salmon	Usually raw, worked with the fingers (lomi), seasoned and mixed with onions
Lono	God of agriculture and harvest
Lopaka	Robert
lu'au	Hawaiian feast named for the taro tops always served at one
Luka	Luke
mahoe	Twins
Ma'ili	Pebbly; town in Waianae on west coast of O'ahu
Makaha	Fierce; valley and town in Waianae on west coast of O'ahu
Makaio	Matthew
Makaleha	Eyes looking about as in wonder and admiration; mountain in Kawaihau district bordering Kalihiwai Valley of Kaua'i
Makawao	Forest beginning; land section, district and forest reserve in Haiku quadrangle, Maui

makua	Parent; or any relative of a parent's generation: uncle, aunt, cousin
Malaekahana	Name of the mother of Princess La'ieikawai and also an image in the Halemano Legend; land division and stream in Kahuku, Oahu
Maleko	Mark
Manoa	Vast; stream and land section on Honolulu, Oahu
manu	Bird; any winged creature
mapuana	Fragrance; especially windblown fragrance
Maui	Named for the demigod, Maui; second largest island in the Hawaiian group referred to as the Valley Isle
Maunakea	White mountain; highest mountain on the island of Hawai'i
mawaena	In the middle; center; field at the center of Kamehameha Boys School
mele	Merry
mileka	Millet
moana	Ocean
mo'i	Supreme; name of scrimmage team for Company A at Kamehameha and printed on green tee shirts
mokihana	Small leathery, cube shaped fruit used for leis from a native tree found only in Kaua'i, belonging to the citrus family
Moloka'i	Legendary child of Hina; One of the smaller islands that make up the Hawaiian group
mo'opuna	Grandchild

mu'umu'u	A loose gown worn by Hawaiian women
Namahana	The twins; high peak, land section and valley in Hanalei district, Kaua'i
Nanakuli	Look at knee; land section in Waianae, O'ahu
nani	Beautiful
Ni'ihau	Tooth gulch; One of the islands of the Hawaiian group in Kaua'i county; privately run where only island born residents are allowed
Nu'uanu	Cool height; section of Honolulu where King Kamehameha fought his famous battle of 1795 driving 300 warriors to their deaths
O'ahu	Gathering place; name of ancient chief; most populous island of the Hawaiian group where Honolulu is the main city and state capital
'ohia'ai	Mountain apple, a forest tree that grows up to fifty feet high with red or white apple like fruits
'okole	Buttocks; bottom
Olohena	Land division and ridge in Kawaihau district in Kaua'i
'o'opu	Fish found in fresh or salt water, included in the families of the *Eleotridae*
'opelu	Mackerel fish
pa kini	Tin pan container
Pa'ia	Noisy; quadrangle, village, bay on East Maui
palaka	Block print cloth or shirt of this material
pali	Cliff
Palolo	Clay; valley in Honolulu, Oahu

paniolo	Spaniard; originally the name for the Spanish cowboy or vaqueros who came to the Parker Ranch, but eventually what the Hawaiian cowboy was referred to
panoa	Touch freely
papale lauhala	Hat made from hala leaf; in this story the wide brimmed high crown hat of the cowboy
papale	Hat
Pauahi	Destroyed fire; Princess Pauahi was named after her aunt (mother of Princess Ruth) who was saved as a child from fire
pikake	Arabian jasmine introduced from India with small white flowers and a very fragrant smell, used for leis, particularly in weddings
pilikia	Trouble of any kind
pipi	Bull; beef
poi	The Hawaiian staff of life and main staple made from cooked taro corms, pounded and thinned with water
po'o wai u	Activity of Hawaiian paniolo when a bull is captured and tied or strapped to a tree, also an event at rodeos
pua mae'ole	Never fading flower
Puakea	Shortened word for ho'opuakea which means to appear bright or to shine
puna	Shortened version of kupuna which means grandmother
punahele	Favorite

Punahou	New spring; private school established by Hiram Bingham in 1841 at the request of Ka'ahumanu for chief's children and missionary children
Punalu'u	Coral dived for; village and beach park in Kahana quadrangle, Oahu
pune'e	Couch bed
Puohokamoa	Falls located on the road to Hana, Maui
pupu	Hors d'oeuvres
tutu	Grandparent
'ukulele	Leaping flea; nickname of the person who popularized the musical stringed instrument from Portugal
umi	Ten
Wa'ahila	Name of a chiefess who excelled in a dance named for her; ridge separating Manoa and Palolo Valleys
Wai'alae	Mudhen water; avenue and country club on O'ahu said to be named after a spring
Wai'ale'ale	Rippling water or overflowing water; highest mountain on Kaua'i
Wai'anapanapa	Glistening water; forest reserve and state park in Hana, Maui
Waikiki	Spouting water; section and beach in Honolulu, Oahu
Waikoloa	Duck water; land section in Puako quadrangle, island of Hawaii
Waimea	Reddish water; land division, homestead in Waipi'o, Hawaii

Wainiha   Unfriendly water; land division, river, valley, in
                     Hanalei district of Kaua'i

Waipi'o   Curved water; land section, valley, stream, bay in
                     north Hawai'i (Big Island)

Sources

Most Hawaiian words have several meanings. Translations are those appropriate to words used in the text and come from the following sources:

Elbert, Samuel and Kawena-Pukui, Mary *English Hawaiian Dictionary* Honolulu: The University of Hawaii Press 1964

Elbert, Samuel and Kawena-Pukui, Mary *Hawaiian-English Dictionary* Honolulu: The University of Hawaii Press 1957

Elbert, Samuel and Kawena-Pukui, Mary and Mo'okini, Ester T. *Place Names of Hawaii* Honolulu: The University of Hawaii Press 1974